The Book, the Film, the T-Shirt

Matt Beaumont lives in London with Holly, Sam and Maria. He drives a blue Saab with a beige leather interior. He smokes fags.

e
The e Before Christmas

Matt Beaumont

The Book, the Film, the T-Shirt

HarperCollins*Publishers*

HarperCollins*Publishers*
77–85 Fulham Palace Road,
Hammersmith, London W6 8JB

www.harpercollins.co.uk

This paperback edition 2003
3 5 7 9 8 6 4

First published in Great Britain by
HarperCollins*Publishers* 2002

Copyright © Matt Beaumont 2002

Matt Beaumont asserts the moral right to
be identified as the author of this work

ISBN 0 00 712768 5

Set in Minion and Franklin Gothic

Printed and bound in Great Britain by
Clays Ltd, St Ives plc

For Patricia Theokritoff, my mum.
Wish you were here.

acknowledgments

Massive thanks to everyone who helped with this book: Susan Opie and Nick Sayers at HarperCollins; Special Agent Lavinia Trevor; Bambos Stylianou (I wouldn't be seen dead in anyone else's slingbacks); Sarah Martin; Matt Weller; Caroline Natzler and Jean Hunt.

Above all, gratitude to Maria Beaumont, who contributed countless ideas, big, small and all sizes in between. She came up with the title, too. Didn't leave much for me to do, really. Few can be a Maria, but we should all try to get ourselves one.

Finally, thanks to Wanda.

And to Mr Matt Ryan.

one:

rolf harris, tampons, drugs

JUDITH OTTLE, HM CUSTOMS & EXCISE: My job has made me blasé about celebs. Terminal Four is like Madame Tussaud's some days and I've been through enough of their bags to realise they wear knickers and Y-fronts like anyone else. But when they told me that she was coming through, I was chuffed. Dean, my eldest, was dool-ally about her. It was his hormones, I suppose, though *that* poster has to take some of the blame – smothering her in lather and giving her a loofah to fondle doesn't require much of a fifteen-year-old's imagination.

As I stood in the customs hall waiting for her I imagined the look on Dean's face when I gave him her autograph. I was also hoping I wouldn't find anything – 'I am arresting you on suspicion of importing a class A drug and, by the way, can I have your autograph?' wouldn't sound right however I said it.

She flew in on the lunchtime flight from LA. We'd had an anonymous tip-off that she'd be carrying coke. We didn't take it too seriously but we couldn't ignore it. I'd been designated to pull her aside. They thought I was one of the more sensitive ones who could handle her with a lighter touch. We didn't want this one to go off in our faces.

Ha!

When she walked into the hall she looked like she did on the telly. She had the hairdo that no normal woman can copy without spending a month's wages (God knows I've tried), and the still-perfect-after-eleven-hours-in-the-air makeup (after a ten-minute bus ride mine looks as if I got Rolf Harris to do it). She was only carrying one small bag but she wasn't travelling alone; among the entourage was a tubby girl pushing a trolley piled with Louis Vuittons.

'Excuse me, madam,' I called out, 'would you mind stepping over here?'

Up close she looked stressed out. She'd flown first class so I don't know what her excuse was. I'd like to have stuck her on a packed charter to Lanzarote along with three squabbling kids and a useless husband. She'd have known what stressed was after that.

I asked for her passport – still British even though she'd made it big in America. As I was leafing through it I asked her, 'What is the purpose of your trip, Miss Richards?'

'Work. I'm making a TV ad.'

'Did you pack your bags yourself?'

(As if.)

'Um . . . no, my assistant did.'

'Can I take a look inside them, please?'

That's when the old bat that was with her piped up.

'Look, lady,' she said, 'I suppose you've got a job to do, but is this really necessary? We're on an extremely tight schedule.'

She reminded me of a teacher I'd had at school. Small and prim with a vicious streak. She used to stick a pencil in my ear and pin my head to the desk if I couldn't remember when the Battle of

Waterloo was. I had to tell myself how thrilled Dean was going to be to stop myself getting sharp with her.

'Could I ask you to move away, please, madam? This will be quicker if I can get on with it uninterrupted,' I said as politely as I could manage.

'I will not move away until you give me a very good reason for this persecution.'

I was being on my best behaviour and she was making me sound like the Gestapo. Or a traffic warden.

'I assure you that Miss Richards is being treated like any other member of the public,' I said.

That was a lie. It was policy to treat everyone the same – it didn't matter whether they were Cliff Richard or some poor Nigerian woman with a bum full of heroin. But I was treating Rebecca Richards with kid gloves.

'Give me your name immediately,' the old bat demanded.

'Officer Judith Ottle,' I said calmly.

Rebecca Richards turned on her then. 'Freddie,' she snapped, 'let's just get on with this. I don't want to be stuck here all day.' The old bat backed off.

By now a traffic jam had built up. Normally people can't get through the green channel fast enough, but when they spotted Rebecca Richards they couldn't resist stopping to gawp at her. She was getting self-conscious. Me too. I was wondering how the hell I'd be able to ask for an autograph with half of Heathrow looking on.

TYRONE EDWARDS, INNOCENT BYSTANDER: I'm wheeling my bags into customs and I'm sweating. I done this a million times before but this time it's bad. Straight up, I'd never seen so many customs guys and I'm sure they got me, man. Fuck, I'm thinking, they got your mug shot, Tyrone, they been tracking you all the way from Jamaica. Interpol, the FBI, the CIA, MI5, the SAS, they're all onto you. I stop my trolley and think. Turn back now, dump the bag on a carousel, no one'll ever know. So I spin round and go back and I think, can't do that, they're all watching you walk the wrong way like a fucking retard and anyway you can't dump the bag because it's got them Polaroids in it – you on the beach with that white bitch.

I turn round again, take some deep breaths and go into the green. Come on, Tyrone, you done this a million times, I'm telling myself. That's when I see the crowd looking at her. I know her, I'm thinking, but where from? Not New Cross. We got some class chicks but she was Premier League. Then it hits me. She's that bird off the telly, Rebecca with the hair that even black girls try to copy. And the tits. They try to copy them too.

I'm carrying a block of Colombian as big as a brick. I should be cruising through because customs ain't giving a shit about me, but I don't. I stop for a look. Rebecca whatsername off the telly is getting done and I don't want to miss a thing, do I?

OFFICER JUDITH OTTLE: She opened the first case for me. There wasn't a thing in there without a designer label that said, 'You can't afford me, you underpaid civil servant.' Even her tampons were in a beautiful little Gucci purse. Something we had in common – periods, not the Gucci purse.

I went through her stuff as quickly as possible. I didn't think I was going to find anything. You get a nose for these things – her luggage smelled of the Harvey Nicks perfume department. Finally only her little shoulder bag was left. I asked her for it but she clutched it tightly to herself.

'It's personal stuff.'

'I'm sorry but I do need to look inside.'

She handed it over reluctantly. It was just personal. A wallet, bits and bobs of makeup and an address book. I had a quick flick and spotted Kate Hudson, Ben Stiller and five different numbers for Warren Beatty. There was also a small, battered leather book. It had those plastic photo leaves inside. I glanced through it – family shots mostly but one or two of Joe Shirer were still in there.

'They're none of your business,' she snapped, trying to snatch it from me.

She was right – they weren't. I handed it back to her and that's when it fell out.

Bugger, I thought.

TYRONE EDWARDS: I'm standing maybe fifteen feet away but the experienced eye can spot these things. I can't believe what I'm seeing fall out of the little book. Extra large Rizlas. Rebecca is packing spliff. You know what runs through my mind now? If only I can get to her once we is on the outside, I can make a deal. I don't know what shit she smokes in Hollywood but I guarantee she ain't had nothing like what I can score. This is the big one, man. LA, get ready. Tyrone is coming!

OFFICER JUDITH OTTLE: Extra large Rizlas aren't illegal, but we all know that they're only used for one thing. I was gutted. With so many officers looking on, I couldn't pretend I hadn't seen it. It meant I'd have to give her a rubdown – a personal search.

'Would you mind coming with me, Miss Richards?' I said.

She followed me without a word. She was upset though. Stars love the stares when they're strolling down the red carpet on Oscar night. They're not so keen when they're being busted. As we were walking away I heard the old bat say to another officer, 'Haven't you idiots got some proper drug smugglers to catch?'

TYRONE EDWARDS: So I'm standing there watching that fit arse being marched off. I'm well gutted. My sweet Hollywood deal is walking out on me. I feel a hand on my shoulder. Shit. Game over. It's your fucking turn now, Tyrone. Why didn't you cruise on while you had the chance? Then this customs guy says to me, 'What do you think this is? A cabaret? Move along, sir.' I don't say nothing. I could. Where I've just flown in from guys get their throats cut for less. But I know when to shut the fuck up. I just got outta there like Maurice fucking Green.

OFFICER JUDITH OTTLE: We got to the interview room and I asked her to remove her jacket. I went through the pockets. Nothing. Then I started the search. I hate this bit of the job. You don't want to know some of the places people hide stuff, places you'd really rather not stick your hand.

I asked her to hold her arms out to the sides, and as I moved in I noticed she was crying. I wanted to stop there and then and say, 'It's all been a terrible mistake. I'm sorry. But before you go . . . It's for my little boy.' I didn't though. I checked her arms and worked my way down her ribs then back up to her bra. I put my hands on her boobs and had a feel. You often find little wraps of this and that stuffed into bras but there was nothing hidden in hers except for perhaps a couple of pounds of silicone. I'd read the articles about how hers were natural, but they were far too firm – lovely boobs, but I'm sorry, Dean, definitely shop-bought.

That's when she lost it. 'Get your fucking hands off me!' she yelled, taking a step back. I moved towards her. She held up her hands to stop me and said, 'You have no idea of the time I've been having and now this. I fly home and I'm treated like a fucking junkie.'

She was really blubbing now. I didn't know what to say so I just went back to work. I asked her to take her shoes off and I looked inside them – nothing. Then I worked my way up her legs, feeling through her trousers. God, I thought, these bloody pins go on forever. Eventually I reached her upper thighs, still nothing. I was nearly home, just a couple of inches away from her fanny and 'Would you mind signing this for me, Miss Richards?'

That's when it happened. I can't honestly be certain whether she hit me deliberately or whether she was just flailing wildly. Whatever, she caught me full on the face. It wasn't actually that hard, but the huge sapphire on her middle finger left me bleeding like a stuck pig.

I didn't find any gear on her but I had no choice other than to custodise her. It was in the cops' hands now. And while she was stewing in a cell she might have been dwelling on the fact that, if she hadn't been so bloody daft and had kept her head, the next day's papers would have been full of some rubbish about *EastEnders* or whatever instead of her right hook.

And my Dean wouldn't have been sulking in his room acting as if I'd personally ordered her execution.

two:

marrakech, monkeys, benny out of crossroads

GREG FULLER, CREATIVE DIRECTOR, FULLER SCHEIDT ADVERTIS-ING: I'd just arrived at the office and hadn't even sat down when Lola came in with an armful of tabloids.

NANCY STARK, PA TO GREG FULLER: Before we start, let's just get one thing straight. My name is not Lola. Only one person has ever called me Lola and that was Greg Fuller. He'd called me it from my first day at Fuller Scheidt – my porn star name apparently. If you'd tied him to his chair, stuck a gun against his head and threatened to pull the trigger unless he told you my real name, I'll bet his brains would have ended up on his desk because he wouldn't have been able to remember.

Thanks for letting me get that cleared up.

GREG FULLER: 'Do you have to, sweet pea?' I asked her as she arranged the papers in an attractive fan. 'This desk cost the best part of five grand and you're covering it with chip wrap.'

'Count yourself lucky,' she said. 'At the bus garage where my dad works a bloke got fired for reading *Sporting Life* between breaks. You're getting paid to do this.'

She had a point. On a better day it might have struck me that this was a pretty cool way to make a living. That particular Friday was nothing remotely like a better day. As Lola left me, a cursory glance at the headlines confirmed the fact.

'REBECCA RICHARDS ARRESTED' – the *Mirror*.

'BECCA BLOWS IT' – the *Sun*.

'IS THIS THE END FOR REBECCA?' – the *Express*.

'CUSTOMS AND EXCITE – BUSTY BECS FELT UP IN DRUG BUST' – the *Star*.

Trust the *Star* to get to the nub of a story. Actually, none of the papers was anywhere near the bloody nub. If one of them had carried a headline that said, 'REBECCA RICHARDS' ARREST POSSIBLY FINAL NAIL IN COFFIN FOR ADLAND'S GREG FULLER WHOSE ONCE GLITTERING CAREER IS IN NO POSITION TO SUSTAIN ANOTHER SETBACK AND WHOSE PERSONAL LIFE IS IN A RIGHT STATE AS WELL – WE'RE DOOMED, I TELL YOU, DOOMED, SAYS FULLER,' then they might have been close. Not one of them so much as mentioned my name though.

Let me explain my fairly convoluted connection to Rebecca Richards. I'll try to keep it brief. I'd written a TV commercial. It was all my own work and I don't think I'm being unreasonably boastful if I tell you it was very good. It featured a boy and a girl on a blind date, one where she happens to be wearing a rubber frock – not the standard blind date attire but this was advertising.

The commercial was for Blackstock Tyres, though it didn't feature any tyres – just cute young man and vulcanised date.

Bear with me. I'm getting there.

Client saw script. Client liked it. Client said he'd be more than happy to stump up several shedloads of money to shoot it. At that stage I could have cast two unknowns but I didn't. I got ideas above my station and reached for the bloody stars.

Wouldn't it be wonderful, I thought, to cast a famous couple; say Lenny Henry and Dawn French or Neil and Christine Hamilton? OK, maybe not, but how about Rebecca Richards and Joe Shirer from that sensational global TV hit, *All Our Lives Before Us*? They were an item on screen as well as off and the day rarely passed when they weren't splattered across the red tops. They made Posh and Becks look like shrinking violets. They'd cost, but I'd yet to meet a client that wasn't a closet starfucker.

NANCY STARK: Greg was such a starfucker. He once wrote a lager ad for Sheridan Morley because he'd had an entertaining lunch with him at the Groucho. Sheridan Morley in a lager ad? Please.

The truth was that Greg had been gagging to get Rebecca Richards in an ad ever since he'd walked in on one of his creative teams as they'd watched her workout tape. Later they told him that before she was famous she'd allegedly done a porn flick. No one had ever seen it but some bloke in Romford swore he'd bought a car off the bloke who'd done a bit of building work for the bloke whose brother was the cameraman. After that it was only a matter of time before he wrote a script that was 'just right' for her.

GREG FULLER: The client, Bob Bull, was the most irredeemable starfucker of them all. He actually started to drool when I proposed Shirer and Richards.

But the ink had barely dried on their contracts when their off-screen personae split up. It was far from amicable.

Never mind, I consoled myself, they're still TV's hottest pairing – they're even due to get married in the next series. They're professionals, I thought, they'll surely show up, perform like troupers and collect fat cheques for their trouble. Not for one moment did I imagine that one of them would show up and swing for a customs officer.

Instead of being banged up in a police cell, she should have been on her way to Soho, where she was supposed to dust herself down with talc and slither into the rubber frock. The wardrobe call was crucial. We were scheduled to start shooting the ad on the following Monday, and rubber wasn't polyester when it came to making alterations – or so I'd been led to believe.

Rebecca's incarceration wasn't my only problem that Friday. As I surveyed the damage in the press, my partner, Max Scheidt, burst into my office to remind me of the rest of the shit on my plate.

NANCY STARK: I'd have stopped anyone else waltzing into Greg's office unannounced – guarding his door was written into my job description. But you didn't stop Max waltzing anywhere.

GREG FULLER: 'What the fuck are you reading the papers for? Haven't you found Paul and Shaun yet?' he bellowed. Max always bellowed. I think a congenital defect prevented him from lowering his voice and it didn't necessarily mean he was in a bad mood. That morning, though, his mood was foul.

'Morning, Max,' I said far more calmly than I felt. 'Seen what our leading lady's been up to? Don't let anyone tell you Vinnie Jones is the only psycho we've exported to Hollywood.'

'What are you going to do about it? Go down there and bust her out of jail with a stick of cartoon dynamite? This isn't *Dukes of Hazzard*. Sort out the fucking problems you can control. Find me Paul and Shaun.'

'Lola's working on it as we speak,' I lied.

NANCY STARK: Max had hardly been in there thirty seconds but he was radiating heat through the plate glass that divided me from Greg. I thought I'd better stick my head in before it reached critical levels. 'Coffee, Max?' I asked breezily.

GREG FULLER: Ever the mistress of comic timing, my Lola.

'Paul and Shaun?' Max yelled at her.

'I think they might be in Marrakech,' she replied. Max looked at me with both eyebrows raised.

'That's what we heard, Max,' I confirmed. At that moment confirmation seemed the best policy.

NANCY STARK: I've no idea where Marrakech came from. I wasn't even sure where it was, let alone whether it was the kind of place that Paul and Shaun would have gone to lick their wounds.

GREG FULLER: It struck me that Lola was probably bang on the money. Marrakech was exactly the kind of one-star, once-fashionable pisshole that they'd flee to.

Some further explanation is required at this point. Paul and Shaun, known only to me as Piss and Shit, were a creative team in my department. They were one of the less talented pairings on Planet Advertising. Why did I suffer them on the payroll of my smooth, sexy and fabulously successful advertising agency? I'll tell you why in three words: Universe of Sofas.

Though they won't shout it from the rooftops, every profitable ad agency has a Universe of Sofas, an account for which they squeeze out shit week after week and in return rake in the loot.

At Fuller Scheidt we had the original Universe of Sofas, whose concrete and steel aircraft hangars were piled to the rafters with ugly approximations of furniture that you could buy now and pay for some time in the next millennium on extremely favourable credit terms. In fact, I may be right in saying that they'd been known to pay *you* to take their crap off their hands.

Universe of Sofas depended on us to tell the nation about their unbeatable deals in the most breathless way possible.

We depended on them for a suicidally high percentage of our revenue.

And I depended on Piss and Shit to write ads that placed second-rate models on third-rate furniture and did the business.

Or at least I had. A couple of days before Rebecca's arrest I'd fired them.

I knew it was a mistake as the words 'You're as sad a pair of gits as ever soiled my office and you're fired' spilled from my mouth. It was a moment of madness. Honestly, I'm not usually that stupid but, in case the fact that I called them Piss and Shit wasn't enough of a clue, I hated them.

NANCY STARK: He really hated Paul and Shaun, even though there was nothing hateful about them. Apart from Shaun's sweat problem they were quite nondescript. Maybe that was their downfall. Greg had filled his department with surfer wear, pierced eyebrows and coloured barnets. Paul and Shaun were a bit Levi 501s, Gap sweat-shirts and sensible trainers – you know, ones that actually look like trainers. They spoiled the aesthetic.

They didn't like Greg either and they made the mistake of letting it show. They were experienced enough to know that sincerity has no place in advertising, but they'd spent the best part of four years crawling up the arse of the Universe of Sofas client and they believed they were untouchable.

Greg loved proving people wrong, even if it meant signing his own death warrant.

GREG FULLER: 'I could hire fucking monkeys to do what you do for me,' I told them. They knew I depended on them, however, and as soon as they were out of the door they rubbed the fact in my face. They called the client and told her what I'd just done. It didn't matter that any pair of monkeys could have done their jobs, because the marketing director at Universe of Sofas happened to love my ex-monkeys. She immediately called Max to ask him what the hell we were playing at. News to him, I'm afraid, and he immediately demanded to know what the hell *I* was playing at.

I felt for him actually. This was a lousy time to have our most profitable piece of business threaten to walk. We were in the midst of negotiations with a buyer. Gruppo Tigana, an Italian agency group, had made an offer for our shares in Fuller Scheidt. Max and I had set up the company four years before with a bold mission statement: we were going to build a radically different ad agency; create an environment in which individual visions could be realised without interference from the money men. This, of course, was bollocks. We'd set up with only one dream in mind: that one day a company like Gruppo Tigana would come along and offer us, say, £28 million.

NANCY STARK: *Twenty-eight million fucking quid!* All right, Fuller Scheidt might have been hot, but twenty-eight-million-quid hot? And Greg was due to collect a quarter of that. I heard him moan about the capital gains he'd have to pay. Poor lamb.

GREG FULLER: The Italians wanted us because we were sexy, won awards and we'd give them a British presence. But mostly they wanted us because we were very, very profitable. I've already mentioned how much of that was down to Universe of Sofas, so no more explanation is needed for Max's reaction to Piss and Shit's firing.

He handled the situation the way he usually did – he lied to the client. He told her what a rascally pair of japers Paul and Shaun were. Of course they hadn't been fired. In fact they'd been sent to a secluded five-star retreat where, surrounded by the finest pampering known to man, they would come up with the Universe of Sofas campaign to thrash all Universe of Sofas campaigns. And, absolutely, it would be ready by Monday week.

My mission (and I had no choice other than to accept it) was to come up with the promised campaign in a little over seven days. Then don my deerstalker and find Piss and Shit to present it. Oh, and while I was at it, get a flaky Hollywood actress out of jail to shoot an award-winning and, therefore, potentially arse-saving ad. And, if I could possibly squeeze it in, save my tottering marriage.

I haven't told you about my tottering marriage, have I?

Nancy Stark: Max blew out of Greg's office as I was going in with a jug of coffee.

'Are they in Marrakech?' Greg asked.

'Haven't a clue. All I know is they're not at home.'

'Well, we'd better bloody well find them.'

'Don't worry, we will. What're you going to do about Rebecca?'

'Jesus, pressure, pressure, pressure.'

'I guess that's what you get paid for, Greg,' I said, 'not for reading the papers.'

Greg Fuller: If you read the biographies of great men – generals, world statesmen, billionaire tsars of software empires – pressure is very often the thing that brings out the best in them. Personally I think it's a pain in the arse.

Nancy Stark: Then he said to me, 'I'm going through hell here, Lola. No calls, no visitors until further notice.'

I'd been with him three years and knew the score. I drew his blinds, got his Evian from his fridge and shut the office door behind me.

That's what Greg's particular hell involved: sitting in a darkened office and drinking Evian from the bottle while he tried to think his way out of whatever mess he was in. He'd usually put something soothing on the stereo – classical or maybe, if he was feeling stressed in a more hip kind of way, one of those Ibiza Chill Out compilations.

If he'd bothered to stick his head out of his door, he'd have seen a very different kind of hell: a one-woman re-creation of the opening thirty minutes of *Saving Private Ryan*. It was total war out there. There'd be blood, severed limbs and corpses, and it wouldn't let up until Greg finally composed himself and was ready to face his public again.

I had to fend off the army of invaders, all desperate to see him. They'd try any trick, make any sacrifice in order to do it. But the bastards would have to get past me first. They all hated me for it and I hated that part of working for Greg but, as I said, Guardian at the Gates of Doom was in my job description.

Usually I'd get a couple of minutes' peace before it began, but that morning the onslaught started the second I heard him put on *Balearic Bliss, Volume III*.

The phone rang. It was Carrie, wife of the man at that very moment burning in hell.

'Sorry, Carrie, he's in meetings . . .' (If you can't stand the lying, don't answer the phone – I'm positive some famous adman said that.) '. . . I've no idea when he'll be free. It's frantic here.'

'When isn't it, Nancy? When you get a chance, ask him if we might get to see him this weekend? If he doesn't improve his attendance, the first time he'll see this baby I'm carrying will be at the christening.'

Carrie was six months pregnant with her and Greg's third.

'How are you feeling?' I asked.

'You really want to know?'

'Of course.' I wasn't lying this time. I liked her and, besides, pregnancy fascinated me in a God-that-could-be-me-one-day kind of way.

'Bloated. Elephantine. They'll do for starters. Actually I feel like I'm Ann Widdecombe and I've accidentally stumbled into the final of Miss World alongside the slimmest and most stunning woman in history.'

'How do you mean?' I asked. Even pregnant Carrie could never have been described as Widdecombe-esque.

'The fact that Greg is spending the next week shooting an ad with Rebecca Richards isn't doing wonders for my self-esteem.'

'Well, he might not be. Have you seen the papers?'

'Call me selfish, but I hope they throw away the key.'

'Beep, beep,' in my ear.

'I've got to go, Carrie – another call.'

It was Toddy Gluck, Fuller Scheidt's head of TV and the producer on the Blackstock Tyres ad.

'Nancy, where the hell's Greg? He should be here.'

'Where's here?' I knew where 'here' was but I liked doing dumb insolence with Toddy.

'French Films . . .' (Kevin French was the big-shot director on the Blackstock ad.) '. . . I feel like a total idiot making excuses for him. Can't you ever organise him properly?'

'Under the circumstances he assumed the wardrobe was cancelled, Toddy.'

'Of course it's been cancelled, but there are a million things to discuss, not least what we're going to do if the silly cow isn't let out of jail.'

'Look, I'll see if I can get him out of his meeting here and down to yours at some point.'

'You do that. And remind him that Kevin French is far too important to treat like this. I'll phone you back in fifteen.'

Even before I put the phone down I had incoming. It was on e-mail from Max's PA, Mandy.

```
Nancy - MM* wants status report on whereabouts of
P&S. Delivery time: 5 mins ago. Don't delay. Code
red - Mands
```

(*Translation: Mad Max)

I had no time to deal with it because the phone rang again. It was Bob Bull, Greg's client at Blackstock.

'I must speak to him. I can't believe he hasn't phoned me.'

'I'm terribly sorry, Bob, but it's wall-to-wall meetings here – you know what Fridays are like. As soon as I can get to him I'll make sure he calls.'

Yes, you're right in thinking that this was my client voice.

'He'd better. The whole thing's going phenomenally pear-shaped. Just remind him that I had severe, no, *phenomenal* misgivings about the Richards woman from the outset. I'm sure that's on the record somewhere and if it isn't I want it on the record as of now.'

I think I could actually hear him sweating.

'Greg is as concerned as you, Bob. I know for a fact that he's working on the problem right now,' I said. I could hear Greg's fridge being opened, so actually what he was working on was his second bottle of Evian.

Bob's front crumbled. 'For heaven's sake, what am I going to tell the board in Akron? All our balls are on the firing range and waiting to be kebabed.'

I think that was what Greg would have called a fatally mangled metaphor – a sign of a desperate client.

As I was saying goodbye I rattled off a rapid reply to Mandy's e-mail – the ability to do two things at once was essential to survival in the Fire Zone.

```
Mands – tell MM I'm tracking P&S down to precise
hotel in Marrakech. Hope good news soon – Nancy
```

I clicked 'send' and the phone rang again. It was Toddy.

'Hi, Toddy, was that fifteen minutes?'

'Don't get fresh with me. I'm not in the mood.'

But then she never was.

'He's still stuck in his meeting,' I said as I heard Greg take off the trance in favour of a calming aria. Calming, my arse – warbly soprano in one ear and Toddy screeching in the other was giving me a bloody headache.

'He'd better not be long, darling.' Only Toddy Gluck could make the word 'darling' send a shiver down your spine. 'Our director won't stand for much more of this. *And* he and I still have matters to attend to.'

I bet they did, I thought. She and Greg didn't know that I knew they'd been screwing for eighteen months. Greg had made a feeble effort at ending it when Carrie caught him just before she got pregnant. No, she didn't find out about Toddy. She discovered the one with Makeup Girl at a shoot. Not even Toddy knew about her, and Greg had no idea that I'd inadvertently helped Carrie find out. Makeup Girl was just after Headhunter at the awards bash, but just before Junior Client at the marketing seminar. Makeup Girl, Headhunter and Junior Client almost certainly weren't aware of each other. Junior Client and Makeup Girl weren't aware of Carrie or Toddy, but Headhunter definitely knew about Carrie – she'd been round to Greg's house for dinner. But Headhunter didn't have a clue about Toddy. I think Toddy suspected Headhunter but she could never prove it. Greg knew that I knew about Headhunter but he thought he'd fooled me on Junior Client.

Confused? There were plenty of times when I was.

And I definitely disapproved. Not because I'm anti-sleeping around. Greg could have had an even more tangled sex life (if that were physically possible without something dropping off) and I couldn't have cared less if it hadn't been for Carrie.

I really, really liked her.

And she was *pregnant*, for fuck's sake.

But what could I do? I was just the Guardian at the Gates of Doom.

Which brings me back to the phone. This time it was Letitia Hegg, aforementioned Headhunter.

'Greg hasn't forgotten our *petite* luncheonette has he, sweetheart?'

Don't 'sweetheart' me, you old trout, I thought but didn't say. I wasn't being bitchy. Even Greg used to call her 'mutton dressed as Britney Spears'. I know he'd screwed her but blokes are like that – anything with a pulse. Actually I don't think Greg was even that choosy.

'I'm sorry, Letitia, but I think he's going to have to reschedule. It's going mental here.'

'I'm mortified, angel. You have no idea of the trouble I've had getting a decent table at Opium.'

I could imagine actually – it probably involved falling to her knees in front of the maitre d', which wouldn't have been too hard – she'd had the practice.

She rang off with, 'Tell him I'll just have to make do with Andrew Cracknell. He always drops everything for me.'

Cracknell was another creative director and, again, I could imagine.

There was no time to get the taste of her out of my mouth before the phone rang again. This time the enemy was launching a final suicide attack.

'Nancy, get off your arse *this minute* and tell Greg that if he doesn't come down here *immediately* we will not have a director on Monday. That is not a request. *It's a fucking order.*'

You know, if Toddy had been on Hitler's staff he might not have got hammered.

TODDY GLUCK, HEAD OF TV PRODUCTION FULLER SCHEIDT ADVERTISING: You will not believe the pressure I was under. I don't know how many times I had to tell Greg's airhead PA that Kevin French was not a man you kept waiting. He was Hollywood now. That morning I heard him on the phone to his agent cancelling lunch with Kevin Spacey. Excuse me – *Kevin Spacey, Oscar winner.*

Fair enough, he and Greg had a history. They were both forty-one and had grown up together in the business, but Kevin had moved on. Anyone could see he would. He had a vision that couldn't be contained by thirty-second TV spots.

His first feature had been a huge success. An action film called *Body Matter*. Not my thing at all – far too Hollywood. I went to see it simply because it was Kevin French and I was staggered by it. He'd given it something you didn't see in that kind of film. Kevin had such a poignant way of framing his shots and an instinctive sense of when to leave a scene. Mind you, I should think the subtleties would have been over the heads of the spotty teenagers that flocked to see it.

NANCY STARK: Toddy and I saw *Body Matter* at about the same time. She'd been to an industry screening with champagne and nibbles. I'd queued up with my mates at the UCI in Edmonton. Afterwards she talked to me about it. I tuned out about two sentences into her review. Poignancy wasn't my strong point, and I hadn't a clue about when to leave a scene (at the end?).

I stopped her and said, 'Do you know my best bit? It was when Joe Shirer was hanging off that tower with his arm around that kid – didn't you *love* that kid? – and the helicopter couldn't get close enough for him to make a jump. I thought they were going to die. The whole cinema cheered when he did it. Apparently he did all the stunts himself. He must have been mad. And didn't he look *massive* in his CKs in the motel bit?'

She just looked at me as if I was talking Chinese.

'You probably didn't understand it, Toddy,' I said. 'It didn't have subtitles, did it?'

TODDY GLUCK: *Body Matter* was a global hit, and by the time he was working on our ad he was fighting off the offers. To be honest I think he was harbouring misgivings about having to shoot Blackstock and, despite the fabulous script that Greg had written him, I could see his point.

But he was a man of his word and he'd agreed.

He was doing it out of loyalty to Greg and because of his new bond with Joe Shirer – not exactly my type, but Kevin had made him glisten in *Body Matter*.

NANCY STARK: I was sick of the tosh about how Kevin French was doing the ad out of loyalty. He was also doing it for thirty-five grand a day. For that money I'd be asking, 'How loyal would you like me to be?'

TODDY GLUCK: But with Rebecca Richards in jail and Greg at the office in 'meetings', Kevin was rapidly running out of patience.

'I don't give a flying fuck how many films he and I have cut together, Toddy,' he said at one point. 'I'm giving him fifteen minutes to show, then I'm on the plane to LAX. I had a face-to-face with Jerry Bruckheimer last week and *he* waited for *me*.'

That was when I got on the phone to Nancy and bawled at her until she physically pushed Greg into a taxi. I'm afraid that a raised voice was the only thing she understood. God knows why Greg put up with her.

I loved the man but I despaired of him sometimes. It was one thing for him to carry a waste of space like Nancy, but I couldn't work out why he'd stayed with his wife. I suppose his loyalty was endearing but I had no idea what he saw in her. She was terribly sweet but she wasn't in his league. If she had been, then he wouldn't have been with me – clearly I met needs that she couldn't. Carrie just drudged around looking after his kids when God knows they could have afforded a house full of nannies. She should have taken advantage of the lifestyle Greg worked so tirelessly to give her. She should have got out there and made an effort; bought some decent facials, sorted out her wardrobe, learnt a language, anything to give him a bit of stimulation to come home to.

I felt sorry for her really. Well, she was a teacher when they met. God, don't get me wrong, it's a terribly important profession. But, be honest, you meet someone at a party and they admit to being a schoolteacher and what's the first thing you do? Exactly. Look over their shoulder for someone more promising.

I was desperate for him to leave her but only for his own sake. He could have done so much better. I cared for him too profoundly not to want the best for him. My own emotional needs definitely came second. There were some vile whispers that I was only with him because of the Italian buy-out, but nothing could have been further from the truth.

NANCY STARK: Greg was an intelligent man but when it came to Toddy he turned into Benny out of *Crossroads*.

Here are some facts presented exactly as I knew them.

Fact one: a friend of a friend was an estate agent with some poncey outfit in Knightsbridge. He told me about a client who'd come into his office. She was thirty-ish, thin and just about the most stunning woman he'd seen since he'd sold a mews house to Liz Hurley. He doesn't know why he remembered this but she was wearing Ungaro. She asked him for the details of a flat just off Sloane Street. Price: £1.4 million.

Fact two: I also knew a thin, thirty-ish, Ungaro-wearing and (I hate to admit it) stunning woman back then. She earned good money but nothing like enough to fund a mortgage that big.

So what, you might say, London is full of expensively dressed, attractive women. OK, smartarse, here's fact three: both women answered to the name of Toddy.

As the wide-mouthed frog said to the crocodile, you don't see many of those around here.

TODDY GLUCK: When Greg finally appeared that morning Kevin forgot his anger. He was bigger than that. It was all slapped backs and high fives. Kevin phoned for some coffee and we got down to business. At last, I thought, a meeting. I love meetings.

YASMIN FISH, RUNNER, FRENCH FILMS: If you don't count working in Homebase in my summer hols and helping my mum and dad in their greengrocer's, French Films was my first proper job. I'd only been there a week and I was serving coffee to Kevin French. If you'd asked me a month before, I wouldn't have had a clue who he was. Well, who looks at the 'Directed by' bit on the titles? You just want them to get on with the film, don't you? But I'd seen *Body Matter* and it was brilliant. And there I was serving coffee to its director, *and* I was about to spend four days in a film studio with its star *and* Rebecca Richards.

You might not think it was a big deal, but I did. I mean, look at all my mates. Kerry had a permanent job at Homebase, Tyler, my boyfriend, was out of work (but he *was* putting his band together), Michelle worked at Carphone Warehouse, Jules was a trainee hairdresser at Turning Hedz on Streatham High Street and Andie (Androulla) worked for her dad (accountant).

And I was *in films*. Well, I was a production assistant. One of the lads there said, 'No, you're not, you're a runner.' I asked him what the difference was and he said, 'You don't assist. You run – mostly to Valerie's on Old Compton Street for Kevin's special brioche.' But I didn't care. When I took Kevin French his tray of coffee, I looked at the ad agency's producer. She was gorgeous and I thought, one day I'm going to do your job. I wasn't even sure what a producer did but it must have been good because it meant she got to dress like something out of *Vogue*.

TODDY GLUCK: Kevin got the ball rolling. 'I've dealt with talent that won't come out of its trailer but I've never had an actress who can't get out of jail. What the fuck do we do about her?'

Greg didn't get a chance to answer because the runner brought in the coffee. She started pouring and Kevin stopped her.

'Is that Alta Rica, babe?'

'Er,' she dithered, 'it's coffee.'

I ask you, where do they find these people?

YASMIN FISH: I didn't know what he was on about. All right, I know now. But back then I just thought coffee's coffee – you've got Nescaff and you've got the stuff you stick in machines. I must have looked like a right pillock and Kevin went spare.

'Forget the fucking coffee. Just get me tea. And make sure it isn't that Typhoo piss.'

Apart from throwing up in Tyler's mum and dad's front room the first time I met them it was definitely the worst moment of my life. So far.

TODDY GLUCK: She fled with her tail between the legs of her baggy combats (*so* Top Shop) and Kevin picked up the thread. 'Even if they release her, she'll be a bitch to shoot. Everyone on the Coast says the bird's a bag of neuroses. Mind you, if Hollywood's taught me anything, it's this: run a fucking tight set. First hint of the Mariahs and she's toast.'

Music to a producer's ears.

'At least we won't have to worry about Joe,' Kevin went on. 'He's a director's dream. Give the kid his lines, point the camera at him and you'll get it in two takes, three max. Eleven weeks on location on *Body Matter*. In Utah we didn't even have a hole in the ground to piss in. I didn't hear Joe whinge once.'

GREG FULLER: We spent the next hour listening to tales of Kevin and Joe. The comradeship. The mutual respect. The bond in blood.

I'd known Kevin for well over ten years and this was to be the fifth commercial we'd shot together. In a former life he'd probably flogged fruit and veg in Albert Square or run with the Krays. Or maybe both. What you saw was pretty much what you got and he'd remained refreshingly uninfected by Adland bullshit.

I hoped that in his keenness to land the director's gig on *Body Matter II*, he hadn't caught the far more virulent Hollywood strain.

three:

flowers, farrah, dennie

TISH WILKIE, ASSISTANT TO REBECCA RICHARDS: Rebecca Richards!

The Rebecca Richards!

The most beautiful star in the whole of *Hollywood*! Well, apart from Cameron. And Jennifer. And Julia. And Angelina (who's a bit weird and lesbian-ish if you ask me but let's not go there). And Gwyneth. Maybe. No, forget Gwyneth. Whatever, Rebecca was definitely one of the most beautiful. *Definitely*.

And the most famous hairdo, like *ever*! Since Farrah Fawcett anyway and she was way before my time.

And *I* was her assistant! Not Farrah's. Rebecca's.

Like, who'd have thunk it?

That's what was going through my head as I was wheeling her luggage through Heathrow. I was watching her from behind and she was walking like only a *real* star can walk. I can't explain it. It was just kind of . . . I don't know . . . star-ish I suppose. Put it this way. If I'd been a top movie producer, which I wasn't, and she'd been a cocktail waitress, which she wasn't, and I saw her walking towards me with my Tom Collins with a twist or whatever, I'd definitely, *definitely* have wanted her in my next multi-multi-million dollar mega-motion picture.

But it was *so* awful. Only minutes after I was thinking those lovely thoughts she was being treated like a crack dealer. Like, it was so *totally* out of order. I wanted to scream actually. I wanted to shout out, 'Hey, I did all her packing and you won't find anything in there apart from some of the most beautiful, *exquisite*, designer-type items, which, by the way you'd better be *damn* careful with because I'm sure most of them are like *totally* far more than you could ever *literally* afford.'

I didn't say anything though. I thought it best to keep quiet. And I hate to admit it, but it crossed my mind that if they *did* find something, which of course they *definitely* weren't going to, and I'd owned up to doing her packing, well, who was everyone going to blame? *Exactomundo.*

VERONICA D, HAIRDRESSER TO REBECCA RICHARDS: I couldn't believe how Freddie was playing it at the airport. We had a situation and she was making it ten times worse. I was standing with Grant, Rebecca's bodyguard, and her new assistant, Tish (what kind of name was that? Sounded like a sneeze), and I decided to blend in. Grant stepped forward but I grabbed his arm. What was he going to do? Beat them up? Then I could sense Tish edging forward. I whispered to her, 'Honey, hold back. Freddie's got a shitload more experience than you and she's screwing up like a dream.' I couldn't figure out why Rebecca had hired Tish. Let's just say I've seen brighter.

TISH WILKIE: I'd only been working with Rebecca for a couple of weeks. I still couldn't believe I'd landed the job. But it seemed *so* perfect. We had so much in common for a start. Here's a list of our similarities (I *so* love lists and, believe me, a *Personal* Assistant to a Major Star, which I most definitely was, absolutely so depends on them):

1. We were both from Essex – she came from Chelmsford and I'm from Loughton, which, even though loads of footballers live there, is still lovely.
2. We were both Virgo – doesn't that just tell you *everything* about us?
3. We'd both gone to LA to seek our fortunes. OK, I went to stay with my friend Kryztal (who used to be Carol but it didn't sound very LA) and had a zillion stupid jobs before I ended up in a production company, while she shot straight to mega-stardom in *All Our Lives Before Us*. But it wasn't really *that* different.
4. Both of our mums were called Katie. Spooky or what?
5. It gets spookier. When we were little girls we both had a crush on Dennie in New Kids on the Block.
6. And guess what we both called our cats. *Dennie*! See? We totally *belonged* with each other.

VERONICA D: After I'd met Tish, I pulled Rebecca aside.

'Honey,' I told her, 'your life's in a crisis. You need to surround yourself with experience, guys with know-how. Just look at her. She named her cat after Donnie Wahlberg.'

'So did I,' she said.

'Uh-huh, but you didn't call yours *Dennie*.'

'I know, Veronica, but she's English. I think I must have been feeling homesick when I interviewed her.'

'Listen,' I said, 'you got hurt badly by Anthea. I don't wanna see you go through it all over again.'

She gave me a look so I just held up my hands and said, 'Hey, I only fix your hair, which happens to be the most famous and copied head of hair on the planet. Pay no attention to me.'

TISH WILKIE: It was *so* brilliant how I got the job. Her last assistant left very suddenly. She did a kiss-and-tell thing with the *National Enquirer*. Isn't that the most disgusting thing? When someone in a position of trust turns into an utter Judas? Trust is literally *everything* in this job.

I was at the production company that made *All Our Lives Before Us*, and one of Rebecca's people came in and said she needed a new assistant, like *pronto*, and had anyone done that kind of thing before? My hand shot up. I'd never been an assistant but I *knew* I'd get it. That's what was so good about LA. It had made me, like, *so* can-do.

Kryztal told me I was crazy. 'You're too nice, Tish. She'll just *so destroy* you. If you go with her to England, you won't come back.'

'Rubbish,' I told her. 'This is my big break. It's what I came to LA for. Anyway, I bet you anything she's lovely.'

Kryztal just laughed. 'She's a flake, Tish. Didn't you read what her old assistant said in the *Enquirer*?'

'I bet all of that's *so* not true,' I said.

'OK, look how she's been since the Joe Shirer thing,' Kryztal said.

I had to admit her life was in a bit of a state. The Joe Shirer thing! I'll give you it in list form:

1. Rebecca and Joe both starred in *All Our Lives Before Us* – I told you that already, didn't I?
2. They were the leads *and* they were going out with each other on the show.
3. In fact in the season that had just finished Joe had proposed to her. It was in the episode when he won some big cycling race and he was all dreamy and glistening in his Lycra outfit and he got down on his knees and Rebecca cried and then she said yes and then they both cried and they fell into each other's arms and the sun was setting behind them and the soundtrack was a fantastic

Christina Aguilera track or maybe it was Mariah but anyway it was so the most beautiful thing I'd ever, *ever* seen in my entire life.

4. They were also going out with each other in real life and it just seemed like they were the *most perfect* couple ever. Well, at least since Tommy and Nic before they had the *tragic* divorce.

5. And then Joe got a part in an action movie called *Body Matter* and he was *brilliant* and apparently did *all* his own stunts including this totally *amazing* one where he saved a little boy or a puppy stuck on a tower and the film was a massive, mega-hit and Joe was suddenly the biggest bee's-knees since Keanu was after *The Rock* or *The Mummy Returns* or something.

6. So, even though he was still in *All Our Lives Before Us*, now he was an all-action-mega-mega-star and he and Rebecca started to drift apart.

7. There was a girl in *All Our Lives Before Us* called Greta Bastendorff and she was really pretty and sweet – though, if you ask me, not nearly as beautiful as Rebecca.

8. And she didn't have the hair.

9. Anyway, Joe started seeing her.

10. And Rebecca found out.

11. Then they had a *massive*, blazing ding-dong in Spago.

12. And Rebecca walked out on him.

13. Or maybe it was Joe that walked out on her.

14. Whatever, doesn't matter, they were *finito*.

15. But Rebecca didn't really get over it and couldn't bear seeing Joe and Greta with each other on the set. God, that must have been so, so hard for her it still makes me cry.

16. Then the rumour about Joe appeared in the *National Enquirer*. You know, about his thingy. OK, I'll spell it out. People said his whatsit wasn't as big as it looked in those Lycra shorts on *All Our Lives Before Us*.

17. And I think that Joe thought that Rebecca must have started the rumour.
18. She denied it of course and I believed her, like, *totally*, 110 per cent.
19. And then they both had to come to England to make a stupid TV ad that they'd agreed to do when they were still in love and Rebecca didn't want to do it but she had to and that's more or less where I came in.

Isn't everything *so* much clearer when you do it as a list?

VERONICA D: You only need know two things about Joe Shirer and Rebecca Richards. One: Joe was a rat who was as cheap as any piece of white, black or brown trash that ever crawled out of a trailer park onto *Springer*. Two: however much he'd hurt her, Rebecca had too much decency to blab about his wiener.

TISH WILKIE: The flight to England was terrible for Rebecca. We weren't actually sitting with each other – she was in first and I was in club with Grant, her bodyguard, and Veronica D, her hairdresser (I really wanted to ask what D stood for but I was a bit scared of her). Freddie was sitting with her. I think they must have had a bit of a ding-dong because when we got off the plane they were barely speaking. Poor Rebecca was terribly fragile and in no state to be searched. I'm 110 per cent *positive* she never hit that horrible customs woman but if she did, and I'm *sure* she didn't, I couldn't say I'd have blamed her. Ordinary people just have no idea what the pressures on a star are like.

VERONICA D: After she'd been arrested I thought, if I know Rebecca (and I'd been fixing her hair for four years so I figured I did), she hit the bitch. Maybe she was asking for it and maybe she wasn't. Whatever, Rebecca hit her. It was just the kind of dumb-ass thing she'd do when she was strung out. She'd always regret it two minutes later.

We all do dumb things from time to time, but it doesn't matter much for two reasons. Most of us don't much care what the whole world thinks of us – if you're an actress, what the world thinks is *everything*, whether you like it or not. Second, even if we did care, most of us don't have *Hard Copy* telling the whole world every little thing we do in the first place.

Like I said, Rebecca always regretted her bad behaviour pretty much as soon as it had happened. A few times on the *Lives* set she'd come on like a diva and piss people off. You know what she always did though? She'd run up to me flapping her arms and say, 'Shit, Veronica, I've done it again'. Then she'd rush off and order everyone flowers. I could see her brain whirring and it was telling her: 'done-dumb-ass-thing-must-buy-flowers'.

I don't think anyone ever told Tish she'd need to find a good florist and make him her best friend.

Rebecca was a long, long way from the career stage some stars reach. The one where so many people are telling them they can do no wrong, they think they can act like twenty-four-carat assholes and it won't hurt them.

Take Tom Cruise or Will Smith. Take P Diddy, Eminem or just about any other guy who's sold a million-plus rap albums.

And don't forget Joe Shirer.

Joe was amazing, a Hollywood phenomenon. He turned into a twenty-four/seven prick after one blockbuster. It took Cruise until *M:i–2*.

Joe was the reason Rebecca was so strung out after the flight to England. She and I hooked up after we'd got off the plane and she told me a tidbit that Freddie had fed her up in first. She'd said Joe had negotiated himself up to exec producer on *Lives* and wanted Rebecca out. After *Body Matter* Joe really didn't need the show any more. Rebecca, on the other hand, had nothing else – she needed *Lives* bad. So why didn't Joe just walk off, be the next Cruise and let her have her little TV series?

Why did he have to do the twenty-four-carat asshole thing?

Why do dogs lick their balls?
Because they can.

TISH WILKIE: On the Friday morning after we'd arrived I was at the Dorchester where the ad agency had booked us in. Poor Rebecca was still locked up. She'd spent a whole night in jail, which must have literally seemed like an *eternity*. I imagined her being victimised by all the ugly prostitutes and druggies sharing her cell and I felt *so* guilty that there was nothing I could do to help. But Freddie had told me and Veronica to stay put while she and Grant went to the police station to sort things out.

I'd had the papers sent up to our suite and they all said disgusting, *totally* untrue things about her but I read them all anyway. Then I ordered full English breakfast for Veronica and me. I was starving and I ate mine but Veronica only had her grapefruit juice – she was *so* making a point, if you ask me. Then I checked all Rebecca's things for the zillionth time.

VERONICA D: Tish was prowling round the suite looking for something to do. She was bored and it was getting on my nerves.

'Tish,' I said to her, 'how many times you gonna check her stuff? It ain't been switching closets since the last time you looked.'

'I want everything to be just right for her when justice is finally done and she's set free.'

'I figure the last thing she'll care about is whether you put her panties in the top drawer or the bottom. She'll be too busy worrying about this shit,' I said, holding up one of the papers. 'These guys are vicious, girl. You wouldn't think Rebecca's one of their own.'

'Are you going to eat that?' she said, looking at my breakfast.

'No way,' I said. 'My stomach ain't on duty till lunch.'

I read some more while Tish ate my breakfast – shit, that girl could put it away. Then I got up and said, 'How about you take me to the shops?'

'No thank you, I'm staying here. Rebecca will need me when she gets back.'

Like a hole in the head, I thought.

'Well, I guess when justice is done she won't be wanting her hair fixed first thing. I'm outta here.'

TISH WILKIE: I must say that I was glad when Veronica went out. She'd been getting on my nerves. She was *so*, like, super-slim for a start. I mean, I could understand Rebecca watching her figure – she was a star – it was *expected* of her. But Veronica was only a *hairdresser*. Was it really necessary? It wasn't just that. She was *so* protective of Rebecca. She was only her *hairdresser*. Who did Rebecca *choose* as her *Personal* Assistant? *Exactomundo*.

God, don't get me wrong, I'm *terribly* PC, and I'm all for cultural whateveritscalled. How could I be anything else? I'm Californian now. So I don't want you to think I'm against coloured people – sorry, 'African Americans'. *No way*. I've got literally *millions* of 'African American' friends. So when I say that Veronica got on my nerves it had *absolutely, positively* nothing to do with her 'African American-ness', which I was completely, *110 per cent* comfortable with.

After she'd left I phoned my mum and dad in Loughton. I hadn't told them about my new job. My mum answered.

'Hiya, it's me!' I said.

'Tish? It must be the middle of the night over there. Is something the matter?'

'I'm not over there, Mum. I'm over *here*, the Dorchester.'

'You didn't tell us you were moving back. Why aren't you staying with us?'

'It's my new job – it's *so* exciting.'

'You're working for the Dorchester. Very flash . . . Tish is working for the Dorchester, Maurice,' she called out to my dad.

'No, silly,' I said, 'I'm working for a *star*. I'm her *Personal* Assistant! I do literally everything for her and we're really close and everything. It's *brilliant*.'

'Who is she?'

I'd decided not to mention who she was yet. My dad read the *Express* and they'd been really beastly about her. It would only have upset them. I was going to keep it a surprise. I knew that once they met her they'd *totally* fall in love with her.

'She's mega-famous, Mummy,' I said, 'She's in a TV show. We're filming an advert in Hounslow next week. Come to the shoot and I'll introduce you. You'll absolutely *adore* her and I know she's *dying* to meet you.'

I told her I'd arrange for a car to bring them to the studio and said goodbye. I was *really* chuffed actually. They *so* worried when I went to LA. I knew that they'd be thrilled that I'd literally become a really successful top Hollywood Assistant.

My mood got even better when I turned on the telly and flicked the channels. There she was on Sky News. Rebecca! She was surrounded by cameras on the steps of a police station. Grant was pushing the photographers out of the way and helping her into a car. Poor Rebecca, I thought. She looked as if she hadn't had a wink of sleep. How could she have with all the filthy druggies wailing for their fixes?

I switched off the telly. I knew *exactly* what she'd need and I went to run her a lovely, deep bath. The Dorchester had the sweetest baskets full of the *yummiest* foams and oils.

four:

jag, bmw, electrolux

CARRIE FULLER, ADVERTISING WIDOW: The kids had their jackets on. I'd put half the contents of the Waitrose deli counter in a hamper. Highgate Woods was waiting for us. It was the first sunny Saturday in May and definitely the first day of the year that the Fullers had resembled a happy-ish family, one complete with two parents, both genetic at that. We were halfway out of the door when the phone rang.

'Let the machine get it,' I said.

'I'd better,' Greg replied and he went back indoors before I could argue.

I waited by the car with Ryan and Hope and he came back out a couple of minutes later. He had that look on his face. The one that said, 'Work – what can I do?'

GREG FULLER: What could I do? The call was from Toddy. She said that Rebecca had agreed to give us half an hour, no more, for wardrobe. We were expected at the Dorchester in forty-five minutes. What was I going to say? 'Give them my excuses, Toddy. Tell them I'm playing Frisbee in Highgate Woods in a belated attempt to save my marriage'? No, I thought, Carrie will have to wait because Rebecca Richards obviously won't.

CARRIE FULLER: 'It's Saturday morning,' I said feebly after he'd explained about Kevin French's call. 'Anyway, why is the director calling you? I thought you had producers to do all that.'

'Like you say, it's Saturday. Job descriptions go out of whack at the weekend.'

'Normal people have weekends off, Greg.'

'I'm sorry but I'm as pissed off as you are. This wardrobe was supposed to happen yesterday.'

'How long are you going to be? Shall we wait?'

'I wouldn't. We'll be two or three hours with our precious star, then Kevin says he wants to go through the storyboard with me. I probably won't make it home before six, maybe seven. Why don't I call you?'

'Why don't you do that?'

He said goodbye to the kids, who looked even more gutted than I felt, and then to me. As he climbed into the car and drove off the baby kicked me violently in the stomach. It was telling me, 'Fight back, woman. Don't let him treat us like this again.'

'Sorry, baby,' I replied. 'This bloody pregnancy is leaving me too knackered to fight.'

I was going mad. I've heard of bonding with your unborn, but I was having full-blown conversations with mine. Since I hardly saw my husband, I suppose I had to talk to someone. We discussed all sorts: TV, new colour schemes for the living room – we once had a heated debate about government penal policy (Unborn was of the short, sharp shock tendency).

As we were going back into the house, Hope piped up.

'Why does Daddy have to go?' she asked. She was six then and couldn't be expected to appreciate the full horror of advertising.

'It's his job, sweetheart, he has no choice.'

'Why?'

'Because he has to watch the most beautiful woman in the world pour herself into a rubber dress.'

'Wouldn't he rather come to the woods with us?'

'Of course he would,' I told her as if I really meant it. 'What man wouldn't?'

TODDY GLUCK: Kevin and I were kicking our heels in the Dorchester reception with the wardrobe girl. Heaven knows what Greg was doing. It was the second time in two days that he'd kept Kevin waiting, and all because of his precious wife and kids.

'Why don't we start without him?' Kevin fumed, looking at his watch. 'I've canned a lunch for this bollocks.'

'Let's give him a couple more minutes, Kevin,' I pleaded.

'Five minutes. Then I'll be on a plane to LAX. I'm not pissing about here.'

Greg arrived twenty minutes later.

'Sorry, but I had a shunt on Hyde Park Corner,' he said. 'A black guy in a Beamer rear-ended me. The cocky sod wouldn't give me his details. He just bunged me a twenty and drove off.'

'God, are you OK, Greg?' I asked. 'He didn't pull a knife, did he? You hear so many stories.' I was genuinely worried – if anything had happened to him, you have to know I'd have been devastated.

'It was fairly boring, Toddy. No knives, not even an Uzi. I'm fine. I'm just sorry I've kept you.'

'Don't worry, mate,' said Kevin. 'Richards has kept us waiting for over twenty-four hours. Now it's her turn to hang about. She'd better not complain either – the bitch has already cost me a lunch.'

'Who was it with?' Greg asked.

'Oh, no big deal, just Sid Pollack. He's in Europe for a few days checking locations.'

He was blowing out *the* Sidney Pollack. Kevin French had definitely arrived.

CARRIE FULLER: Greg hadn't even left me with a car – the other one was in the garage – so Ryan, Hope and I had the picnic in the garden. They made a fast recovery. They were used to last-minute let-downs. As they played in the sun I remembered how perfect my marriage had seemed until six months before.

What the hell am I talking about? It wasn't perfect. For a start I hadn't seen much of Greg since he'd founded Fuller Scheidt four years before. Whenever I complained he'd say he was only doing it for us.

'What "us"?' I'd reply.

Men don't build business empires to provide for 'us', their families. They do it for the same reasons as schoolboys have pissing contests up the urinal wall – I used to be a teacher and I know all about it. It's an ego thing. I sometimes imagined Greg and Max still at it in the executive toilet, seeing who could get the highest.

His non-appearances weren't my only whinge, but all of them put together didn't amount to anything too threatening. And anyway, I'd think, name me one whinge-free couple. So, while it may not have been a perfect marriage, it was pretty good.

That all changed the day I got pregnant. It was also the day I found out about the makeup girl.

TYRONE EDWARDS: I been back from JA two days and my life's going down the toilet. I knew that cruise through customs was too good to be true, man. Saturday morning I'm in my pit and I hear Yvonne screaming. I think, pigs, man, it's a bust, gotta flush my stash. I run into the living room but Yvonne's on her own and she jumps me, starts hitting me, pulling my locks, scratching me. She works in a nail parlour so them claws are doing serious harm. I chill her a bit and ask what's up. Then she shows me the Polaroids. Fuck. She's found the pictures of me on the beach. With the white bitch. Tyrone, man, I'm thinking, they shoulda busted you at Heathrow cause it woulda saved your balls being ripped off now.

CARRIE FULLER: I'd spent years watching friends' marriages crumble because of affairs. I'd always express my sympathy but inside I'd feel a little smug – not me and my Greg.

The bastard. How dare he make me feel smug? I hate smug.

I didn't make a scene when I found out, but only because I was on my own and lacked an audience. Ryan had a school trip that day and needed money. My purse was empty so I looked in Greg's desk drawer where there was usually cash. I found a tenner for Ryan and I also found a receipt. He always had receipts that would pile up until he could be bothered to pass them on to Nancy for his expenses. I never paid much attention to them. I still don't know what made me look at it. It was for a room at the Charlotte Street Hotel. I couldn't work it out. However late he worked, Greg never stayed in town. We only lived in Primrose Hill and he'd always roll home at some point. I wasn't immediately suspicious – he might have picked up the bill for a visiting client – but I was curious.

I checked the date – the previous Thursday. I opened my diary, feeling like Fuller of the Yard. Thursday: Ryan to dentist; Hope to drama after school; best friend Clara round at 8.00. She was keeping me company because I had Greg down as spending the night in Wales – a two-day car shoot that had turned into three. He'd phoned me up on Thursday afternoon and told me about the overrun. He'd said he'd be back late Friday.

Curiosity turned to suspicion. Why would he have been at a West End hotel when he'd told me he was two hundred miles away? Greg had an exceptional brain but it hadn't yet got round to inventing teleporting.

TYRONE EDWARDS: You damn fool, I'm thinking, why didn't you chuck them stupid snaps? It wasn't even like you was keeping them because the bitch was fit. You got a fucking death wish, Tyrone?

CARRIE FULLER: I couldn't wait until Greg showed up that night to confront him. I phoned him. Nancy answered as usual and said he was in a meeting as usual.

Since I was now DI Fuller of the Yard, I asked her, 'By the way, Greg's black leather jacket. Has he said anything about leaving it in Wales last Thursday? I can't find it anywhere.'

'He was back at the office last Thursday. Don't you mean Wednesday?'

Up to that point I'd been fully prepared to believe a picking-up-the-tab-for-the-client-type explanation.

TYRONE EDWARDS: Yvonne's going mental again and whacking me on the head and I'm saying, 'Darling, it ain't what you're thinking, straight up it ain't,' and she's screaming, 'So if it ain't what I'm thinking why is your filthy hands all over the dirty white slut?' I'm telling her, 'OK, it was just the one time, sweetheart, straight up, maybe two times tops and she don't mean nothing, I swear on my mum's life she don't.'

CARRIE FULLER: That afternoon I picked up Hope and Ryan from school and took them straight to my mum's. I'd ordered Greg home early, something I'd never, ever done. I wondered if Nancy had realised her slip-up and told him. I imagined him driving home, cooking up his story. He didn't have a clue though. At first he tried to deny it but after a while he crumbled.

Her name was Mew (*Mew*). She'd been doing makeup on the shoot. He'd never met her before. They'd slept together on the second night. On Thursday he'd got greedy and taken her to the Charlotte Street for seconds.

I felt destroyed. Absolutely fucking crushed. I felt I didn't know him at all. I was re-evaluating everything he'd ever told me and I knew I'd struggle to believe anything he said after that.

I yelled at him, threw a mug at the wall. Then I cried. Then he did. He said she meant nothing; it had never happened before;

would never happen again; he loved me, only me; I *had* to believe him.

When I'd calmed down he said it had just happened. I told him that was rubbish. Nothing just happened. Ryan didn't just fall over. He mucked about and then he fell over. Hope wasn't just sick. She ate a dozen Mini Mallows and then she threw up. Neither did Greg and Mew (*Mew*) accidentally end up in bed like the random meeting of two particles.

'Carrie,' he pleaded again, 'it was the biggest mistake of my life. It will never happen again. *You have to believe me.*'

I so wanted to.

TYRONE EDWARDS: She stops hitting me but she's still screaming so I'm thinking, lover man, turn on the old Tyrone charm. It's worked before and it's gonna do the business now. So I'm telling her, 'Yvonne, babe, you know you're the only one. I'll do anything for you, you have to believe me,' and she chills a bit. You still got it, Tyrone, big time. Then I put my arms around her and she's melting and I'm thinking it's time for some sexual healing.

CARRIE FULLER: I still can't believe we had sex that evening. Right there in the kitchen where we'd been rowing.

I used to teach maths and a bit of science but I didn't need my experience to be able to work out when I'd conceived.

After that Greg did make an effort. He came home earlier. We even had a few weekends that went the full two days. I made an effort to trust him, as well as to look at myself and work out if there was anything I could change to avoid a repeat. But gradually it petered out. Max and Greg went into negotiations with the Italians and work took over again with a vengeance.

By the time of the Blackstock shoot nothing had been sorted out. True, I'd had no more evidence of straying and there wasn't a pocket, drawer or e-mail in-box that I hadn't searched. But we hadn't moved on from *Mew*.

TYRONE EDWARDS: After we finish Yvonne says, 'Tyrone, if this is gonna work you gotta straighten your life out. No more fucking around.'

'No more, I swear,' and, man, she's wagging that evil nail at me and I mean it.

'And you gotta get yourself a proper job. No more flying off to JA. You been lucky so far but that ain't gonna last. Sooner or later you're gonna get busted and I ain't waiting around for you to come outta Brixton.'

'I know, sweetheart, I'll get a job. Don't worry.'

'I mean *now*, Tyrone. Not sometime maybe never. And you ain't getting no job where there's women in the place, you hear me?'

'That's cool, sweetheart.'

'No white women, no black women, no women. I want you working where I know where you are and I can phone you any time I like and it ain't gonna get picked up by some slut saying, "Tyrone, he's tied up right now, darling".'

'Cool,' I say.

So I'm thinking, if I'm gonna get a job, I'm gonna need a new suit. And if I'm gonna buy a suit I'm gonna need some cash. I still ain't been paid by – nah, you don't wanna know his name – for the kilo I bring in last week, but I remember Ashley in Shepherd's Bush owes me three hundred from a deal I did a few weeks back. So I go to see my brother, Cedric, in Camberwell and borrow his wheels: '88 BMW 635, fuel injected, anthracite black, full leather, tinted glass, Alpina wheels, *mint* condition. I head off west and I'm a new man. This is the new Tyrone, I'm thinking, you are gonna make Yvonne proud.

That's when I hit the flash wanker in the brand new XK8 on Hyde Park Corner.

GREG FULLER: She'd give us half an hour, no more, her gnarled agent had told Toddy. A woman like Rebecca Richards didn't make her own appointments. I imagine she didn't even take a dump without taking legal advice beforehand and having a full makeover afterwards.

So if her schedule was so tight, why were we waiting for over an hour in her suite? Something was awry. We could hear her talking in the bedroom with her agent. Sometimes the voices were raised and we went quiet in an effort to hear them – no joy.

At one point, gnarled agent stuck her head round the door, gave us a false smile, introduced herself as Freddie and said her mistress would be two minutes. That was forty minutes before she appeared. Kevin twitched and glowered in a drug-enhanced strop. In a business that ran on narcotics, prescription or otherwise, Kevin had long stood as a role model. As one assistant director once put it, 'That geezer should have a haz-chem warning tattooed on his arse.'

'He doesn't look at all well,' Toddy whispered to me. 'Do you think I should take him out for some air?'

'Leave him be,' I said. 'If he spontaneously combusts it'll be one less diva to worry about.'

'Stop it, Greg, he's your friend,' she hissed. Then she changed the subject. 'Are you and I going to have some quality time after this, darling? There're things to discuss. *Properly*. We could go back to mine, relax on the terrace, Pinot Grigio, crab cakes, then maybe a little shagerooni . . .'

'Fine, sweet pea, if we ever get out of here.'

Jesus, I thought, I am sick of all the things I had to discuss with people. *Properly*.

Max wanted a proper discussion on Universe of Sofas. On Friday afternoon he'd rumbled Lola's Marrakech bluff. He'd got it out of Mandy, probably with the aid of thumbscrews. He'd had a shitfit. I'd promised Lola I'd sign for two full weekends of overtime if she spent Saturday tracking down Piss and Shit.

The Italians were due at Max's country pile on Sunday, where I was to join them for a proper discussion on our continued involvement with the agency once the deal was done. I hadn't yet told Carrie about that lunch.

My Blackstock client, Bob Bull, wanted 'a frank, cards-on-table, no-stone-unturned-type chinwag' regarding 'the potential consumer takeout ramifications of the Rebecca Richards post-arrest media phenomenon.' Roughly translated this meant, 'Help, I'm shitting myself.' He had a new CEO. Roger Knopf was fresh off the plane from Akron and didn't like the ad we were shooting. What's more he was probably a member of the Alabama Church of All Sinners Will Fry in Eternal Damnation, so he certainly wouldn't have approved of Rebecca's brawl. Bob was right to be scared. However things turned out, I gave him two months before he was clearing his desk and dusting off his CV.

Carrie didn't so much want to discuss anything as she wanted our life back. But I'd put her on permanent hold because I was inundated at work. And also, if I'm honest, because I was deferring the hard work that rebuilding our lives would involve.

Then there was Toddy, who wanted to discuss the exact date I'd tell Carrie I was leaving – and, by the way, had she shown me the details of the simply perfect little flat she'd found off Sloane Street, an absolute steal at one point something million?

I don't know why I let it get so out of hand with Toddy. Lola, my conscience, considered her to be shallow, grasping and, to all intents and purposes, the Enemy of All Things Good and True.

That's how Toddy came across to most people – the price she paid for her desperate ambition. She was a good producer but, rather than let her talents take her to the top naturally, she'd fitted a rocket booster-pack and sod anyone unlucky enough to get caught in the blast. Three months before the Blackstock shoot our head of TV had left. Before Max and I had had a chance to draw up the brief for his replacement, Toddy was making her pitch. She did an amazing sell on herself. Max, who'd only ever noticed her legs before then, was impressed. So was I, but I didn't want to make the decision – I'd seen more than her legs and I didn't think I could be objective. I let Max make the call.

Once the top job was hers I thought she might ease off the throttle. Maybe Stalin's associates thought the same about him –

'Now that he has achieved his dreams and has the Politburo at his beck and call, Comrade Joseph will show us his cuddly side.' They were dead wrong and so was I. After she'd reduced one of her PAs to a sobbing jelly I suggested she lighten up.

'You don't understand, do you?' she said. 'I'm still only twenty-nine. I have to *prove* I can do it. They have to respect me.'

'Toddy, they're terrified of you.'

'You see, it's working already, Greg.'

My point is that what Lola and the rest saw as malice for the sake of it was actually Toddy's sincere attempt to be the best. She put maximum effort into everything she did.

Everything.

For instance, they used to say nothing sucks like an Electrolux. Then along came Toddy.

TODDY GLUCK: It was so frustrating to have to sit there and wait. Greg was inches away on the sofa – so near yet so far. One could feel the electricity crackle between us. All either of us wanted to do was to go somewhere private and tear each other's clothes off – well, not exactly *tear* in my case – I was wearing a gorgeous little Prada two-piece.

GREG FULLER: Kevin was looking at his watch every thirty seconds or so. He was close to eruption. Suddenly he sprang up and announced, 'The bitch is taking the piss now. There's a flight to LAX in three hours. I'm on it.'

That was the moment the bedroom door opened and Rebecca appeared. It was the sort of entrance that careers are built on. Toddy was the last woman to credit a fellow female with anything, but even she was left short of breath by it.

TODDY GLUCK: Personally I couldn't see what all the fuss was about. The Donna Karan she had on looked much better when Victoria H had worn it to my birthday do at the Met.

GREG FULLER: Rebecca ignored Toddy and me. She knew where the power was and she veered towards it like a heat-seeking missile.

'Kevin, I've been dying to meet you,' she gushed. 'I can't believe we're shooting together. I *love* your work.'

(His 'work' consisted of a bunch of commercials and one cheap-thrills actioner – hardly a body to rival Scorsese's, but we'll let that pass.)

'Rebecca, babe, Bobby Zemeckis told me he couldn't believe I was getting you first.'

(Which didn't exactly square with the 'she ain't much of an actress – more Jessica Rabbit than Jessica Lange' comment he'd made earlier, but we'll let that pass.)

Air kisses were exchanged, and then Kevin turned to us to make the introductions. Nice of him to remember we were there.

VERONICA D: Rebecca was something, she really was. I'd been waiting in the other bedroom with Tish while she talked to Freddie – they were going over the *Lives* mess. I could hear them through the wall and it wasn't pretty. Rebecca had spoken to me about it Friday night, and the not-knowing if she still had a job was killing her. She'd also told me that when she'd been in jail one of the cops let slip that the search wasn't routine – there'd been a tip-off. She was at the end of her rope.

She was no better Saturday when those guys turned up for the wardrobe call. But then she stepped out and turned it on. She did it every time. She could've been bawling, raging and PMT-ed up to her eyeballs, but when she had to do the star thing it was like flicking a switch – set phasers on stun.

They bowed and scraped like she was Lady Di. I heard the guy called Greg say, 'I love *All Our Lives Before Us* – the show defines the promise of youth and *you* define the show.' I couldn't see a man like him, who must've been at least forty, setting his VCR for a high-school soap but we'll let that pass.

We went back into the bedroom with the wardrobe girl and I

fixed her hair while she put on the dress. It took some pushing and squeezing, but it was worth it. Hot? In that dress she could've had Pope John Paul up against the Vatican walls.

GREG FULLER: When she reappeared in rubber it reminded me of why I'd come into advertising. Name me any other profession where you can draw up a wish list and then make it come true. You want some sun? Write an ad that begins with 'Open on palm-fringed beach'. You have an unfulfilled need to inform (insert name of preferred masturbation fantasy, male or female) how much he or she means to you? Write, say, 'Marie Helvin pours a trickle of oil onto her naked stomach'. I did the latter when she was in her prime. Someone bet me that I couldn't get a supermodel into a chip-fat ad. I ended up with £100 and the cherished memory of a corn-oil-basted Helvin.

Now here I was in a suite in one of the world's finer hotels watching Rebecca Richards make squeaky noises in sprayed-on latex. The words happy, pig and shit came to mind, and I awarded myself a smug pat on the back for being the clever boy who'd come up with the idea in the first place.

CARRIE FULLER: It was starting to rain so I got the kids inside. In the cynical mood I was in it struck me as bitterly ironic that it should be Greg at the Dorchester and not me. By way of explanation, I'll replay a conversation we'd had some ten or so months before. Fuller Scheidt had been pitching for Blackstock and about five days before the meeting Greg came home in a temper. When I asked him what was up he said, 'Blackstock.'
'Why is it so difficult?'
'It's tyres, the least interesting thing on a car.'
'Well, why are you starting with the car?'
He looked annoyed. There he was struggling with his art while I washed dishes and arranged flowers or whatever it was he thought I got up to, and I was belittling his efforts by making it sound simple. But, I'm sorry, it did seem simple to me.

'How do you mean?' he snapped.

'How about this? Tyres are boring so don't think about them. Think about what they're made of. Rubber's quite interesting. I once taught a lesson on how many applications there are for the sticky goo that oozes from a tree.'

'Go on,' he said. He was still a bit snarly but I could tell he was vaguely interested.

'Well, there're rubbers as in pencil erasers, or as in johnnies – OK, maybe not. There're squash balls, wellies, whoopee cushions, industrial flooring, surgical gloves . . .'

'Is this going anywhere?'

I had no idea actually but I carried on anyway. 'There's a whole field of sexuality devoted to the stuff.'

His ears pricked up then, an instinctive male reaction.

'Hey,' I carried on, 'wouldn't it be funny if you had a vamp-ish sort of girl on a blind date with someone who works at Blackstock – a nerdy scientist. She misunderstands his interest in rubber and turns up in a fetish dress. No idea how you pull it back to flogging tyres though. Probably nothing in it.'

The rest, as they say, is history.

GREG FULLER: It was all over in ten minutes. Everyone agreed that the frock made Rebecca look stunning – certainly nothing like she'd ever looked before. Apart from, perhaps, in the alleged porn film that no one had ever seen and that I'd regretfully filed under Urban Legend, cross-referencing it with Hollywood Myth.

TODDY GLUCK: How did she look? I'd seen tarts in Shepherd Market with more class. Well, at least the thing fitted. Music to a producer's ears. When it was all over I grabbed Greg and suggested we adjourn immediately for our 'meeting'.

CARRIE FULLER: Greg arrived home just after nine.

'How did she look?' I asked casually.

'OK, I suppose.'

As if, I thought. 'Just OK?' I said.

'It fitted, anyway.'

'How was Kevin?'

'Jesus, that man can bore for Hollywood. All afternoon and half the bloody evening poring over storyboards and shot lists. Look, can we talk about something else? Today's been a total fuck-up for all concerned. I'm sorry it turned out like this.'

'So am I,' I said. 'Clara and Sam are coming over for lunch tomorrow. What shall I cook?'

'They're not tomorrow, are they? I've got to go to Henley. Max is having the wops round. I told you about it days ago.'

You may choose not to take the word of a woman crazed enough to converse with her unborn baby, and you may also believe the story that pregnancy kills off brain cells causing forgetfulness but, no, he hadn't told me.

I protested but it was futile. I had as much chance of taking on the corporate armies of Italy and their £28 million as I'd had earlier against Rebecca the Rubber Goddess.

five:

mariah, britney, george clooney's socks

TIM LELYVELDT, ASSISTANT TO JOE SHIRER: I was sitting in business on the flight from New York to London. I was actually glad I wasn't in first. Joe was up there and, though it was Sunday morning GMT, he was still pissed about Friday night EST.

VERONICA D: 'Seen these, honey?' I said, tossing the Sunday papers onto Rebecca's bed. 'These Brits are vicious. You'll love 'em.'
   'What is it?' she asked, still half-asleep.
   'Shirer walked off *Letterman* on Friday.'
   'Why, what happened?' She was waking up now.

TIM LELYVELDT: Before Joe would agree to go on the show the usual army of PRs had gone over to CBS to agree the questions. Routine stuff but they did stress one thing: under no circumstances will Letterman bring up the *Enquirer* story, also known as Dinky

Dick. Letterman's people assured them, 'Hey, c'mon, David wouldn't dream of going there.'

So they were taping the show and it was Joe's slot. Letterman was joshing him about his stunt work on *Body Matter* and asking if he was up for the sequel. Then he asked him whether he was going to stay with *Lives*.

'*All Our Lives Before Us* has been great to me, Dave, it's like family,' said Joe. 'I've had some incredible offers since *Body Matter* but I –'

He was still mid-answer when Letterman leant forward and asked quietly, 'So tell us, Joe, whatcha packing down there? Salami, Baloney, or d'you prefer an old-fashioned pair of rolled-up socks?'

That was it. Joe was out of his seat and it was 'cut to commercials'.

VERONICA D: 'Ain't it beautiful, Becca? They're ripping him to pieces.'

'It stinks, Veronica. I mean, it's just so personal. I know we're in the public eye, but hands off our genitals, please. It's no one's business.'

'You're too kind to him, girl. It's about time the sharks feasted on Shirer.'

'No, I may hate the guy but I feel for him,' she said. 'He did right walking off.'

'Hey, what do I know? I'm just the girl who fixes your hair. Anyway, David Letterman has knocked you off the front pages. At least you could thank him for that.'

TIM LELYVELDT: After *Letterman*, Joe went into hiding. He locked himself in a suite at the Paramount and didn't come out until it was time to leave for JFK. It suited me. The do-not-disturb sign meant that I didn't have to deal with him.

Joe hadn't been happy since the *Enquirer* piece on *his* piece. When he read it he wanted to kill the writer, a woman called Erika Mack. The only thing that stopped him was the fact that the name of her source would die with her. Since then his rage had subsided and only erupted when someone like Letterman relit the fuse.

But Joe was a difficult boss even when he was happy. He didn't create hell over the big things so much, but I didn't have to deal with those – they were what he had management and lawyers for. I was left with the details, and they were what Joe really fretted about.

I'd have to make sure that the bowl of organic jellybeans in his dressing room had been purged of the lilac ones. I'd have to take his jeans to the Denim Doctor to have the size ticket switched to something slimmer. When we were on location on *Body Matter* I'd had to make sure that the shower tank in his trailer was filled with mineral water. And I'd had to go to Tiffany to choose the sapphire that would express his undying devotion to Rebecca.

VERONICA D: After we'd finished with the papers I ordered juice from room service, and then I asked her what I'd wanted to ask for a couple of days. 'At the airport. I know they never charged you, but did you do it?'

'What, hit her? Afraid so. I regretted it the instant my fist started to fly through the air, but it was too late. I didn't realise this could do so much damage.' She flashed the sapphire. That ring had started wreaking havoc the day Joe gave it to her.

'So, who set you up? Couldn't've been Joe,' I said.

'No, Joe wouldn't stoop to that,' she replied. 'That's what he's got Lelyveldt for.'

TIM LELYVELDT: More recently I'd had to phone the British customs service to let them know that Rebecca Richards might be carrying more than expensive toiletries and designer items. Why did he do it or, rather, get me to do it? Payback. He was convinced she was behind the *Enquirer* story. Personally I thought that, however much he'd hurt her, she wouldn't have stooped to that. But I never argued with Joe when it came to the details.

Joe was delighted with the outcome. He was in the Green Room at CBS. One of the bookers came in and told him about her arrest. He said, 'Poor Becca. That's terrible, man. Tim, send her a bouquet, the best. You know she loves flowers.'

Oh, yes, he was delighted.

I did all right that time, but woe betide me if I ever screwed up on the tiniest detail of one of the details in Joe's life. The mineral water in the shower tank? On the first day I got the wrong brand – came within an inch of losing my job.

I didn't suffer alone. I knew one assistant who did get fired – because she didn't know the difference between regular and skinny latte. Actually she did know but she simply failed to appreciate that it would matter *that* much to her boss, a macho studio exec. When I first met her she was convinced she'd be the next Sherry Lansing. She ended up back home in Sioux City, working in a mall. That was the price of a Starbucks fuck-up, and it tells you pretty much everything about being an assistant.

But for every one of us that ends up in a Sioux City mall, there are a thousand more ready to slip into our shoes. Such is the lure of fame by association. There's an adrenal buzz to assisting that even repeated abuse can't take away. Who could deny the thrill of telling their college friends they helped, say, George (as in Clooney) to pick out his socks?

Everyone in Hollywood who isn't making it (and that means most of us) wants to hook onto someone who is. Successful actors, producers and directors are one-person welfare-to-work schemes. It cuts both ways though. Just as people are lining up to kiss celebrity ass, the stars welcome us with open pocket books. They *need* the entourage, and the bigger the better.

It's a statement. Given that it isn't yet fashionable for a star to pull his dick out of his shorts and lay it on the table in the Sky Bar, he has to make do with displaying his people. If the rumours about Joe were true (and I swear I had no idea), he had more reason than most to rely on his posse as a penis substitute. Joe's posse was *big* – if it had been a schlong it would have dangled some way past his knee.

Joe may have needed the entourage, but on the trip to London so did I. It gave me somewhere to hide. It wasn't as big as the Hollywood crew, being a slightly downsized-for-travelling-purposes version. All of their expenses were being met by the extraordinarily generous folk at Blackstock.

VERONICA D: Tish had taken the day off to see her folks, so Rebecca and I had some peace. She ordered us a massage in the suite. We were laid out on the slabs getting pummelled and I asked her, 'So who d'you think Joe's bringing over with him?'

'I don't know. Should I give a shit?'

'Course you should. We're talking entourages. Size is everything. You're a starlet, girl. You know that.'

She did know that. There was a contest on *Lives* about which of them could get more of their people on the payroll. The crew took bets on who'd come out in front. On Rebecca's side I think the pressure came from Freddie. It was a scam – she was trying to offload some of her agency's overhead onto the network. I never heard Rebecca complain though.

TIM LELYVELDT: Let me take you through them. First and foremost was Morton Newman, his manager. Morton defined his profession: shrewd, flexible, partisan, barely thirty but clinging desperately to the forever-twenty-one look that *Lives* had made popular – the perfect age – old enough to drink and screw, but still young enough to skateboard and get subbed by Mom and Dad.

VERONICA D: 'He'll have Short Mort with him, for sure. How many face-lifts has that guy had?' I said.

'I heard just the one.'

'C'mon, he's had more tucks than a motel bed.'

TIM LELYVELDT: Next up was his chef. Joe went nowhere without Roland Shen. He also went nowhere without his bodyguard. I knew of no threat to him, but he was deeply insecure. Not because of what an unhinged fan might do, more because he felt that he was becoming the only star without the ultimate accessory – his very own stalker. He was pissed that even Britney had one – 'It's a stunt, man. Who the fuck'd wanna stalk her?' Hollywood didn't have an agency that supplied stalkers to the stars (which, now I think about it, is going on my list of possible ventures for the day I've had enough of assisting). However, Joe could hire the muscle to make him at least look like a target. The man charged with stopping a bullet for him was Chris Shave.

VERONICA D: 'He'll have Shave with him,' I went on.

'I've got Grant. A bodyguard goes without saying.'

'Yeah, but Grant can take care of himself. Shave's fucked unless he can lock 'n' load like Rambo.'

'He'll be truly fucked over here, then. We Brits have quaint views on firearms.'

'Hey,' I said, 'd'you think he'll bring Jake? No, strike that. Not even Joe could be that dumb.'

TIM LELYVELDT: The party wouldn't have been complete without Jake, Joe's driver. He might have brought a personal trainer, a tennis coach or a manicurist. All would have been more use to him in London than a guy who'd never travelled further east than Vegas and who couldn't find his way out of a parking lot without a map.

Joe was also bringing his social life with him. Glenn, Waverly and Danton were his professional friends. In LA their numbers swelled to nine or ten but, as I said, this was the travel pack. Just as friends should be, they were always there for him – a party on call twenty-four/seven. But they were pros in the sense that, if Joe's career dived, they'd swiftly pack up and move on.

As I said, Joe was not bringing his personal trainer, his tennis coach or his manicurist. Other non-travellers were his stylist, his astrologer, his spiritual adviser, his shrink, his vitimologist, his acting coach and his pool cleaner.

VERONICA D: 'I think you'd better be prepared for the worst, honey. You know, *he* might show up with *her*,' I whispered. I could see the masseurs' ears flapping.

'Bring her all the way to London for a four-day ad shoot? I don't think so, Veronica. Anyway, I heard she's supposed to be testing next week for the Farrelly movie.'

'I thought they were talking to you about that.'

'They were. Story of my life. I also heard she's going home to Dallas to get her nose fixed.'

'The bitch's nose ain't all I'd like to fix. Just be prepared, Becca.'

TIM LELYVELDT: I almost forgot the most important element of any A-minus list star's posse. The Trophy Girlfriend. Joe was bringing Greta Bastendorff, who'd been glued to his side for the past six months. She was elfin-beautiful and every bit as sweet-natured as she looked – believe the hype.

Of course, he was also bringing me, Tim Lelyveldt, Executive in Charge of Jellybeans.

VERONICA D: 'He'll have Lelyveldt with him,' Rebecca said.

'Himmler to Joe's Adolf.'

'He's good, isn't he? It crossed my mind to steal him when Anthea left.'

'Well, it ain't too late to arrange a swap with Tish. If you wanna pay Joe back, she's guaranteed to fuck up his life.'

TIM LELYVELDT: We arrived at the Dorchester eventually. I say eventually because Joe insisted Jake drive the lead limo. He gave us a deluxe tour of London's sights before he got us there.

We were walking through the lobby and Joe grabbed my arm.

'She's here,' he hissed.

'Who?' I said.

'She's flown her fucking hairdresser over.'

I looked up and saw Veronica D disappear into an elevator.

Since Rebecca's legendary hair needed round the clock TLC to keep it that way, I wasn't surprised to see her, but Joe turned to Morton and snapped, 'Why the hell didn't you negotiate me a hairdresser?'

Morton floundered for an answer. I wanted to step in and help him out. I wanted to say, 'Because you don't need a hairdresser, Joe. You have only slightly more hair than Bruce Willis. The only TLC it needs involves some schmuck, usually me, putting a blob of gel in his hand, rubbing it into your scalp and mussing it about a bit. Takes all of five seconds,' but I didn't. The first rule of assisting: know when the fuck to butt out.

After a moment Morton got himself together and said, 'A complete oversight on my part, Joe. I don't know what I was thinking. I'll rectify it first thing tomorrow.' Which is exactly what I'd have said in his shoes.

By the way, you may have been wondering what Veronica's D stood for. On the *Lives* set she was known as Veronica Dontevengo-therehoney – her standard reply whenever anyone was dumb enough to ask.

I checked Joe into his suite and unpacked him. He looked exhausted but I knew that – seven o'clock call the following day or not – he wouldn't sleep. He was no insomniac. Not-sleeping was his new thing. He'd met Madonna at some party. She told him that sleep was an indulgence and she operated on four hours a night. Then he'd read an interview with Mariah. She said that because she was a worrier she'd get up at night and write lyrics, do her scales, bath her shih-tzu or whatever. Eventually she'd trained herself to manage on three hours' shuteye a night. 'Fuck the pair of them,' said Joe, never one to be outdone by a couple of mere divas. 'An hour's cool for me.'

As I left his suite he said, 'Tim, set your alarm for two and wake me.'

'You'll be wrecked, Joe,' said Greta.

'Sleep's for faggots, babe.'

He could be very single-minded when he wanted. Or a prime asshole. Depends on your point of view, which in turn depends on whether or not you were on his payroll.

six:

the script that yasmin fish couldn't believe she was going to have something to do with

YASMIN FISH: I can't sleep when I'm excited. Like the night before I saw the Spice Girls (I was only thirteen, all right?), the night before Tyler and me were going to do it for the first time, the night *after* we did it (that was worry – I was sure I was pregnant), and the night before Ashley Cole came to my school to give a 'just say no' lecture (I hated football but I loved Ashley Cole). I didn't sleep a wink the night before the Blackstock shoot.

On the Friday I'd been given a call sheet, which is a list of names and job titles. Rebecca Richards and Joe Shirer were down under cast. Mine was on it too – Yasmin Fish: Runner. It was weird seeing me on the same sheet of paper as them. OK, so there were about forty crew members listed as well, and my name wasn't literally on the same page because the call sheet was about five pages thick, but I was definitely in there.

I was still gazing at it at two in the morning – Rebecca Richards,

Hollywood, Joe Shirer, Hollywood, Yasmin Fish, Streatham. *Wow*. There was a script stapled on at the back. I'd never seen one before and I decided to read it.

---

fuller scheidt advertising / tv script

CLIENT	BLACKSTOCK TYRES	AC. GROUP	HALLEY
PRODUCT	CORPORATE	CR TEAM	GREG FULLER
JOB No.	BS-001		
TITLE	BLIND DATE	PRODUCER	TODDY GLUCK
LENGTH	120''	DRAFT No.	3

Open on DOUG (JOE SHIRER) sitting in a booth in an American singles bar. He seems apprehensive as he waits for his date to show up. He checks his teeth in the reflective glass of the table and pulls at the knot in his tie. Then he looks up, his eyes widening, as ROXIE (REBECCA RICHARDS) appears across the crowded bar. She's wearing a black rubber dress and fetish shoes. She sashays through the drinkers and slides into the seat opposite. She immediately clicks her fingers to a passing waitress, who gestures that she'll be back for her order. Doug clearly can't believe that this woman could be his date.

    DOUG: Hi ... er ... Roxie?
    ROXIE: Doug, so good to meet you at last. Denise has told me
           so much about you. ...

From the moment she opens her mouth we appreciate that Roxie is used to assuming a dominant role in these situations. She leans in close to him and lowers her voice.

    ROXIE: ... including your thing for rubber.

He looks down, embarrassed.

   DOUG: Really?

She puts a soothing hand on his.

   ROXIE: Don't worry, honey. Actually, I find it exciting.
   DOUG: You do? Most women –
   ROXIE: I know, honey, most babes run a mile. But I'm not
          most babes. I want to know all about it. I want to
          know what really gets your juices sluicing.

She has slipped off a shoe. Her bare, painted foot has
disappeared up his trouser leg.

   DOUG: Heck, where do I start? I guess I've always loved
         rubber.
   ROXIE: Go on.
   DOUG: I like its pure blackness, its suppleness, its strength.
         I love the way it grips, the way it clings like no other
         substance.

Doug grows more confident as he talks about his passion.
Meanwhile Roxie's foot has disappeared between his thighs.

   ROXIE: That sounds *sooo hot*.
   DOUG: I always wanted to do something truly exciting with
         it – something the whole world would talk about.
   ROXIE: Mmmm, Doug, baby, you're a *nasty* boy.

Doug sits back slightly, a look of triumph on his face.

DOUG: Last week . . . last week I made the breakthrough.

Roxie gives Doug's hand a passionate squeeze and almost purrs as she speaks.

ROXIE: Tell Roxie, tiger.
DOUG: It's called GoFlat. It means there's no stopping you, even after a puncture.

She looks a little confused but no less interested.

ROXIE: No kidding.

Now Doug has worked up a head of steam. He can't believe he's finally met a woman who shares his obsession.

DOUG: Yeah, you can do up to 50 mph after a blow-out and drive home on the flat. Junk the spare in the boot. The other guys in R&D had been working on it for years, but I –
ROXIE: Baby, are you talking about what I think you are?
DOUG: The Blackstock GoFlat tyre. God, there's nothing we can't do with rubber! There's not a vehicle or a driving situation you could dream up that we couldn't make the tyre for. We can –

An icy veil draws itself over Roxie's face as the scale of the misunderstanding strikes her. She pulls back from him abruptly.

ROXIE: Hold it, Doug, I'm double-parked. I really can't afford another ticket.

She gets up and hurriedly exits the bar, leaving Doug
slack-jawed and crestfallen. The waitress arrives to take the
order.

> WAITRESS: What did you say to her? She find out you're
> kinky or something?

Fade to black and a rolling title:

THIS COMMERCIAL IS DEDICATED TO VICTOR BLACKSTOCK,
THE ORIGINAL RUBBER OBSESSIVE.
WITHOUT HIM OUR 104-YEAR LOVE AFFAIR
WITH THIS AMAZING SUBSTANCE
WOULD NOT HAVE BEEN POSSIBLE.

Cut back to Doug in the booth. He takes a small black rubber ball
from his pocket and bounces it on the tabletop. His expression
switches from deflated to excited.

> DOUG: (to himself) Self-inflating tyres!
> SUPER: *BLACKSTOCK* (logo)

When I'd finished I read it again. It was hard trying to picture all
the words turning into an ad. I couldn't wait to see it on the telly
and I imagined telling my mates that I'd had something to do with
it (didn't know what exactly, mind, and it probably wouldn't be
much, if anything, but still definitely better than working at
Homebase).

seven

NORMAN THE COOK: Connery, Kubrick, Cruise, Kidman, Caine, Ciccone, and that's just the Cs. The movie big-knobs that have eaten my bacon butties must run into the hundreds.

Check the Plate is the name, movie catering is the game. I run the show with Wendy, AKA Mrs Norm. She can't cook to save her life. If it doesn't come from M&S with instructions on its arse, she doesn't stand a chance. She may be Ava Gardner in the bedroom but she's also Ava bloody Gardner in the kitchen. It was her total inability with anything trickier than a Pop Tart that got me started in this line.

I did the grub at home and found I had a flair. I began with the simple stuff – a nice cooked breakfast or a Spag Bol. Then I got a bit more adventurous. Cooking is a piece of piss, if you ask me. You get your bit of meat, fuck it about a bit and before you know it you've got *gratinée* this or a *Provençal* that.

I used to work for Lee Lighting. I was driving a truck all over the shop dropping off the gear for shoots. Then I got talking to the geezer that was catering for *Brideshead Revisited* and I thought, I could do this.

I got a bank loan, bought an old Bedford and roped Wendy in to drive – my knees were going. We haven't looked back.

You name it, we've fed and watered it. Bond movies, telly, pop promos. We did *Queer as Folk*, which was an eye-opener. I'm all for live and let live, but I don't fancy seeing ten takes of two blokes snogging while I'm stirring their *coq au vin*.

No, there's not a lot I don't see from my serving hatch.

It's about six by four, the hatch on the side of my truck. I look out of it and it's like seeing the world in Cinemascope. I reckon I've got one of the best views in the movie business.

It's a delicate balancing act, cooking for the film crowd. On the one hand you've got your typical spark. He'll start his day with an egg, bacon and sausage roll, then have cottage pie, peas and spotted dick for his lunch. Then you've got your luvvie. He or she will have very different ideas as to what constitutes fine fare, and these will almost certainly involve aubergines somewhere along the way. So at one end of my range there's a nice bit of scrag end with two veg. At the other there's blackened Cajun whatsit, ratatouille and some nonsense with Thai spices.

Like I say, a delicate balancing act. Mind you, there's always one greedy Herbert with a tool-belt who piles the luvvies' lime-drenched tuna alongside his steak-and-kidney pie and chips.

Which makes a complete bloody mockery of my ideas of film-set sociology.

My mates are always asking me about my movie experiences. Lads, I tell them, you know what took the biscuit? It wasn't any of the Bonds, the Robbie Williams videos, or even *Eyes Wide Shut* with Kubrick. No, the strangest time I ever had was on a telly ad. By rights we shouldn't even have been there. It was a studio shoot and all the bigger ones have their own canteens. But some pillock in the kitchen at Hounslow had got sloppy with a fryer. There'd been a fire and they'd had to call in Check the Plate. The shoot was for Blackstock tyres.

BOB BULL, EXECUTIVE DIRECTOR IN CHARGE OF MARKETING, ADVERTISING AND PROMOTION (EUROPE, THE MIDDLE EAST & NORTH AFRICA, EXCLUDING LIBYA), BLACKSTOCK TYRES: What a buzz. Rebecca Richards and Joe Shirer from *All Our Lives Before Us* in my ad. A phenomenal coup, totally phenomenal.

It was a humdinger of a script as well, one that truly pushed the old envelope. It took nerves of toughened steel to sell it to the Exec Board in Akron, Ohio. But I laid it on the line for them: 'You took me on to raise Blackstock's sex-quotient. Close-ups of tread patterns will not sauté our sirloins, gentlemen. Rebecca Richards and Joe Shirer *will*.'

There was much huffing and puffing from the old duffers. But all credit to them, they let me take the ball and run all the way to the try-line.

NORMAN THE COOK: Now I think about it, Blackstocks were on my first Bedford. We had a blow-out on the way back from a shoot in the Mendips. Wendy managed to keep it on the road, but it was a bloody mess. The back of the truck looked like a Peckinpah movie – *Sauce Provençal* everywhere. After that I fitted Dunlops. Should have insisted on British in the first place. So what if Blackstock has a factory in Liverpool? There's a McDonald's on every bloody high street, but that doesn't qualify them for British passports, does it?

BOB BULL: I honestly do not believe that there were many market-ing honchos that could have pulled it off. It really does come down to bonding with the creatives. Greg Fuller and I clicked the moment we met. There was a phenomenal amount of common ground between us. For instance, we were both nuts about Status Quo.

NANCY STARK: Greg called me from Hounslow Studios as soon as I got to work.

'Any luck, Lola?' he asked.

'Paul and Shaun? I spent all day Saturday trying. Sorry. Not even Shaun's dad knows where they are.'

'Let me explain how this job works, Lola. You are paid to tell me what I need to hear, just as I am paid to tell the likes of Bob Bull what he needs to hear. Jesus, you should see what he's wearing today. Anyway, I've spent the last ten minutes greasing him up with, "Don't worry, Bob, Rebecca's arrest has already been forgotten. Look at today's *Sun*: EDWARD PLANTS HIDDEN CAMERA IN HM'S LOO," and, "Status Quo, Bob? One of the few bands privy to pop's great secret – you can never have too much of a good thing." Now, Lola, "Sorry, Greg, can't find them," wasn't what *I* needed to hear from you. Next time I call, for fuck's sake give me some good news.'

'I think you could have made the point in half the words,' I said, but he'd already hung up. Good job probably.

BOB BULL: Greg's and my relationship went beyond shoptalk. It was only a matter of time before he, Carrie and the little Fullers were sharing their holidays with us Bulls. I could picture it: he and I sipping Frascati on a Tuscan veranda while Carrie and Jane bathed the sprogs.

The fact that we were about to 'turn over' with no less a director than the great Kevin French on what I confidently believed would be the phenomenon, advertising-wise, of the new millennium, simply confirmed our bond.

Greg was very taken with the satin bomber I was wearing, a rare Foreigner tour jacket. Shoot attire is absolutely key. I'd given my wardrobe a great deal of thought and I was pleased Greg noticed. I told him the bomber was one of the prizes in a promotion I'd once run. That was an experience, taking the competition winner backstage at Earl's Court to meet the band – phenomenal guys, living rock legends.

I'd already earmarked a space in my office for the framed photo of me with Joe and Rebecca. It was going to take pride of place between Foreigner and Michael Barrymore. I once did a supermarket ad with him and he had the crew in stitches for three solid days. 'Awight!' Shirt-lifter or not, I won't hear a word against him.

Oh, yes, hobnobbing with the stars was nothing new to me. Even so, it was still pretty damn special when our leading pair turned up. A lump-in-the-throat moment.

NORMAN THE COOK: The fans at the gate went bananas when Shirer and Richards showed. I'm not surprised. I haven't seen so many limos since the funeral scene in *The Godfather*.

TISH WILKIE: It was so, like, literally *way cool*. I can't describe the feeling of walking in with Rebecca Richards. All those eyes upon us. I wanted to shout out, 'Yes, I'm with Rebecca. I'm her *Personal* Assistant.' I felt almost exactly like Marilyn Monroe must have felt when she walked down the staircase in the big ballroom scene in *Gone With the Wind*.

TODDY GLUCK: No one paid much attention to Joe and Rebecca's arrival. Kevin was keeping us all far too busy. He'd called a crew meeting and I decided to listen in. I wasn't crew so I wasn't strictly invited, but I took my job damn seriously and I knew it would be educational. I was about to go when a little American who introduced himself as Morton Newman, Joe's manager, collared me.

'There are a couple of issues, Toddy. Tiny things that will ensure Joe hits the ground running.'

'Of course, Morton, fire away,' I breezed – I thought it best to get off on the right foot with someone so important.

'Please don't for a second think that he's unhappy, but Joe feels that the ad agency has been just a little negligent.'

'The jellybeans!' I cried. 'Did they not have clingfilm over them?'

'The beans were fine, Toddy. No, it's the hairdresser.'

'What hairdresser?' I was confused.

'Exactly,' he said. 'Joe feels that he should have been provided with one.'

'Really?' I didn't know what else to say. Well, hair wasn't Joe's thing so it had never crossed my mind to ask. I flipped open my Filofax and wrote 'HAIRDRESSER' on a blank page. 'Does Joe have someone in mind?' I asked. 'There are some fabulous stylists in London.'

I immediately thought of my own darling little snipper, Fouzia at Nicky Clarke. I was about to mention her when Morton said, 'Joe would be more comfortable with someone from LA.' He gave me a sheet of paper with three or four names on it. As I looked at it, he added, 'Also, Joe would very much like a bed.'

'Pardon me?'

'A bed. In his dressing room.'

TIM LELYVELDT: There was panic in Joe's dressing room. The only one that wasn't running around like a headless chicken was Joe himself. It was like he'd turned up to play the lead in *Coma*. A combination of Post-*Letterman* Stress Disorder, jet lag and his no-sleep regime meant that behind his shades he could barely keep his eyes open. He crashed on the sofa. No one knew if he'd be fit enough to work. Then Greta suggested a bed.

TODDY GLUCK: 'He's got a number-two crop. What's he want a hairdresser for?' Greg said when I told him.

'It's worse than that. He wants one from LA.'

'Jesus, we haven't even shot the first set-up and it's started. Look, just do it. We'll worry about who pays later.'

'That's not all. He wants a bed.'

Greg started to laugh.

'It's not funny. His manager says it's the new thing in LA. Apparently all the stars have them in their dressing rooms. He called it Karmic Daylight Sleep Therapy. I simply can't believe we overlooked it. I'm normally so up on these things.'

'What's the big deal? You're a producer. Produce a bed.'

'OK, OK, I'll do it, but I'd just like you to know that my morning is in total ruins. I'm missing Kevin's meeting. I so wanted to go to that.'

'Go then, Toddy. I'll get the bed.'

'You complete darling. And thanks for stopping by yesterday on your way back from Max's,' I added in a whisper. 'Twice in one weekend. What have I done to deserve you?'

YASMIN FISH: I couldn't stop myself calling Tyler on my mobile and telling him I'd actually seen Joe and Rebecca. He was still in bed and acted like he couldn't care less but I knew he was jealous. I didn't mention that Greta Bastendorff was there as well. He really fancied her. She was pretty and she was only seventeen, the same age as me.

I read *Heat* and I knew all about Joe, Rebecca and Greta. I felt sorry for Rebecca. I remembered how I'd felt when Tyler and me finished for a few weeks because he wanted to 'get his head together', and then he turned up at the Ministry with that stuck-up slag, Bridget Farmer.

I'd been given a walkie-talkie and I felt like Sigourney Weaver in *Alien*. I wasn't sure what it was for. The studio wasn't *that* big. Couldn't we have just shouted to each other? I was trying to figure out how it worked when Kevin called a meeting.

TODDY GLUCK: Kevin may have been rough at the edges, but the moment he climbed up onto a chair he was an inspiration. He started out by letting everyone know where they stood.

'Some of you won't have worked with me before, so I'll tell you one thing about myself. Guy Richie might like to think he's a geezer, but I'm the real thing. I grew up in Poplar in the days before the City pricks turned it into fucking wine bar. My school was crap and I only got one CSE. But I learned one invaluable lesson: take no shit. It works in the playground when some big cunt is trying to shake you down for your dinner money, and it works in a movie studio. I don't give a dog's cock whether I'm shooting a $100 million feature or a lager ad. I'm a bastard either way. I run a tight set, a fucking tight set.'

Music to a producer's ears.

YASMIN FISH: I was standing next to a couple of sparks. They're like electricians really – basically they plug in the lights. The smaller one whispered to the other, 'I was with him on the Estée Lauder job in Portugal. Tight set, my arse – didn't know his bollocks from a bag of marbles.'

TODDY GLUCK: Then he went on to set out his vision. 'In case any of you were wondering, we ain't making a tyre commercial. . . .'

YASMIN FISH: 'News to me,' the little spark whispered. 'It definitely says Blackstock Tyres on my call sheet.'

TODDY GLUCK: '. . . This is art. And, like it or not, I am the fucking artist. I've got a vision in here,' he said, tapping the side of his head, 'and I'm gonna spend the next four days getting it onto film. Anyone that stands in my way gets a fucking one-way ticket to Hades. . . . Any questions?'

For a moment there was stunned, awed silence, but there's always one idiot, isn't there?

YASMIN FISH: I nudged the little spark and asked, 'What's he on about?'

'It's complicated, darling,' he whispered, 'You'd better ask him yourself.'

I stuck my hand up and said, 'Excuse me, I was just wondering where Hades is.'

He exploded. It was awful. Definitely the worst moment of my life, at least since the coffee thing. The spark was pissing himself.

'What the fuck am I working with?' Kevin yelled. Then he looked round the room and pointed at the little spark. 'You fucking tell her,' he yelled. The bastard stopped laughing then. He asked three or four more people before someone said, 'Hades – it's the island next to Mikonos, isn't it? It's got a little taverna run by the geezer who used to be Ridley's favourite grip.' Obviously the wrong answer, because Kevin was off his chair and storming out.

NANCY STARK: Greg phoned again half an hour later.

'Paul and Shaun – I'm working on it now,' I said before he had a chance to speak.

'I wasn't calling about them, smarty-pants. I want you to get a bed to the studio ASAP. Joe Shirer needs one in his dressing room. Some sort of Beverly Hills therapy apparently.'

'I'm just a secretary. We did shorthand and diary management at college, not beds. Where do I get one?'

'Universe of Sofas does those pullouts. Tell anyone that works on the account to have the client send one over. If they whinge, say there'll be some PR in it for them. They've got a store down the road in Ealing – should have it here by lunch.'

'Isn't this the kind of job that Toddy's supposed to do?'

'She's in a meeting,' he said a bit too defensively.

Of course she was in a meeting. Toddy spent her life, if not actually in meetings, then planning them, shuffling them around or, if she happened to be asleep in her silk-lined coffin in Holland Park, probably dreaming about them.

'Anything else?' I asked before I hung up.

'Tell my department to hang around tonight. I'm coming back to the office to review Universe of Sofas.'

He'd put all his creative teams on the brief. It was official: Universe of Sofas was code red.

'What time will you be back?' I asked. 'Some of them have got families to go home to.'

'Fuck knows when I'll be back. And sod their bloody families. Do you think I've seen much of mine lately?'

CARRIE FULLER: Greg had got home from lunch at Max's at about eleven that Sunday night. I had the TV on but I wasn't really watching. It was just something to stop me talking to Unborn. I'd cancelled lunch with Clara and Sam and it had been a shitty day.

'You act like a doormat, you get treated like one,' Clara had said when I'd called her.

'Greg can't help it. He's never been busier,' I'd replied. I had no idea why I was defending him – habit, I suppose.

As I heard his key in the lock, Unborn piped up. 'Your mate was right with the doormat comparison, you know. You've got "PLEASE WIPE YOUR FEET" tattooed on your forehead.' Just the kick-start I needed: Greg and I started to row before he'd even taken his jacket off.

He hit me with all he had: the pressure he was under, the Italians, Universe of Sofas, Blackstock, the fact that I questioned his every move, put him under constant scrutiny, as well as the fact that I showed no interest any more.

'Are you going to take that lying down, woman?' Unborn demanded, kicking me in the ribs to reinforce the point. 'It's your sodding bladder that should be complaining about pressure, the size of me now. And as for the scrutiny, it wasn't us that shagged the makeup girl, was it? And what about our needs? Do you think I'll be happy sitting in my high chair watching you mope about the house feeling "unfulfilled"? Go on, tell him.'

So I did. It wasn't pretty. As Greg slammed the door and stormed up to the spare room Unborn said, 'Well, I think that went pretty well. Shall we watch some telly now?'

That was the first time I noticed the repeat of *All Our Lives Before Us* that was showing – an episode where Joe's character told Rebecca's how lucky he felt to have her: she was so special, so beautiful; she could have any man she desired.

Including my husband, I thought self-pityingly.

VERONICA D: Rebecca had been in a state when she'd gone to bed the night before the shoot. That's because I'd spotted Greta in the lobby. Well, I couldn't not tell her, could I? On Monday morning we'd managed to get her out of the hotel ahead of Joe, so she hadn't had to talk to him. Then when we arrived we all surrounded her and hustled her inside while Joe and his posse hung around at the fence signing autographs and posing for the press.

Creeps.

However strung out Rebecca was feeling, her dressing room was a sanctuary. Once we were inside she felt safe. Even though she had to work with Joe and Greta was there too I think she felt kind of happy. She was at home. It was the first time she'd shot in Britain since she'd made it in *Lives*. It was her turf, not Joe's.

Well, that's what I figured, but what the hell did I know? I was the girl that fixed her hair, not her shrink.

Anyway it was peaceful in there. I was doing my thing, Dennis, the English makeup guy, was fixing her nails, and we had a Destiny's Child CD playing.

Then Tish rushed in and blew the karma.

'Guys, guys,' she flapped, 'I've made a list.'

TISH WILKIE: I *so* couldn't believe how many people Joe had with him. Literally *millions* more than Rebecca. *So* unfair. I had to be discreet so no one knew what I was up to, but I managed to write them all down.

1. Little man. Wearing suit. Agent/manager/lawyer?
2. Big man. Also in suit. Looks like he works out. Bodyguard?
3. Chauffeur.
4. Greta Bastendorff.

(Though I thought it best to cross her off before I showed it to Rebecca.)

5. Assistant.

(I knew who he was because he'd introduced himself – he seemed really sweet.)

6. Chinese man – probably chef.

(I'd seen him back at the Dorchester and I thought I recognised him from a show on Discovery Home and Leisure. I hate cooking but I totally *so adore* food shows.)

7. Three men in casual dress. Hang around together. Can't work out ID. Possibilities: personal surfing coaches, rock musicians – is Joe forming Keanu-type band?

Poor Rebecca hardly had anyone to help her out. There were just four of us and all Veronica did was hair.

VERONICA D: Tish was closely followed by Freddie. 'Rebecca, I've spoken with Morton Newman. He *happened* to point out that Joe's dressing room is thirteen by seventeen – that's two hundred and twenty-one square feet. He wasn't making small-talk. He must know Joe has the bigger dressing room. I checked your contract, angel, and it stipulates a minimum of two hundred square feet.'

She whipped out a tape she'd stolen from one of the crew, shoved Tish out of the way and measured up.

'I knew it – thirteen by fifteen.' Then she got out her calculator. 'Only one hundred and ninety-five square feet, the goddamn con artists. We'll have the bastards for breach.'

Becca called time out. 'Freddie, I've had Tish going on about the size of Joe's entourage. Now you about the size of his dressing room. Does it really matter?'

'It may only be a few square feet, but believe me, angel, it sets a highly dangerous precedent. And now you mention it, Tish has a valid point as well.'

'Freddie,' Becca said, 'I'm not going to have more people flown over if that's what you're thinking.'

'OK, angel. I happen to think you're wrong, but that's for you to decide. However, we can have something done about –'

'And I'm not having you get the builders in to put an extension on my dressing room either.'

GREG FULLER: It was eleven o'clock and we were nowhere near shooting our first set-up, Rebecca's grand entrance into the bar. Kevin had modelled the set on a fifties musical – when he'd agreed to take the job he told me it was conditional upon him being able to make 'Madame Whiplash meets Doris Day'. It was way over the top. The bar was huge and was going to be populated by nearly one hundred extras. He'd also had some exterior constructed – a bit of street that would be seen through the bar windows. Even more extras had been hired to glide up and down it on rollerblades or to walk designer mutts.

Bob Bull's jaw had hit the floor when he'd clapped eyes on it – perhaps because it was genuinely impressive, but more likely because he was picking up the bill.

'Don't worry,' I bullshitted, 'you're looking at excellent value for money – every penny will end up on screen.'

I hoped he wouldn't rumble the fact that, since most of the action involved Joe and Rebecca in close-up canoodles, it was actually very unlikely that the final cut would feature many rollerblading Pekinese-walkers.

Kevin was choreographing the extras to part like the Red Sea on Rebecca's appearance, but it was looking more Butlin's talent spot than Busby Berkeley. I hid in a corner, trying to crack Universe of Sofas. I wasn't getting anywhere. Retail shit wasn't my forte. That's what I'd had Piss and Shit for, damn the little fuckers . . . I know, only myself to blame.

So when Toddy flew up I was glad of the interruption.

'This is the *worst* nightmare,' she wailed.

'Take me through it, sweet pea.'

She did. The sofa bed had arrived, along with the Ealing branch manager of Universe of Sofas, and a photographer he'd rustled up from the local rag. They'd given us their deluxe model, a three-seater in plush salmon Dralon designed on a scallop theme. The bed was fitted with their premium deep foam Suite-Dreemzzz™ mattress, and they'd thrown in a set of brushed nylon Kotton-esque™ sheets in primrose yellow.

It didn't turn into the photo op the branch manager had been banking on. For a start Joe wasn't a salmon, primrose and scallop-y kind of guy – one look at his ripped singlet and distressed leather jeans in *Body Matter* would have told you that. Nor was he much of a one for synthetics, as the shopping list his manager had given Toddy made clear.

Bed: futon in unbleached organic cotton.

Sheets: organic cotton again, with a weave of precisely ninety threads per inch (I didn't doubt that they'd count them).

Duvet: goose down. Not any old geese either. Only a rare breed found nesting on a single lake in Alaska would do.

'Well, Toddy,' I consoled her, 'I don't imagine they expect you to fly to Anchorage and pluck them yourself.'

This didn't cheer her. 'I should never have left it with you,' she snapped, before disappearing to organise it herself.

I wondered if this was the same Joe Shirer that Kevin had found such a joy to work with in privy-free Utah. Maybe there were two. I went out to the car park for some air and a bit of calm. No chance. Norman the cook was having a shitfit.

NORMAN THE COOK: It had been a quiet morning. After we'd got out the breakfasts, I'd opened a couple of books. Wendy doesn't approve but I've never seen a crew that doesn't enjoy a flutter. The *Letterman* walk-out had been in all the papers so I was running some action on what Joe was packing down his Y-fronts.

Evens – the real McCoy, genuine 100 per cent beef.

Two to one – socks.

Four to one – some sort of custom-made contraption (I knew

a model maker who'd built one for a leading British actor. I'm too discreet to name him but he's got a couple of BAFTAs).

Ten to one – good old-fashioned upholstery foam.

I was also taking bets on who Rebecca would lamp first. Given their history, Joe was the clear favourite, closely followed by Greta; after his strop on the chair, though, the smart money was going on Kevin French.

There'd been a bit of a to-do over a sofa bed but, as I said, otherwise quiet.

Or at least it was until the Chinaman showed up. Another stretch pulled up in the car park at about half eleven and he hopped out. I didn't know him from Mao Tse Tung, and I thought nothing of it. He unloaded some containers from the boot and brought them over to my truck. He hopped up onto the step in front of my hatch. 'Hi, I'm Roland Shen,' he said, sticking out his hand. 'I guess you've been expecting me.'

He didn't sound a bit Chinese – perfect American accent.

'Not exactly,' I said warily.

'I'm Mr Shirer's personal metabolic therapist.'

'Oh, right,' I said. I could see where he was coming from now. 'The studio's that way, mate. If you're here to give him a rub-down or whatever, you'll want to be doing it in his dressing room. You seen all them fans by the gate? They'd go a bit mental if you started lubing him up out here.'

'You misunderstand me,' he said. 'I've come to prepare his mid-day nutritional treatment.'

'You're his bleeding cook?' I asked.

That's exactly what he was, and he expected to use my truck to rustle up some grub, sorry, nutritional treatment. I was furious. That was bang out of order. I had everything just the way I liked it, and no Chinese metabolic bollocks merchant was going to fuck with that.

If you think I was being unreasonable, let me put it this way. Van Gogh is in his studio happily doing his daffodils when Picasso muscles in and asks if he can plonk himself in a corner and paint one of his wonky birds. Oh, and, by the way, would he mind if he borrowed some brushes and maybe a dab of sky blue while he was at it? Do you think Vince would be happy? No, he'd give him a right earful.

TIM LELYVELDT: By the time I got to the car park, the worst was over. Norman, the English chef, was still brandishing his cleaver, but a guy who introduced himself as Greg Fuller had stepped in and calmed things down. He took Norman aside and I think I saw money change hands. When they came back Norman agreed to give Roland some space to do his stuff.

He marked out a tiny corner of his already cramped kitchen, and then warned us, 'I don't want him touching none of my gear though. Some of them knives are lethal in unskilled hands.'

The way Roland ran his finger across the counter before inspecting it, I imagined he'd be touching as little as possible.

NORMAN THE COOK: Plenty of luvvies tip up with personal chefs. Most of them are five-star ponces, but it's no skin off my nose. If a star doesn't fancy my fry-ups, it's one less tosser for me to cater for. But the Chinaman took the bollocking biscuit. For a start he didn't even call himself a chef.

'What's a metabolic therapist when he's at home?' I asked.

He gave me some flannel about studying his client's bio-waves, combining it with his meridian something or others, taking some cosmic readings and then probably doing the hokey-bloody-kokey to come up with a nutritional plan that harmonised diet with mental and physical needs. Basically that meant he did the same as me – he got a bit of grub and fucked it about a bit.

Well, in theory at least. When he'd finished Shirer's lunch and stuck it on the plate I looked at it and said, 'That wouldn't feed an anorexic ant. What is it?'

'Bean curd, pumpkin seeds and grouper fish oil. Mr Shirer's

biorhythms need to be re-synchronised after the trauma of changing time zones.'

'That ought to do it then,' I said. 'Mind you, when me and Wendy came back from Orlando I found that a nice bit of gammon with some chips and a Cadbury's Mini Roll did the trick.'

Before he left he gave me a T-shirt: 'ROLAND SHEN'S WAY TO NUTRITIONAL NIRVANA'.

XXL.

Saucy cunt.

eight:

the one in the middle in destiny's child

BOB BULL: As a keen student of the film-making process I'd spent the morning watching the crew. After the long, gruelling months of preparation, it was so exhilarating to be on the set at last – the smell of the lights, the greasepaint, all the gubbins.

I suppose it was this ability of mine to empathise with the creative process that made left-brained types like Greg relish working with me.

We'd broken for lunch when my mobile rang. I could tell in an instant it was mine – the William Tell Overture. It was mission control, my chief exec., Roger Knopf, a recent arrival from Akron. He was a phenomenal guy and I had huge respect for him. But he was new to the MO in Europe and the script had made him jittery. I'd resigned myself to having to hold his hand through the whole process.

'Roger, how can I be of service?' I asked.

CARRIE FULLER: That lunchtime I got some leftover quiche from the fridge and sat down in the kitchen. I thought back to the night before. I'd said some nasty things to Greg and maybe I was being unfair. He was under pressure and I should be making allowances. Maybe the makeup girl was a genuine one-off and I shouldn't dissect every little thing he did. (It only took, 'Just going to get *The Sunday Times*, Carrie,' to set me off: 'I knew it. Mrs Nawaz at the newsagent. The *whore*. No wonder she's forever sending her husband to the cash-and-carry. How could I have been so blind?') Perhaps the torrent of hormones unleashed by the miracle of pregnancy had turned me into a paranoid neurotic, one under the malign influence of her foul-mouthed unborn child.

Greg and I had been happy before. I remembered when I used to think his wit made him the funniest man alive, not an irritating smartarse. And I remembered when I thought his charm was genuine, not a ploy to talk me round or schmooze any passing makeup girl into bed.

He hadn't always excluded me from his life. He used to take me to client dos and awards dinners and act as if he was proud of me, even though I wasn't a media babe. And Blackstock hadn't been the only time he'd involved me with his work. I don't want to brag but I'd had a hand in a few commercials on his reel. Whenever he was at a dead end we'd talk and sort it out. I never got a credit but he'd always been grateful. More than once he told me I should be doing something more creative.

I took him up on it and wrote a screenplay. He took ages to get round to reading it and wasn't particularly encouraging when he did. But he was preoccupied at the time – two pitches at once or something.

Unborn woke up at that point. 'You didn't tell me you'd written a screenplay. What do you mean the bastard wasn't encouraging?'

'Shut up and go back to sleep,' I said firmly. 'I'm going to give Greg a break. We're going to get our marriage back and I'm not having you talk me out of it.'

Silence.

The baby manuals are right. Show the little sod who's boss and you'll never have any problems.

GREG FULLER: Toddy was recounting the hell that had been her morning but I wasn't listening. An extra was eating her lunch a few feet from us. The way she was dropping peas down her cleavage made me realise what British TV had lacked since Benny Hill had died. I was interrupted when Bob Bull joined us with a plate of cottage pie, chips and chicken curry.

'Greg, you and Toddy are obviously deep in work matters and I hate to intrude, but we need to have a meeting. I think the script might need a tiny tweak.'

Here we go, I thought. I asked Toddy to give us a minute. She hated to miss *any* meeting but she slunk off obediently.

'Don't get me wrong,' he started. 'I'm two hundred per cent behind the ad. It's a phenomenal envelope-pusher. It's just that I think we might be missing a trick.'

I'd been here before. Rough translation: 'I've had Knopf on the phone and he says he can't believe what possessed me to buy this piece-of-shit advertising.'

'I think we should feature some tyre shots,' he went on. 'The GoFlat is actually mentioned in the script. Why don't we show it? And what about the AquaTrak 6000? Phenomenal product. All our research shows that consumers respond incredibly positively to tyre-based imagery.'

Translation: 'All right, I know the research actually shows that punters can't tell one tyre from another, but Knopf says that if the ad doesn't include some groin-tightening close-ups of tread patterns, I'll be fucked all the way to Ohio with a splintery stick.'

'Leave it with me, Bob,' I soothed. 'I'll ask Kevin to park a car on the set. We'll stick some Blackstocks on it.'

'Terrific,' said Bob. 'I know it's just a detail but it'll make all the difference.'

He failed to add, '. . . to my prospects of keeping my job.'

NANCY STARK: Just after lunch I got my first positive lead on Paul and Shaun. It was an e-mail.

```
Nancy - 1 of my photographers has villa in
Andalucia. P&S been there on jollies and are on
promise of unlimited free use in rtn for lucrative
3-pce-suite shoots. Have obtained address.
Couldn't possibly divulge but you're welcome to
attempt persuasion - Olly xxx

PS - you did not - rpt, did not - get this from me.
```

Olivia del Monte (she claimed to be distantly related to the bloke that said 'yes') was a photographers' rep. She'd sink to any depths to get work for her boys and/or a free lunch. Here she was selling out one of her own snappers, and it didn't surprise me one bit. Greg couldn't stand her.

I e-mailed her straight back.

```
How about lunch w/Greg? Ivy OK? - Nancy
```

I could sink as low as she could, and the end justified the means because within sixty seconds she was on the phone.

'Have you a pen ready?' she asked.

YASMIN FISH: Rebecca hadn't been out of her dressing room all day. All that time just to do her hair. At Turning Hedz, where my mate Jules worked, they could do you a Rebecca in half an hour.

VERONICA D: Rebecca was always hours in hair and makeup. If she ever bitched I'd say, 'Honey, most women'd pay three hundred bucks to have what I'm giving you for zip, so shush.'

YASMIN FISH: At around three o'clock Kevin was ready to turn over (start filming – it was like learning a new language) and I was sent to collect her by the first (first assistant director – I suppose he was kind of a foreman: his job was to yell at everyone whenever Kevin wasn't). This was my big moment. Definitely more exciting than when Ashley Cole had said 'No problem, darling', when I'd asked for his autograph. I went to her dressing room and tapped on the door. There was no reply so I banged a bit harder. A gorgeous black woman (she reminded me of the one in the middle in Destiny's Child) stuck her head out.

'Yes, honey?' she said.

'They're ready for Miss Richards.'

'At last. We coulda wrapped *Pearl Harbor II* in the time we been hanging around. Becca, get your shit together. We're shipping out.'

TISH WILKIE: I was just *so totally* in awe when she walked onto the set. I mean, she looked *to-die-for*, literally. I immediately made a list.

REASONS I LOVE WORKING FOR RR

1. RR 110 per cent more beautiful than Greta.

(Who was totally plain in comparison even if she hadn't spent hours on end in hair and makeup.)

2. RR definitely most beautiful woman in world.

(Except for Julia R in *The Wedding Planner*, my best film of all time *ever* and perhaps Callista in *Ally McBeal* – but only certain episodes – definitely *not* the ones where she was just being miserable and eating ice-cream on her sofa.)

3. RR has IT.

(Which most people think means Information Technology. We in the motion picture business know IT means 'Star Quality'.)

4. RR is really kind – esp Romanian AIDS babies charity and panda/mountain gorilla/whatever appeal.

(I put the last point down because she'd been having a really hard time in the papers and people forgot what a total heart of *gold* she literally had.)

YASMIN FISH: She must have been sweating buckets in the rubber dress but she looked amazing as she stood outside the bar door for her opening scene. She rehearsed a few times and then got ready for the real thing. The first yelled, 'First positions, everyone . . . No talking, please. . . .Camera . . . Aaaand action!'

Rebecca did the sexiest walk ever into the bar, the extras parted and it was going brilliantly when, 'Beep, beep!'

My mobile went off – a text message from Tyler.

Kevin screamed, 'Which stupid cunt was that?'

Definitely my worst moment since the last one.

Toddy Gluck grabbed my arm and shrieked, 'No mobiles on the set. Ever! Didn't they teach you anything at school?'

I wish I'd said, 'Well, it didn't come up in maths or English,' but I could write a book on the things I wish I'd said.

TODDY GLUCK: Kevin was too kind. He should have made an example and fired her on the spot. I took her to one side and gave her a talking-to. Take it from me, she wouldn't be doing that again.

That was the only glitch. Kevin had such command of his crew that things could only run like clockwork. Then it was on to Rebecca and Joe's first scene. It took an eternity to get him out of his dressing room. God knows what was going on in there.

TIM LELYVELDT: Joe was awake but he didn't want to go out.

'Kevin hasn't been to see me,' he snarled. 'Jesus, we shoot last year's third biggest picture together and he can't even stop by my dressing room and say hi. What gives? Has the bitch been getting to him? If he wants to shoot *BM II* he'd better figure out whose side he's on.'

None of us mentioned the fact that Kevin had stopped by twice while he'd been out for the count. Instead we agreed that the bitch, AKA Rebecca, had almost certainly been getting to him. Anyone who told Joe what he should hear rather than what he wanted to hear didn't stay around for long. His driver before Jake got into an argument with him over the way to some new club. The driver was right but it didn't stop him getting fired.

It was half an hour before he got his head together.

TODDY GLUCK: Kevin was calmness personified. 'It's cool,' he said. 'The crew on *BM* called him Joey One-Take. He can be as late as he likes and I bet we'll still wrap early.'

YASMIN FISH: I couldn't work Kevin out. He'd spent the whole day yelling at people for nothing. Now Joe was holding everything up and he didn't bat an eyelid.

When he finally came onto the set with Greta, I looked at Rebecca to see how she'd react. It reminded me of when Tyler had walked into the Ministry with Bridget Farmer. I blanked them both and acted like I couldn't care less but Jules and Andie both said they could tell I was gutted from the way I was dancing. Rebecca was amazing though. She went up to him as if nothing had ever happened between them. She kissed him and even gave Greta a little wave. It wasn't exactly like they wanted to have each other's babies or anything, but you couldn't tell she might have hated them both.

VERONICA D: Rebecca was never less than a pro when she had scenes with Joe – playing Romeo and Juliet in *Lives*, they had a few of those. If I'd been her I'd have killed the prick, but she never once let her cool slip.

OK, just the once. The scene had Joe and Rebecca making out in the back of a convertible. The pair of them were stretched out on the car seat and the camera was on a boom looking down on them. On the second take the director yelled, 'Cut! For fuck's sake cut!' We saw why when the car door fell open and Joe rolled out clutching his nuts. I was standing next to one of the producers as he covered his face and groaned. Me? If it ever makes it onto one of those blooper shows, I'm the one you can hear hollering, 'Go, girl!'

YASMIN FISH: I was staring at Rebecca and I didn't realise Toddy was clicking her fingers at me. 'Pay attention! Can't you see Joe's thirsty? Water, *now*.'

I went to the fridge and took out the coldest bottle of Perrier. On the way back to the set I practised the best way to say, 'Here's your water, Joe' and then wondered if 'Mr Shirer' would be more appropriate. I didn't get a chance to call him anything because Toddy barged up to me, grabbed the bottle and handed it to him with a sickly smile. He took one look, and said, '*Sin gas, chiquita.*'

She virtually threw the bottle back at me. '*Sin gas*, you idiot,' she hissed. 'God, give me strength.'

The little spark came up to me. He could see I was confused and said, 'It means without –' I stopped him and said, 'Get lost. You've got me in enough trouble already.'

NANCY STARK: The phone rang again and the display showed the Hounslow Studios number.

'Hi, Greg,' I said, 'what do you want now? A Parker Knoll Recliner for Rebecca? A fitted carpet for Bob Bull?'

'It's not Greg.'

Shit, I thought.

I switched to client-schmooze before he could ask me what I was talking about, 'Hi, Bob, how's the shoot? I wish I could see it.'

'The shoot is phenomenal, thank you.' He didn't sound as if he was enjoying it much, though.

'How can I help?' I asked.

'I wanted to speak to Greg actually.'

'He's with you, isn't he?'

'Of course he's with me.' He was sounding irritated now.

'Well, have you tried, you know, going up to him?' Obvious, but it seemed daft not to suggest it.

'Greg is avoiding me,' he announced.

'Oh, I'm sure he's not. You know how busy things get. He probably hasn't had a spare second.'

This was bollocks, by the way. Agency people have got sod-all to do at shoots. They sit around stuffing their faces, reading the papers and trying to work out what freebies they can pick up from the set. When they come back to the office they complain about how knackering it was. Toddy once went to Miami to shoot an alcopop ad. She came back to work with a perfect tan and £2000-worth of bikinis. I asked her how it was – 'Nightmare, darling. I could sleep for a week.'

'Look, Bob,' I told him, 'I'll be talking to him soon and I'll tell him to make you his number one priority. He'll feel terrible to have given the impression he's avoiding you.'

I got him off the phone and called Greg's mobile.

'This had better be good,' he said. 'I haven't had time to piss here.'

'Bob Bull just called.'

'I've been avoiding him. What's he want?'

'He gave me a list. He wants to know when he's going to be introduced to Joe and Rebecca. He said that he's the bloke picking up the tab and he thinks it's only common courtesy.'

'He's right, but we're already having trouble with our male lead. One look at Bull will have him on the first flight home.'

'He also wants to know where his cars fitted with – let me see if I can get this right – GoFlats and Aquaban 6000s are.'

'It's Aqua*Trak*, sweet pea – Aquaban is for swollen ankles. Anything else?'

'Yes, he thinks Rebecca's dress makes her look a bit "loose" . . .'

'If by that he means sexually active to the degree of gagging-for-it, then that is exactly how she's supposed to look.'

'. . . and he wonders whether Roxie is the right name for her character.'

'Jesus, he's had the script for months. Now that we're shooting the one scene where Joe says her name he decides he's not sure. Anyway, as he's already pointed out, she's dressed like a latex lap-dancer. What's he want us to call her? Daisy?'

'Actually he suggested Jane.'

GREG FULLER: I'd taken Lola's call outside the studio because Kevin was about to turn over. When I went back, the thing I'd feared all day was happening – an unattended Bob Bull was heading for Joe. I'd briefed Toddy to keep him away but she was engaged in more important business. She had about twenty brands of mineral water ranged in front of her and was haranguing a runner about them. Too late to intervene myself, I watched in dread as Bob stretched out his damp hand to Joe.

BOB BULL: I was getting phenomenally cheesed off waiting for someone to show us some respect. Joe must have been as miffed as I was with the situation. He'd flown thousands of miles to make my ad. Don't you think he'd have expected to be introduced to the man signing the cheques? It was never in my nature to pull rank, but I was as good as in charge. Technically.

As it turned out we hardly needed anyone to make the introductions. It went very well. All the thought I'd put into my wardrobe paid off handsomely – he looked at my T-shirt and said, 'Where the hell did you get that, man?'

'Ah, I can tell you're a chap with a nose for a rarity. It's a special limited edition – only 20,000 were ever printed.'

I was about to offer to get him one but he was called back onto the set.

TIM LELYVELDT: On his way back to the set Joe grabbed Mort. I couldn't hear what they were saying but Mort came over afterwards.

'Problemo, Timbo.' I hated him calling me that. 'Joe wants that guy out of the studio.'

'Which guy?' I said.

'The one in the Foreigner jacket. He's also wearing an *M:i–2* T-shirt – a big cheesy mug shot of Cruise.'

Joe loathed Tom Cruise. No good reason. It was just jealousy – it hurt Joe every time he was up for $20 million a picture. It was pathetic. I could understand some guy on a production line working a sixty-hour week wanting to disfigure Cruise's smug face. But Joe who'd been paid $5 million for *Body Matter* and who was on triple that for the sequel? Come on.

'What's the big deal, Mort?' I said. 'Get him out.'

'I can't. He's Blackstock, the client.'

I could see what he meant. It'd be like shooting a Miramax picture and saying you didn't want that slob Weinstein hanging around. Except Harvey Weinstein would never have been seen dead in a Cruise T-shirt and a Foreigner tour-jacket.

'Problemo, Morty,' I said. 'Your department.'

Mort wasn't the only one with troubles. French had Joe to deal with. When he took off his shades his eyes were open but he'd left his brain in the dressing room. Or LA. His first scene was easy. All he had to say was, 'Hi . . . er . . . Roxie?' How many ways can you screw that up? Joe came up with ones that you couldn't possibly think of. French tried to sweet-talk the words out of him, but after thirty takes he gave up and we broke.

NORMAN THE COOK: The crew came piling out for their tea and I was doing a brisk trade in egg sandwiches, Eccles cakes and the contents of Joe's pants. They'd had a good look at him now and, though his jeans weren't giving much away, they all wanted a punt. I also ran a little sweep on how many takes he'd need for his opening line.

YASMIN FISH: Toddy had sent me to the supermarket to buy every bottle of mineral water they had. I'd felt like a camel dragging them back. I didn't join the others for tea. I was too miserable.

I stayed in the studio. It was quiet, but then I heard shouting coming from Rebecca's dressing room. I edged closer to listen, but a fat girl stuck her nose out of the door and glared at me before slamming it shut.

TISH WILKIE: 'Shhh,' I said loudly as I shut the door. Freddie and Rebecca immediately went silent and looked at me. 'I think we've got a spy.'

'C'mon, Tish,' said Veronica, 'the Cold War's over. The Russians are just regular gangsters now.'

Veronica was talking rubbish as usual. I'd worked in Hollywood for long enough to know that the Russians wouldn't spy on Rebecca. I wasn't sure who would – maybe Joe or the TV people or perhaps another Major Star who wanted to know her top beauty secrets. And whoever it was had cunningly recruited an innocent-looking girl that no one without a trained eye could possibly suspect. She was *blatantly* sitting almost exactly outside her dressing room in broad daylight (except there weren't any windows, but you know what I mean), and she was listening to every word we were saying. Well, not we, just Freddie and Rebecca.

Veronica only did hair. What did she know about protecting a Major Star? That, as *Personal* Assistant, was *definitely* my job.

VERONICA D: Freddie and Rebecca were getting heated over the *Lives* situation when Tish came up with the spy drama. They ignored her and carried on.

'Look, angel,' Freddie said, 'it's just a rumour and we've got to treat it as one. All we know for sure is that Joe has agreed to stay for another season in return for exec. producer status and whatever money he can screw out of them. The thing about him using his new position to get you out is no more than gossip.'

'Well, challenge them, Freddie. Get them to confirm in writing that it's not true. This is my life we're talking about,' Rebecca pleaded.

'I'm working on it, angel, believe me I am.'

I believed her – it may have been Rebecca's life, but Freddie had a twenty per cent stake in it.

TODDY GLUCK: My bed arrived at tea. Nancy had made a complete pig's ear with the one from Universe of Sofas. I'd managed to salvage things of course – Greg should have left the problem with me in the first place.

Greg appeared and I said, 'Where've you been? Joe's futon's here.'

'Never mind that. I've been talking to Bull. We need to see Kevin. There's been a slight change of script.'

'God, nightmare. What? Why?'

'Roxie is now Jane,' he said, 'and, believe me, we got off lightly. It took all my powers of persuasion to prevent Jane from being dressed in something ankle-length and high-necked from Laura Ashley.'

GREG FULLER: Kevin was less than delighted when we told him.

'I agreed to shoot this script because I loved it, every fucking word of it including "Roxie". I don't give a toss if the client wants to get his wife's name in the ad. It's not changing. Do you understand?'

I decided to save mentioning Bob's demand for a Blackstock-shod car for another time.

He kept up the rant for a few minutes. 'For fuck's sake, what kind of a name is Jane?' he said as Rebecca sashayed back onto the set.

'Who's Jane?' she asked.

'It's some idiot's idea that you are, babe,' he snarled.

Joe was close behind her and picked up the fag-end. 'Jane? I can work with that, man,' he said. He rolled it around his mouth a few times. 'Jane . . . Jane . . . yeah, now I know why I was struggling with that line. It was that dumb ten-dollar hooker's name, Roxie.'

'OK, let's get to work, you lot,' Kevin yelled. 'Minor script change. Roxie is now Jane.' As about-turns went it got a zero for style, but a ten for shamelessness.

Bob Bull showed up then and stood on the edge of the set beaming. At least he wasn't doing the idiot grin in a Tom Cruise T-shirt. Using my limited acting skills I'd accidentally emptied a Styrofoam cup of coffee on it, and now he was wearing an extremely Shirer-friendly 'ROLAND SHEN'S WAY TO NUTRITIONAL NIRVANA'. I'd also persuaded him to slip out of the Foreigner jacket on the pretext that I wanted to feel 'some really hard-rockin threads' around my shoulders – I was hoping that Joe, still in shades between takes, would no longer recognise him.

Jesus, the things I did in the name of diplomacy.

YASMIN FISH: Joe sailed through the scene when they came back after tea. Rebecca was brilliant – the way she said 'including your thing for rubber' in a sort of half-English, half-LA accent was dead sexy. I didn't even like rubber and I definitely wasn't turned on by women (which Tyler was gutted about because the bass player in his band had told him she was bi), but she made me think about it for five seconds.

I pictured Jules at Turning Hedz, making cups of tea for her blue rinses. I wondered how many slightly lesbian fantasies she'd had that day.

Toddy hadn't yelled at me for at least half an hour, and it was the first time I enjoyed my new job. It couldn't last. Rebecca's assistant came up to me and said, 'I'm watching you, *moley*.'

'What?' I said.

'Don't think I don't know what you're up to. If I read a single one of Rebecca's top beauty secrets in the papers this week, you'll never work in films again.' Then she walked off.

I thought of Jules again. Turning Hedz might have been boring, but at least she didn't have to deal with loonies.

GREG FULLER: Once he'd got the scene, Kevin wrapped. Thank Christ, I thought. We'd managed to get to the end of day one without Kevin hitting the road for Heathrow, Joe hitting the client and Rebecca taking her sapphire knuckle-duster to any poor sod that caught her eye. I was about to jump into a cab to the office when Toddy arrived looking distressed.

'That bed is a *fucking* nightmare.'

'What's wrong with it – even the delivery man was organic, wasn't he?'

'It's the frame.'

'Teak – beautiful – a frame fit for movie legends.'

'Exactly. *Teak* – endangered bloody hardwood. According to Morton, Joe is a committed conservationist.'

'Well tomorrow he can dump the convoy of limos and cycle to the studio, can't he?'

'Stop being a smart-arse, Greg – it isn't helpful. He's decided that since he's in England it would be fitting if he had an antique four-poster.'

'You're joking.'

'Preferably Tudor.'

'Well, Hampton Court is just over the river. Why don't we get him the one that Henry VIII slept in?'

Bob joined us so we didn't have a chance to talk about it any more.

'Phenomenal day, chaps. "Doug" and "Jane" were outstanding in that last session.'

'Outstanding, Bob,' I said, as Joe plus entourage wheeled into view. Joe halted and stared directly at me or, more specifically, at Bob's jacket, which still adorned me. He turned to Morton and said, 'What's that cocksucker doing on my set?'

An alarmed Bob grabbed my arm. 'Crikey, Greg, you haven't been upsetting my star, have you?'

TODDY GLUCK: Poor Greg couldn't get out of there fast enough. He clearly needed a bit of comfort. I decided to put aside my own troubles and share his cab into town. I was cuddling up to him when his mobile rang.

NANCY STARK: 'When are you coming back, Greg?' I asked him. 'The department is getting restless. They've watched all their videos and they've started to vandalise the coffee machine.'

'I'm in a cab now.'

'How's the day been?'

'Stressful.'

'Well this'll cheer you up. I've found Paul and Shaun. They're holed up in a Spanish villa.'

'You were close then. It's only pissing distance from Marrakech. Have you been in touch with the twats?'

'I've tried but it's not on the phone.'

'Are they definitely there?'

'I'm pretty sure. The source was good and I paid top price for the tip – it's costing you a lunch at the Ivy.'

'I can bear that.'

'With Olly del Monte.'

'Jesus fucking Christ, you're an unscrupulous cow, Lola. Anyway what else has been happening?'

'Nothing much. Carrie called a few minutes ago. Wanted to know when you might be through.'

Silence.

I might not have been able to hear her but I could tell he had Toddy with him. I could sense the whiff of evil down the line – Chanel.

TODDY GLUCK: He hung up and I said, 'Darling, switch off the phone. We need some quality time,' but before he got a chance the bloody thing rang again. It was Carrie – so needy. He tried to push me away but I wasn't going to budge – I was there first.

CARRIE FULLER: 'I wanted to say sorry,' I said. 'I had a miserable weekend, but it wasn't fair to take it out on you when you got home last night.'

'No, it was my fault,' he said.

'Let's try and start afresh. Nancy told me you'd be reviewing at the office, but I'll wait up. I'll open some wine.'

'Yes, that's good.'

'You can drink it – I'll just make do with the smell.'

'God, yes, that's fantastic.'

'Well, it'll only be something plonky. Anyway, do you think you'll be long?'

'Jesus, no, I'm coming now.'

As I hung up, I thought that he was probably overcompensating for our row, but at least we were talking again.

TODDY GLUCK: 'Bloody hell, Greg, you could have given me a bit more warning,' I shrieked, grabbing a tissue. 'This jacket is Byblos.'

TIM LELYVELDT: Joe's body clock had switched to vampire-mode: when we got back to the Dorchester he was all set to take Greta and his three professional friends out to 'show this Third World town how Hollywood rips to the tits.'

He hadn't reckoned on the visitor who was waiting for him in the lobby. Doctor Nandlal Jobanprutter, eminent psychiatrist and frequent guest of Oprah, had been sent by the network. They'd been concerned about Joe's mental health after *Letterman* and wanted reassurance that their new executive producer would be fit to resume his *Lives* life in a few weeks.

Joe refused to see him and locked himself in his bedroom with Greta. He came out after an hour, still mad as hell. 'They think I'm some kinda fucking fruitcake.'

'Of course they don't, Joe,' Mort said, trying to be conciliatory but straying dangerously close to antagonistic. 'They're only concerned about the pressure you're under – as we all are.'

'Fuck em, Mort. They're screwing with my head. I want that shrink out of here now . . . *Now!*'

'Sure, Joe, he's on his way,' said Mort, stepping back rapidly onto safe ground. 'Anything else?'

'Yes,' said Joe after a pause, 'I want my own therapist on the next flight to London.'

nine:

four in the morning stuff

YASMIN FISH: I woke up on Tuesday and put on 2Pac – 'Keep Ya Head Up'. It was one of Tyler's CDs. I'd grown out of the Spice Girls and I got my Girl Power fixes from other stuff. Girl Power/ dead gangsta? Sounds stupid but it worked – try it sometime. I bounced round my bedroom, and put on my Baby Phat T-shirt, Diesel jeans and Buffalo trainers – mind you, with six-inch plat-forms, the only training they were good for was being-taller practice. I took off Baby Phat – too soppy – and put on Phat Bitch. Then my dad thumped on the bedroom wall and shouted, 'Turn down that bloody din.' Well, it was four in the morning and he didn't like hip-hop at the best of times.

I was determined that Tuesday was going to be a better day. I was going to leave my mobile off. I wasn't going to ask Kevin French any stupid questions – I wasn't going to ask him *any* questions. I wasn't going to screw up on water, biscuits, tea or coffee – definitely not coffee. And if Toddy said one thing to me I was going to give as good as I got. I definitely, definitely wasn't going to have a single worst moment of my life.

When I arrived at the studio Kevin was going through the camera move for the first scene. 'We'll start ECU on Rebecca's kisser as she says, "I want to know what really gets your juices sluicing", pull back, dolly down under the table and zoom in tight on her foot as it scoots up Joe's strides. Fuck, I'm getting hard just talking about it. She'll look well tasty.'

That's when Toddy ran up to him and whispered in his ear.

'I don't give a rat's cock who she is or how much you're paying her,' he yelled, 'I'll tear the tart limb from fucking limb.' Then he stormed out of the studio.

'Don't sound like she'll look too tasty to me,' said the little spark.

TISH WILKIE: Monday night was terrible. Rebecca called me at four in the morning and told me to get to her suite, like, pronto. I literally *charged* down the corridor in just my Dorchester dressing gown – that thing was just so incredibly *fluffy*, I decided I was going to buy, like, *three* to take back to LA. When I got to her she was in the bathroom in absolute floods.

TYRONE EDWARDS: It's four in the morning and I'm flying, man. Yvonne's asleep but I done some charlie I scored off Ashley and it's blown me away. No way I can sleep. My sister-in-law, Paula, has fixed me up with this interview at a record company her brother works for. Eddy says they need a guy to do the letters and stuff but I know I'm in there. The interview's first thing so I try on the suit. Cost me three hundred notes but worth every one. There I am in the bathroom mirror. Five foot seven of raw sex in pure steel-blue silk. That job is yours, Tyrone, I'm thinking. You are the Man, the one that is going to discover the next TL-fucking-C – or the next Honeyz, anyway. That's when it fucking happens.

TISH WILKIE: I remember thinking how *fantastic* this was. Of course, I felt totally *devastated* that she could be *so* upset. But you have to admit that this was a special moment for me. No, for *us*! Look at it this way. Rebecca woke up in the middle of the night, far, far away from home. She was experiencing a *serious* crisis. And who was the *first* person she reached out to?

Me, me, me!

Rebecca Richards needed *me*!

VERONICA D: 'Why didn't you call me?' I asked her later.

'I tried, Veronica. Your phone was off the hook. Do you honestly think I'd have turned to Tish if I'd had a choice?'

TISH WILKIE: I rushed to her side and put my arms around her.

'Rebecca, it's OK. Tish is here now. What is it? Was it a nasty dream? Tell me, sweetie.'

Kryztal had told me I had a *very* soothing voice. It seemed to do the trick because she calmed down as I hugged her.

'It hurts, it really hurts,' she blurted.

'What does, sweetie? Is it a broken heart? A horrid boy?'

'No, it's not a boy. It's my *bleep*.'

TYRONE EDWARDS: That's when my fucking nose explodes. I never seen so much blood. It's doing *Reservoir Dogs* all over my new white shirt. All over my brand-fucking-new £300 suit. I'm grabbing toilet paper but it ain't stopping and I'm yelling, 'Yvonne, get in here. I'm dying.'

TISH WILKIE: OK, she didn't actually call it a *bleep* but I can't bring myself to use that word.

She pointed down there through her dressing gown. You know, *down there*. All right, I'll say it. She pointed at her *front bottom*.

I have to admit I felt a bit lost.

'Rebecca, hate to be a pain and everything but I'm not with you.'

'Jesus, Tish, do I have to spell it out?'

'Would you mind terribly?'

'I've got a *bleeping* rash on my *bleeping bleep*.'

Then she did an *incredible* thing. She just *whipped* up her gown and showed me her whatsit.

'Look at it!' she shrieked.

I shrieked too. I know I was like *totally* Californian but I've never been comfortable with nudity. I had a harrowing experience when I was fourteen and I can't even begin to tell my therapist about it yet. Of course, Rebecca didn't know any of that but there she was displaying her *thingy*. And, my *God*, you should have seen it. I mean, no, you *shouldn't* have because it was awful. Like, *yeuch*!

TYRONE EDWARDS: Yvonne runs in and grabs a towel and puts it on my face. 'I'm dying, baby,' I tell her, but she can't hear me through the towel and she suffocates me with it and says, 'Stop writhing around, Tyrone, you're getting blood on my extensions.'

TISH WILKIE: I'd never, *ever* seen a rash *there* before. She turned around and it was all over her bum and her back as well.

'What is it?' I asked.

'How should I know? I just woke up with it. *And it hurts like hell*.'

I decided it was time to be totally blunt.

'Well, do you think it might have something to do with, you know, S, E, X?'

'Since I haven't had S, E, *bleeping* X in nearly six months, I very much doubt it, Tish.'

'What do you want me to do?' I asked.

'I want you to call a doctor.'

TYRONE EDWARDS: It's still pouring out of my nose and I say to Yvonne, 'Get me a doctor. I feel weak, baby. I think I'm bleeding to death,' and she says, 'You ain't bleeding to death. You just done too much charlie. How much you put up your nose tonight?'

I tell her, 'A couple of little lines, no more, I swear. I don't know what's in that shit of Ashley's, but it's killing me.'

'There wasn't nothing wrong with it, idiot,' she says. 'You just done too much. You got half of Colombia up there.'

'Baby, I'm *dying*. I don't know how much longer I can last. Get me a doctor!'

TISH WILKIE: The doctor arrived in no time. I suppose they have to be quick when they're dealing with stars, especially since Lady Di. I hate to sound cruel but no one is going to miss an old lady if she passes away in the night but a gorgeously beautiful mega-celeb, well, obviously that's different. I'm talking about grief on a *world scale*. Obviously.

He was with Rebecca for about half an hour. When he came out of her room he gave me a prescription.

'Get this for Miss Richards as soon as the chemist opens. It's an ointment.'

'My God, doctor! What is it? Is it incurable?'

'No, no, not at all. It'll clear up by itself in a little while. She won't experience a recurrence just so long as she stays away from rubber. The poor girl's allergic.'

TYRONE EDWARDS: Yvonne never calls a doctor but she stops the bleeding. I'm feeling weak but I think I'm gonna live. I look at my suit. 'My suit. *My interview*. What the fuck am I gonna do?'

'I'll phone Eddy and tell him you're sick,' says Yvonne. 'I never wanted you working there anyway.'

'C'mon, baby. This job is my dream.'

'Postboy? You're dreaming big. Anyway, that place is full of sluts in hotpants. You wouldn't last a week before I murdered you.'

BOB BULL: It came to me during the night as it often does. That's the creative mind for you – never switches off. I woke up at four and everything seemed phenomenally clear. I rushed downstairs to grab some paper. First I wrote down 'MEMO TO SELF: KEEP PAD AND PEN ON BEDSIDE TABLE FOR FUTURE MIDNIGHT BRAIN-WAVES'. Then I jotted down my brainwave.

It had absolutely nothing to do with what Roger Knopf had said to me about the script. I wouldn't have been much of an Executive Director in Charge of Marketing, Advertising and Promotion (Europe, the Middle East & North Africa, excluding Libya) if I'd caved in to every little quibble from my CEO, would I? No, I had niggles of my own and I'd finally worked out a solution.

TIM LELYVELDT: The phone woke me at 4.05 am. It was Morton: 'Problemo. Joe's pulling out of the ad.'

I got to Joe's suite in five minutes. I was the last to arrive. Morton was already there of course, his little head sticking out of a sea of towelling Dorchester dressing gown. It made him look like a drowning man – and in truth he probably was. Greta was giving Joe a head massage. Danton, Waverly and Glenn were there as well, though only Glenn was still awake – he was rubbing his nose so I could see how he'd managed it. It took me a minute to pick up the plot. Joe and Greta had been reading through the script when Greta had drawn his attention to something.

BOB BULL: It was only a small thing but it was phenomenally important. The problem lay in Rebecca's reaction when she worked out what Joe's true interest in rubber was. As the script stood, she was so turned off that she couldn't get out of the bar fast enough. It just didn't ring true.

TIM LELYVELDT: 'Joe plays a total loser,' was how Greta put it.

'I wouldn't say that, Greta,' I said, regretting it as soon as the words were out of my mouth. Disagreeing with Star's Babe is just about as serious as disagreeing with Star.

Greta looked hurt and Joe jumped in. 'What makes you William fucking Goldman all of a sudden? Have you even read it? Have you seen what I play? A nerd. A geek. A total loser.'

I watched Morton sink deeper into his sea of fluffy towelling but I was stuck on this course now and – even though my life was in danger – I had to continue. I said, 'You're not a loser at all, Joe – you're a top research scientist.'

'Exactly – science is for losers.'

I tried reasoning. 'That's not so, Joe. Think of Goldblum in *The Fly*.'

'He turns into a fucking bug,' said Joe.

'Fucking loser,' agreed Glenn between sniffs.

'OK,' I said. 'What about Hoffman in *Outbreak*?'

'That big-nosed fuck?' said Glenn, loud enough to wake Danton and Waverly.

'Well, he can act,' I said.

'So?' said Joe.

I desperately flailed around for something, anything, to save me. 'And he thwarts a military conspiracy and saves the world – *and* he gets the girl.'

Morton had been close to sinking completely, but now his head shot out from the gown as if he'd just seen Pamela Anderson in a bright red swimsuit knifing towards him through the Malibu surf.

BOB BULL: In reality shouldn't Rebecca's reaction have been the exact opposite? Let me put it this way: if you found out that your blind date was a key research scientist at a company as dynamic as Blackstock, wouldn't your response be more, 'Wow, let me get to know this fascinating man'?

TIM LELYVELDT: 'Hoffman gets the girl. You might have something there, Timbo,' said Morton.

'Yeah,' agreed Joe, 'if I can get the girl in this script, I might consider doing it.'

BOB BULL: You see, that is the power of creative thinking. The tiny change that had come to me in my sleep would do far more than simply make the script more believable. It would have the effect of putting the Blackstock product offering centre stage, making it seem that much more exciting, which it clearly was.

Now, I wouldn't have been much of a marketing wiz if I hadn't cried 'hear, hear' to that, would I?

fruit, veg, porn

TODDY GLUCK: How could she not have known that she was allergic to rubber? This is the age of safe sex – *condoms* for God's sake. I can't stand them myself, but even I'd used them once or twice.

Kevin was livid. Even Greg, who doesn't snap that easily, was shaking. I pulled the pair of them aside for a crisis meeting, but Bob Bull was hovering in the background.

'Greg,' I hissed, 'we can't discuss this with him there.'

'Bob,' he called out, 'Joe should be arriving any minute. I know he'd be thrilled if you greeted his limo.'

'OK, Greg. There is something I want to discuss – very minor script tweak – but I suppose it can wait. Can't escape my diplomatic chores, can I?'

As he walked off I said, 'What did you say that for? Joe will have him thrown out of the studio.'

'Hardly. You see what he's wearing?' Greg replied. 'He looks like he's modelling for Shirer's official merchandise catalogue.'

NORMAN THE COOK: The Blackstock geezer tipped up in a *Body Matter* satin bomber and a pair of 'As seen on *All Our Lives Before Us*' cyclist's leggings. His arse looked like two lumps of wholemeal dough wrapped in turquoise Lycra. I couldn't take my eyes off his T-shirt though. It was one of the Chinaman's. He wasn't the only one either. Half the crew were wearing them and I was getting seriously narked.

'Calm down,' said Wendy. 'It's only a sodding T-shirt. Just look at them all. Nothing's changed. They're cramming down your bacon-and-egg rolls like they're going out of fashion.'

'Right now they are, yes. But give it a day and they'll want to re-balance their sodding meridians. They'll be rolling up and saying, "Norm, do us a nice bit of tofu with extract of jellyfish in a granary bap. And hold the HP." You mark my words.'

'You're losing it, Norm.'

'No, Wendy, I am only trying to protect our business. I ain't taking this lying down. I'll give the Chinese bastard nutritional fucking nirvana. I'm calling my brother.'

GREG FULLER: Kevin's first reaction was to stomp off to consider his options – a toss-up between the afternoon and evening flights to LAX. Mine was to watch my life pass before me on fast forward. Normally I'd have kept my shit together, but that morning there was a tangible sense of the walls closing in and, though I'm not particularly proud to admit it, I lost it. 'The whole shoot's out of the window,' I very nearly sobbed to Toddy.

Whatever anyone else said about her, and they said plenty, Toddy was an excellent producer. Her initial hysteria quickly gave way to a sustained bout of practical thinking. 'Pull yourself together, Greg,' she snapped. 'There's always a way to save things. I'm sure our insurance will cover us for the extra time we'll need. First things first – we need to call a meeting.'

'Call a meeting. Yes, excellent idea.' For once I meant it. 'What about? Who with?'

'Kevin for a start. We can't shoot anything without him. You've been friends for years – you can calm him down. We also need to round up wardrobe, the lighting cameraman, the art director and anyone else with anything constructive to say. We might even need a casting agent.'

'Casting agent?' I said with an unbecoming squeak of panic. 'We're not going to get rid of Rebecca, are we?'

'No, Greg, but we might need a body double.'

My mobile rang and Max's name flashed up on the display.

'Take the call, Greg. I'll check the insurance and call the meeting.'

I watched her walk away – one of the best producers I'd ever worked with. It's also worth mentioning in my mitigation that, if there'd ever been an England Ladies' Blowjob XI, Toddy would have been both coach and team captain.

My composure restored, I picked up my mobile and said, 'Morning, Max. How's Soho?'

'Fuck that, Greg. How's Universe of Sofas? You reviewed it last night. It'd be nice if you told me how it went.'

'I saw some very interesting ideas,' I said.

CARRIE FULLER: 'How did the review go then?' I asked Greg when he finally got home on Monday night.

'Some interesting ideas,' he replied, 'all of them way beyond the comprehension of a client with the wit of a learning-impaired earthworm.'

'Not suitable then?'

'It'd have them diving for the windows within the first five minutes of the presentation.'

GREG FULLER: 'I've seen a couple of clear contenders for presentation, Max. Very Universe of Sofas,' I went on. 'I simply need to make sure they tick all the boxes on the brief.'

'Just be certain we get the regulation leggy blonde on sofa,' said Max.

CARRIE FULLER: 'How far off-brief were they?' I asked.

'How far is it from here to Pluto? Jesus, all I want is a script containing a pretty blonde parking her arse on a leatherette sofa beneath a luminous '0 PER CENT CREDIT – WRITTEN DETAILS ON REQUEST' starburst. All I fucking get are animated aardvarks, Mongolian contortionists and thrash-metal soundtracks.'

I watched him slump – a change of subject was due. 'I dug out my screenplay this afternoon and I think –'

'Fuck, Carrie, I'm days away from losing our largest account, I'm in the middle of the biggest shoot of my life and all you want to do is talk about your fucking screenplay.'

'I was going to say I want to do some more work on it before the baby's born, and then when you have the time I'd like you to read it again. You can forget it now.'

'I'm sorry –'

'No, forget it. Blondes on sofas come first.'

'Not when Greg's screwing them they don't,' Unborn chipped in gratuitously.

'Shut up, you dirty-minded sod,' I snapped.

'I didn't say a word,' said Greg.

I was definitely going mad. At that point I didn't know who was going to arrive first – the baby or the men in white coats.

GREG FULLER: 'We're nearly home and dry then, yes?' said Max. 'I look forward to seeing the work.' He felt reassured, which was good because there was no point in both of us feeling doomed. 'What about Paul and Shaun?' he went on. 'Any sightings?'

The Diuretic Duo, of course, were my only hope, and I decided to go for it. 'Yes, good news. Lola tracked them down to Spain. She's flying out there today.'

Which was exactly what she would be doing just as soon as I told her.

I got Max off the phone and remembered my client and his mention of a 'very minor script tweak'. If I knew Bob Bull – and sadly I did – that could only mean one thing: he was sitting in the cab of a fifty-car freight train waiting to drive it through my award-winning (and, therefore, arse-saving) TV commercial.

BOB BULL: Much as discussing the script with Greg was the morning's top priority, my diplomatic mission to Joe Shirer was also key. After Greg had failed to make the appropriate introductions on day one, I was glad that he finally appreciated my need to ensure Joe was fully on-message, brand-strategy-wise. I was waiting as his limo pulled up.

'Joe, welcome once again to Hounslow. I trust you slept well,' I said. He seemed tired, and I hoped the strain of appearing in a top TV ad wasn't getting to him. He looked admiringly at my attire – the Lycra leggings had been Jane's idea, and I must admit the little lady played a blinder there. Then he asked, 'And you are?'

I was disappointed that he'd forgotten me so quickly but, as an in-demand top-level executive, I knew how easy it was to forget a face.

'I'm Bob Bull, Executive Director in Charge of Marketing, Advertising and Promotion at Blackstock.' (I missed out the Europe, the Middle East and North Africa bit – that would have been unnecessarily showy.) 'I just want you to know that, if there is anything I can do to aid the artistic process, performance-wise, you have only to say the word.'

'You the guy sorting out my bed?' he said.

Before I could ask what he meant, his manager stepped in and said, 'No, Joe, that's the Barbie doll's job.' Then he took my arm and led me away.

'We haven't been formally introduced. I'm Morton Newman,' he said, shaking my hand with a reassuringly firm grip. 'There is something Joe is concerned about.'

'Fire away,' I said.

'Did you have anything to do with this?' he asked, taking the script from his suit pocket.

It was immensely flattering to be identified as the creative brains, but I shouldn't have been surprised. As I have said, that is where my true talents lay. A man as obviously intuitive as Morton would have read it in my body language.

'Well, I don't suppose I exactly wrote it,' I protested, 'but I was responsible for lighting the blue touch-paper, inspiration-wise.'

'Whatever,' said Morton. 'Joe has an issue with the way his character has been developed. He feels there may be one or two more heroic qualities that the script in its current form doesn't fully exploit.'

Now I was concerned. I had been involved in enough commercials to know that rule number one is to make sure that cast members are totally on board with the motivations of their parts. I once commissioned a sanpro film where my leading lady had to dress up as a panty-liner. Luckily she was RADA-trained and could identify 100 per cent with what it meant to be super-absorbent yet unobtrusive and discreet.

Clearly Morton and I had some serious chinwagging to do. I grabbed two coffees and sat down at a table near the catering truck. 'We need to fully explore this, Morton. Let's dig around the issues and see what the manure of fresh thinking can do.'

'Joe is disappointed that his character isn't more of a match for Rebecca's,' explained Morton. 'We've carried out a number of focus groups vis-à-vis the Joe Shirer brand phenomenon and we've found that the persona our core audience responds to with the most positivity is the go-getting winner.'

Morton may have been young and just a touch flashy for my taste, but I was beginning to warm to him. He spoke the lingo of the smart operator.

'Joe feels the film would be much stronger if he were to, as it were, get the girl,' he said.

'Bingo!' I couldn't help thinking. I didn't say so, of course. What I did say was, 'You might just be surprised to learn, Morton, that, as the executive responsible for the whole kit and caboodle, I have been rethinking my script along very similar lines.'

NORMAN THE COOK: After breakfast I lit up a fag and picked up the *Sun*. Shirer was in there. The headline said, 'WHAT'S JOE PACKING IN HIS LUNCHBOX?' They had pictures of a lookalike in Lycra shorts with food shoved down the front: a cucumber and two tomatoes, a jumbo Frankfurter with a couple of plums, a banana and . . . you get the gist.

'You seen this, Wendy?' I said.

'That's disgusting,' she said as she looked over my shoulder.

'Too right, darling. As a catering professional I'm appalled. It's downright unhygienic.'

TIM LELYVELDT: We left Morton with the client and headed for Joe's dressing room, where a guy was erecting a four-poster bed. It was huge, roughly the size of the USS *Nimitz*. There was hardly room for Joe, Glenn, Danton, Chris Shave, Greta and me in there as well. Waverly had gone for the coffees, and when he squeezed through the door a couple of minutes later he was clutching a tabloid. 'I think you should see this,' he said to Joe. I looked over his shoulder as he and Greta took in the lookalike with a deli down his shorts. Greta started to cry. Joe threw the paper to the ground and said, 'See what the bitch is doing to me?'

We all knew who the bitch was. We also knew that he had no evidence that she'd planted the rumour, but no one had ever contradicted him.

'She's destroying you,' said Danton.

'It's an assault on your dignity, dude,' said Glenn.

'It's bang out of order, mate. No man should have to take it.' Shit, even the guy erecting the bed was joining in.

'You're fucking right,' said Joe. 'OK, everybody out. I need some space to get my head together.'

Where he was going to find space in there was beyond me, but we all did as we were told.

'No, you stay, Tim. I got an idea.'

How many times had I heard that before and shuddered?

NANCY STARK: I'd been to get his sandwiches, his dry cleaning and his traveller's cheques. He'd sent me to bookshops, record shops and sweetshops. I'd been out to buy birthday presents for Ryan and Hope, and kiss-and-make-up gifts for Carrie (which meant I'd got to know her taste in perfume, earrings and lingerie better than he did). He'd sent me to the V&A, the Tate Modern, the Natural History Museum and the insect house at London Zoo in the name of research. Once he even sent me all the way to a taxidermist in Northampton to pick up a stuffed horned toad.

And now I was at Gatwick, about to catch a plane to Malaga on a mission to find a missing creative team. Definitely the most bizarre errand Greg had ever sent me on.

And the most fun.

YASMIN FISH: 'You,' Toddy yelled across the studio, 'can you write?'

'B in GCSE English. Will that do?'

'There's no need for cheek. Come with me. I'm chairing a very important meeting and I need you to take notes.'

The word had spread about Rebecca's rubber allergy, so I knew what this was going to be about. Everyone was laughing about it, but I felt sorry for her. I remember when I ate a crab-paste sandwich on the day of Tyler's band's first-ever gig. I came out in the worst rash ever. I could have gone if I hadn't minded looking like something out of *Evil Dead II* in a sequinned halter-neck. I sat at home itching. And crying. It got worse the next day when I found that Bridget Farmer had been there – slag.

I followed Toddy to the production office. Kevin French was in there with Greg Fuller. So was the lighting cameraman (bloke who spends hours having a light moved one millimetre, then a few more hours having it moved back again), the art director (bloke who builds the set – well, who farts around like the long-haired ponce on *Changing Rooms* while a bunch of chippies do the actual work), the first (explained him already – hope you were paying attention) and the wardrobe girl (obvious what she does).

The meeting was nearly over and Toddy looked gutted. Kevin had calmed down and was back to his normal self. Still rude and bossy, but I'd worked out that was normal for him. He went over what had been agreed.

'We'll order a new dress in PVC. It had better look like fucking rubber, Lucy, or I'll –'

'Absolutely it will, Kevin. The dressmaker gave me his word,' said the wardrobe girl.

'We'll put out a casting call for a double. We'll use her in the long shots and some of the close-ups. She'll need a wig, Lucy, a proper one, not a Wogan.'

'Are you getting this down?' whispered Toddy.

I nodded. It didn't seem that hard. I'd written:

1. PVC dress. Must be brill or KF will do something evil.
2. Body double.
3. Wig. Not T Wogan.

'With luck we'll have Richards back tomorrow. And she'd better kiss my arse or I'll personally tear her a new one,' Kevin said. I couldn't resist writing:

4. New bum hole for RR.

'As for today,' he went on, 'we'll do whatever close-ups and one-shots of Joe we can, and we'll shoot some ambient stuff around the set.'

'We can't turn over on Joe until this afternoon at best, Kevin,' said the first.

'Why the fuck not?'

'His hairdresser doesn't get in until midday. He refuses to go in front of camera until he's had some styling done.'

'Jesus Christ, I'll give the . . .' he snarled, but he stopped himself from finishing. Then he said, 'His barnet could do with a touch-up.

We can wait. All right, let's get to work and see if we can salvage some art from this dog-mess.'

VERONICA D: 'Jesus, you look like an overripe pomegranate,' I couldn't help yelping when Rebecca lifted her T-shirt.

'I guess I won't be getting the Clinique contract in a hurry,' she said.

'I gotta ask you, Becca. How did you not know?'

'What, that I was allergic to rubber? I've never worn it. I've had boyfriends who've wanted to dress me up in all kinds of stuff. Stockings, maids' outfits, leather. I had one who wanted me to wear skateboarder's pads on my knees and elbows.'

'What was that all about?'

'Don't ask – nothing to do with protecting me from carpet burns, though. Anyway, none of them tried to get me into latex.'

'Yeah, but what about rubbers? You must've used them.'

'Never. Sounds reckless, but I've always been on the pill and well, you know, you think it's never going to happen to you.'

She paused for a minute.

'Hang on, I did once. It must have been about the second or third time I had sex. I was fifteen. It took him about ten minutes to get the Durex on and the sex lasted less than three.'

'Well, honey, if he hadn't had a rubber numbing his dick he'd have lasted less than one. Didn't you react to it?'

'I did. It was really unpleasant. I didn't put it down to the Durex. I was convinced I had VD, but it cleared up in a day or so and I forgot about it. Stupid, huh?'

'Not stupid,' I said, 'just fifteen.'

Tish came into the suite with a huge bunch of lilies.

'Aren't they yummy? They're from French Films,' she gushed. Then she read the note. '"Rebecca – the shoot can wait because nothing matters more than the health of our brightest star – Kevin, kiss, kiss, kiss," Isn't he the *sweetest*?'

'I bet he ain't saying that on the set,' I said.

Rebecca ignored me. 'They're lovely. Thanks, Tish. Anything else?'

'Yes, I made a list.' She took some paper from her pocket and read. 'One: ad agency's insurer wants to send doc. I suppose they want to make sure you're not putting it on just so you can have a lie-in! Two: make sure RR uses ointment. No, that's a note to me. Three: Freddie. I think she wants to chat about *Lives*. Probably about your look for the next season. So *mega*-exciting?'

'Is that it?'

'No, one more thing. Four: knickers. Sorry – another note to me. I didn't pack enough. Oh, and five: order bouquet. No, ignore that too. That's what you asked me to do last night.'

'I hope you did something discreet, Tish – I don't want to freak the woman out,' said Becca.

'Absolutely, Rebecca. I asked for the tiddliest bunch going and the note was like *so* understated.'

JUDITH OTTLE: When I opened our front door I couldn't see the delivery man for lilies, forsythia, and shocking pink gladioli.

'Got these for Judith Ottle,' he said. He shoved them at me and I nearly collapsed under the weight.

'Who are they from?' I asked.

'Dunno, love, but they've done my back in. I gave up the removals job because my lower vertebrae couldn't hack it. I thought I'd be safe at a florist.'

I dragged the flowers into the kitchen and I was looking for a note when Dean wandered in.

'Shouldn't you be at school?' I asked.

'Study day,' he lied. He saw the bouquet. 'They from Dad? What's he done now? Must have been bad.'

'I don't think they're from your dad.'

I found an envelope and opened it.

'Oh my God,' I gasped.

Dean snatched the card from me and read it out.

'"Please accept this as a teensy reparation for my literally unforgivable behaviour – Rebecca Richards." Loads of kisses too. Wow! She writes a bit funny but cool flowers.'

You don't know my Dean – 'cool trainers', 'cool groove', yes. 'Cool flowers', never. The boy was more in love than I'd thought.

VERONICA D: Tish and lists. I'd been in her room and it was knee-deep in little scraps of paper.

'What's with all the bits of paper?' I asked her.

'Lists, Veronica. As a *Personal* Assistant lists are like *so* essential for organisation and clarity. Literally. This one here, for example,' she said, holding up a scribble on the back of a room service menu, 'is my master list. It tells me exactly where I can find all my other lists. You only do hair, so I don't suppose you understand.'

'No, I get it, Tish. They got the same system at the Pentagon so they don't lose any of their nukes.'

'*Exactomundo.*'

And the Brits say we Americans don't get irony.

GREG FULLER: I watched with dread as Bob Bull and Joe's manager approached me. They had the joined-at-the-hip look of new allies – Tweedledumb and Tweedledumber.

Breathlessly they unveiled their shimmering new vision for my script, a version where Joe gets the girl and I get to be the target of bread rolls tossed by my mocking peers at the next adland awards bash. I argued my corner, but I was pissing into a force ten. If it had been Bob on his own I'd have blinded him with polysyllabic bullshit. He'd have slunk off to regroup with the help of the *Pocket Oxford Dictionary*, and I'd have bought enough time to keep things as they were.

But together they were awesome, an irresistible force – 'phenom-enal', 'envelope-pushing' and 'outstanding brand/endorser synergy' in quadraphonic surround-sound. What else could I do but wilt under the onslaught? Anyway, as well as a terrifying arsenal of vacuous marketing speak, they were armed with a weapon of mass destruction – Joe Shirer. It was clear from the outset that if I insisted on shooting the original script, I'd have to do so without the talents of my leading man.

If I acquiesced, on the other hand, Kevin's first move would be a call to the BA reservations desk. The gap between rock and hard place was the merest sliver, but my not-quite-as-slim-as-it-used-to-be frame was wedged in good and tight.

I had one straw left to clutch at. It was likely to disintegrate at the faintest touch, but it was my only hope of maintaining my creative dignity and keeping both star and director on the set. It was the old 'let's shoot it both ways' routine – tried, trusted and as likely to succeed as a turd in a talent show. ('I enjoyed the seven-year-old Celine Dion and the paraplegic plate-spinner. Didn't think much of the turd, though – just sat there and steamed a bit.')

VERONICA D: 'They must think I'm pathetic at the studio,' Rebecca said when Tish had left us.

'Course they don't, honey,' I lied. I knew that she could be dying of cancer and the crew would be moaning that the spoilt bitch just wanted a day off. Too many stars had behaved like assholes down the years and she was picking up the check for all that bad behaviour.

She looked at her rash and said, 'Well, it can't get any worse, can it? At least I'll know what to say if they offer me Cat Woman in *Batman VIII*.'

TIM LELYVELDT: The guy had finally got the four-poster up and I left Joe asleep with Greta curled up beside him. They looked so sweet and I couldn't believe what I was about to do for him.

I picked up the tape from the counter, took it onto the set and found the video playback girl. She was picking her nails and reading the tabloid story about Joe's shorts. She flipped the page when she saw me coming and pretended to be engrossed in a photo-story about a guy whose girlfriend did the cooking in her bra, panties and heels – the agony page, I think, though I couldn't see what the guy's problem was.

'You look bored,' I said.

'This job is dull at the best of times,' she replied without looking up, 'and it's turning out to be a slow day. Anyway, what can I do for you?' she asked.

'Nothing for me, but some guys were asking for you out by the catering truck.'

'OK, thanks,' she said, getting up and walking out.

I put the tape on top of her VHS machine, making sure the label was facing out. It read 'TITANIC – SCREEN TESTS'. There was no way in the world she'd be able to resist looking at it.

GREG FULLER: By the time I'd rewritten the script I was resigned to losing Kevin on the next available flight. No point in fannying around, I thought, so I took him to the production office and plunged straight in. The opening was pretty much the same but the sentiments changed somewhat about halfway through:

> DOUG: You can do up to 50 mph after a blow-out and drive home on the flat. Junk the spare in the boot. The other guys in the lab had been working on it for years, but I . . .
> JANE: Doug, are you talking about what I think you are?
> DOUG: The Blackstock GoFlat tyre.
>
> Jane, now even more fascinated, leans closer to her date.
>
> JANE: Wow, I thought you were . . .
> DOUG: Some kinda pervert? I had you going then, huh? I'm in R&D at Blackstock.
>
> Jane laughs at her date's mischievous sense of humour.

```
JANE:    That's amazing, Doug. Excuse me while I powder my
         nose, and then you can tell me more about your
         fascinating work.

As she walks off the waitress arrives to take the order.

WAITRESS: Boy, she's putty in your hands.
```

Not your average blind-date conversation, but one that was apparently commonplace in the pick-up joints frequented by Bob and Morton, his intellectual doppelgänger.

'I have to credit you, Greg,' Kevin said when he'd finished, 'you've got some bottle showing me this. It's squirrel shit.'

'I know, but if I hadn't written it you'd be reading Bull's version – the one where Jane flutters her eyelashes and says, "Gosh, I've always wanted to meet the chap behind the phenomenal state-of-the-art technology that's responsible for making roads safer and protecting the lives of countless innocent children." Trust me, this is the least worst option.'

'And you expect me to shoot it?'

'What are we talking about? The same set-ups with half a dozen alternative lines of dialogue. We'll cut both versions – they're bound to go for the original when they see how much sharper it is.'

'Bollocks, and you know it.' Kevin was as familiar as I was with that old routine. 'Sorry, Greg,' he went on, 'we may be mates, but if you want to shoot this pony piece of writing you can find some other prick to point the camera at it. I've got better things to do.'

I decided that it was pointless to beg. 'I've known you for too long to expect you to start compromising now, but I don't see that I have any choice but to shoot it, Kevin.'

'Have you shown this to Joe yet?' Kevin asked as he got up to go. 'He doesn't like having rewrites dumped on him mid-shoot. If I know him, he'll be on the flight with me once he reads it.'

'Didn't I explain?' I said. 'These changes are as much Joe's doing as anyone else's. Believe me, if it had just been the client I'd have talked him out of it.'

'Fuck my arse,' he said. He slumped back into his chair and sat there in a daze.

After a moment I said, 'Can I ask you something, Kevin? What is it with you and Joe?'

'How do you mean?' he said defensively.

'I know you, remember? I've never seen you put up with crap from anyone. Over the last day and a half I've watched Joe feed it to you by the pound.'

He leant towards me and said, 'This doesn't leave the room, right?'

'Of course not.'

'Joe's got me by the bollocks.'

'What are you talking about? You did an amazing job on *Body Matter*. You could shoot whatever you want now.'

'You don't know Hollywood, do you, Greg?' He was right, I didn't. 'Unless he fucks up large, Joe's on his way. The studio's chucking money at him to sign up for *BM II*, and every hopeful twat in Tinseltown is sending him their script. You might think I'm shit-hot but I'm just another gun for hire out there. There're hundreds of us. We're all shit-hot. I need *BM II*, and Joe knows I do. That cunt has got me.'

I didn't know what to say so I didn't say anything. Kevin broke the silence. 'We'll shoot the bastard both ways, then, and hope for a fucking miracle. Just promise me one thing. If the shit version goes out, you'll swear on your deathbed that I had fuck-all to do with it, right?'

'I promise, Kevin. Thank you.'

I put my hand on his shoulder as he gazed at his feet.

'You got any drugs?' he asked quietly.

Kevin and I had been through much over the years, but never any shared drug experiences.

'Nothing stronger than Vick's Sinex,' I said.

'Not what I had in mind.'

'I don't suppose it was . . . but it does work for up to eight hours.'

'Go on then, mate. It's better than nothing.'

I gave him my inhaler and he stuck it up his nose. Then I hit him with the car.

'I'm not parking a fucking car on my set,' he snarled, back to his old self.

'It is a street, Kevin. Cars are pretty much the norm.'

'It'll fuck with my rollerblade routine. It's beautiful – Torvill and Dean meet *Rollerball*.'

'Please, just one car. You can hide it at the edge of the frame, have the rollerbladers leap over it, whatever.'

'Stunts? That might work,' he conceded grudgingly.

I honestly didn't know I still had it in me.

YASMIN FISH: Kevin reappeared on the stage and announced, 'Right you lot, we're gonna have to shift up a gear. There're some extra lines to shoot. And another change of plan – I want some wheels. Something retro. A Thunderbird. No, a Mustang – pre sixty-five.' The art director clapped his hand to his forehead. I supposed it must have been his job to find a Mustang Pre 65, whatever one of those was. Kevin pointed at a couple of the rollerbladers. 'You and you, reckon you can clear a motor on those things?'

I knew it would be another two hours before they turned over (I was getting the hang of the language now), so I wandered off to see what else was going on. A few people had gathered by the video playback girl. (It was her job to tape every take and then play it back to Kevin. He'd squint at it and say something like, 'Not fucking bad at all, babe. Now let's see if we can get one where the extras look like they're enjoying it and not moping about like cunts in a bus queue.') She was holding a videotape.

'What's that?' I asked.

'I don't know. I found it on my table a few minutes ago.' She held it up and I read the label – 'TITANIC – SCREEN TESTS'.

'I *loved* that film,' I said.

'It was toss,' said the clapper-loader (the bloke who holds the little board in front of the camera and says, 'Slate three . . . yawn . . . take thirty-six', which is what he'd got up to when Joe kept screwing up his opening line). '*Blue Lagoon* with special effects and a bit of carnage. Anyway, stick the tape on.'

'Go on, then. Nothing else to do,' she said. She put it in the slot and pressed play. A wobbly title came up – *Going Down on the Titanic*. 'It was never going to be called that,' she said.

VERONICA D: Not long after Rebecca's 'things can't get any worse, can they?' comment, they did. Freddie appeared in her suite.

'Rebecca, angel, how are you doing?' she said.

'OK, I suppose. I should be fit to shoot tomorrow.'

'Excellent. I talked to Kevin this morning and he's terribly concerned. He'll be so pleased to hear it.'

'You've got bad news, haven't you?' said Rebecca, reading her like a trashy airport novel.

'You're ill – now isn't the time.'

'Like hell it isn't. Whatever it is, I want to know. *Now*.'

'All right. I suppose you'll have to find out sooner or later.' She sat down next to Rebecca and held her hand. 'My network source called me last night. It's not looking good. He confirmed that Joe has exec. producer credit.' She paused.

'And?'

'And the writers have been asked to come up with – how did he put it? – "Some dramatic and unexpected outcomes for Rebecca and Joe's relationship".'

'What the hell does that mean?'

'Angel, they want to kill you in episode four.'

YASMIN FISH: After the title there was a scene in a cabin. An actress was bent over an open trunk – we couldn't see her face. The cabin door opened and a bloke in a sailor's uniform came in. He looked at the woman and rubbed his hands together. He walked up to the woman and stood behind her as she unpacked. Then he dropped to his knees and lifted up her long skirt. She was wearing fishnets underneath and it was getting a bit weird – I mean, *Titanic* was PG, wasn't it?

'Jesus, is this what I think it is?' said the clapper-loader.

The sailor pulled her knickers down and stuck his face . . . You know where he stuck his face. The woman still hadn't turned round but now she spoke: 'Able Seaman Lash – I'd recognise that tongue anywhere.'

'It isn't!' shrieked the video playback girl, recognising the voice.

Then the woman turned round.

'It fucking well is,' said the clapper-loader.

It fucking well was and all.

eleven:

the white-hot blowtorch of publicity

VERONICA D: Freddie and her bad news were long gone, but Rebecca was still crying. 'It's gonna be OK, honey, you'll see,' I said as I hugged her. 'No more faking it on film with Joe. . . . And you're gonna have a ton of offers, a *ton*. . . . And, hey, you'll be able to change your hair. You said yourself you're sick of it – God knows I am.' But I was flailing and the tears were getting worse.

'This is the end,' she said between sobs. 'I'm being fired and every tabloid in the world had me beating up that customs woman. How much worse can it get?'

'Get a grip, Becca. Wake up to Hollywood. It's just one little battle after another. Joe's won this one. He's stiffed you; you've got to pick yourself up and move on. You're beautiful, you act like a dream. There're better parts out there for you.'

'There's nothing out there. I'll be lucky to get a walk-on as a junkie joyrider on *The Bill* after this.'

I had no idea what *The Bill* was, but it didn't sound good.

YASMIN FISH: I'd seen Pamela Anderson and Tommy Lee's home movie. The drummer in Tyler's band had downloaded it – 'Tommy's a drummer too. It's research, all right?' – and we'd watched it on his PC. That didn't shock me – from what little I could see they were only doing stuff that me and Tyler had already got up to.

But watching *Going Down on the Titanic* left me in a daze. When Rebecca and Able Seaman Lash were done, they were joined by two other blokes. I could just about get my head round one woman with three men – just about. But three men *all at once*?

TODDY GLUCK: Greg and I had barely got the day back on track when the girl from reception came up to us.

'I'm sorry to bother you,' she said, 'but there's a couple of blokes here from the *Daily Mirror*.'

'Well, send them away. This is a closed set,' I told her.

'They say it's been arranged.'

'Not with me it hasn't. You know that everything comes through me. *I* am in charge here.'

'They say it's been arranged with Blackstock Tyres.'

Greg sighed and said, 'What the fuck has the Timmy Mallet of international marketing been up to now?'

BOB BULL: I did think that Greg was being unreasonable to fly off the handle. OK, so it had slipped my mind that the *Mirror* chaps were coming, but I was a phenomenally busy man. At the same time as supervising the shoot, I had marketing and promotional balls to keep in the air across Europe, the Middle East and North Africa (excluding Libya). Greg had no idea what a key player I was, juggling-wise.

He should have been chuffed about the *Mirror*. Not only excellent PR for Blackstock, it shone the white-hot blowtorch of publicity on Fuller Scheidt as well. In return for an exclusive, they'd promised me a double-page feature with plenty of name-checks for the Blackstock product offering. I wouldn't have been much of a head marketing honcho of the world's fifth largest tyre company if I'd turned down an offer like that, would I?

GREG FULLER: What the hell was he thinking? The first rule of PR is Present Your Best Side. You don't open your door to the press with two-day stubble, halitosis and your dick hanging out of your winceyette jim-jams, do you? The shoot was heading down the pan and he was inviting a tabloid to witness the pulling of the chain.

YASMIN FISH: The next scene had her with another woman. 'She's fucking insatiable,' the clapper-loader said. 'Thank God they weren't carrying livestock on that ship.'

BOB BULL: I must admit that the timing could have been a tad better. I could only offer the journalist and his photographer access to one star, singular.

Greg had flounced off in a creative tizzy, so it was clearly up to me to do the schmoozing. Fortunately I'd had plenty of experience in the tricky field of media relations.

'Gentlemen, welcome to Hounslow's famous studios. I think I can promise you a treat,' I announced as I prepared to give them a tour. 'It isn't every day the press glimpses Premier League envelope-pushers at the front line of lateral thinking.'

YASMIN FISH: 'I thought this film was about a ship. I haven't even seen the sea yet,' I said as the video showed Rebecca letting herself into the captain's cabin.

'You haven't watched much porn before, have you?' said the clapper-loader.

I didn't answer. I was struck dumb by what was on the TV. Rebecca was on her knees and the captain was unzipping himself.

'Fuck,' said the playback girl, 'now I know why it's called *Going Down on the Titanic*. He is *big*.'

It wasn't just the captain that was massive. It hit me then exactly what it was we were watching. Rebecca was a Hollywood star and we weren't watching her simply take her clothes off and bounce around a bit like Sharon Stone in *Basic Instinct*. We were watching her *really do it. Repeatedly.*

Now that was BIG.

I was still trying to get my head round it when there was a loud crash. We looked across the studio to where Kevin had been rehearsing the rollerbladers. He'd put a Citroën Xantia on the set to stand in until the Mustang arrived. The legs of one of the rollerbladers were sticking out of the car's sunroof. Two of the grips were trying to haul the poor sod out. Kevin was yelling at the crew. He obviously didn't know who'd screwed up, so he covered himself by blaming all of them. No one seemed to notice a photographer flashing away.

BOB BULL: When you've been to as many shoots as I have, you develop a nose for when things are going awry. My experience combined with my cat-like reflexes enabled me to avert disaster. I swiftly got them out of the studio and sat them down with coffee. 'That's the amazing thing about filmmaking,' I explained. 'What to the inexperienced eye appears chaotic is actually precision-engineered efficiency. Now, I'm sure you must have dozens of questions. Please, fire away.'

'Actually we were more interested in talking to Joe and Rebecca,' the reporter said. 'Any chance of meeting them?'

'Ah, there is a small problem there. Unfortunately Rebecca is indisposed. The poor girl is ill.'

I'd decided it was best to be hazy about the precise reason for her absence. They'd only make mischief out of her being allergic to the material at the core of our business.

'A touch of Delhi belly,' I said, nodding towards the catering truck. 'Yesterday's cottage pie wasn't quite kosher. All is not lost, though. I'm sure I can get you in for a chinwag with Joe. Just give me a minute and I'll see if I can swing it.'

TIM LELYVELDT: Mort was giving me the news on Rebecca's death. The producers had got it down to a play-off between an eve-of-wedding car crash and a sudden, fatal embolism at the altar. We were interrupted by the Blackstock guy. 'Pardon me, chaps, but I have a favour to beg.'

'Name it, Bobby,' said Mort.

'A reporter from the *Daily Mirror* is here. He'd love to meet Joe.'

'Boy, that's a toughy,' said Mort. 'Joe never speaks to the press without his publicist. I'll have a word, but I doubt he'll be keen. Anyway, he's with his stylist at the moment.'

Joaquin Montoya, guardian of Winona Ryder's and Nicole Kidman's lush locks and creator of *el Montoya*, was at that moment addressing his greatest challenge yet – Joe Shirer's half-inch of dark brown stubble.

Mort came back a couple of minutes later with a big smile on his face. 'You're in luck, Bobby,' he said. 'Joe has asked Joaquin to take five. He'll give your reporter fifteen minutes.' Then he looked at me. 'Timbo, I need you to tape it – necessary precaution.'

I dug out my Dictaphone and checked the batteries. I had a shrewd idea as to why Joe had agreed to his first unprotected interview in years.

NORMAN THE COOK: One of the geezers who'd been having coffee with the Blackstock client rolled up to my truck while he was gone. 'What can I do for you?' I said. 'You're a bit early for lunch but I could sneak you a portion of chilli.'

'No thanks, we won't be eating,' he said. 'I'm from the *Mirror*. I wonder if I could ask you a few questions? Just some background. We're interested in Rebecca Richards.'

'No offence, mate, but I have a reputation to consider. If I start spilling the beans on my stars, well, it won't be long before I'm slinging burgers on a lay-by on the A40.'

'Oh, it's nothing like that,' he said. 'Actually, I was wondering what she had to eat yesterday.'

'Haven't you got some real news to report?' I said, 'I mean, whether Rebecca Richards chose the stir-fry or the brisket is hardly up there with the debate on the euro, is it?'

'I know,' he said, 'but our readers can't get enough celebrity trivia. Besides, there's been an allegation that her illness is the result of your cooking.'

'You fucking what?' I said.

No one has ever been ill because of my cooking. Well, apart from one producer who spent a couple of weeks on the khazi. That was intentional, though – he'd wound me up something rotten so I kept a choice bit of fillet out of the fridge overnight and made sure the twat got it rare.

'Her stomach upset has been linked with your cottage pie,' said the hack.

'You should get your facts straight before you go accusing people. She isn't shooting today because of her fucking allergy.'

'To cottage pie?'

'No, you plonker, to rubber.'

GREG FULLER: As the broken glass was being swept up from the studio floor and the broken rollerblader was being put in a cab bound for A&E, I wondered whose dumb idea the stunt had been. Then I looked at my watch and said to Toddy, 'Joe is spending longer in hair and makeup than Rebecca.'

'When he's through with that he's talking to the *Mirror*,' Toddy replied. 'We'll be lucky to turn over at all, darling.'

TIM LELYVELDT: I pressed record and sat back.

Reporter: 'I'd just like to say thanks for doing this at such short notice. Do you mind if I start with *Body Matter*?'

Joe: 'Shoot.'

Reporter: 'Clearly what excited audiences the most were the stunts. Is it true that you did them all yourself?'

Joe: 'It was no big deal.'

Reporter: 'Leaping from a three-hundred-foot tower to a moving helicopter was no big deal?'

Joe: 'Sure, I was surrounded by experience. The stunt team was the cream – the Navy Seals of stunt work.'

Reporter: 'Moving on to something more personal, can I ask you how you feel about some of the more unpleasant media coverage you've been getting recently?'

Joe: 'I ignore it. A guy in my position can't respond to every cheap shot. You've got to float above it – don't let it screw with your karma.'

Greta: 'It makes me sick, the things that have been written about Joe. I think he's taken it amazingly.'

Joe: 'It's not worthy of comment, babe.'

Greta: 'Totally not worthy.'

(I should point out that as she said this Greta was holding her hands apart like a fisherman doing the one-that-got-away thing.)

GREG FULLER: I was actually glad that he'd agreed to the interview. At least the hacks would be going back to Canary Wharf with more than just shots of the rollerblade fiasco. Who knows, I thought, perhaps we'll get some decent PR out of this after all.

TIM LELYVELDT: Reporter: 'I hope you don't mind me finishing with a question about Rebecca Richards.'

(Greta stiffened.)

Reporter: 'It has been rumoured that she may be written out of *All Our Lives Before Us*. Can you offer any comment?'

(Greta relaxed.)

Joe: 'First of all, let me say that it's all talk. Secondly, the producers know my feelings on this.'

Reporter: 'And they are?'

Joe: 'If she leaves I'll be cut up. We're pros and we've never let our differences get in the way of work. Rebecca's a major talent – *Lives* wouldn't be the same without her.'

GREG FULLER: Meal breaks are the high point on any shoot. You can send a crew to film swimwear on a Caribbean beach, and at the first sign of doughnuts the cast of curvy models will be trampled in the stampede. So, when Kevin called a lunch break and Toddy and I headed for the car park, we were surprised to have the catering truck to ourselves. We found out why when we returned to the studio and saw them gathered at the video playback station. Toddy dived into the mob to find out what was going on. When she re-emerged her face was several shades whiter.

'What's the matter?' I asked.

'They're playing a tape of Rebecca,' she said. 'Fucking –'

'Fucking what?'

'*Fucking*, Greg. It's that porn film.'

'I knew it existed,' I said triumphantly. 'And you never believed me.'

Then I saw the journalists emerge from Joe's dressing room and rejoin Bob. I had my second panic attack of the day.

'I'll divert them,' Toddy said. 'You get in there and confiscate that tape.'

I plunged into the mob and hit the off switch on the VCR.

'Where the hell did you get it?' I asked the video playback girl.

'It was left on my table,' she said.

'You'd better let me have it. Is it the only copy?'

'Yes,' she said, and I hoped to hell she wasn't lying.

BOB BULL: The *Mirror* chaps joined me to say their goodbyes.

'It's been a terrific morning,' said the reporter. 'We've got some good stuff.'

'Glad you could witness history in the making, celluloid-wise,' I said, hoping they hadn't noticed that no actual film had been shot. Toddy joined me as they went and I said to her, 'Well, that wasn't so bad, was it? I don't know why Greg made such a ballyhoo when they arrived.'

GREG FULLER: 'Did you get it?' said Toddy when she rejoined me. I patted the tape that I'd stuffed inside my shirt. 'Thank God,' she said. 'That was too fucking close.'

'I didn't see it when it was playing – I was too busy finding the off switch. How bad is it?' I asked her.

'Worse than you could imagine.'

'I've got quite an imagination, Toddy.'

'I know you have, darling, and believe me, it's worse.'

Even if she was only half-right, I knew that I was holding the video equivalent of a neutron bomb – leaves buildings intact but vaporises careers.

TIM LELYVELDT: The reporter was waiting for me in his car. I leaned through the window and said, 'I have your word that you'll make Joe look like a prince tomorrow?' The reporter nodded. 'And you'll hold on Rebecca, the Early Years, until the day after?' He nodded again. I handed him the tape. 'No one ever finds out where you got this, right?' I said as he wound up his window.

Joe didn't need a publicist to negotiate a great deal with the press. He just needed Tim Lelyveldt, Executive in Charge of Jellybeans.

the one with the pierced eyebrow in 5ive

NANCY STARK: It was only Puerto Banus in May, but as far as I was concerned it was heaven. I sat down on my sunbed and undid my bikini top (Knickerbox, Gatwick North Terminal – it didn't fit that well but I only had five minutes between duty-frees and 'Will Passenger N. Stark please proceed to gate sixteen *immediately*?'). I was lubed up with Hawaiian Tropic (Boots, North Terminal again) and ready to soak up the last couple of hours of sun. I slipped on my pop-star shades (Sunglass Hut, ditto) and put Usher (HMV, ditto) on my CD Walkman (Dixon's, ditto). That's when my mobile vibrated against my arm.

All right, which idiot had the bright idea of making mobiles work abroad?

'Hi, Greg,' I said as I sank into my super-thick towel (from the hotel's We-Saw-You-Coming-Sucker luxury boutique – doing my exes after this trip was going to be fun).

'What are you doing right now, Lola?'

'Just checked in and I'm waiting for a cab to take me to Paul and Shaun's pad. Should be here any minute.'

'You're not sitting by the pool, are you?' he snarled.

'Of course not,' I said.

'Anyway. Piss and Shit. What are you going to say to them when you see them?' he asked.

'I'll talk about the money, of course.'

'Do you really think that's what this is all about?'

'What else?'

'You're right. Every time they look at the shiny Maseratis they'll undoubtedly buy with their pay rises they'll be reminded what a twat they made me look. Remember, no higher than fifty per cent without talking to me first.'

'I won't. Anyway, how's it going back there?' I asked.

'Where do you want me to start?' he replied. 'Kevin is about to wrap on a day in which we've exposed less than three seconds of film. Do you want to know the most stupid thing? We've spent upwards of thirty grand flying Joe's hairdresser over from LA. Said stylist spent nearly four hours working on his client's barnet, and when said client finally made it onto the set I'd have defied Vidal fucking Sassoon himself to spot the difference.'

'Bad day then,' I said. (I'd have made that 'bad hair day', only he wasn't in the mood.)

'That's the least of it. You don't want to know the rest.'

He was right. I didn't. At that moment the most beautiful man I'd seen since the one with the pierced eyebrow in 5ive walked past. He smiled at me.

'Gotta go, Greg. My ride's here.'

GREG FULLER: I flicked my phone off just in time to see Joe take a stroll around the gleaming powder-blue 'sixty-two Mustang that had arrived moments before.

A few minutes later Morton joined Kevin and me. 'Guys, Joe has one tiny concern,' he said. 'He feels the car is kinda old.'

'It's bloody ancient,' said Kevin. 'That was the idea. Never been a pussy wagon like the sixty-two Mustang.'

'Joe feels that it doesn't quite mesh with the Shirer brand-profile that he has so carefully developed.'

'Jesus, what the fuck is he? An actor or a can of Coke?' asked Kevin. If Joe had him by the balls, this was clearly a squeeze too far.

He'd made a fair point, but it was going to get us nowhere. It was time for me to play Kofi Annan. I shot Kevin a look that was intended to convey 'It's only a bloody car that's going to be entirely peripheral and you didn't even want it in the first place, so does it really matter what the make, model and serial number is?' It was a lot to ask of slightly narrowed eyes and a furrowed brow, but it seemed to do the trick and Kevin backed off.

'What would make Joe comfortable, Morton?' I asked.

'A Dodge Viper would be in the right ballpark,' he replied. 'Say, the American Club Racer, eight-litre, Koni shocks, one-piece aluminium wheels.'

'Stunning choice, Morton. Sounds like we'd have a fine mesh on our hands,' I said. 'Anything else?'

'Make it red,' said Morton.

Toddy joined us. 'Everything OK?'

'Perfect,' I said before Kevin could open his mouth.

'Our taxi's here,' Toddy said. 'We don't want to be late.'

We were heading for the offices of French Films in Soho, where flesh awaited. We were hoping that we'd find one young woman who was the spit of Rebecca Richards, at least in the region between ankle and tits.

Bob Bull appeared as I was climbing into the cab. 'Greg,' he said, 'one tiny concern with the car.'

'I know, way too old. Don't know what came over us. Don't worry, though – a shiny Dodge Viper will be here first thing.'

He looked relieved – he was a car drone (he told me he actually *wept* when *Top Gear* was canned) and, unlike me, he not only knew what a Dodge Viper was, but he also gave a shit.

CARRIE FULLER: It was after eleven o'clock and I hadn't heard from Greg all evening. Unborn and I were alone in the sitting room.

'Tell us about this screenplay then,' he said.

(I had no idea whether *he* was a boy or a girl, but Unborn sounded exactly like Ben Kingsley in *Sexy Beast*. I'd have preferred something sweeter, a little less psychotic – Ben Chaplin, say, in *The Truth About Cats and Dogs* – but you never get the child you wish for, do you?)

So we sat on the sofa and while I channel-surfed I said, 'OK, I'll tell you. Are you sitting comfortably?'

'Pins and needles in my little legs, but that's as good as it gets in here. Shoot.'

'It's about coincidences,' I began. 'I once heard a story, probably apocryphal but it got me thinking. A driver ran out of petrol in the middle of nowhere and he set off to find a garage. As he was walking, he passed a phone box. It rang. He couldn't ignore a ringing phone so he stopped and answered it. It was for him.'

'Nah.'

'The call was for him. A friend wanted to talk to him. She called him at home but misdialled. Out of every number she could have rung, she got the phone box. She was connected at the exact moment he walked by.'

'What are the chances of that happening, eh?'

'I used to teach statistics and I tried to work it out. Believe me, it's so remote it doesn't bear thinking about. But it isn't impossible.'

'So how did you get a film out of it?'

'I thought, wouldn't it be interesting to write about someone whose life is plagued by coincidence? I nicked the phone box story, changed the man to a woman, and took it from there.'

'What happens?'

'At first my heroine is party to fairly benign coincidences. The consequences are positive. There's the phone box, for example, and her car has a shunt with her childhood sweetheart's – she hasn't seen him in years and they fall in love again over a broken headlight and a dented wing.'

'Sounds icky.'

'It is, but gradually things turn black. A train crashes, killing dozens of passengers – she'd have been on it if she hadn't tripped over her nephew's model railway and sprained her ankle. Later she goes to hospital for something minor – ingrown toenail or whatever. Unbeknown to her, a woman with the same name is in for a hysterectomy. Their details get mixed up and they end up having each other's ops.'

'Jesus, poor bitch.'

'Then a year to the day after her car hits the childhood sweetheart's, he's killed in a crash at the same junction –'

'That's sick.'

'– And she's driving the car that hits his.'

'Correction: *you're* sick.'

'It gets worse. Much worse. I'm not sure I should tell you at your age. Anyway, it freaks her out. She becomes a pariah – everyone thinks she's the focus of some supernatural wickedness. Even she starts to believe it.'

'How's it end then?'

'She disappears. Changes her name, moves house, starts a new life. The coincidences stop. She's free.'

'Thank fuck for that.'

'Until years later when she runs out of petrol in the middle of nowhere. . . .'

'Setting yourself up for the sequel? What's it called?'

'Nothing clever, I'm afraid. I named it after my central character – *Rebecca Edwards*.'

'Rebecca? You're kidding.'

'God, I'd never thought of that. See? Life's packed with coincidence.' I glanced at my watch. 'Look at the time. Where the hell's Greg?'

NANCY STARK: I was drifting off to sleep when my mobile rang again. I looked at my watch – midnight.

'Hello,' I said.

'Who's that?'

'Nancy. Who's that?'

'*Nancy*! It's me, Carrie. I meant to phone Greg but I must have hit the wrong button on the speed dial. I've woken you, haven't I?'

'Don't worry, I was just dozing. Are you OK? You're not –'

'No, still three months to go. I'm just trying to track Greg down. You don't know where he is, do you?'

'Sorry, haven't a clue. I spoke to him at the shoot this afternoon. No idea what time he finished. Universe of Sofas is still crap, so he probably headed for the office.'

Beep, beep – the battery warning on my phone.

The body next to me stirred and mumbled, 'Who is it, Lola?'

CARRIE FULLER: I heard it. I distinctly heard it. *Lola*. Only one person on the planet called her that. The fucking bastard, I thought. *The fucking bitch.* All that time being my friend, a pillar of support. I choked and hung up.

NANCY STARK: The phone went dead – batteries, I assumed. I turned to the body next to me. 'It was no one, Dieter. Just a friend. You fancy raiding the mini bar?'

Dieter. Thong boy from the pool. Came from somewhere called Wiesbaden. Even sexier than Pierced Eyebrow in 5ive. Didn't speak much English. Given that we had as much dialogue going on between us as the average blue movie, it seemed appropriate to give him my porn star name.

thirteen:

fluffy clouds, peanut butter, toxoplasmosis

NORMAN THE COOK: My brother had done me proud. He was on my doorstep at sparrow's fart on the Wednesday morning.

'Hope these are what you're after, Norm,' he said, handing me a big cardboard box. I opened it and looked inside.

'They are the dog's,' I said.

Wendy appeared in her dressing gown and fluffy mules.

'What are you doing here, Ray? It's not even five yet.'

'Got fifty T-shirts for Norm. I had to put off a bulk order from Willesden Weight Watchers to do them in time. Have a gander.'

He pulled one out of the box and held it up.

'Look at that, darling,' I said. 'The unmistakable work of Kilburn's finest T-shirt printer.'

'It's West Hampstead, Norm, and it's bespoke T-shirt art,' Ray corrected.

Whatever the fuck, the boy had done a bang-up job. 'NORM's

F-PLAN DIET (one tast and your diet's f****d)' it read over a picture of a juicy mixed grill.

'Just wait till the metabolic shit-shoveller sees the crew wearing these beauties,' I said. 'He'll be lost for words.'

'Oh, I think he might have something to say, Norm,' said Wendy. 'Like "Isn't there an e in taste?"'

GREG FULLER: I got up just before five. I dressed and, as I tiptoed to the door, I heard a mumble.

'Come back to bed, Greg.'

'Go to sleep,' I whispered.

'You're going to *her*, aren't you?'

'I have to put in an appearance. She is pregnant.'

'But Toddy needs you,' she pouted.

'Go back to sleep. I'll see you in Hounslow soon enough.'

In the cab to Primrose Hill I got my story straight.

Eight pm to ten-thirty pm: casting for a body double.

(This bit was true – it was an outrageous success, as it happened. I was surprised how many girls had the body, if not the presence, of Rebecca. In the end it was a toss-up between Sonia from Bethnal Green and a Polish model called Agnieszka. Sonia got the gig on the assumption that the Pole's name would give the crew nightmares.)

Ten-thirty pm to five am: closed session, do-not-disturb-on-pain-of-being-shouted-at-very-loudly brainstorm with my creative department in the Fuller Scheidt boardroom. Mission: find solution to Universe of Sofas problem or die in attempt.

(Partially true – that was exactly what I was doing until shortly before midnight. Toddy was waiting for me and I could see her through the plate-glass partition. After yawning affectedly for a while, she went into the kitchenette and returned with a jar of queen olives. She placed one carefully between her front teeth and proceeded to stone it by drilling it with her tongue. As she knew it would, her party piece served to remind me of the other minor miracle of which her mouth was capable. Combined with the mind-numbing tedium of the brief, it caused me to throw in the towel and flee to her Holland Park fuckpad.)

My alibi sorted, I switched on my mobile and checked my messages. There was just the one: 'I know exactly what you've been doing, you shit. If you bother to come home you'll find the door bolted. I never want to see you again.'

How the fuck did she rumble me? was all I could think. Then again, perhaps she was bluffing in order to trick me into an unnecessary confession. My mother used to do that – make an accusation that I'd flushed, say, her concrete porridge down the toilet when she could have had no actual evidence, apart from a barely discernible hairline crack in the U-bend.

Perhaps someone had talked, though who it could have been escaped me. Lola? Unlikely. She was in Spain. Anyway, she didn't know about Toddy, did she? Had Toddy herself squealed? Knowing that she wanted to upgrade the aforementioned fuckpad to a Sloane Street model and that she'd need me – or rather my bank account – to do it gave her motive.

There was one other possibility: that Carrie hadn't got wind of Toddy at all. Maybe she'd discovered the toast crumbs I'd left in the peanut butter the previous day – a habit that needled the hell out of her. She'd let it fester, her antenatal flood of hormones feeding her rage, until it became a firing issue.

By the time the cab pulled up outside my house I'd convinced myself. It *was* the crumbs in the Sunpat. Such is the power of wishful thinking. I imagine that when the police turned up to arrest Kenneth Noye for the road-rage murder he was thinking, 'Bugger, I should have paid those parking tickets.'

True to her word Carrie had bolted the front door. I thought about ringing the bell, but only briefly. I sat down on the step and was pondering when the milkman arrived.

'She locked you out?'

'Something like that,' I replied.

He reached down for the empties and found a scrap of paper tucked behind them. He looked at it.

'This'll be for you then. Either that or she's had it up to here with my gold top,' he said, handing it to me.

I read the note: 'I THOUGHT I TOLD YOU TO FUCK OFF' in the spiky, splenetic hand that Carrie reserved exclusively for bad hair/husband days.

I'd asked the cabby to hang on and I told him to take me to Hounslow. I got him to stop on the way so I could get the *Mirror*. It wasn't my usual read, but I couldn't fail to be attracted by the front page puff, 'Joe and Becs in rubber rumpus. Exclusive interview and pictures, page 4.'

NORMAN THE COOK: 'Wendy, I'm in the paper,' I hollered.

She looked over my shoulder at the photo. 'You could have put the knife down,' she said.

'Tool of the trade, darling,' I explained.

'The way you're waving it at that reporter, it doesn't look like you're dicing carrots. And you've got a bloody fag hanging out of your gob. Environmental Health will be round here like whippets when they see that.'

Obviously jealous. 'I don't see your picture here,' I said.

'That's because I've got some sense. Now what do you want me to do with these stupid T-shirts?'

'One free with every breakfast,' I told her, 'and don't forget to tell them it's the American spelling of "taste".'

GREG FULLER: The feature opened with a shot of Kevin yelling at the legs of the rollerblader as they projected uselessly from the car sunroof. I cursed the advance of colour repro technology – every pulsating vein on our director's purple face was discernible in high-res detail.

There were plenty more pictures. I won't describe them. Let's just say I've seen footage of motorway pile-ups that was less distressing.

However, though she hadn't even been present, the portrait of Rebecca Richards took the biscuit. They'd used a file photo of her in a skimpy bikini and superimposed the effects of a rubber allergy. The one-word headline read 'B-LIST-ER', which would have made me smile on any other day. The fact that they hadn't laid their hands on a still from her only period drama – you know, ship meets iceberg/girl meets boys – was a minor comfort.

As if the photographs weren't sufficiently damaging, the reporter had gone to town with several hundred choice words. He signed off with, 'Blackstock? Better make that laughing stock.'

All of that was on pages four and five. There was a special treat on page six.

YASMIN FISH: 'Gordon Bennett,' said my dad, choking on his corn-flakes, 'I thought this was a family paper.'

My mum grabbed it from him. 'That's bloody lethal, that is,' she said. 'Just you keep well away from him, Yasmin.'

'He should have a licence for it,' my dad agreed.

I reached for the paper and looked at the picture they were getting so hot and bothered about. I couldn't help blushing. Joe's pecs and abs looked amazing, but they weren't what had caught Dad's eye. Tyler had exactly the same pair of Tommy Hilfiger underpants, but he didn't fill them like Joe.

GREG FULLER: The headline over Joe's 'exclusive and revealing' interview was 'JOE: "SIZE *DOESN'T* MATTER"'. This was about as sincere as writing 'JORDAN: "I WISH THE PRESS WOULD LEAVE ME ALONE"' over a shot of said media whore arriving at her fifth premiere of the week.

I hoped that by the time Max worked his way down from the *FT* to the *Mirror*, he'd be so mesmerised by the scale model of K2 in Joe's shorts that he'd overlook the PR disaster preceding it. In the likely event that he didn't, I had my excuse buffed up and ready: 'Inviting the *Mirror* over wasn't my idea, Max. Thank our esteemed client for that.' For once I wouldn't be lying.

BOB BULL: I was on my way to the shoot when the call from Roger Knopf came through. I wouldn't have been much of a multi-region marketing wiz if I hadn't been primed. I muted *Anthology: The Very Best of REO Speedwagon*, and took it on the hands-free.

'I take it you've seen the *Daily Mirror*,' he said.

'Rog, I'm as infuriated about it as you are. I recommend we take it off all our media schedules with immediate effect.'

'I wasn't aware that our ad-spend was going their way.'

'Well, it's not exactly, but I'll be spelling it out to them in no uncertain terms that, if it were to have been, then we'd take great pleasure in withdrawing it.'

'What I want to know, Bob, is how the heck a gutter tabloid was given an access-all-areas pass to our movie set.'

'You're not the only one, Rog. I am making it my personal mission to find out what our ad agency was playing at when they invited them.'

NANCY STARK: My mobile had been switched on while it recharged overnight and its ring woke me up. I looked at my watch – seven-thirty. The display on the phone showed 'GREG HOME'. 'Shit,' I thought, and I flicked the air-con to max. I hoped it would sound vaguely like the inside of a cab and I could say I was on my way to Paul and Shaun's villa.

I needn't have worried. It was Carrie.

'Having fun, are we?' I thought it might be the line, but she sounded cold.

'Well, it's hardly a holiday, Carrie,' I replied, looking down at Dieter asleep beside me.

'You bitch,' she said. It wasn't the line then. 'How could you do this to me? I thought you were my friend, someone I could depend on. Now this.'

'Now *what*?' I said.

'You know exactly what I'm talking about, *Lola*.' (She'd never called me that before.) 'Do you know what I've been doing all night? I've been replaying every conversation we've ever had. "Sorry, Carrie, Greg'll be late – he's with a client ... Sorry, Carrie, the meeting's overrunning. Don't expect him for dinner ... *Sorry, Carrie*."' It was scary – she had my voice off perfectly. 'And I believed every lying word.'

Shit. *She knew about Toddy.*

'I'm so sorry, Carrie.' It sounded feeble and it was.

'Oh, fuck off. Sorry doesn't even come close.'

'I knew how hurt you'd be. I should have done something but I couldn't bring myself to–'

'I don't want to hear this now. I only wanted you to know how much I despise you,' she said before she rang off.

'The stupid bastard,' I said out loud. 'He's fucked everything up.'

'Sorry, Lola,' Dieter mumbled. 'Four times at one night is too many.' He rubbed his groin to make sure I got the point.

'Not you,' I said, 'Greg.'

'*Gott*, you have a husband?'

BOB BULL: Greg was reading the *Mirror* when I arrived.

'I think you should dispose of *that*,' I told him.

'Who was it yesterday that said, "All publicity is good publicity"?' he blustered, trying to shift the blame.

'A figure of speech. Anyway, how was I to know that they'd show up on the day the shoot fell apart?' I protested. 'I must say there is one thing that the *Mirror* got spot on. Your handling of events leaves much to be desired – not what a company like Blackstock expects of its advertising agency.'

'I didn't invite the paper down here, Bob.'

'That's as maybe, but you should have stopped them. This is your domain. You are supposed to be the flipping expert.'

He knew I had him there because all he could do was splutter.

His mobile rang. 'I'd better take this call,' he said. He wasn't going to get off the hook that easily, though.

NANCY STARK: 'Your timeliest intervention yet, Lola,' Greg said when he answered. 'I was just about to throttle our client. Give me good news. Tell me that, having checked Piss and Shit into the baggage hold, you're about to board your flight home.'

'You are such an idiot, Greg.'

'Why? What have they said about me?'

'Paul and Shaun haven't said anything. I haven't seen them yet. Carrie doesn't think much of you, though.'

'You've talked to her? What did she say?'

'She knows about you and the Wicked Witch of TV.'

'How did she find out? Hang on, how did *you* find out?'

'I've known for ages. You two are crap at covering your tracks.' They were as well. Toddy marked her territory. I think she had a special gland that sprayed Chanel.

'Carrie definitely knows then?' he asked.

'*Definitely.*'

'Shit. My hopes were pinned on the peanut butter.'

'I don't know what you're on about, Greg, but you'd better deal with this. You will never, ever meet another Carrie. If you lose her and end up with that shallow bitch you'll be more of a prat than I thought.'

Silence.

'Greg?'

'I'll deal with it, OK? By the way, why the fuck haven't you seen Piss and Shit yet?'

I was hoping that, with his marriage crumbling, his mind might have been taken off them. I should have been so lucky.

Lucky, lucky, lucky.

NORMAN THE COOK: The Blackstock client came up to the truck for the Norman Number One Belly-buster and I handed him his T-shirt.

'Cheers,' he said. 'You should be in marketing, you know. Loyalty reward programmes – a major growth area. The classic free T-shirt – on a cost-per-prospect basis, the most effective incentiviser in the game. You can never make the corporate bean-counters understand that. The number of T-shirt promotions I've had die at the hands of the accountants is a tragedy.'

'Too right, mate,' I said, though I didn't know what the fuck he was talking about.

He unfolded the shirt and held it up. 'Is that a rude word?' he said. 'Don't you think the press has made us look stupid enough without everyone running around with rude words on their flipping chests?'

'That's not a rude word,' I said. 'It was supposed to say, "one taste and your diet's *finished*". My brother printed them. He ran out of letters but he had a job-lot of them asterisk whatsits.'

'Ah, I see. Very droll,' he said.

He was right. I should have been in marketing. With tossers like him running the show, I reckon they could have used some brains.

VERONICA D: Rebecca's rash had almost cleared by the time she woke up. Her mood hadn't improved though. It was worse than when she found out about Joe and Greta. However upset she was then, she knew deep down that he wasn't the last guy on the planet. But now she was acting as if *Lives* was the last job on TV; the only roles she'd ever be up for would involve wearing chicken outfits and handing out KFC flyers in malls.

She didn't say a word in the limo. Tish filled in the silence, though.

TISH WILKIE: I'd decided to work on Rebecca's self-esteem issues. If she was going to be at her best she needed to be made whole again. Veronica glared at me. She was so, like, *duh*. What did she know about handling a star's fragile ego?

Veronica said Rebecca was simply depressed because she'd lost her job, but even a thicko could see that deep down she was a *very* unhappy person. She'd obviously caught Paradise Syndrome, which was literally sweeping Hollywood like AIDS only worse. You catch it when you have everything: fame, money, beauty, but you still feel like there's a huge, nothingy void in your life. You've probably never heard of it, but why would you have? You have to be a mega-celeb to be at risk and you probably work in a shop or factory or whatever.

I'd already decided to find out if there was a support group for it when we got back to LA. Celebrities Anonymous or something. If there wasn't, I'd start one. Rebecca and unhappy stars like her deserved our help. Alcoholics have their own group and they *choose* to drink. Stars don't choose to be millionaires and have chauffeurs and the best restaurant tables, etc. OK, they do sort of, but you know what I mean. Don't you?

I'd been reading an *amazing* book. It had *totally* changed my life. It was called *World Peace Starts with Inner Calm*. There was a *brilliant* bit about how to cleanse yourself *completely* of anger. It was exactly what she needed.

'Rebecca, I want you to try this exercise,' I said. 'Close your eyes and imagine your dark feelings as fluffy clouds.'

She turned her head and looked out of the window. I think she'd closed her eyes but it was hard to tell.

'That's right, fluffy little clouds,' I said soothingly. 'Now think of a lovely golden sun shining on the clouds. One by one they'll fade away and disappear . . . fade away . . . and disappear.'

VERONICA D: Rebecca sighed ominously, so I decided to snap before she did. 'Tish, honey, right now Becca is dealing with Hurricane Shirer. I don't think a few goddamn fluffy clouds are gonna cut it. Why don't you give it a rest, huh?'

TISH WILKIE: Ever since Rebecca called *me* in the middle of the night about her allergy, Veronica had been so jealous of our bond.

But I wasn't a spiteful person and I decided to work on her too. There was literally an *entire* chapter in *World Peace* about winning people over with 'positive bio-waves from within'.

CARRIE FULLER: 'We'll be better off without him, you'll see,' announced Unborn as I put an egg on to boil.

'So you fancy being brought up by a single mum? Queuing up for benefits, pariah of the state and the *Daily Mail*?' I replied.

'This gaff isn't council and you're no Waynetta Slob.'

'You're right . . . we'll be well shot of the bastard. Can you believe him, screwing his bloody secretary?'

GREG FULLER: Toddy swept into the studio wearing store-fresh Valentino. She was the only woman I knew who didn't wear the shoot uniform of T-shirt, jeans/combats and Timberlands. We once went on location to the Sierra Nevada and I had to admire the way she climbed three hundred feet of scree in three-inch Jimmy Choos. It took her all day and we'd almost wrapped by the time she reached the top, but it was admirable all the same.

'We've got to talk,' I said to her.

'God, yes,' she replied. 'That Dodge Viper looks ghastly – red – so *nouveau*. I think we have to call a meeting.'

'Not about the car. About us. Carrie knows.'

'You told her? That's marvellous,' she squealed, flinging her arms around me.

'No, I didn't tell her. I thought maybe you did.'

'I did *not*. What do you take me for? Look, it doesn't matter now. She knows,' she declared. 'She'd have worked it out for herself months ago if she hadn't been so self-obsessed.'

CARRIE FULLER: 'How could you not see it?' Unborn demanded. 'She's right there on his doorstep, bringing him coffee and dough-nuts, wearing those tight tops, going, "Whoops-a-daisy, dropped a pencil," and giving him a flash of her knickers.'

'I'd sooner not go there, thanks,' I shuddered.

'Will you stop shuddering, please? It's claustrophobic enough in here without you firing off like a pneumatic drill. Look, you said yourself she's a babe. And he calls her *Lola*, for buggery's sake. If I was a barrister that would be Exhibit sodding A. How could you not see it?'

'I've been a little preoccupied with you, for starters. Anyway, I thought Nancy was my friend. It's something called trust. You'll learn about it when you get out.'

'Not from you I won't. I can see you're no expert.'

GREG FULLER: 'Trust me, Toddy,' I said as she sobbed on my shoulder. 'It's for the best.'

'Why though, Greg?'

'Because she's about to have our third kid. I owe it to her to try and make things work . . . if she'll let me.'

'You'll come crawling back in a couple of weeks. You always do. No one understands you like me,' she sniffed.

'Not this time, sweet pea. I have to give it a go with Carrie – some proper time.'

CARRIE FULLER: 'How long are you planning to give it?' Unborn asked.

'The usual three-and-a-half minutes,' I said, lifting the egg from the pan.

'*Three-and-a-half minutes*! Haven't you heard of Salmonella? While you're at it, you might as well chew on a bit of raw pork and you can give us both toxoplasmosis.'

'What the hell is that?'

'You don't want to know. It's vicious – the scourge of us foetuses.'

fourteen:

kate winslet, sex hypermarkets, the british banger

VERONICA D: Our arrival at the studio was one of those Black-Bart-walks-into-the-saloon moments. The place was buzzing, but it went silent when they caught sight of Rebecca. If there'd been a honky-tonk piano player in the corner, he'd have stopped mid-bar.

TIM LELYVELDT: You never feel the same about someone when you've seen them naked, do you? Poor Rebecca – the day before everyone had seen her, while not exactly bare, clothed only in fetish wear. Worse still, they'd also seen her giving it, taking it and swallowing it, as well as being spanked quite hard with a hairbrush. So when she arrived it was as if they'd all had a drunken fuck with her and once they'd sobered up they were too ashamed to make eye contact.

VERONICA D: Rebecca seemed too spaced to even notice it, and she cruised through to her dressing room on autopilot. I set about her hair. She didn't usually say much when I styled her. I know most girls go to the hairdresser and expect to gossip, but when you spend over two hours of every working day having the same bitch do the same stuff to the same hair it doesn't take long before you run out of vacation and boyfriend stories.

That morning she didn't even grunt, not even an 'Ouch, Veronica, go easy with that comb' – quiet as a mouse for more than an hour.

Then, out of the blue, as I was about to give her a blast with the dryer, 'Fuck, Veronica, no one even looked at me.'

'Uh-huh, sweetheart.' I couldn't lie.

'They must know.'

'How could they?' I said. 'You ain't even been told about the decision officially.'

'They know something.'

BOB BULL: I couldn't believe that it hadn't clicked before. I was rarely off my game but I felt like such a twit when I overheard two of the lads talking about Rebecca's remarkable performance in that phenomenal film. Not that I'd have described her character as 'filthy' or 'horny' – more proud, and yet vulnerable.

I was surprised that Jane hadn't pointed it out to me. Why hadn't she said something all those weeks before when I'd told her our new commercial was to feature Rebecca Richards, the star of her all-time favourite motion picture? She wept buckets every time she listened to the Irish-y Barbra Streisand theme song. I'm not sure she'll thank me for telling you this, but she'd even insisted we 'recreate' that raunchy scene in the back of our Scorpio when we'd parked up on the Dover–Calais ferry. I'm not usually one for 'performing' in public, but I think I acquitted myself rather well.

I made a mental memo to self to compliment Rebecca on her performance the moment we finally had a chance for a chinwag. I'd tell her that both Jane and I thought she and Leonardo di

Capriati made the most romantic screen couple ever. I'd also compliment her on the weight she'd lost since she'd made *Titanic*.

Not that I like them too skinny. I'm a chap who prefers his ladies a little rounded. Give me something to grab hold of, as I never failed to tell Jane whenever I caught her diving into the chocolate ginger nuts.

TIM LELYVELDT: 'How am I doing then, Tim?' Joe asked me.

'Ace,' I replied.

He'd already taken away her job. With the imminent international exposure of *Going Down on the Titanic*, he was also about to strip away any dignity the poor bitch had left. I'd say he was definitely having a good day.

'Yeah, I'm doing OK,' he mused. 'But wouldn't it be cool if the tyre company guy had another look at her résumé – the version that includes her early career.'

Jesus, I thought, he'll see it along with the rest of the world tomorrow. Can't you wait?

'Sure,' I said, 'that'd be cool.'

VERONICA D: After the silence, the floodgates opened. I couldn't stop Rebecca talking.

'You know what, Veronica? I actually couldn't give a damn who knows.'

'Why the change of heart?'

'Everyone thinks they know everything about me anyway. What would it matter if they found out ahead of time that I've been fired? Maybe losing this job isn't the end of the world. I shouldn't feel like a failure, should I?'

'No way.'

'And I shouldn't care what everyone is saying.'

'Now you're talking, honey.'

'I'm really proud of what I've done on *Lives*. In fact, I've never done anything to be ashamed of.'

She was definitely talking herself round.

'Well,' she said after a pause, 'except for one thing.'

BOB BULL: I was beginning to feel that I'd got everything back on track. Greg's card had been marked and the crew were working like nig –. I can't use that word, can I? They were working phenomenally hard to get the show on the road again. We weren't far off shooting the day's first scene when Morty came up to me.

'Bobby, can I have a discreet word,' he whispered, 'on a matter that is giving Joe a great deal of trouble?'

It was telling that he should look to me as a confidant. Not Greg, not Kevin French, but Bob Bull. At that moment it was crystal clear who exuded the authority in the studio. We found a quiet corner and Morty laid it on the line.

'Bobby, there's no good way to put this, so I'll cut to the chase. You're clearly a man who values directness.'

I braced myself for the worst.

'It has come to Joe's attention,' Morty went on, 'that his co-star has been less than candid with him.'

'I thought the two of them were ... you know ...' I fumbled for a suitably delicate way to put it.

'Oh, Joe and Rebecca have long since ceased to be an item, Bobby, but they have continued to enjoy a close professional relationship. Think Bob and Bing, Fred and Ginger.'

'Or Terry and June,' I said, picking up the thread.

'Their rapport has been built on mutual respect and trust. I'm sure that a man of your sensitivity must appreciate that the on-screen chemistry they spark could not exist without that.'

'Absolutely,' I nodded, 'phenomenal trust.'

'You must also appreciate that the Joe Shirer brand has been developed with care. It's clean but sexy, youthful but virile, apple-pie-American but with a touch of good-natured mischief.'

'All the qualities that make Joe and Blackstock the perfect fit at the brand/consumer interface,' I agreed.

'Any hint of sleaze would destroy all that fine work.' Mort paused and took a deep breath. 'This morning Joe learned something about Rebecca that places a major question mark over the future of their working relationship.'

'My God,' I said, 'what has she done?'

VERONICA D: What Rebecca said next was strange: 'Do you think porn exploits women, Veronica?'

'Porno? Honey, you ain't *that* desperate.'

She ignored me and said, 'Because Hollywood's biggest irony is that it's the only branch of movies where women earn more than men.'

'I've never thought of it like that.'

'Imagine some producer telling Nicholas Cage that Angelina Jolie was getting six mill more than him and when he asks why he's told, "Let's face it, Nick, no one's queuing for two blocks to see *your* tits." That's how it works in the porn business.'

'Becca, what's brought this on?' I asked.

She didn't answer straight away.

BOB BULL: 'Early in her career, Rebecca appeared in a low-budget film of questionable morality,' said Morty.

'Not a video nasty,' I said, feeling myself deflate.

'More of a video very nasty.' I must have looked confused because he added, 'She did a porno ... a skin flick ... a stag movie ... triple-X ... hard core.'

'You mean a sex film?' I was flabbergasted. 'However did she land the lead in *Titanic* after that?'

VERONICA D: 'I did a porno once, you know,' she said in the kind of casual voice you'd use to tell someone you once wore lilac.

'You never did,' I yelped, cutting off a quarter-inch too much from her fringe.

'I told you I had one thing I'm ashamed of.'

'Nothing explicit, right?' I said. 'Just a bit of dry humping, yeah?' I was looking for reassurance but she didn't give me any. 'Jesus, Rebecca Richards. Please don't tell me you've done a triple-X.'

'Times three,' she winced.

'My God, girl. How the fuck did you manage to keep that one to yourself?'

'Well, when I was testing for *Lives* and they asked me what I'd done before, it did cross my mind to say, "Oh, not much. I was Woman in Car Crash in *Casualty* and I've done a couple of TV ads and a *Titanic* tribute movie where I gave the captain a blowjob." But then I thought, no, best to keep schtum about that.'

'OK, so you're not gonna tell all to Larry King, but these things always come out one way or another. Look at Kevin Costner, Sly, Madonna – we've all seen their skin flicks.'

'I've been lucky. The guy that produced it got his break at the same time as me – same week, in fact. He'd been grubbing around doing porn for years, but he really wanted to be in mainstream TV. He was forever punting programme ideas to the networks over here. Nothing ever stuck. Then out of the blue he got a commission from the BBC. Funnily enough he was like me – he hadn't mentioned his fuck movies on his CV. He could have made a fortune from it when I got the part in *Lives*, but he was as keen to keep it buried as I was. It was never released.'

'So, what sort of TV does the guy make?' I asked.

'That's the funniest bit. He's a big hit with the under-fives. He produces something called *The Shaggles*.'

'What the hell are they?'

'Kind of *Teletubbies* but shaggier, and with a custard-pie fetish. He's rich now – probably makes more money from the merchandising alone than he ever did from porn.'

TYRONE EDWARDS: 'What are you playing at, Tyrone?' Yvonne screams.

'What you doing back? I thought you'd gone to work.'

'Forgot my Walkman. Anyway, why the hell are you watching TV?'

'It's *The Shaggles*.'

'What the fuck are you? Three? Get off your skinny arse and find yourself a job.'

'I was just thinking,' I tell her. 'These guys must make millions dreaming up this shit. It's gotta be easy. Stick someone in a monster suit, sing some kiddies' songs, chuck some pies. I could come up with one of these.'

She throws the Yellow Pages and it hits me in the face.

'Fuck, Yvonne, that hurt,' I say.

'Good – it was meant to. There's people in that book that gives people work – even lazy, useless criminals like you.'

'I'll get a job, I swear, but you've gotta give me time.'

'I'll give you some time. You've got till I get back tonight,' she says, and she slams the door.

I open the Yellow Pages, S – scrap-metal merchants, screw manufacturers, secretarial, security services.

Security. That gives me an idea. I grab my jacket. I'm going to see Hakkan.

BOB BULL: I was thinking clearly again and I was ready to give my response. 'This is potentially a phenomenal crisis, Morty. First I must see the film for myself and work out precisely what we are dealing with. If experience has taught me anything, it's that one mustn't rush to judgement in these delicate matters.'

'I hear you, Bobby. Look, as far as Joe is concerned he doesn't want to make waves. He's upset with Rebecca, but he'd like to keep that between the two of them. As his manager, though, I have to look at the big picture and ask the tough questions: what will his association with her do to his career? Frankly, my advice to him would be to distance himself from her. Is there any possibility of a termination scenario being played out with regard to Rebecca's contract?'

'Blackstock has a proud heritage. It has served the family motorist for over a century in a way perhaps unrivalled by any other corporation in the automotive arena.'

'So you'll ice her, then?'

'If the tape contains the faintest whiff of inappropriate behaviour . . . absolutely,' I assured him.

'I can breathe easier knowing that, Bobby,' said Morty, and he handed me the tape.

VERONICA D: 'Why are you telling me this now, Becca?' I asked.

'Because you're my friend and I trust you. I haven't told a soul since I came to LA.'

'But why are you telling me *now*?'

'Because I'm trying to explain why being fired doesn't seem like such a big deal.'

'I'm not with you, honey.'

'Well, whenever something bad happens I think of the porn film and feel better.'

'Now I'm definitely not with you.'

'I was desperate when I made that. It wasn't a happy time. However bad things get, I'll never be that low again.'

BOB BULL: I'm no puritan. I had no objection to a bit of Page Three-type titillation, and had no time for the killjoys who demanded an end to a cheerful bit of cleavage. But any decent human being knows that a line must be drawn. Correct me if I'm wrong, but surely that line was crossed when a motion-picture event as important as *Titanic* was reduced to smut.

I went off in search of Greg. He was about to discover that Blackstock hadn't recruited me for my strategic vision alone, but also for my guts of toughened titanium.

It ran through my mind that Maggie must have felt much the same when she was told the Argies had invaded. She didn't buckle, and neither would Robert Gerald Bull.

VERONICA D: Then Rebecca announced, 'I really don't care what anyone thinks of me. I'm going for some breakfast.'

'But I ain't done with your hair,' I said as she got out of her chair. 'And you don't even eat breakfast.'

But she was out of the door.

CARRIE FULLER: I tried to ignore the phone but I couldn't.

'Carrie, I know you're mad, but you've got to let me explain,' he blurted before I'd even managed a 'hello'.

'What are you going to say? I'm six months pregnant, you're a piece of shit – that's all the explanation I need.'

'You're right to hate me. Fuck, I hate myself. I'm sorry.'

Silence.

'I'm so, so sorry.'

More silence.

'We have to talk. You must know I love you.'

'Burn in hell, Greg,' I said, and I hung up.

GREG FULLER: I was toying with the idea of calling Carrie back when Bob appeared and saved me from my indecision. He was clutching a VHS.

'Have you seen this? I want that perverted hussy out of my film *now*,' he demanded. 'I'm also seriously questioning the judgment of the agency that cast her.'

I looked at the scribbled *Titanic* label on the tape's spine. Obviously the copy I'd confiscated the day before hadn't been the only one in existence.

I took a deep breath and said, 'Not the James Cameron version, I take it, Bob. Yes, I have seen it. Have you?'

'Well, no, but –'

I knew then that this was a situation I could salvage. I started as I invariably do with the logical arguments. 'Bob,' I explained, 'Rebecca's appearance in that film was an aberration, a decision that she now regrets deeply. The Rebecca on that tape is not the Rebecca who will grace your commercial.'

He didn't look convinced but, given his opening position, he couldn't reasonably be expected to back down straight away.

I put this to him. 'Pornography isn't what it used to be. It's a new age, and porn is the new Disney. Across Europe sex hyper-markets are springing up like IKEAs. They even have crèches.' (I made up that last bit. However, it didn't seem too far-fetched to suppose that in the suburbs of Amsterdam, next door to the Dutch equivalent of Universe of Sofas, there were children drowning in pits of brightly coloured plastic balls while their parents browsed the aisles for some well-shot sodomy.) 'I'd be prepared to bet that any tracking study will show a marked improvement in Blackstock's approval rating should the public ever discover Rebecca's exhi-bitionism.'

It seemed highly unlikely that Roger Knopf, let alone his geriatric board in Akron, would ever see porn as just another choice in the varied menu of family entertainment alongside Nickelodeon and Ker-Plunk!; nevertheless, I could sense a slight thawing in the Bull demeanour. Only slight, so I pressed ahead.

'Of course that day is unlikely ever to arrive. The film has stayed buried for this long, and we've confiscated every copy that surfaced here. Actually, I should dispose of that one, too.'

Amazingly he handed the tape over – he was dafter than I'd thought.

'Thanks, Bob. I'll give it to Toddy to incinerate.'

Bob did look a little reassured at that point, but not convinced. It was time to bring a little sweat to his palms.

'If you choose to, I'll fully understand you blaming us. That's what we're here for. "Taking the rap" isn't explicit in Fuller Scheidt's terms of service, but perhaps it should be. I'll be very sad to lose the Blackstock business. But you don't require me to tell you that, just as you need to blame us, your board will be looking for a scapegoat too. It would be a tragedy if you had to leave at the point when you were beginning to make a very real impact in the tyre sector.'

As this was sinking in, I spent a moment reminiscing.

'To think it was only a few months ago that you gave us your business. That was some celebration, Bob,' I smiled.

'A phenomenal night out,' he agreed.

'A superb dinner.'

'Superb.'

'Then Tramp.'

'Seeing Chris de Burgh *and* Rod Stewart – a dream come true,' he sighed.

'And the perfect night-cap at Honeydew.'

He looked slightly discomfited at the mention of the table-dancing club where we'd finished our evening, but he still managed a tepid smile.

'Did you know that Max has a stake in that place?'

Bob had no idea, but why should he have had? Max had fingers in many pies. He'd tell anyone who'd listen about his extra-curricular interests in restaurants and health clubs. However, he was less forthcoming about his more dubious ventures, of which Honeydew was just one.

'Don't tell Max,' I went on, 'but I'll let you into a secret. There are security cameras all over that club, even in the private rooms. He likes to acquire the tapes for a little home entertainment.'

I had to stop then because Kevin appeared. Bob said he'd have to think about his final decision, but I didn't for a minute doubt that he'd end up seeing things my way. If and when he was asked to justify his decision he would, of course, cite all the logical reasons. He wouldn't mention that he'd based a major business decision not on hard-nosed logic but on the fact that he was scared shitless of the world and his wife (especially his wife) discovering that Rebecca Richards wasn't the only person whose genitalia had been committed to video.

TISH WILKIE: I was finally having a positive effect on Rebecca. After our chat in the limo she'd literally floated off to her dressing room. The fluffy clouds were working.

I was also making inroads with Veronica. I'd summoned up all my positive bio-waves from within and asked her what the D stood for. She'd never told anyone that, not even Rebecca. But she clearly felt the warmth I was transmitting and she told me. It was Dontask, which sounded Polish or something. I hadn't realised that Poland had any of her sort, but I suppose that hers must have been one of the few African-American Polish families that weren't wiped out by the Nazis. So sad – clearly I'd have to be extra-sensitive in my dealings with her.

I was congratulating myself on my progress when disaster struck. I spotted the awful picture of Rebecca in the *Mirror*. They'd made her look like a hideously diseased alien. I knew she'd be devastated if she saw it, so I got some scissors and went round the studio, cutting it out of every copy of the paper I could find. Some of the crew were a bit funny but I explained, 'Look, there's only a boring old article about Terry Blair on the other side – it's not as if you'll be missing anything.'

NORMAN THE COOK: Want to know my most treasured memory from a lifetime in the film business? *Sense and Sensibility*: the sight of Kate Winslet in a boned frock cramming a sausage-and-fried-egg roll down her neck. Not in the film – that would have been daft – outside my catering truck. Winslet wasn't unusual. It doesn't matter what poncey power-diet a star is on, there's something about the smell of a knob of dripping melting on a hotplate that gets them every time.

I had that Catherine Deneuve in the back of my truck once. She was something of a sausage connoisseur and she wanted to see for herself what it was that made the British banger so special.

'You French chop up your meat too coarse, love,' I explained. 'The secret is to mince those pig's innards into a really fine mulch.'

The cream of the acting community has enjoyed my breakfasts

so I wasn't surprised to see Rebecca Richards turn up for the high-fat treatment. She wasn't in the best of moods, but she seemed perkier after a bacon roll. Didn't make much of an impression on her, though – still skinny as a bookie's pencil.

'Here, you're not going to do a supermodel on me, are you?' I asked.

'What's that?' she said with her mouth full.

'One time we was shooting this bra ad with a bunch of them. They shovelled my belly-busters down their necks but ten minutes later they were forming an orderly queue at the Portaloo.' I put two fingers down my throat by way of demonstration.

'God, no. This is too good to waste.' Then she asked out of the blue, 'So why's the crew acting weird today? They can't even look me in the eye.'

I decided it wasn't my place to bring up the fact that everyone reckoned they knew her at least as well as her gynaecologist, so I said, 'You must be imagining it. The crew love you.' I wasn't lying, either, though I don't suppose it was the kind of love she was after.

'You're very kind,' she said, 'and you make a mean bacon roll.'

'You're not so bad yourself. Here, have one of these,' I said, tossing her a T-shirt.

'Thanks.' She unfolded it. 'It's cool. I'll wear this later. What's "tast"?'

'It's the American . . . Nah, you won't fall for that. It's my idiot brother. Sticks slogans on T-shirts for a living and he can't spell to save his life.'

She laughed and headed back into the studio.

YASMIN FISH: I don't know what had got into Toddy, but when she came up to me she had a face on her like she'd just been dumped by her boyfriend or something. 'Get the heel fixed on this,' she snarled, and she shoved a broken slingback at me.

Welcome to the wonderful world of film, I thought – limos, stars, heel bars.

On my way out of the studio I passed the video playback girl's table. She was showing Rebecca's porn movie to two of the chippies that hadn't managed to catch it the day before. I couldn't help being drawn to it again. We were watching with the sound off, so I was shocked to hear Rebecca's voice.

'Jesus, this takes me back.'

I turned round. She was standing behind us with a bacon roll in her hand. I'd thought she was still in hair and makeup.

'I wasn't happy with this scene. The money shot could have been much stronger. You guys are in the business. A top shot would have worked, huh? I wanted the director to retake, but no one seemed up to it. By the way, has anyone got a cigarette?'

Nobody knew where to look – anywhere but at Rebecca. One of the chippies fumbled in his pocket and gave her a Camel. Then she walked off.

She was *so* cool.

And I felt *so* embarrassed.

fifteen:

eastenders, emmerdale, waterworld

TISH WILKIE: I went to the dressing room to make sure Rebecca hadn't seen that awful picture but she wasn't there.

'She went to get some breakfast,' Veronica said, 'but that was ages ago. Wardrobe are doing their nuts. They need to see her in the PVC and I need to finish her hair.'

'I'll go and look for her,' I said.

TYRONE EDWARDS: Hakkan and me went to school together and we're tight as anything. We got into martial arts when we were thirteen – Tai Kwan Do. OK, I only did it for a couple of weeks. Too much discipline. Waste of fucking time. Just punch the fucker, man. Hakkan got into it big time, though. He was like Glasshopper in *Kung Fu*. He'd done the whole *Way of the Dragon* thing – pilgrimages to Korea, herbal tea that smelt like dog shit, the lot. When he left school he did bouncing at clubs and then got his own outfit – Securicool. He must be doing OK, cause the only other businessmen that drive around New Cross in gold Lexuses with chromed alloys ain't in the Yellow Pages, if you know what I mean. Even though he's straight we're still mates. OK, we might not go pulling at the Electric Ballroom no more, but I know he's always there for me.

I walk into his offices and clock his secretary – a babe, just like the skinny bird in *Ally McBeal*, which is shit but it's Yvonne's favourite thing on the telly. I see the sign on his door – 'HAKKAN HAKKI, CEO'. Whatever the fuck a CEO is, this is definitely big-shot stuff. Ally McBeal shows me in and we do the high fives. He's really fucking made it cause on his desk he's got one of those things with the steel balls that whack together.

'Hakkan, man,' I tell him, 'you is doing OK for a short-arse Turk.'

'It's cool, Tyrone,' he says. 'What about you though?'

He's looking at the black eye that's coming up – Yvonne with the phone book.

'It's nothing, man,' I say, rubbing the shiner. 'A guy owed me money and tried to leg it. You should see him now – he ain't winning no beauty contests.'

'Anyway,' says Hakkan, 'what can I do for you? You ain't never come to my office so it must be important.'

'No big deal, man. I was just wondering if you could fix me up with any bouncing work.'

'We don't do bouncing,' he says and I think he's pissed off. 'We're Security and Personal Safety Facilitators.'

TISH WILKIE: I couldn't find Rebecca anywhere. It was as if she'd literally vanished into thin air. I thought that maybe she'd been kidnapped or something, and I was starting to panic, but I told myself, 'Tish Wilkie, you are a top *Personal* Assistant. It is your duty to stay calm.'

Then I went to the loo – I was, like, *so* bursting. I could hear crying from the cubicle next door. It sounded like Rebecca. Total shock horror. What was a Major Hollywood Personality doing in a toilet for *ordinary* people? It didn't make sense. Then I looked under the partition and I saw her high heels.

'Rebecca, is that you?' I said.

She didn't reply. She was still crying. Damn, I thought, she must have seen the picture in the *Mirror*.

'Rebecca, I know how upset you must be,' I said.

'It's a nightmare,' she sobbed. 'Has everyone seen it?'

'Well, I'm not sure,' I said. 'I tried to get to all the copies before everyone could have a look.'

'Jesus, Tish, how long have you known about this? Why the *bleep* didn't you tell me? I just walked in on a bunch of them staring at it . . .' She started sobbing again. Who'd have thunk she'd have taken a silly photo in a newspaper *that* badly.

'Rebecca, I know it's disgusting, but it's only a stupid little picture.'

'What are you talking about?' she wailed. 'It might be low budget, but the last thing I'd call it is a "stupid little picture". It was a disaster movie from my point of view.'

She was getting hysterical now. I mean, she was literally talking nonsense. It was a time to get firm.

'Rebecca,' I said in my best calm but firm voice, 'get *over* it. It is only a *silly* photograph in a *stupid* newspaper.'

'God, you're on another planet, Tish. You haven't seen it, have you?' she said.

'Seen what?'

'The tape.'

'What tape?'

'The tape of the film that I've lost more sleep over than anything else in my entire life. Worrying about the day it might come out, worrying about what my parents would say, never mind the rest of the world. Now a *bleeping* film crew is watching it.'

Lightning quick I switched from firm to sympathetic. 'Everyone must have at least *one* movie they wish they'd never done but they move on. I mean, you won't find Brad Pitt crying over *Waterworld*, will you?'

'Tish, let me give you this in list form because it's the only thing you seem to understand. Number *bleeping* one, Brad Pitt doesn't lose sleep over *Waterworld* because he wasn't in it. Number *bleeping* two, *Waterworld* didn't have its male lead humping his way through half the population of Romford.'

'I still don't get it,' I said.

'You don't get much, do you? It's a pornographic film.'

'Oh my giddy aunt,' I squeaked. I wished I hadn't. Why do I always sound like my mum when I'm in shock?

She burst into tears again. It was time to take control.

'Stay there while I get help,' I told her decisively.

As I got up to go, I got my second massive shock. Smoke was rising from Rebecca's cubicle. What on earth was she playing at? I mean, literally *no one* smoked in LA any more. 'Rebecca,' I said. 'Do you know how dangerous cigarettes are? Your career could be finished. Literally.'

'Tish, will you please just go,' she shouted.

She was obviously in denial – typical addict behaviour. It wasn't the time to deal with it, though, and I said, 'OK, I'll find Freddie.'

'For *bleep's* sake, not her,' she said. 'I've never told her about it. Get Veronica.'

I wasn't sure that Veronica would know what to do – I mean, it wasn't like layering or highlights would help. But if that's what she wanted . . .

'Shall I tell her to bring her scissors?' I asked.

TYRONE EDWARDS: 'I can do security and personal safety facilitating – no problem,' I say to Hakkan.

'Tyrone,' he says, 'I don't want you to take this wrong, but you're a dealer, man. That ain't exactly facilitating safety. Anyway, I've got guys working for me who are ex-SAS. They are *fit*. I bet the last time you worked out was in PE, and you bunked off that half the time.'

'I'm in the best shape of my life. There ain't a minute when I ain't pumping.'

'Look, even if you've got the body of Naz under them sweats, there's another little problem.'

'What's that?'

'The guys that work for me who ain't ex-SAS are ex-Met.'

'That's cool. I don't mind the filth,' I lie.

'I'm not sure they'd feel the same about you. Most of them have probably arrested you at least once. Security ain't what it used to be. It's a respectable business now. Anyway, why do you want a job? I thought you were happy doing the drug shit.'

'You know how it is, man. I feel like I've achieved all I can and it's time to move on . . . and Yvonne told me to.'

'You still with Yvonne?'

He winces when he says it and I know why. At school no one ever got the better of him in a rumble except for this one time when he needed six stitches on his head. He never said who jumped him, but it was when he was seeing Yvonne's baby sister, Venetia. Me and Hakkan were eighteen, but Venetia was only thirteen. That was the sort of thing a girl's big brother would beat you senseless for. With Yvonne around, Venetia didn't need brothers.

'No promises, man, but I'll see what I can do.'

'Cheers, Hakkan. You ain't gonna regret this.'

I get up to go and he says, 'I don't know what you did to piss her off, but you're lucky she let you off with a black eye.'

TISH WILKIE: I stepped out of the cubicle and – bizarre or what? – my mum was standing there.

'Mum, what are you doing here?' I shrieked.

'A chauffeur brought me, dear,' she said.

'But, Mum, *what* are you doing here?'

'You invited us, didn't you?'

I'd completely and utterly forgotten – *literally*.

'Your dad's outside looking at all the film bits-and-bobs, but I was desperate for a pee.' (Small bladder – hereditary I think.) 'Anyway, where's this celebrity of yours? I'm dying to meet her. We've been racking our brains to think who she might be. Is she in *EastEnders*? I hope it isn't Cat. We don't like her.'

God, parents – *so* embarrassing.

'No, she isn't in *EastEnders*. She's a *real* Hollywood star. Mummy, this isn't exactly a brilliant time.'

'Oh, we won't be any trouble. You'll hardly notice us.'

'OK, let's go and find Dad and I'll get you a cup of tea.'

I tried to shove her towards the door but she said, 'Aren't you going to let me spend a penny?' and pushed past me into the cubicle next to Rebecca's. I waited for her by the basins. I've no idea where I get my quietness from because my mum just doesn't know when to shut up. She was still wittering when she was in the loo. 'I made your dad and me a nice packed lunch. I cut a few extra sandwiches. I bet you've missed my cooking in America, haven't you? Anyway, where is she then?'

I couldn't tell her she was in the next-door cubicle in a state over a dirty film, so I said, 'She's in her dressing room, Mummy – *preparing*.'

'Quit the bull, Tish,' said Rebecca icily, 'I'm next door.'

'Gosh,' shrieked my mum, 'I'm in the presence of a star and my knickers are round my blooming ankles. Lovely to meet you, dear. And you are?'

'Rebecca Richards.'

'Oh, the pretty blonde in *Emmerdale*. I must say you don't sound a bit like on the telly. You do a very good Yorkshire accent.'

'I'm in *All Our Lives Before Us*. It's American.'

'Oh, we don't go for American shows. We went off them when they stopped showing *I Love Lucy*. It's all loud music, guns and girls taking their clothes off these days. You don't take your clothes off do you?'

Rebecca's cubicle door flew open.

'Jesus, Tish, I can't believe I'm having this conversation. Why the hell did you invite your mum?'

'I thought it would be OK,' I said. 'I didn't know everyone was going to see your whatsit film today.'

She pushed past me and went to the mirror, where she tried to get rid of the makeup streaks on her face.

'Do you still want me to get Veronica?' I said.

'I think it's a bit late now. I'm going to my dressing room. Don't let a *bleeping* soul disturb me.'

As she left, my mum came out of the loo.

'She seemed a bit funny, dear,' she said. 'She's not having problems with her plumbing, is she?'

NANCY STARK: It was almost eleven o'clock. I'd sent Dieter packing and it was time for my first cocktail. I didn't normally drink that early, but the waiter at the pool bar was really toned and his forearms looked gorgeous when he did his Tom-Cruise-with-the-shaker thing. He was mixing a Singapore Sling. I wasn't sure I'd like it but I didn't care – it involved some bloody vigorous shaking and, anyway, Greg was picking up the bill. It was appropriate that he chose that moment to call me.

'Well?' he said.

'You're having a nightmare there, aren't you, Greg? I can't leave you alone for a minute.'

'How the fuck do you know?'

'The wonders of technology – I picked up the European edition of the *Mirror*. Anyway, I've got some good news for you. Piss and Shit have gone fishing.'

'Why the hell didn't you go after them?'

'They're somewhere in the middle of the Med catching swordfish, Greg. I thought about calling out the Spanish Navy but I reckoned, however important the Universe of Sofas brief is, it probably wouldn't get them cancelling their siestas.'

'Lola, cut the sarcasm. I am in the deepest shit here.'

'I know, I read the paper.'

'The *Mirror* didn't even get the worst bit. Remember the urban legend about Rebecca's porn film? It had its premiere in Hounslow.'

'Wow,' I said, 'who's seen it?'

'Everyone, including the leading lady. She's in her dressing room and I'll be surprised if she ever comes out. I wouldn't if I were her. I watched the tape and she's depraved.'

'I can't believe you. You're the depraved one. Your marriage is collapsing and you're watching porn. Have you even spoken to Carrie?'

'I tried. She doesn't want to know. Will you talk to her?'

'I'll do your typing and look after your diary. I don't even mind collecting your dry cleaning and stray creative teams, but I don't think I can save your marriage.'

'She likes you. She'll listen to you. At least try and break the ice for me.'

'I think she hates me as much as she does you. I'm Satan's Little Helper as far as she's concerned.'

'Please, sweet pea.' A desperate man – he rarely said please.

'All right, I'll try. But don't hold your breath.'

TIM LELYVELDT: Everything should have been right on Planet Joe. Everything was going his way, wasn't it? But he was edgy. Morton and I had had to tell him that his shrink couldn't make it over.

He was called Stryker Queenan. He had the movie star name but he also had the Pillsbury Doughboy gene, so he'd had to settle for a career counselling movie stars – just Joe, actually. As you can imagine, the work took it out of him. He'd taken advantage of Joe's absence from LA by fleeing to Wyoming, where he was hiding in a sensory deprivation tank, one with a big 'do not disturb' notice on it. Not even Joe's threats could get him on a plane to London. Joe took it out on us, of course, but it wasn't enough, so he started on French and the crew.

They were shooting the Viper and he stood by the camera as it rolled. As they were boarding take six, he interrupted.

'Something ain't right, guys,' Joe said.

'It's sex on four wheels, babe,' said French. 'What's the problem?'

'It's the colour.'

'You asked for red,' said French. If he'd gritted his teeth any more they'd have shattered in his mouth.

'I know but now I see it it's *too* red, man,' said Joe.

GREG FULLER: I heard Toddy whisper behind me. 'I said that, but would anyone listen?' She was talking to the continuity girl, but I was clearly the intended audience.

'My character is cool, confident,' Joe went on. 'He wouldn't drive a red car. It's too in your face, too *nouveau*.'

'I said that, I said that.' Toddy was on a loop now.

'I have to agree,' piped up another voice behind me. 'It's been nagging at me all morning. Joe's managed to put the problem into words phenomenally well.'

The new and unholy alliance between Bull and the Shirer camp was unlikely, but it was proving mighty effective.

'What colour would you like, boys?' said Kevin. He really shouldn't have asked, because five minutes later we were breaking early for lunch while the art department re-sprayed the car in discreetly cool, confidently un-*nouveau* Electric Candy Blue.

TIM LELYVELDT: 'Colour is crucial,' Joe explained as we went back to his dressing room. 'That red was fucking with my karma.'

Then he saw her standing on the other side of the studio and he couldn't believe it. Neither could I. There she was, swathed in black rubber, surrounded by fawning film crew. She looked hot, but how could that combination of hair, latex, tits and legs on porn-star spikes not?

'Fuck, I didn't think the bitch would have the *cojones*, said Joe, and I had to agree. We figured that if she ever set foot outside her dressing room it would be to jump straight into a limo heading for the airport.

YASMIN FISH: She was called Sonia and she looked stunning, like Rebecca from the neck down. I could never be someone's body double. All right, that's mostly because I don't have anyone else's body, except for J.Lo's bum, according to Tyler. But if I did look like a celeb, I'd never want to be paid to be her double. There's something sad about being someone else.

Stars in Their Eyes is my mum's favourite show, but it depresses me. Tyler calls it *Shit in Their Pants*, and I have to say he's about right. They look terrified, and I feel sorry for them. They might have OK voices, but they're so desperate to get on TV they put on stupid wigs and pretend to be someone much better than they are. Except when they impersonate Emma Bunton. I feel especially sorry for them – why would anyone want to be someone so crap?

TIM LELYVELDT: The moment it dawned on him that rubber babe was Rebecca's double, Joe turned to Morton and said, 'Why the fuck haven't I got one?'

'Excuse me?' asked Morton, not unreasonably.

'A double. The bitch has one. Why the fuck haven't I?'

'Er, I guess because –'

'Get me one, Mort.'

'But –'

'Now!'

I'd become accustomed to hearing bizarre and outrageous demands from Joe. In this respect he was hardly setting a precedent. The bizarre and outrageous demand is a Hollywood tradition every bit as honourable as the concrete handprint outside Grauman's Chinese Theatre. We were shooting a TV commercial that contained scenes involving neither physical risk nor explicit nudity, and the fact that Joe was now demanding a double put it right up there with the Badoit in the shower tank.

Ironically, the more bizarre and outrageous the demand, the more likely it is to be acted upon. This is the way it works in

Hollywood. Nicole Kidman's sweetly reasonable request for a cup of tea might be overlooked in the hubbub of film-making. However, should she ask for, say, an orchestra of Bavarian nose flautists to serenade her through the ardour of hair and makeup, they'll be on the studio lot within the hour, clutching the sheet music to 'Waltzing Matilda'. This is because turning her down would entail telling her she's completely fucking loco, and I don't imagine there'd be many volunteers for that job. There certainly weren't any when it came to Joe. Thirty minutes after he'd turned to Morton and grunted, 'Where the fuck's mine?', the search for Joe Shirer's physical match was on.

NORMAN THE COOK: When the metabolic fuckwit tipped up with his magic wok I was ready for him.

'Rolly, I wouldn't mind a bit of metabolic peace and harmony in the old truck today,' I explained, 'so I've got a couple of rules. Number one – you don't turn your nose up when I use a dollop of honest British lard, and I won't say a dicky bird when you sauté your loin of sea slug or whatever. Agreed?'

'Agreed,' he nodded.

'And number two – you stick this on.'

I gave him a T-shirt.

He took one look and said, 'I can't, not with this picture.'

'The mixed grill. Britain's greatest culinary export.'

'It's meat.'

'That's what I do, mate. I cook meat.'

'But I don't. It's murder.'

'Look, there'd be no such thing as pigs, cows and fluffy lambs if we didn't breed them to whack on the plate with our two veg. You lot in the Linda McCartney brigade conveniently forget that. If you ask me, the animals should be grateful.'

'Grateful for being slaughtered?'

'Humanely knocked off,' I corrected, 'and only after they've had the life of Riley. They get dry straw to kip on, food on demand, vaccinations. If it wasn't for us humans they'd be grubbing around in the forest and looking over their shoulders for the fucking bears.'

He started to argue but I said, 'I'd love a debate, Roland, mate, but I ain't got the time. I've got a queue a mile long waiting for their veal casserole. You've got a choice. Either wear the T-shirt or Mr Shirer has his tofu hotdog raw.'

NANCY STARK: I'd booked myself a massage in the hotel spa. I'd clocked the masseur. Dutch and gorgeous. It was going to be a toss-up between him and the barman. I was finding out that you have to make some tough calls on these business trips. No wonder Greg always came back from them looking so drained.

Booking the massage hadn't been totally frivolous. I still had to phone Carrie and the prospect was giving me a tension knot the size of a grapefruit. I downed my drink and picked up my phone. It was now or never. I was hoping she wouldn't answer and then I could flop back on my sunbed with a clear-ish conscience – 'I tried, Greg, really I did'. She picked up on the sixteenth ring, though.

'Carrie, it's me, please don't hang up.'

She didn't say a word but she didn't slam the phone down.

'I know you're mad, but all Greg wants is a chance to talk.'

'So he drafts you in as a marriage-guidance counsellor? That's guaranteed to calm me down, isn't it? I can't believe he was stupid enough to put you up to it and I can't believe you had the front to agree.'

'I'm doing this because you're my friend, Carrie.'

'My friend? How can you say that? I don't know what planet you're on, but this is not what friends do to one another.'

'Maybe I should have told you about it, but you've got to appreciate the difficult position I've been in.'

'I don't think telling me about it is the issue here. What I'd like to know is why the fuck you did it in the first place?'

'Did what?' She was confusing me now.

'Don't play dumb, *Lola*.'

She must have been able to hear the sound of the penny dropping down the line.

'Hang on a minute, Carrie. You think I –'

'Don't deny it. I may be a dull housewife, but I'm not brain dead.'

'Carrie, Greg's in London and I'm in *Spain*.'

'Handy that you're on a mobile, isn't it? You could tell me you're calling from Venus and I couldn't prove otherwise.'

'Carrie, I'm in Spain, honestly.'

'Don't insult my intelligence. I heard Greg calling you your fucking sex name at gone midnight and no amount of lying's going to get you out of it. Goodbye.'

I could feel the blood draining from my face. The barman came over and asked, 'OK, señorita?'

'Not really,' I said. 'I've just found out how the Birmingham Six must have felt.'

He didn't have a clue what I was talking about. He pointed at my empty glass.

'Thanks, I think I need another one.'

NORMAN THE COOK: The Chinaman may have been away with the fairies, but he was a man of principle. I had to take my hat off to him for that. He wouldn't wear the T-shirt. He marched off to the camping shop across the road and came out ten minutes later with one of those titchy one-ring gas cookers. Wendy stood next to me as we watched him disappear into the studio with it.

'How to win friends and influence people, eh, Norm?' she said. 'You're already in the paper waving your knife around like Jack the Ripper. Now you've started a diplomatic incident with China.'

'He's Chinese-American. Anyway, he was getting on my tits. We're well shot of him.'

NANCY STARK: 'Thanks a million,' Greg said when I'd explained the mix-up. 'You've really dumped me in it. Why would anyone else call you Lola?'

'I didn't realise you had a copyright on it. Anyway, don't blame me. It's not my fault you only have to glance in the general direction of another woman and Carrie thinks you're having an affair – blame yourself for that. Besides, you are having an affair. She just got the wrong suspect.'

'Well, didn't you tell her that you're in Spain?'

'She didn't believe me.'

'Jesus, the shit you've landed me in. Phone her back and make her believe you.'

'No, Greg, *you* phone her. I've fucking well had enough of this. I really like Carrie and right now she hates my guts. This is your mess. You sort it.'

I flipped my phone shut before he could say anything. I'd never lost it with him before. By now my entire body was so tense that I must have looked like something out of the *Boy Scout's Book of Very Complicated Knots*. I needed a big Dutchman and about a gallon of scented massage oil.

GREG FULLER: After Lola had hung up on me, I took a moment to review the dog's dinner that constituted my life.

Marriage: Lola was bang on the money. Who was turning Carrie into the pregnant poster girl for Victims of Bastard Husbands? Guilty as charged.

Rebecca Richards: bonus points for keeping her porn movie out of the papers. A big kick up the arse for failing to keep it hidden from her.

Joe Shirer: We were looking for his body double. Why? Because he'd told us to. By that stage of the sorry, desperate mess, if he'd demanded a flight of RAF Harriers to provide air cover on the drive from studio to hotel, Toddy would have been on the phone to the MOD, paying the necessary bribes.

Universe of Sofas: I had only abject failure to report on the blonde-plonked-on-sofa front. And where were my saviours? Gone fishing.

Back on the set, Kevin was actually exposing some film. Sonia the double was good, and watching her slither in front of the camera almost lulled me into thinking that all was dandy. But, fine as she was, she could only do so much, and the time inevitably came for Ms Richards's close-up. This was a moment I'd been dreading. Only God and her stylist knew what was going on in her dressing room, but I was prepared to bet that it wasn't her new PVC wardrobe and her best professional smile.

sixteen:

elvis

VERONICA D: Rebecca had been mad ever since she'd returned from her walkabout. She didn't say much but her body language screamed rage. The wardrobe girl had squeezed her into the PVC and Dennis had finished her face. She was nearly ready. I hadn't said anything, but I couldn't stand by and watch her die on a film-set.

'Becca, sweetheart,' I said, 'I know I just fix your hair, but can I tell you what I think? You don't have to do this.'

'Do what?'

'Go out there.'

'What do you think that bastard wants me to do? He wants me to run away. Why the fuck should I give him the satisfaction?'

'You're right, honey, but are you sure you want to put yourself through it? If I were you I'd be on the first plane outta this dump.'

'No, Veronica, he's taken everything else from me, but I've still got some pride. He's not having that.'

'If that's what you want, go kill him, girl. I'll be glad to zip up his body bag.'

YASMIN FISH: Kevin told me to fetch Rebecca and I panicked. It was a million times worse than having to fetch Joe on day one – he hadn't caught me watching him in a porn film, had he? I knocked on her dressing-room door and her hairdresser stuck her head out.

'Two minutes, honey,' she said, and pushed the door to.

VERONICA D: The wardrobe girl and Dennis walked out and Becca stood up to follow them. 'Hang on, let me arrange your wisps,' I said. 'You know, after everything he's done, no one would blame you if you'd planted the rumours about his schlong.'

'Maybe . . . but I didn't do that.'

Then she was quiet. She stared at the door as if she was plucking up the nerve to get on out there.

YASMIN FISH: I watched her through the crack in the door while she had her hair finished. She could see me and she smiled. Then she spoke to Veronica, but the whole time she was staring at me.

'I've never slagged him off, Veronica, but . . . just this once,' she said. 'Don't repeat this to a soul, OK?'

'I'm leak-proof,' said Veronica, zipping her lips.

'You know Joe did all his own stunts on *Body Matter*?'

'How could I forget what a hero the piece of shit is?'

'It's bullshit. He didn't do one of them.'

'No way.'

'He had doubles for everything.'

'But I've seen the interviews with French. He talked up Joe like he deserved a Purple Heart.'

'He's a liar. Sold his soul for the sequel.'

'This is too much. You mean he didn't do a thing? Sliding down that roof, dropping on his ass into the car, flying through those windows . . .'

'Doubles.'

'Swimming through the storm drain?'

'Can't swim.'

'Hang on, Becca. I saw the "Making of" vid. That was Joe on the tower making the jump.'

'Veronica, how long have you been in Hollywood? Don't ever tell me *I'm* naive again. If they can cheat it in the movie, they can cheat it in the documentary. It was all a set-up. The producers saw how well the hero-for-real stuff played for Cruise on *M:i-2*. It was a way of breaking Joe into the big league.'

'Fuck, Rebecca, I do not believe this. The guy's a fraud.'

'More than you'll ever know.'

I couldn't believe it, either. I'd been completely taken in. So had Tyler. Joe was his hero. I'd never be able to tell him. It would be like telling him that Slipknot, his favourite band ever, belonged to a knitting circle. He'd be destroyed.

Rebecca said, 'Come on, let's get out there and finish this fucking ad.'

They came out together and I tagged along behind. 'Remember, Veronica, keep it zipped,' she said. Then she turned round and smiled at me again.

TIM LELYVELDT: Hollywood Moments, the bits in movies that are too perfect, too scripted to happen in real life. Here's one: *An Officer and a Gentleman*. Richard Gere walks into the plant, sweeps Debra Winger off her feet and carries her out to an ovation from the entire workforce. We all watched that and loved it/threw up (according to taste), while at the same time knowing it was too good/cheesy (again, according to taste) to be true. In reality Gere would have been stopped at the gate by security wanting to see his ID. If he'd got past first base, Winger's co-workers would have sneered, 'Look at the stuck up bitch with her "officer". She thinks she's better than us now.'

Could never happen.

Except that it did when Rebecca walked onto the set. The whole crew had assumed they wouldn't see her again – not after they'd seen *so much* of her on video.

TISH WILKIE: She looked *so* defiant, like Joan of Arc. Or Jennifer Beals in *Flashdance*. My eyes welled up. They weren't tears of pride though. Ever since I'd found out about her thingy film I'd felt *terrible*. Please don't get me wrong. I'm like *literally* Californian now and I can completely respect anyone's decision to take most or even all their clothes off and perform disgusting sex acts on camera. But in Rebecca's film she like, you know, 'kissed' other women. I'm 110 per cent un-homophobic, but she'd totally crossed the line there. How could I ever unpack her knickers and do other really private Personal Assistant to a Major Star-type things knowing what she'd done?

When the crew applauded her, the floodgates literally opened. My mum was next to me and she said, 'What is it, Tish?'

'Mummy, it's Rebecca. She's disgusting.'

'I know, dear, that dress is awfully lewd. Terribly practical, though. Just wipe it clean with a J-Cloth.'

TIM LELYVELDT: It started with one of the carpenters – a slightly embarrassed hand clap. Then, when no one told him to shut up, he put more energy into it. It didn't take long to explode into a twenty-four-carat Hollywood Moment.

VERONICA D: As they cheered, I said to her, 'Sarah Michelle never gets this on the *Buffy* set, babe – you should do porno more often.'

TIM LELYVELDT: Even Joe and Greta applauded. They didn't want to, but the undertow was irresistible and they were sucked right in.

YASMIN FISH: Half an hour later there was a break. Rebecca was talking to Kevin and the agency people. Joe was with his posse –

not far away but not close enough to join in. She stopped the conversation and said, 'Dinner, tonight. How about it? I'll take you all out.'

Everyone looked at Kevin – it was his shoot and nobody wanted to say yes first. He seemed startled, though. He looked at Joe, then Rebecca, then Joe again. 'I dunno. We're supposed to be casting Joe's double tonight,' he said, glaring at Joe. Then he smiled. 'No, fuck that. The agent can take care of the casting, and we'll look at the tapes in the morning. Going out's a great idea, babe. I'm due some fun. How about the Ivy? I can always get a table there.'

'It's crawling with paparazzi, Kevin,' said Rebecca. 'Do you mind?'

Toddy suggested a place called the Sanderson. 'It's very *of the moment*, darling, *très* celeb-friendly.'

'I don't fancy a media crowd,' she replied.

I was standing in the background and I'd assumed I wasn't part of the conversation, but she looked at me. 'Where do you go for a night out, Yasmin?'

She knew my name. I couldn't think straight. I usually went to Pizza Hut but I didn't suppose that was what she had in mind. 'Um . . .' I had to think of something. '. . . Er . . .' Quick. '. . . I went to Chinese Elvis for my sixteenth,' I said.

'Any good?'

'We had a brilliant time.'

'Great. Book a table . . . And include yourself.'

TODDY GLUCK: Chinese Elvis.

The Old Kent Road.

Oh my fucking God.

What the hell was she thinking? We were in a city packed with some of the world's most sophisticated restaurants. Why on earth did she ask the runner?

Oh my fucking God.

YASMIN FISH: I started to hyperventilate. It took me ten minutes to calm down enough to call the restaurant. A Chinese woman took the booking.

'Tableforsevenpeople? Whatime?' she said.

'Nine o'clock, please.'

'Whaname?'

'Rebecca Richards.' *Rebecca Richards* – I loved saying that.

'Howyouspell?'

I don't think it made much of an impression, though.

GREG FULLER: With Chinese Elvis, Rebecca proved she had a sense of humour as well as some spunk. She shot like a dream for the rest of the afternoon. Kevin was now in awe of her and Joe seemed cowed. Jesus, I thought, this is like being on a proper shoot – one where you actually make a commercial. Or more accurately, thanks to the rewrites, two commercials.

It couldn't last.

The last set-up of the day was an ambitious crane shot – Kevin's spectacular finale to my original script. It started tight on Rebecca as she jilted Joe at their table. The camera then swept up over the crowd and finished on the door. The idea was that, having moved off Rebecca at the table, she'd stalk back into the shot on her way out of the bar. Kevin rehearsed it and then he was ready to roll. I stood next to him as he watched on the playback monitor. I thought we were going to get it first take. Or at least I did until the end of the move when Kevin yelled, 'What is *he* doing in my shot?'

I studied the monitor and I could make *him* out standing by the Dodge Viper. He was in his sixties, sporting bifocals and a comb-over. In a sea of extras, all of them safely under thirty, he stood out like a dog's wrinkled bollocks.

Apartheid still flourished in Adland. We were in a strictly youth-only zone. Bifocals Man had no business being outside his home-land, a place where he might have been able to grub some work in daytime TV ads for incontinence pants.

Kevin pushed his way through the extras and yelled, 'Who the fuck are you and what are you doing on my set?'

'I'm Maurice Wilkie,' he said calmly. 'You do realise that this car isn't legal, don't you? It's a death trap, and with the lack of suppression on the exhaust you wouldn't get half a mile before the police pulled you up.'

VERONICA D: As Rebecca slid out of the PVC, I asked, 'Who's this Chinese Elvis?'

'It's a restaurant. Cheap Chinese food and Elvis songs. I went years ago – I must have been Yasmin's age. I remember liking it. That lot we're taking will probably hate it.'

'Why are we going then?'

'If I'm honest, I don't know why we're going out at all. It was spur of the moment – it seemed like a fantastic way to piss Joe off. Now I wish I were going back to the hotel to hide. I just want today to end.'

'Get Freddie to make your excuses,' I said. 'That's what you pay her for.'

'She's not talking to me at the moment. Since she found out about *Titanic* I think she's been regretting turning down Jennifer Aniston because she was too busy with me.'

TIM LELYVELDT: When we'd wrapped Joe turned to Morton and said, 'What the fuck's Kevin doing? After his casting session tonight, we're meant to be hooking up.'

Joe had been given the first draft of *Body Matter II* a week or so before. He hadn't read it all, just the scenes with his character – but they were the only ones that mattered. He hated it. He was desperate to discuss it with French. Morton scurried off. He came back with his bad-news face. 'Kevin says he can't wait to discuss the script, Joe, but he's too shattered to go there right now. He wants a rain check.'

'Does the guy want to work? Did you tell him we've got directors queuing up for this picture?'

'He knows that, Joe. He says he's absolutely confident you'll make the right choice.'

'Arrogant fuck,' Joe grunted. Then he turned to me and said, 'What's Chinese Elvis? Some kinda members-only gig?'

'I've no idea, Joe,' I said. 'I can find out.'

'Do that. If it sounds cool, we'll hit it. It'd be cute to see Rebecca party before she crashes and burns tomorrow.'

NANCY STARK: My Dutch masseur was a credit to his profession. His hands could have worked the tension out of a Palestinian peace summit. They had bugger-all effect on me, though.

Afterwards I lay on my bed and pictured Carrie torturing herself. My thoughts weren't entirely for her. It was eating me up to think that she believed I was The One.

Then I sat bolt upright and said out loud, 'You fucking idiot, Nancy. Why didn't you think of that before?' I dialled Carrie's number. There was no reply, so I left a message.

'Carrie, this is Nancy. Please listen to this because it's the truth. I *am* in Spain and I was here last night as well so I couldn't have been with him. If you don't believe me, call me here. I'm *not* sleeping with Greg. I never have and I never ever would. Please call me.'

I left the hotel number and waited.

A few minutes later there was a knock on my door.

'You ready, Lola?' said Dirk the Dutch masseur.

I looked at the phone . . . 'I'm expecting a call.' . . . then at his piercing grey eyes. 'But it can wait.'

CARRIE FULLER: I listened to Nancy's message as she left it.

'Sounds like bollocks to me,' said Unborn.

'I don't know. Now I think about it, if you're going to invent an alibi, Spain is a little over-elaborate.'

'Why didn't you pick up the phone then?'

'Because it asks more questions than it answers.'
'You've lost me now, Carrie.'
'Please, *please* call me Mum.'

seventeen:

sesame toast, prawn balls,
spring rolls, fried seaweed,
honey barbecued spare ribs,
beef in black bean sauce,
sweet-and-sour pork hong kong-style,
szechuan chicken, shrimp chow mein,
fried pork with ginger and spring onions,
squid in oyster sauce, special chop suey,
sliced duck with mixed vegetables,
braised chinese mushroom with bean curd,
singapore noodles, egg-fried rice

oh, and lawdy miss clawdy

GREG FULLER: I bumped into Bob Bull outside the studio.
'Phenomenal day at the finish, Greg.'
'Not bad was it, Bob? I'm sure we'll lose the old codger in the edit.'
'How about a jar? There's a pub round the corner that pulls a

smashing pint of Old Peculier. You can bring me up to speed on Max's wheeling and dealing. A phenomenal entrepreneur, that man. I'd love to get my hands on his secret.'

The only thing that Bob wanted to get his hands on was a videotape. One that showed him with a lap dancer sitting on, well, his lap probably. I'd have liked to help him out but, frankly, I had no idea whether such a tape existed. Max did have an interest in Honeydew, but he was very much a sleeping partner. Yes, all that stuff I'd told Bob earlier, I'd made it up.

What can I say? I'm in advertising.

I certainly didn't fancy having a conversation about it. Besides, I hadn't told him about our date with Rebecca. Since he was paying her hefty wages, he'd have been miffed to discover he hadn't made the guest list.

'I'd love a beer, Bob, but ... er ...' I saw Toddy approaching. '... Toddy and I have tomorrow's logistics to discuss.'

'Your dedication never ceases to astound me,' he smarmed. 'Don't work too hard, you two.'

'What was he talking about?' she demanded as he walked off.

'I'm sorry, I needed an excuse,' I said. 'You were the nearest one to hand. You going tonight? Chinese Elvis doesn't sound like your bag.'

'It fucking well isn't, Greg. But I *am* the producer. It would be *totally* unprofessional if I didn't show up.'

'You could always have one of your tactical tummy bugs.'

'Stop being facetious. Don't you think you've hurt me enough already?'

'Sorry. Do you want share a cab there?'

'I'd rather hitch a ride with John Prescott.'

TODDY GLUCK: I'd given him two weeks, but there he was crawling back already. I wasn't going to make it easy for him, though. I climbed into my taxi and looked back at him as we pulled away. He was talking to the runner. If he imagined he could upset me with her then he must have been completely stupid.

YASMIN FISH: Greg Fuller looked lost.

'You OK?' I asked.

'Fine, thanks. Just waiting for a taxi. You hit the jackpot with Chinese Elvis.'

'God, it was the only place I could think of,' I said. I could feel myself blushing.

'Rebecca liked it well enough. Anyway, it's the last place on earth the tabloids will look for her. How are you getting there? Want to share a cab?'

'I don't think I have enough money.'

'Don't be silly. Bob Bull's paying.'

BOB BULL: I slid into the seat of my Scorpio and headed for home and Jane. I maxed the volume on the Pioneer, but not even the phenomenal voice of Bryan Adams belting out that driving classic, 'Summer of '69', could lift my spirits. It had been some bombshell that Greg had dropped on me. I'd forgotten all about Honeydew, but now a harmless cuddle was threatening to blow my life sky-high. She was called Fiona and was actually a business studies student. We spent our time together discussing her desire to climb the greasy pole of management. As I recall, I gave her some jolly useful tips on CV presentation.

Just because she happened to be wearing a thong and high heels and I'd loosened my belt on account of a rather large dinner doesn't mean that what took place wasn't perfectly innocent. Why is it that two like-minded souls can't have a simple chinwag without it being totally misconstrued?

TIM LELYVELDT: On the way to the Dorchester Joe asked me, 'So, what've you found out about this club?'

'It's a restaurant as far as I can figure – a kind of Chinese tribute to the King – soundalikes and stuff.'

'Cool.'

'I'm not so sure,' I said. 'I hear it's a bit of a dive.'

'You don't get the Brits, do you? They love all that Vegas shit. Makes 'em feel superior. Take it from me, this Elvis place is cool. We'll go after we've eaten. I'm fucking starving.'

Roland Shen might have been working miracles on Joe's meridians, but he didn't seem to be doing much for his stomach.

CARRIE FULLER: I did call Nancy eventually, but there was no answer from her room. The receptionist confirmed that she was booked in. I was relieved, but I also felt stupid – even though I was sure that Greg was up to something, it obviously wasn't with his PA. There's nothing worse than blaming the wrong person.

I decided to call him.

'Where are you?' I said when he picked up.

'In a cab on the Hammersmith flyover. I'm glad you phoned. Me and Lola? What were you thinking?'

'I know. I just rang her in Spain. You've still got a lot of explaining to do, though. You'd better be on your way home.'

'I've got a late one, I'm afraid. It's a shoot thing. Schmoozing the players and all that. There's no avoiding it.'

There never was.

'Who's going?' I asked with all the warmth of cod fillet.

'Oh just a few of the production company, some of Rebecca Richards's hangers-on, Rebecca.'

Rebecca. He just *had* to go out with a young, charismatic, beautiful, gazelle-legged, pencil-waisted, melon-breasted celebrity. There was *no* avoiding it.

In that instant everything clicked into place. Of course, he hadn't been screwing Nancy. Why would he settle for his PA when the star prize was on offer?

'I'll be home as soon as I can,' he went on. 'Wait up and we'll talk then.'

'In case you hadn't noticed, I'm pregnant. What that means is that by ten-thirty I'll be so shattered I'll barely be able to drag my bump upstairs to bed. Don't worry, though – while I'm elevating my swollen ankles on a pile of phone books and putting ointment on my haemorrhoids, I'll be thinking of you and Rebecca.'

'Carrie, please don't be like this.'

'What do you expect? I've been going out of my mind wondering where you were last night. Now I find out your biggest headache has been where to take Rebecca fucking Richards for dinner.'

'Carrie, please –'

'Oh just go, Greg. Eat your dinner. Screw your starlet. But don't expect to come home and tell me what a bind it's been – the door will be bolted.'

YASMIN FISH: He put his phone away and I asked, 'Are you all right?'

'Fucking mobiles,' he said. 'Lost the signal.'

'Me and my boyfriend argue too,' I said, 'but it's always really special when we make up.'

He didn't answer.

TYRONE EDWARDS: Yvonne comes in from work, kicks her shoes off and says, 'If I see another damn nail extension I'll –'

I butt in. 'Put on something bootylicious, sweetheart. We're celebrating.'

'Celebrating what, Tyrone? You manage to make a whole word on *Countdown* today?'

'I got a job.'

'Don't wind me up. I ain't in the mood.'

'Straight up, sweetheart. I'm a Security and Personal Safety Facilitator. I went to see Hakkan and –'

'You're a bouncer? You are winding me up. I seen you in a rumble. Look at your eye. That was just me. How you gonna handle six gorillas with baseball bats on a night-club door?'

'It ain't about fighting, babe,' I tell her. 'The security business has changed. It's about people skills, diplomacy – that kinda shit. Hakkan says I'm ideal material.'

'I believe you, Tyrone. The six gorillas with baseball bats won't. So where are you taking me tonight?'

'It's booked, sweetheart – Star of India.'

'Old Kent Road? You know how to spoil a girl. There was me thinking you was gonna try and buy me off with the Ritz.'

GREG FULLER: Yasmin and I arrived at Chinese Elvis to see an ambulance parked outside. The driver was up front reading the *Standard*. The fact that the restaurant appeared to keep one on standby didn't bode well for our evening. Inside, Chinese Elvis was singing 'Devil in Disguise', but no amount of lip-curling could shift his accent from Canton to Mississippi. Toddy was already there with a Bloody Mary for company. She took a sip and said, 'God, haven't they heard of Tabasco?' Yasmin made a plucky attempt to break the ice by shoving the prawn crackers towards her and saying, 'Go on, they're really nice.' Toddy, ever gracious, replied, 'Have you any idea how many calories are in just one of those things?'

Kevin arrived and, as he took in the potpourri of B&H, MSG and blended vegetable oil, his nostrils flared. Or perhaps they were making room for the coke. Hard to say.

'I parked my Aston round the corner,' he said as he sat down. 'What's the betting it's on bricks by the time we leave?'

He'd be lucky if the wheels were all that were gone.

Kevin's opener was Toddy's cue to come to life. 'It's the pits, isn't it, darling? I suppose we should give Rebecca the benefit of the doubt, though – she's been away for years. Still, some of us should know better.' She glared at Yasmin, who'd sunk so low in her chair that she was in danger of disappearing under the table. I was about to defend her, but Kevin did it for me.

'What are you on about, Toddy? I love it here. I've had it with the media brothels I normally go to.'

'OK, I admit it has a certain irony, but don't you think we'd have been more comfortable at the Sanderson?' asked Toddy.

'The Sanderson,' snorted Kevin. 'The *bierkeller* of the fucking Style Nazis.'

'But you can't argue with Starck's design,' Toddy protested.

'Philippe fucking Starck,' he snorted again – the charlie was kicking in now. 'Here and fucking now I'm declaring a fatwah. One million big ones to the first sod to ram one of his fatuous fucking lemon squeezers up his fatuous fucking arse.'

Yasmin probably didn't know Philippe Starck from Phil Mitchell, but she perked up at that.

VERONICA D: I looked out of the limo and said to Rebecca, 'Jesus, honey, where have you brought us? It looks like the bits of the Bronx that even Busta Rhymes is too scared to show in his vids.'

'You didn't think London was all Albert Halls and Big Bens, did you? You've been watching too many British movies. Get real,' she replied.

Tish had been jammed into a corner, as far away from Rebecca as possible. She'd never been so quiet but she spoke then. 'Veronica has a point, Rebecca. Maybe Grant should go out ahead of us and do his search-and-destroy thingy.'

'Stop being wet, you two. Let's get out there and rock.'

Rebecca wanted that dinner date even less than Tish and me – she must have put on her brave face with her makeup.

GREG FULLER: We watched Rebecca climb out of her twenty-foot pussy wagon. 'Amazing, Greg,' said Kevin. 'How the fuck does that very small piece of fabric hold up that very large amount of tit without the aid of scaffolding?'

VERONICA D: The whole place downed chopsticks and looked at her as she walked in. I could see them going through the 'That looks like . . . Is it? . . . My God, it *is* her' thing. It wasn't the sort of restaurant that was blasé about Hollywood stars.

GREG FULLER: Kevin and I watched Rebecca's PA waddle in her boss's wake. 'Must be a clause in her contract that says "the employee will at all times dress like six sorts of shit in order to make the employer look gorgeous." Her frock looks like a body bag with a couple of sows wrestling inside,' Kevin observed.

'You're too cruel,' I said. 'One sow would have made the point.'

TIM LELYVELDT: Outside the Dorchester, Joe watched his crew file into his stretch. It was like a military op. Or the scene in *Aliens* where the space marines climb into their little ship, ready to kick extraterrestrial ass. We were Hollywood Special Forces and we were going deep behind enemy lines. The mission: locate target and terminate her career with maximum prejudice. GI Joe had his grunts: Waverly, Glenn, Danton and Chris Shave. He also had Jake, the driver, who could find his way anywhere just so long as it was called Sunset Boulevard. And he had me. I liked to think of myself as the unit's intelligence officer in as much as I had some.

Jake pulled out onto Park Lane, and Joe surveyed us, his fawning entourage, proudly. At that moment, I was reminded of Hollywood's greatest truth: if you look around the dinner table (or, indeed, around the stretch taking you to the dinner table) and see that everyone there is on your payroll, then you truly are an A-list prick.

YASMIN FISH: Probably because I was nearest, Rebecca sat next to me. Toddy had pulled out a chair for her on the other side of the table, and she got her hands trapped as Tish plonked herself down in it. Is that fat-ist? I don't care. Tish was fucking enormous.

GREG FULLER: Nobody is faster than me when it comes to cerebral undressing. While most men are mentally struggling with a bra clasp, I'm settling back for my post-shag fag. On any other night that is what I'd have been doing – gazing across the table at Rebecca,

Veronica and Yasmin, concocting the fantasy foursome. Yasmin would have played the pretty ingénue. Veronica, the slightly scary Amazon posing suggestively with her curling tongs. Rebecca Richards would have starred as herself with the dress winning a best support prize. Me, I'd have been somewhere in the tangle of bodies.

Not that night, though. My conscience was stirring, reminding me that I had one. And reminding me that I also had Carrie. I should have been at home and I knew it. Chinese Elvis didn't help when he launched into 'Hound Dog'.

TODDY GLUCK: I looked at Greg staring at Rebecca and I knew what was going through his mind. I'm not going to let the bastard get to me, I thought. I'm going to rise above this and do the only thing I can. I took charge and busied myself with the menu, ordering drinks and generally producing the whole act. I was a producer, after all: one of London's finest. Whatever attack my emotions were undergoing, I could always seek refuge in my work.

TIM LELYVELDT: 'You sure you know where we are, Jake?' Joe shouted.

'Sure, boss.'

I wasn't the only one who'd spotted that we were driving over the same bridge for the third time. Jake had a map beside him, but it might as well have been an atlas of Venus written in Venusian hieroglyphs for all the help it was. To American sensibilities, London is a huge, meaningless sprawl. Nothing like US cities, which were founded on the 'Let's have a city and let's have it right here' principle, and whose planners must have had Jake in mind when they came up with the idiot-proof grid.

We crossed the bridge for the fourth time, hung a left, and were swallowed up by a maze of narrow streets that led us into a canyon of black warehouses. Without warning it opened out onto a new vista of dilapidated apartment buildings – what in the States would be called the projects.

'We're very close now, boss,' Jake announced confidently.

We were definitely fucked.

YASMIN FISH: Apart from giving her direction, Kevin had virtually ignored Rebecca for the last three days, and he'd been horrible about her whenever she hadn't been on the set. Now he was totally into her. Veronica leaned behind Rebecca and tapped the side of her nose. 'Bullshit powder,' she whispered.

'I love this place, Rebecca,' Kevin told her. 'Big respect on your –'

GREG FULLER: I honestly thought Kevin was going to say 'tits', because by then his eyes were like lasers, attempting to cut the spaghetti straps that were all that stood between Rebecca's breasts and the immutable laws of gravity.

YASMIN FISH: '– choice.'

'Oh, thank Yasmin,' Rebecca said, putting her arm around me. 'If it weren't for her we'd be in the Sanderson.'

I just melted into her at that point.

TISH WILKIE: I looked at Rebecca cuddling up to the production company gopher and I felt sick. I no longer cared that the gopher was almost certainly a mole in the pay of a top Hollywood rival. I couldn't breathe and I simply had to get away. I went to the loo and locked myself in a cubicle. Then I took a pad from my bag and made a list:

PROS	CONS
1. Best tables in top restaurants	1. Being seen at best tables with lesbo
2. Mingle with other A- and B-list Personalities	2. Who might also be lesbos or (if male) homo
3. Privileged access to RR's top star beauty regime	3. RR 'comes out', goes butch, stops waxing, etc
4. Help out on celeb causes, e.g. cancer, baby seals, etc	4. Get roped into gay pride and/ or other homo 'causes'
5. Meet George Clooney	5. Meet George Michael
6. Hand-me-down star freebies	6. Catch AIDS from hand-me-down freebies
7. Celeb tennis lessons w/Chris Evert	7. Celeb tennis lessons w/Martina Navratilova
8. Get treated like VIP	8. Get treated like lesbo

When I read it over, everything suddenly seemed clear. I knew exactly what I had to do the next day.

YASMIN FISH: Rebecca changed the subject. 'Tell me, Kevin, what's next for you?'

'*Body Matter*, babe, Sequel City. My agent's got the bones of a deal. I'll whack my name on the dotted any day now.'

'*Body Matter* was amazing, Kevin. I loved it,' she said.

'You're sweet. It wasn't bad, was it?'

He couldn't have sounded less excited if he'd tried, and Rebecca said, 'I'm getting a vibe that you're not one hundred per cent enthusiastic about *BM II*.'

'Oh, sure I want to do it. I'd be crazy not to. They're doubling the budget, the script's cool, Joe's a dream to work with, blah, blah, blah. Anyway, it's about establishing myself with the studios so that they'll eventually let me shoot the picture that I really want to make.'

'You have a screenplay?' Rebecca asked.

'No, just a bunch of ideas. I wouldn't mind doing something with some dialogue. I reckon there's more fucking rabbit in the ad we're shooting than there was in two hours of *Body Matter*.'

'Well, good luck, Kevin.'

Kevin took a big swig of beer and said, 'Don't take this the wrong way, Rebecca, but I reckon you're just about the bravest bird I ever saw.'

'What are you talking about? I'm the original coward.'

'Take it from me, the way you strutted onto the set after . . . you know. It was a fucking privilege to witness it. If I'd been in your place, I wouldn't have had the bottle.'

I looked at Kevin and tried to imagine him in a porn film. Shouldn't have gone there, Yas, I told myself, and I felt the prawn crackers coming back up. Rebecca must have read my mind because she said, 'Kevin, I have trouble imagining you in my place, but I'm sure you have plenty of courage.'

'Bollocks.'

'You could prove otherwise.'

'What, you want to see Kevin in a hardcore?' asked Greg.

'Hardly, Greg. I mean that Kevin could do something really courageous just by saying no.'

'I'm listening, babe,' Kevin said. So was I.

'Say no to *Body Matter II*.'

VERONICA D: Maybe Rebecca was right when she'd said I was naïve, because I should have seen that one coming.

YASMIN FISH: 'The first movie was stunning, it truly was,' Rebecca explained. 'No doubt the sequel will do great business, and it might even be as good. But I've learned one thing in LA: the further you travel down a road, the harder it is to get off it. You keep making action movies, Kevin, and, however good they are, they're all you'll ever make. That's fine if they're what you really want to do. But you said yourself it's not. Whatever they're offering you for the sequel, turn it down and make the film *you* want to make.'

VERONICA D: Translation: 'If you're not completely stupid, Kevin, you must know that I loathe Joe Shirer. I want to damage him every bit as badly as he's damaged me. He's desperate for *Body Matter II* to be massive. He's an insecure little fuck and, however much he's been dicking you around, he's only doing it because he thinks you need him more than he needs you. No one has ever said no to him. Be the first on the block.'

YASMIN FISH: Kevin looked as if he couldn't believe someone so beautiful could say something so smart. Then he said, 'Food for thought, babe.'

'Talking of food,' said Toddy, who'd been trying to get our attention for ages, 'would we all be happy with egg-fried rice or does anyone want plain boiled?'

TIM LELYVELDT: Joe finally came out with it. 'Jake, dude, you're lost, aren't you?'

'Kinda, boss. All these apartment blocks look the same.'

'I think that's cause they are. We've been cruising round the same ones for a while now,' said Joe with rare insight.

The road that had led us there had disappeared. We were trapped. As we went in circles, the homies were getting to know us. They must have priced up the limo already, and moved on to speculating how much they could get for the schmucks inside.

TYRONE EDWARDS: Yvonne looks the business. Tight top that shows plenty of what Tyrone likes, black leather mini and the boots with the spike heels that I like her to leave on in bed but she says will rip the sheets so we have to do it standing up and I have to climb on a box because she's taller than me especially in them boots and I end up doing my hamstrings.

We stroll out of the flat and the lift is broken again.

'We'll have to walk, babe,' I say.

'You expect me to walk down fourteen floors in these heels? You wanted me to wear them, Tyrone – you can give me a piggyback.'

TISH WILKIE: I was beginning to question Rebecca's judgement. There was the 'kissing' girls thing, but there was also the dump she'd brought us to. I'm *so* not a snob, but we were surrounded by total lowlifes. They were crazed by alcohol and monosodium glutamate and were probably armed to the teeth. Goaded by the presence of a Major Hollywood Personality, they were capable of literally *anything*.

I felt sorry for Toddy. She obviously thought the restaurant was totally unsuitable, but she was making such a brave effort sorting out the food. No one was paying her the slightest attention, though, and I decided to give her a hand. 'Toddy, do you want me to make a list? I always find that helps.'

'God, would you, darling?' she said. 'We're never going to eat at the rate we're going, and as far as I'm concerned the sooner we order and get out of this hole, the better.'

'*Exactomundo*,' I said.

TYRONE EDWARDS: How can I say this without seeming rude? Yvonne is kind of big boned. So by the time I've humped her to the sixth floor, I'm fucked.

'Gotta take a breather,' I say. I put her down and lean on the wall.

'You think I lost some weight then, sweetheart?' says Yvonne, smoothing down her skirt.

I say, 'Definitely . . . pant . . . you is definitely . . . puff . . . slimmer since . . . pant . . . the last time the lift broke.'

Then I look down into the street.

'Hey, babe,' I ask, 'what's that limo doing in the Bob Marley?' I point at the big white stretch that's doing about five miles an hour.

Yvonne clocks it and says, 'Probably one of your dealer friends made it big and he's come home to show off.'

'And you want me to go straight, huh?'

TISH WILKIE: I'd finally got the order. I stood up with my pad and said, 'OK, everyone, pay attention. This is what we're having. Sesame toast, prawn balls, spring rolls, fried seaweed, honey barbe-cued spare ribs and those scrummy shrimp parcel things to start. Main courses: beef in black bean sauce, sweet-and-sour pork Hong Kong-style, Szechuan chicken, shrimp chow mein, fried pork with gingery bits, squid in oyster sauce, special chop suey, sliced duck with mixed vegetables, braised Chinese mushroom with bean curd, Singapore noodles and egg-fried rice. OK . . . OK?'

They ignored me and Kevin turned to the waiter: 'Set menu C for seven, extra noodles, sorted.' So *completely* rude.

I sat down next to Toddy and said, 'I've got a totally *amazing* idea. Let's get squiffy. I always find that helps.'

BOB BULL: As Jane served up her usual splendid fare, I couldn't get Honeydew off my mind. If the videotape came out, how would I ever make Jane see it for the innocent business discussion between battle-hardened corporate operator and keen young student that it most definitely, categorically and without a shadow of a doubt was? It was a humdinger of a conundrum, worst-case-scenario-wise.

'What's the matter, Bo-bo?' Jane asked. 'You've hardly touched my Quorn stir-fry.'

'It's Greg,' I explained. 'He's handled things badly today. He's not a deft hand, man-management-wise. A major commercial shoot is rather like a supertanker, and the signs are that the wheels are coming off this one.'

'That doesn't sound like my Bo-bo. He's lucky to have you down there. Step in and take charge. Remind him who's boss.'

'You know, you're flipping well right, Jane. That's exactly what I'm going to do.'

'That's more like it. Now eat up. There's crumble for afters.'

I looked across the table at her, my loyal, sweet Jane. How could I ever hurt her? I had to get my hands on that tape.

TIM LELYVELDT: We cruised towards the same group of teenagers for about the twentieth time. Chris Shave turned to Joe and said, 'Why don't I ask these kids where the hell we are?'

Joe shrank back into his seat. 'I don't think that's a good idea. Look at 'em. This place is crack city.'

'Don't worry, boss. Protecting your ass is what I'm here for.'

TISH WILKIE: Toddy and I were on our second bottle of house white.

'This wine is disgusting,' she said, draining her glass.

'God, *way* disgusting. Probably full of genetically modified E numbers,' I agreed as I finished mine.

Toddy looked at Rebecca, who was flirting completely openly with Veronica and the gopher. 'How long have you been working for her, then?' she asked me.

'Oh, only a few weeks, but we clicked instantly,' I said. Then I quickly added, 'But we didn't click in *that* sort of way.'

'What sort of way, darling?'

'You know, *that* sort of way.'

'I don't know what the *bleep* you're talking about, darling,' said Toddy, who was squiffier than I'd realised, 'but, if you want my advice, don't get too close.'

'Oh, I *so* won't,' I said, but she ignored me and rambled on.

'You give them everything, your heart, your soul, your *bleeping* body, *everything*. Then, when you have no more left to give, they throw it back in your face. The *bleeps*.'

I had no idea what she was talking about, but it sounded awful and somehow so *very* sad.

TYRONE EDWARDS: We get to the ground floor and I am knackered. If I didn't have to walk up fourteen floors with Yvonne on my back I'd fuck the curry and go straight back home. Yvonne is waiting for me to get my breath back and she's looking at the limo. It's pulled up by Richie Jones and his crew.

'I told you it was one of your dealer friends,' she says. 'He may have made the millionaire club, but he can't stop himself selling £5 wraps to them poor kids.'

'Well, he don't want to be selling nothing to that mad fucker, Richie Jones,' I say.

The door opens and a big white guy climbs out. He's no one I know.

TIM LELYVELDT: 'Chinese Elvis, we're looking for C-h-i-n-e-s-e E-l-v-i-s,' Shave said to the nearest kid like he didn't speak English.

The teenager said, 'There ain't no chinks round here.'

'He must mean the old guy in the chippie,' said another.

'Nah,' said the first one. 'He don't look like Elvis.'

'What about that dealer over in Berdmonsey?' said another. 'He's into that rock 'n' roll shit.'

'Fuck off, he's Triad,' said the first one.

TYRONE EDWARDS: Richie Jones is standing back from the others, but he decides to take a tour of the stretch. He walks around it and then he hops up onto the bonnet.

TIM LELYVELDT: Jake must have forgotten that the limo was a rental, because when the kid who hadn't spoken climbed on the hood, he leapt out and went at him like he'd spent his life savings on it.

'Get the fuck off my wheels,' he yelled, giving him a shove.

TYRONE EDWARDS: I'm thinking he ain't from round here, because if he was he wouldn't do that to Richie Jones.

TIM LELYVELDT: The kid slid off onto the road, but he wasn't down for long. He jumped to his feet, flashing a knife. He moved behind

Jake and pressed the blade against his throat. The other kids started shouting. 'Easy, Richie, these guys are with the Triads.' Shave reached into his jacket where he would normally have had his gun – nothing. He had to make do with, 'C'mon, kid, there's no need for this. Put the knife down.'

I was in the anti-gun lobby – I'd signed petitions, sent hate mail to Charlton Heston, the whole nine yards – but right then I wished Shave had been packing, say, a Kalashnikov with grenade launcher.

I climbed out of the limo and so did Waverly, Glenn and Danton. It was beginning to look like *West Side Story* minus the thrilling choreography, Oscar-winning score and Natalie Wood.

We badly needed the Joe who'd once nailed a 250-pound gangsta with the line, 'One move and your ho will be sucking lead from your fat ass.' But that was in the movies. Back in the real world our man was cowering in the limo.

TYRONE EDWARDS: 'This is your moment, Tyrone. You're a security and personal safety facilitator now,' says Yvonne.

'You taking the piss? That's Richie fucking Jones.'

'Stop being a pussy. Go and do some facilitating,' she says, and she shoves me in the back.

TIM LELYVELDT: The stand-off continued, but then I saw a little guy stumbling towards us. Shit, I thought, we're all going to die. I wasn't looking at him, though. I'd just seen his girlfriend.

TYRONE EDWARDS: Diplomacy and people skills, I'm telling myself. Hakkan says it's all about diplomacy and people skills. I look at Richie, then the knife, and then at the little trickle of blood that's running down the driver's neck and onto his nice white shirt. I think back to the nosebleed that went all over my suit and I remember I don't like blood. I turn to Yvonne and say, 'Babe, I booked the table. We're gonna be late if we don't –'

But she ignores me and starts yelling.

TIM LELYVELDT: She was big, WWF big, and she was armed with fingernails from hell. She shouted, 'Richie Jones, put that knife away now.'

The kid replied, 'What if I don't?'

'I'll get your mum down here before you've had a chance to shit your pants and the pair of us will kick you from here to Deptford.'

I believed her. So did the kid. He pocketed the knife.

'It was just a laugh, Yvonne. I wasn't gonna to do nothing.'

As soon as the kid stepped back, Shave leapt in. But Yvonne was faster and got between them. 'And you leave him alone, you big bastard,' she shouted. 'He's only fourteen.'

From behind the safety of Yvonne, the kid goaded Shave: 'You look like Tony Soprano, you fat *cocksucker*.' But Shave had the sense to know when to call it quits and ignored him.

The teenagers moved away. They decided there was probably something more interesting happening under another street light and wandered off.

TYRONE EDWARDS: 'You OK, babe?' I say to Yvonne. 'You should've let me handle that. I was just about to –'

'If I'd waited for you, they'd be chalking the guy's outline on the road now. C'mon, let's get that curry.'

TIM LELYVELDT: Shave checked out Jake who was falling apart on the sidewalk. Waverly, Glenn and Danton had got back into the limo with Joe, who was transforming himself back into a movie star. 'Let's get the fuck out of here,' he yelled.

'Let's find out how, otherwise we'll just be driving round in circles all night,' I said in my capacity as intelligence officer. I walked after Yvonne and her boyfriend.

'Hang on, you guys,' I called out and they turned around. 'Thanks for saving our lives just now. . . . And can you help us? We're lost. We were heading for a place called Chinese Elvis.'

'What you wanna go to that dump for?' said Yvonne's friend.

'I was wondering that myself,' I said.

'It's five minutes from here,' said Yvonne.

'It might as well be five hours. We can't find our way out of this place, and it looks as if we don't have a driver any more.' I pointed to Jake who was retching on Shave's shoes.

'We're heading for the Indian across the street,' said Yvonne. Then she turned to her friend. 'Tyrone, reckon you can make yourself useful for once and drive that lily-white tank?'

'No problem,' he said. 'Who's in that thing anyway?'

'My boss,' I told him, 'a guy called Joe Shirer.'

'*The* Joe Shirer?' screamed Yvonne.

'Uh-huh,' I said.

'Joe Shirer with the huge –'

'The very same,' I said.

TISH WILKIE: By the time we'd finished the third bottle, Toddy was completely blotto. She leaned on me and said, 'Tish, tell me this is a nightmare and I'm going to wake up.' *Yeuch*, I thought, it *is* a nightmare. I was literally surrounded by *them*. I tried to pull my chair away but I'd tucked the tablecloth into my cleavage to stop the sweet-and-sour sauce going onto my dress. It was a Stella McCartney – a *total* sack on the hanger but *so amazing* on. My bowl started to slide off the table and Toddy was sliding towards my bosoms. I didn't know which one to stop first.

GREG FULLER: Toddy and alcohol had never got along. She and Rebecca's PA were locked in a race to see who could fall off her chair first. I decided to split them up before it got out of hand.

TISH WILKIE: Greg must have sensed my panic because he came over and literally saved my life. He sat between us and propped Toddy up in her chair. *Perfect*, I thought – a bit of harmless *heterosexual* flirting would prove to her that I wasn't into kissing girls in anything other than an air-type way. I put my hand on his and gave it a squeeze. It was the *tiniest* little squeeze, and all Greg did was smile at me, but Toddy went crazy-ape-poo. 'How can you be so *bleeping* cruel, you *bleep*?' she said.

.God, *such* an overreaction. It wasn't as if I'd told her I was a *lesbian* too and wanted to have her *lesbian* babies. I leaned across Greg and was about to give her a few home truths but he pushed me back into my chair and said, 'Look at Rebecca.'

GREG FULLER: I never thought I'd be so overjoyed to see a middle-aged, tone-deaf, Cantonese Elvis Presley impersonator.

YASMIN FISH: Chinese Elvis had finally homed in on Rebecca. He serenaded her with 'Love Me Tender' and Rebecca whispered to me, 'I don't know whether to love this or die of embarrassment.'

I whispered back, 'I'd love it if I were you – it'll probably get worse.'

When he'd finished he took her hand and pulled her up from her seat. She tried to stop him but Veronica gave her a shove and she was on her way.

VERONICA D: They did a duet – 'Teddy Bear'. The whole restaurant tuned in. It was *Rebecca Richards – Unplugged*. After a shaky start she improved. Not exactly Mary J, but she wasn't Courtney Love either. I guess in that bit of London, Rebecca Richards karaoke nights didn't come along like those big red buses, and every diner with a camera was flashing it at her. One of them had a rig that looked too big to have fitted into her purse, but it didn't click right away that she was a pro. When they were through the crowd wouldn't let Rebecca get to her seat, and she had to stay up for an encore – 'Lawdy Miss Clawdy'.

YASMIN FISH: Rebecca was up for it by the end, and she'd have done a full set if a waiter hadn't appeared and whispered in her ear. She nodded and followed him to the kitchens. Veronica said, 'What the hell is she doing now? The washing up?'

She came back out with a birthday cake. The waiter led her to a big party at a table on the other side of the restaurant. Chinese Elvis joined her and they sang 'Happy Birthday' to a pale-looking girl. The woman on the next table leaned over to me and said, 'That kid has only got a month to live. They let her out of St Thomas's for a few hours because it's her sixteenth. There's an ambulance waiting outside to rush her straight back. How many stars off the telly would trek down here to give the poor girl a memory like that? Your friend Rebecca is a very special lady.'

My 'friend' Rebecca – *wow*.

I looked at the girl and saw that she was connected to a portable drip, the sort you see people wheeling along hospital corridors. By then she was crying. So were her entire family and almost the whole restaurant. I nearly held my lighter up. Look, you just had to be there, all right?

Toddy's eyes glazed over and she said, 'God, I think I'm going to be sick.'

I'd had enough of her, and after a couple of beers I didn't give a toss any more so I said, 'Just for once can't you be nice about someone?'

'You don't understand,' she said, '*I think I'm going to be sick.*'

She jumped up from the table and ran for the loo, but she only got halfway before there was sweet-and-sour prawn balls and egg-fried rice all over the floor.

VERONICA D: Rebecca eventually made it back after signing every napkin in the restaurant. As she sat down I said, 'You planned this, didn't you, honey?'

'No way. It just happened.'

'Celebrity karaoke, the sick kid – this is PR from paradise. You telling me you didn't call the paparazzo?'

'What paparazzo?'

'The one that snapped every moment of your show.'

'I swear I didn't. I didn't even notice. I'm just having a good time. Maybe the restaurant rang the local paper.'

I believed her, really I did.

We watched the agency's supermodel producer struggle back to the table with sick down her silk blouse. Rebecca said, 'I think it might be time to get the check.'

YASMIN FISH: Outside the restaurant everyone was climbing into taxis and limos. Except me. I didn't know how I was going to get home. Greg wasn't going to offer me a lift again – he was too busy helping Toddy into a cab. I was looking for a bus stop when Rebecca came up to me and said, 'Where are you heading, Yasmin?'

'Streatham. I think there's a night bus,' I replied.

'Come back to the Dorchester with us.'

'I couldn't,' I said, and I prayed that she didn't say, 'OK then, see you tomorrow.'

She didn't. She said, 'Yes, you could. I want to thank you properly because I don't care how many Oscar parties I go to, this will always be one of the best nights of my life.'

I'd never been in a limo before, and I felt like a pop star. As we were pulling away I looked out of the window and saw another big white stretch. It had huge scratches down its side, its wing mirrors were hanging off and it had lost its bumpers.

Veronica said, 'Hey, ain't that Joe's?'

TYRONE EDWARDS: We make it to the Star of India and Yvonne is so mad at me she can't even speak.

'Babe, how was I to know the limo would be too wide for that gap? I ain't never driven one before.'

'It said "WARNING – MAXIMUM WIDTH FIVE FOOT SIX INCHES" in big letters,' she hisses at me. 'What the fuck did you think you were doing, you idiot? For the first time in my life I'm sitting in a limousine, and you get us stuck between two stupid posts. An hour waiting for a tow truck to haul us out – a whole fucking hour.'

'But, babe, you had a whole hour with Joe whatsisname.'

'And he's too terrified to say anything to me. He's thinking we've set him up for a mugging. You got a lot of making up to do, Tyrone Edwards.'

I feel her spike hit my foot like a pickaxe.

'Fuck, that hurt,' I shout.

I forgot that sex ain't all them boots is good for.

eighteen:

vomit, ninja, basildon bond

GREG FULLER: I woke up and smelt the sick. The memories came flooding back: prising Toddy's encrusted body from mine and depositing her on her bed; checking into a cheap tourist hotel round the corner from her flat; no toothbrush; no Carrie.

Max rang as I fought a losing battle with the shower controls. He'd decided to dispense with treating me as his business partner. Now I was his juvenile son – the bone idle one that still hasn't tidied his room after the fiftieth time of asking.

He, of course, wanted to know where his Universe of Sofas campaign was.

I, of course, promised that he'd have it by the end of the day, first thing Friday at the latest.

Then, of course, I buried my head in my hands and despaired.

YASMIN FISH: I woke up on Rebecca's sofa. She was already up and Veronica joined us for coffee and orange juice. I told her that she looked like the one in the middle in Destiny's Child.

'Beyoncé? You're kidding me.' I could tell she liked that. 'We got the same hairdresser.'

Weird – a hairdresser to the stars who had her hair done by a hairdresser to the stars.

Then I asked her what the D stood for.

'Don't ask, honey,' she said. 'There are three things I tell no one. One of them is my surname.'

'What are the other two?'

'I ain't telling you that, girl.'

'Yasmin,' Rebecca interrupted. 'I'm probably as close to Veronica as anyone, but I gave up asking about the D years ago. Better it remains a mystery.'

I sat beside Rebecca in her limo on the way to the studio and I thought that life couldn't get any better. My mum always used to tell me to go out in clean knickers just in case. Well, Mum, that morning I didn't have any fresh ones, so Rebecca had given me a pair of hers. Pale blue satin. My bum had never felt so special. Or squashed – they were two sizes too small.

NORMAN THE COOK: If some of them psychologists spent a bit of time watching where everyone sits down to eat on a shoot, they'd find more answers to life's questions than they do up their own arses, which is where they normally look. There's a pecking order to shoot seating arrangements. No one puts out place cards, but everyone knows exactly where to plant their arses.

At breakfast on the Thursday morning a few of the crew were eating their fry-ups at the tables in the car park. So far so normal. Then Rebecca showed up with tissues round her neck to stop the slap going on her kit. She got two bacon rolls, went straight up to the lads and asked if she could join them.

Now, rule one is that talent never sits with crew, especially when the talent has a star on its dressing-room door.

At first the lads didn't know where to look, but she warmed

them up and soon enough it was like the snug on a Friday night. Then the focus-puller asked her, 'You seen the *Mirror* today?'

TIM LELYVELDT: I climbed into Joe's new limo. 'You got it?' he said. I nodded and handed him the paper. He looked at the front page. The big story was about a man who'd left his wife for a horse, but a red flash announced 'THE REAL REBECCA RICHARDS – EXCLUSIVE STORY AND AMAZING PICTURES page 5'. Joe cracked his first smile of the morning.

NORMAN THE COOK: 'No, I haven't,' Rebecca replied. 'What's in it?'
  'You are. You're amazing,' said the focus-puller. 'The world will see you in a new light today.'

TIM LELYVELDT: 'What the fuck is this?' Joe threw the paper at me. I picked it up and looked at it. The headline read, 'REBECCA AS YOU'VE NEVER SEEN HER BEFORE'. So far so good. The main picture showed her giving a blowjob as well, just not the one that Joe had in mind. She was extinguishing the candles on a birthday cake alongside a wan teenager on a portable IV. The caption explained, 'Rebecca gives brave Lisa a birthday present she'll treasure forever.' (Which, in Lisa's case, looked to be about a month.)

There were plenty more shots: Rebecca serenading sickly Lisa; Rebecca helping a waiter serve a surprised party with their chow mein; Rebecca rocking with Chinese Elvis; Rebecca with her arms around the production company's girl gopher and the Barbie-doll producer, who looked ready to collapse.

Only days before, she'd been all over the papers for maiming an innocent customs officer. Now she was Princess Di mark II. An army of LA's silkiest-tongued publicists couldn't have effected a makeover that good that quickly, yet she'd managed it all by herself.

By the time we reached the studio we needed another new limo. Joe had put his foot through the glass partition that divided us from Jake.

NORMAN THE COOK: For an amateur psychologist like me, things started to liven up when Shirer showed his face. The posse was with him. They headed for a patch of lawn where he got started on a Jackie Chan routine. Now, my knowledge of this stuff doesn't stretch beyond the chorus of 'Kung Fu Fighting', but to my untrained eye it looked like Shirer's mastery of the inscrutable arts was pretty fucking limited. His kicks were not as fast as lightning and he was definitely not a little bit frightening.

It was obvious that he wasn't doing this for his own benefit. No, it was for us lot. The trouble was that he had to contend with the Rebecca Richards Breakfast Show and he wasn't getting a look-in.

It doesn't take Stephen Hawking to figure out that the moment a star stops being treated like one, he's no longer a star. And, if you happen to be a star, that moment will be about as welcome as sitting on a plane and hearing Osama bin Laden's voice announce, 'This is your captain speaking.'

YASMIN FISH: My mobile rang. I looked at the display: MUM. Shit. I'd forgotten to tell her I wouldn't be home.

'Hi, Mum. Look, I'm really sorry. I completely forg –'

'You look lovely, Yasmin, I'm so proud.'

'What are you talking about?'

'The picture of you with Rebecca in the *Mirror*. I'm going to have it blown up and framed. I'll get them to cut off that drunk-looking woman with the sick down her front, though.'

NANCY STARK: When Dirk the Dutch masseur left to start his shift, I decided to call Greg before he called me.

'I've booked Paul and Shaun's flights,' I told him.

'Fantastic,' he said. 'So you'll be back today?'

'No, early tomorrow. I didn't realise their fishing trip was overnight. I'll be waiting at the marina when they get back this afternoon.'

'How can you be so sure they'll come with you?'

'Trust me, Greg. You wouldn't have kept me on for so long if I couldn't get things done, would you?'

I didn't tell him that, actually, I could have delivered them that day, but I needed a bit more time. The tan on my front was coming along, but my back had a bit of catching up to do.

CARRIE FULLER: I returned from the school run to find Clara on my doorstep. I hadn't been expecting her, but she had a way of sensing when she was needed (even when she wasn't).

'Stick your coat on. I'm treating you,' she announced. 'I've just blown bloody thousands on membership to the Chelsea Club. It's incredible – a spa that thinks it's a five-star Caribbean resort. You can be my first guest. They won't give you a massage in your condition, but you can have a deep-cleansing mud bath. It will honestly make you believe you're Cameron Diaz.'

'My pores are fine,' I said.

'You're missing the point. It has nothing to do with pores. It's designed to cleanse your system of bastard husbands.'

TISH WILKIE: As soon as we got to Hounslow I went to the shops. It was so important to do this properly and I spent ages finding the right bits and bobs. I bought a pad of Basildon Bond in classic pale blue, matching envelopes and a Parker biro. I went back to the studio, found an empty office and started to write.

Dear Rebecca,

No, far too personal under the circumstances. I tore off the sheet and started again.

Dear Ms Richards,
   It is with a literally deep feeling of regret that I

That read like one of those awful letters you write when someone has died. I threw it in the bin and went to get a coffee. Obviously this was going to be harder than I'd imagined.

TIM LELYVELDT: Joe had calmed down enough to order Morton to call the *Mirror* and find out why they hadn't run with *Titanic*. He also decided that the studio was unsafe – not enough heavies to keep reporters and fans at bay. He demanded reinforcements.

'He's freaked. What happened last night?' Morton asked me, before adding, 'southeast London can't be that bad.'

'Maybe,' I agreed, 'but Joe acted as if it was southeast Asia, circa nineteen sixty-nine.'

YASMIN FISH: I was still gazing at the photo in the *Mirror* when Sonia, the body double, came and sat down next to me.

'Gorgeous, isn't she?' she said. I suppose she was complimenting herself as well as Rebecca. 'Mind you, I hope she doesn't have another boob job. I don't fancy going through that again.' Then she asked, 'So, which one of the blokes here do you fancy?'

'No one really,' I replied. 'I've got a boyfriend.'

'What's that got to do with it? You have to fancy at least one of them. It's the only thing that stops you dying of boredom at a shoot. I quite like the ad agency guy.'

'Greg Fuller. He's sweet,' I said, 'but he's old enough to be my dad. No, he's *older* than my dad. Married as well.'

'Old and married is cool. They know what to do with it when they've been round the block. Greg is definitely cute.' She paused and then said, 'But I think I'll go for the director.'

'Kevin French? He's revolting.'

'He picked the right side of the camera to work on, didn't he? But he *is* the director.'

'So?'

'Best bit of advice I ever got was from another model. She said if you can't screw the producer, shag the director.'

Then she was off.

Great career advice. I remember when Tyler got a job in a hotel kitchen. He was told that if he wanted to make it in catering he'd have to start by sticking his hand down the drain and scooping out the congealed fat. Tyler quit on the spot. But I'd have sooner cleaned that drain than screw Kevin French.

TIM LELYVELDT: 'We've got to do something or he's going to self-destruct,' Mort said to me. This was after we'd watched Joe order Joaquin to fire up his clippers and shave his head. We'd talked him out of it – just. The continuity arguments didn't work. It took Greta pointing out that the tan on his scalp wouldn't match the one on his face to make him realise it was a poor idea.

'What are we going to do?' I said. 'Put out a contract on Rebecca, because that's what it'll take?'

'I like your thinking Timbo. I'll get onto it when we get back to LA. In the meantime, though, we could fly someone over.'

'Someone else to make him feel loved up? He's already got his girlfriend, his chef, his hairdresser, his buddies and us. And we've tried to get his shrink to come.'

'Queenan. Remind me what happened there.'

'Couldn't reach him – the "no cell phones in sensory deprivation" rule. Anyway, it's Thursday. Even if we could get him, by the time he arrives we'll be flying home.'

'That's beside the point, Timbo. For Joe the therapy won't be what he does when he gets here, it'll be knowing that he's on his way. You track down Queenan and I'll tell Joe he's coming.'

NANCY STARK: I cursed the day that Greg had surrendered to Bob Bull's need to be able to be in touch twenty-four/seven and had given him my mobile number. I was hardly out of the shower when he phoned me.

'I wish to register a strong complaint re Greg,' he announced.

'I'm a bit busy at the moment, Bob,' I said, drying my hair. 'Can't you tell him yourself?'

'I'm not talking to him,' he sniffed.

'Oh dear, what's he done?'

'He went to dinner with Rebecca Richards last night. It's all over the flipping paper this morning.'

'Greg does feel that a crucial part of his job is keeping the cast happy,' I said, hinting at only a tenth of the truth.

'Yes, but what about his clients? I should have been there. He must know that fostering productive relationships at the brand custodian/brand spokesperson interface is key to achieving desired outcomes, marketing communication programme-wise.'

And there was me thinking he was simply miffed because he'd missed out on free grub with celebrity totty.

'I'm sure he had a perfectly good reason not to involve you. Maybe he thought a little dinner was too trivial, given all your other incredibly important responsibilities.'

'Maybe,' he said, slightly appeased. 'As it happened, I was far too busy to have been able to attend. Just tell him that I should at least have known of his plans, strictly for informational purposes, of course.'

'Of course, Bob. He'll be very concerned about your concerns, as am I.'

What really concerned me, though, was what the hell Greg was playing at gadding about with Rebecca Richards when he should have been at home with Carrie.

'Anything else?' I asked.

'Yes, actually, there was one little thing. I was wondering what you knew about Max's business interests.'

'Not a lot, Bob. Why do you ask?'

'Oh, it's no big deal. I had a thought for a promotion. You know the kind of thing, buy a set of tyres, win a night out in a top London night-club. I know Max has fingers in multiple pies, business venture-wise. I wondered if he had any clubs we might do a tie-in with.'

'I've no idea, Bob. You'll have to ask Max.'

Tyre promotion, my arse. I knew exactly what he was driving at. Greg had pulled the Honeydew scam again. Bob Bull was the third client who'd fallen for it.

TIM LELYVELDT: Morton came into Joe's dressing room just as he was falling asleep.

'I can't disturb him,' I said. 'He'll kill me.'

'I wanted to tell him about the *Mirror*,' said Morton. 'I spoke to the editor. Charming guy – sounded very Merchant Ivory for a tabloid jock. Anyway, they were set to run with *Titanic* but then they were tipped off about the Chinese. It was just too juicy to ignore. He assured me they haven't spiked the porno. It's all part of setting her up before they knock her down.'

'I don't think Joe can wait even a day,' I said. 'You know he's not big on patience.'

'Well, there is some good news to keep him going. By the time he wakes there'll be an extra ten operatives beefing up the security presence.'

TYRONE EDWARDS: I'm sitting in the back of a Transit with nine other guys. I am one of the elite. A Professional Security and Personal Safety Facilitator. Hakkan briefed us up at HQ. We are going in to a film studio. We are going to be discreet. We are going to be cool. We are going to take no shit from no one. We are going to make them film people feel well fucking safe.

Then he took me aside for my special instructions. 'Tyrone,' he said, 'I only called you because I had no choice.'

'I know, man,' I said, 'you needed a guy you could trust with your life.'

'No, I needed *guys*, bodies, fast. These film gigs are hard to score and when they come you've got jump in. Keep a low profile and, *please*, don't fuck this up for me.'

'Have I ever let you down?

'Apart from that time when the skinheads jumped us?'

'There was at least six of them, Hakkan.'

'Yeah, and after you scarpered there was only one of me. Don't blow it today.'

'I won't, I swear.'

And I won't, I'm thinking. I am the Facilitator.

GREG FULLER: The last thing I was expecting was a good idea. The supposedly creative left side of my brain had spent the week on strike. It was sick of being clever – all that jumping-through-hoops lateral thinking; couldn't it be in charge of dumb stuff like choosing the TV channel?

Then, on Friday morning, it stirred into action and hit me with the perfect sofa solution. It wasn't so much an idea as a reminder that I had, in fact, already had the idea.

Before I teamed up with Max I'd been a creative group head at Saatchi & Saatchi, where I'd worked on a pitch for Galaxy of Suites, the chain of edge-of-town stores stacked to the rafters with crap furniture (not to be confused with Universe of Sofas, the chain of edge-of-town stores stacked to the rafters with crap furniture). I, or, if I'm being honest, Carrie and I came up with a line, 'home suite home'. I turned it into a campaign, executed in the style of Victorian samplers and featuring needlepoint illustrations of Dralon sofas. The Galaxy of Suites mob wasn't impressed, though, and the business went elsewhere. But the idea didn't die. It was merely resting in a brown envelope in the proverbial bottom drawer.

It took no leap of imagination to remove the Galaxy of Suites logo and replace it with Universe of Sofas.

I am a fucking genius, I thought to myself. Provided none of the marketing arseholes at Universe of Sofas happened to have worked for Galaxy of Suites at the time of the Saatchi pitch (not such a long shot, given the whore-like promiscuity of that profession), I was surely home free.

There remained only one hurdle. The brown envelope had to

make the journey from Primrose Hill to Hounslow ASAP. That would require the help of she who didn't like me very much.

CARRIE FULLER: I was up to my neck in mud and beginning to feel, if not exactly like Cameron Diaz, then perhaps a little like her older and plainer sister. Peace at last.

Then Unborn kicked me.

'It's doing my head in. I can't stop thinking about it.'

'Thinking about what?' I asked.

'Rebecca.'

'Stop it, will you? I'd just about managed to clear my head of that Hollywood bitch.'

'Not her. *Rebecca Edwards* – that bloody screenplay of yours. It's sick.'

'I knew I shouldn't have told you about it.'

'Jesus, they say your parents fuck you up – I haven't even been born and you've started.'

GREG FULLER: There was only one thing for it – I dialled my home number. The machine picked up. I was torn between relief that I didn't have to talk to her and agony that I wasn't immediately going to get the precious brown envelope. The tone sounded and I said, 'Carrie, we badly need to talk. I want to sort things out as much as you do. But first you've got to save my career. I desperately need those old Galaxy of Suites ads – they're in the bottom drawer in the study. If you're in, please pick up. If not, please, *please* don't ignore this when you get back. And, Carrie, whatever's been happening, whatever you think of me, I love you.'

Even though I was speaking to a machine, it was the most heartfelt thing I'd said in months – every word of it, even the last three.

Next I called her mobile. Voicemail. I left more or less the same message.

Then I waited.

VERONICA D: Rebecca was the happiest I'd seen her in a while. Partly because her dressing-room was so calm. Freddie had stayed at the hotel and Tish had disappeared as soon as we'd arrived.

'You're having a good day, aren't you?' I said to her.

'Not bad, thanks.'

'Just watch yourself when you get out there. Joe's dangerous when his stock's down, and I'd say he's dropped about two hundred points on the Dow this morning.'

'I can handle him. He's just an inadequate, vindictive cunt.'

'So is Saddam Hussein, honey, but he's also a dictator. Joe's a movie star and that's almost as powerful.'

TISH WILKIE: I'd finally finished and I read it back to myself.

> *Dear Ms Richards,*
>
> *I have so enjoyed the two and half weeks I have spent being your Personal Assistant. I feel that I have really got to know you both as an employer and as a friend. So it is with a literally heavy heart that I sit down to write this.*
>
> *I have just received the totally devastating news about my mother, who by the way was so bowled over to meet you yesterday and will treasure the memory forever. She needs to have a life-saving operation. She has been bravely suffering in silence for months but yesterday she told me that she's on a waiting list for a new heart . . .*

I'd originally written 'liver', but I decided it made Mum sound like an alcoholic.

> *. . . Now a donor has been found and you will appreciate that I must stay by her side at this awful time.*
>
> *Please accept my resignation. I am sorry to leave you 'in the lurch' like this, and I wish it could have been different. I will watch your future career with great interest, and I am*

positive you will get over the 'situation' that has arisen with
'All Our Lives Before Us' and go on to brilliant things.
Literally.
   Yours sincerely,
   Tish Wilkie

Perfect. Now all I had to do was find the right moment to give it to her. I didn't want to do it when we were alone just in case she was overcome with emotion and expected me to hug her or something. But I also didn't want to do it in front of everyone else and publicly humiliate her. God, you have to be *so* sensitive when you're a Personal Assistant to a Major Star.

Though, with everything that had happened, perhaps she wasn't a very Major Star any more.

GREG FULLER: OK, so I didn't wait long – I was desperate. Fifteen minutes later I phoned home again.

'Hello, Mr Fuller.'

It was Jenny, the cleaner at Fuller Mansions.

'Jenny, is Carrie there?'

'No, she's out, Mr Fuller. I let myself in. There's no note about when she'll be back.'

'OK, maybe you can help. You know the chest in the study?'

'I only dust the surfaces. I never go through your drawers.'

'I know, Jenny, but today you can make an exception. If you look in the bottom drawer, you'll find a brown envelope. When you've got it, put it on a bike.'

'Oh, I'm not sure I'd know how to do that.'

'Don't worry, I'll organise it. A man in a crash helmet will turn up. Give him the envelope and he'll bring it to me.'

'Brown envelope, bottom drawer, man in crash helmet. That sounds fine.'

I hung up. Now, I thought, how the hell do you organise a bike?

NANCY STARK: I was lubing myself up with factor two when I remembered Bob Bull wanted me to talk to Greg. I thought it probably wasn't a great idea if client and agency went the whole day not speaking, so I picked up my phone.

'Thank fuck you called, Lola. How do I organise a bike?'

'Oh, that's a hard one,' I said. 'You'd better write this down. You phone Despatch and say, "Can you get me a bike, please?" Remember the "please", otherwise they take all day.'

'Can you do it?'

'You want me to organise a bike?'

'Yes.'

'From Southern Spain?'

'You *are* my PA. Just do it. Anyway, why are you calling?'

'Because you haven't heard a squeak from Bob Bull this morning, have you?'

'I know. God knows what I've done to piss him off, but it's been blissful. I take it he's spoken to you though.'

'He's deeply hurt that you didn't invite him to dinner.'

'It was only a meal, not an audience with the Pope.'

'Only a meal? I've seen the pictures, Greg. What were you doing there? You should have been at home.'

'Don't start.'

'OK, I won't, as long as you promise to go home tonight and grovel like you just invented it.'

'I promise.'

'And give Bob Bull a kiss while you're in making-up mode. By the way, you haven't pulled the Honeydew scam on him, have you?'

'That's a legitimate business technique, Lola.'

'If you say so. One more thing. Was that what it looks like on Toddy's blouse?'

'I'm afraid so.'

'That's funny. She finally gets her chance to be a tabloid It Girl alongside Victoria, Tara and Tamara and she blows it by throwing up.'

'I hadn't thought of it like that.'

'You can bet that she has, though.'

TODDY GLUCK: My life was in complete ruins. How could I ever face any one of my friends ever again? Of course, none of them would dream of reading the *Mirror,* but I was sure that their publicists would let them know about it. Those bloody prawn balls. The runner had probably laced them with botulism.

I didn't even have Greg to comfort me. He'd simply dumped me on my sofa and left. All he could think about was rushing home to Carrie. She was only bloody pregnant. What did she know about pain and suffering?

YASMIN FISH: Sonia the body double couldn't have made her intentions clearer if she'd been wearing a T-shirt printed with 'I'M KEVIN'S SHAG'.

(My friend, Debbie, had that printed on a T-shirt she wore to a party. She'd been trying to get off with Kevin Little for weeks, but he'd been blanking her. It didn't work. It turned out he was dyslexic and he ended up in the bathroom with Bridget Farmer – I told you she was a slag.)

Kevin loved the attention. What bloke wouldn't like a woman who looks almost like a beautiful celebrity rubbing her boobs against his arm? What bloke wouldn't prefer the real thing, though? When Rebecca came out of her dressing room he dropped Sonia like a big stack of bricks.

She was supposed to be shooting a scene with Joe, but he was still in his dressing room. Kevin didn't seem bothered – he had Rebecca. But after fifteen minutes the first went up to Kevin to try and get things moving. Kevin said, 'OK, let's rock 'n' roll. Send the runner to knock for him.'

That would be me, I thought. Shit.

GREG FULLER: When I was a kid I'd rise at dawn on my birthday and squat on the doormat. I'd stare through the letterbox, willing the postman to arrive with my cards and presents. However, the anticipation I'd felt as a child was nothing to what I was experiencing as I waited for a man in a crash helmet to show up with a dog-eared manila envelope.

You could say that I took my eye off the ball.

YASMIN FISH: Ten minutes later I was back on the set. Without Joe. I heard Toddy mutter, 'Useless bloody girl.'

'What's the hold-up?' Kevin asked me.

'He won't come out as long as . . .' I couldn't say the next bit.

'Yeah?' snapped Kevin, who was turning into his usual unpleasant self again – it didn't take much.

'As long as Rebecca is here.' Then I looked at her and said, 'I'm sorry – that's what his assistant told me.'

Rebecca gave a helpless shrug, but Kevin lost it and yelled at me, 'How the fuck am I supposed to shoot dialogue with one fucking actor? I'm a film director, not David fucking Copperfield.' I was about to burst into tears, but then he completely shocked me. He apologised. 'I'm sorry, babe. I don't know why I'm giving you grief. It ain't your fault.'

'Actually, I wouldn't be surprised if it is her fault, Kevin,' Toddy interrupted. 'She's probably got the wrong end of the stick again. I'll deal with this.'

BOB BULL: 'No, I'll damn well deal with it,' I said. I couldn't stand back and watch the fiasco a moment longer. Greg had gone AWOL. Heaven knows what was on his mind, but it certainly wasn't my envelope-pushing, multi-million-pound TV commercial. Toddy looked at me and said, 'Bob, I know you're trying to help, but I think you should leave this to the professionals.'

'I've been leaving it to the "professionals" all flipping week, and look where that's got us.' The fact that I was swearing made my feelings clear and she shut up. 'Joe and I have a relationship,' I went on. 'I have earned his trust. If he won't come out, he must have serious issues with some of the people around here.'

I glared at Rebecca. I wanted the tramp to know that I hadn't risen to Executive Director in Charge of Marketing, Advertising and Promotion (Europe, the Middle East & North Africa, excluding Libya) without knowing how to deal with a woman who treats all and sundry to a night out but neglects to ask the man who's paying her wages.

Toddy came back with, 'Bob, why don't we have a meeting?'

'The time for meetings has passed,' I said. 'Now is the moment to act.'

I marched off towards Joe's dressing room, making a mental memo to self to use that line more often.

YASMIN FISH: Kevin ripped off the lens he wore round his neck and threw it across the set. 'That's the last shit I'm taking from Shirer,' he muttered and marched off. Toddy chased after him. 'Kevin, darling, we should sit down calmly and have a meeting.'

'*You* have your fucking meeting, Toddy,' he yelled back, '*I've* got a fucking plane to catch.'

NORMAN THE COOK: I watched Kevin French stride towards his Aston. The chippie who was having an early gander at the lunch menu said, 'That's a score you owe me, Norm. I had a fiver at four to one on French being first to take an early bath.'

YASMIN FISH: Toddy looked at me through narrowed eyes and hissed, 'Now look what you've done, you idiot.'

Greg Fuller appeared at the same moment, clutching a brown envelope. He looked at me with tears in my eyes, at the crew with their mouths hanging open, at Toddy pulling a bottle of pills from her Burberry bag and at Rebecca sitting in a director's chair while Veronica fiddled with her hair.

'What have I missed?' he said.

'Let me see,' said Toddy. 'Joe Shirer won't leave his dressing room, Bob stupid Bull is trying to talk him round, Kevin is on his way to LA and I am having a nervous fucking breakdown.'

'Nothing we can't handle then,' he said with a smile. Then he turned round and walked out of the studio.

GREG FULLER: I did have a plan and, half-baked as it was, I was confident I could pull it off. There was no good reason for my optimism, but the safe arrival of the brown envelope had restored my faith that somehow everything would turn out right.

It was the same when I was a child. It didn't matter how long I'd been numbing my arse on the doormat, when postie finally turned up, I'd believe that all my wishes would be realised. Valerie Page would let me catch her in kiss-chase, I would win the *Tour de France* on my Chopper and one day I would finally open a pack of bubble-gum football cards and find the Gary Sprake to complete my Leeds United eleven.

Thirty years on, little had changed. I was certain the Blackstock ad would sink under the weight of the awards it would garner and the Universe of Sofas mob was going to rise as one to salute my genius at Monday's meeting. I was also convinced that Carrie was going to fall limp with love into my arms as I banked an obscenely large cheque from the Italians.

As faith went, mine carried a white stick and was fluent in Braille.

I walked out to the car park and looked for the wannabe Carl Foggerty who'd delivered my envelope. He was still there, helping himself to tea from Norman's urn.

You see, my plan was working already.

I looked at his bike. It was lime green. The word Ninja was writ large on the tank. I knew bugger-all about motorbikes, but this one looked as if it had the power to take out a bus queue with a flick of its rider's wrist.

'How fast can you ride that thing?' I asked.

He gave me a psychotic grin that resembled the 'after' shot in a pictorial entitled 'Before and after gargling with sulphuric acid'. That sold me – Dougie Deathwish had the job.

'There's a silver Aston Martin on its way to Heathrow,' I explained. 'If you can catch it, there's five hundred quid in it for you.'

'A poxy Aston? Piece of piss,' he said, downing his tea and slipping on his helmet. 'What am I delivering?'

'Me.'

nineteen:

chuck norris, major matt mason, tupperware

TYRONE EDWARDS: The Transit pulls through the studio gates and the driver has to steer hard left as a bike shoots out past us. It's doing nearly a ton but I get a look at the guy on the back and I think I seen him somewhere.

We park up and walk into the studio behind Hakkan. I'm a pro. I'm moving like them commandos I've seen in Cedric's Chuck Norris vids. I scope the place. I'm checking out every geezer in there, working out which ones is just a bit dodgy and which ones is the full-on psychos. I'm looking for the spots that'd make the perfect hiding place for a loony fan with a machete. Nothing gets past the eagle eyes of the Facilitator.

Then I spot someone else I know – the bird with the tits and the extra-large Rizlas. When Hakkan briefed us up he said to expect the unexpected. But I definitely wasn't expecting her.

CARRIE FULLER: Clara and I were having our pedicures. I didn't see the point. I was more or less prevented from seeing my toes by my expanding bump. But Clara insisted and I was enjoying having my calluses sanded – pathetic, but I was grateful for any attention.

'So, what are you going to do about Greg?' Clara asked.

I'd managed to avoid the subject all day, but he had to come up at some point.

'I don't know,' I said wearily. 'Make up I suppose.'

'But he's having an affair with that actress. This isn't a row over soft furnishings.' (The sort of thing that she and Sam argued about.) 'You can't just "make up".'

'I don't know if he's having an affair. I was convinced he was screwing Nancy but I was wrong there, wasn't I? Maybe I'm paranoid.'

'You are not paranoid. He's done it once – at least. He can do it again.' Clara was a *Mail* reader and wasn't a believer in rehabilitation. 'You can't let him get away with it.'

'Clara, I didn't tell you this because it's embarrassing. Not long ago I was sure he was seeing someone. I was even fairly certain who she was.'

'My God, Carrie, who?'

'Actually it was you.'

'How could you even . . . ?' Lost for words, she trailed off.

'I told you. Paranoid. I'm sorry. Remember when you came for dinner with Sam and we argued about abortion?'

'I was a bit of a Nazi that night,' Clara said, blushing.

'When Greg jumped to your defence, that did it – all the proof I needed that the two of you were days away from announcing you'd put down the deposit on the love nest. I didn't get it out of my system until the following Saturday. Greg said he was going out to buy a CD player. I was sure he was going to see you so I bundled the kids into the car and followed him.'

'You didn't.'

'All the way to the Hi-fi Hut on Tottenham Court Road. I'm telling you, I'm paranoid.'

Clara didn't say anything for a while after that.

YASMIN FISH: It was like none of it had ever happened. Greg strolled back into the studio with his arm around Kevin French and, apart from the fact that Greg's hair was sticking out straight behind him, they looked as if all they'd been doing was having a cup of tea. At the same time the client walked onto the set with Joe. They were smiling too.

Kevin said, 'What the fuck are we waiting for then?' and the first jumped out of his chair. 'OK, first positions, everyone,' he shouted, though he obviously couldn't believe the words were coming out of his mouth.

My mouth was still dangling open when Toddy rushed up to me and said, 'Chop, chop, girl.'

'What?' I said.

'Joe's water. Let's try and get one thing right today, shall we?'

That did it. The woman was fucked. Well and truly.

TYRONE EDWARDS: Things are getting even unexpecteder. I'm only just getting used to seeing Extra-large Tits and Rizlas again when the bloke from last night walks in – the one whose limo needed a respray; the one Yvonne reckons is hung like a donkey. And I'm just getting over that when I see the bloke on the motorbike again. I work out where I know him from. Saturday. Hyde Park Corner. Flash wanker in the XK8 that also needed a tickle-up in the body shop. Hakkan has told me to keep a low profile. Too fucking right, man, and I hide behind a big light at the back of the studio.

GREG FULLER: When we hit the speed bumps on the road outside the studio, I knew a man could fly. Normally an excursion with Dougie Deathwish would have left me with the constitution of raspberry jelly. However, nothing was normal that morning, and sitting behind Dougie as he attempted to reach Earth-escape velocity was strangely exciting – in a non-homo-erotic way, of course.

'How did I do?' I asked him after we'd flagged Kevin down.

'A bit girly, pal. Only my bird holds me that tight, and that's cause she's trying to give me a rock-on.'

I turned to walk back to Kevin's car and he called after me. 'I don't think you need that any more.'

'Cheers,' I said, taking Norman's Tupperware bowl off my head – Dougie Deathwish had reckoned that at 150 mph it would look indistinguishable from an MOT-approved helmet to any police patrols we passed.

Kevin was so shocked to see me clinging to the back of a Kawasaki Ninja in the fast lane of the M4 that he almost drove us off the road. He put up only a nominal struggle when I begged him to return. Everybody likes to feel wanted (ironically the more successful and, therefore, wanted you become, your need to feel it is all the greater). My dance with death with only a pale yellow salad bowl for protection was proof enough of how much I wanted him.

As we arrived at the studios he said, 'You know, if I do shoot *BM II*, your motorbike chase is a cert for the script.'

'Oh, I don't think it was that earth-shattering by Hollywood standards,' I replied.

'No, it wasn't, but I'd love to see that self-adoring cunt, Shirer, in a Tupperware skid-lid.'

BOB BULL: Don't ask me how I managed to persuade Joe to carry on. I wouldn't be much of an Executive Director in Charge of the Whole Damn Shooting Match if I gave away trade secrets to any sneaky Johnny working for the competition. I will say that I felt inspired by Jane's words of the night before. I also used all my interpersonal skills, honed over many an Interpersonal Skills for Senior Management seminar.

By the end I had Joe eating out of my hand, and he nobly agreed to continue working with the tramp who was making all of our lives a misery.

Tim Lelyveldt: I would imagine that to this day the Blackstock guy doesn't have the faintest clue as to what persuaded Joe to step back onto the set. It took me a moment to figure it out, and I pretty much roomed inside Joe's head.

Bob Bull tried everything. He had Morton helping him out as well – he was dreading the breach-of-contract suit he'd have to deal with if Joe didn't finish the job.

Bull offered him more money (a lot) and even suggested that a curtain be strung across the bar-room table between him and Rebecca – 'We can get rid of it in post-production,' he said, as if he knew what he was talking about.

But it wasn't about money, or even Joe's dislike of Rebecca. However much he loathed her, he could face her so long as he felt he had the upper hand. But he couldn't deal with her that morning because she'd beaten him. Joe had done everything within his power to drive her out and the woman was still there. Ronald Reagan must have felt the same when he sent the F-15s to waste Qadafy and the next day the grinning colonel popped up alive and mocking on Libyan TV.

Bull tried a last desperate throw of the dice. 'Joe, how would you feel if I got our new CEO down here to tell you how much we appreciate your involvement with the Blackstock corporate mission? Roger Knopf – a fellow American, a bit of a Bible-basher but a really top-rate chap.'

'Sure, why not?' said Joe. 'It'd be cool to meet the guy.' He rose and prepared to be an actor once again.

Two little words swung it. They weren't 'fellow American'. They were 'Bible-basher'.

Greg Fuller: The only words that Joe and Rebecca were prepared to say to one another were the ones that appeared on the script or, rather, scripts – but that was enough. We were shooting again. All was right in our little corner of Adland. Job done, it was time to inspect the gems that lay within the brown envelope.

I sat down, lifted the flap and reached inside for salvation, for a passport to the Italian millions, for . . . *shit*.

TYRONE EDWARDS: I'm still hiding behind the big light. Even though I'm busting for a piss, I ain't going nowhere as long as Donkey Dick Movie Star and Flash Wanker in the Jag is both there.

The camera's rolling and Donkey Dick says to Extra-large Tits and Rizlas, 'I always wanted to do something truly exciting with it – something the whole world would talk about.'

Then she purrs back, 'Mmmm, Doug, baby, you're a *nasty –*'

'Shit!' yells someone who ain't Donkey Dick Movie Star or Extra-large Tits and Rizlas. Everybody stops and looks round at Flash Wanker who's sitting in a chair staring at some papers. He ignores them and yells again. 'Shit, shit, fucking shit!'

I'm thinking, fuck, man, if he's this mad over a few bits of paper, I definitely ain't saying sorry for whacking his Jag.

YASMIN FISH: Greg looked suicidal. Whatever he'd been reading, it must have been bad. I remembered the row he'd had with his wife, and I thought that maybe they were divorce papers.

Kevin, sympathetic as usual, shouted, 'If anyone fucks with my film again, I will rip their head from their shoulders and piss in the hole. I don't give a steaming pile of elk shit who the fuck they are.'

Which was my cue to stitch up Toddy.

GREG FULLER: I tossed the envelope and went to the car park for some air. It wasn't literally the end of the world, but for a few minutes it felt like a dry run for Armageddon. It had been the same on my ninth birthday. Nirvana when postie arrived; apocalypse when I ripped open the first package to discover that my aunt had sent me not the requested Major Matt Mason but a pathetic Action Man.

As I stared into the abyss, Sonia the double joined me.

'Cheer up, it might never happen,' she said with irritating perkiness.

'It already has,' I replied.

'Oh dear. What is it? Tell me. I'm a great listener.'

'Just an admin cock-up. I've been sent the wrong package.'

'Can't you get the right one?'

'Probably, but it means waiting.'

And it means talking to my wife, I thought.

'Tell you what,' she suggested, 'I'll give you an Indian head massage. I learnt it off a video and I need to practise.'

CARRIE FULLER: My calluses had been buffed to oblivion and my toenails were now a rich royal blue (or so I'd been told). Clara and I were having lunch. She was over the shock of discovering that I'd thought she was Greg's bit of fluff, and had conceded that I just might be paranoid.

'I can't go on like this,' I announced with a mouth full of club sandwich. 'I have to sort it out. I'm going to call him.'

'Not now,' pleaded Clara. 'Wait till tonight. This is your Greg-free day.' She wasn't prepared to let him off the hook so easily. But then he wasn't the father of her kids.

And she didn't love him.

I ignored her protestations and switched my mobile on. It immediately flashed that I had a message. I listened to Greg's plaintive voice. He sounded desperate – about work, sure, but also about me. I listened to it again. And then again. I dialled his number. He didn't answer.

'I've got to see him,' I said. 'He's in trouble.'

'Don't be so melodramatic and finish your lunch.'

'Clara, you didn't hear his voice. I've got to go.'

'You're letting him walk all over you,' lectured Clara.

'She's right and you know she is,' agreed Unborn.

'He'll lose any respect he has left and he'll treat you like this again . . .' Clara continued.

'Doormat, doormat, doormat . . .' chorused Unborn, as if it was a football chant.

'. . . and again and again.'

'. . . doormat, doormat . . .'

'Shut up, the pair of you,' I shouted.

Silence.

'You are not my mother, Clara,' I snapped. Then I looked down at my bump and said, 'As for you, this is not *Look Who's* bloody *Talking*.'

I started to shake. Clara put her hand on my arm and said, 'Sit down and I'll get you a herbal tea.'

'I'm sorry, Clara, but I am going fucking mad. That's why I've got to see him. Thanks for today. I'll call you.'

I turned round and walked out.

'Can I just say . . .' Unborn ventured in his politest tone to date.

'Not another word.'

twenty:

burberry, nokia, mother bloody teresa

YASMIN FISH: It was the last scene in the original script (I think – I was confused). The one where Joe had to bounce a rubber ball on the bar table and then catch it. We were up to take eighteen because he couldn't catch. He claimed Rebecca was putting him off. I couldn't see how because she was on the far side of the studio, reading. But Kevin asked her to move and she went back to her dressing room.

The crew set up for take nineteen. Joe psyched himself up like he had to do that big speech in *Hamlet* that I could never be bothered to learn at school. The first yelled, 'First positions . . . Quiet, please . . . Camera . . . Aaaand action!'

Joe bounced the ball.

He caught the ball.

Kevin French was so relieved he mouthed, 'Thank fuck.'

Joe got as far as saying, 'Self-infla –' when a mobile rang.

Kevin screamed, 'Find that phone NOW!' Toddy, chief of police, leapt into action. 'I cannot believe anybody could be so moronic,' she yelled. About two seconds later the little spark held up a Burberry handbag and pulled out a dinky Nokia.

Toddy died.

I reached into my trouser pocket and pressed 'cancel' on my phone. The Nokia stopped ringing.

Definitely the best moment of my life so far.

VERONICA D: 'I thought you were hanging with your new fans on the set,' I said to Rebecca when she walked into the dressing room.

'I was, but Joe could hear me breathing from forty feet. It was putting him off.'

She had a wad of typed paper and she sat down to read it.

'What's that, honey?' I asked.

'Shh, I'm concentrating.'

Conversation closed.

YASMIN FISH: Toddy had left her flashy Burberry bag lying around the studio all week. It hadn't been hard to reach inside and flick on her mobile. It didn't take Sherlock to find her number either – it was next to her name on the call sheet.

Kevin walked over to the little spark and took the phone from him. Then he turned to Toddy, handed it to her and said in a really calm voice, 'You will now get the fuck off this sound stage and you will never, ever set foot on a set of mine again.'

Definitely, *definitely* the *best* moment of my life so far.

TYRONE EDWARDS: At lunchtime I find Hakkan and say, 'You gotta get me outta that studio, man. Them lights is baking.'

'You're not cut out for this, are you?' he says. 'Tell you what. I'll swap you round with Tony on the front door. Reckon you can handle some fresh air?'

'No problem. What do I have to do?'

'Nothing. Do *nothing*. Just keep the fans and the photographers out and let the other guys check visitor IDs.'

'Don't worry, Hakkan. I'll be a tiger out there.'

'Whatever, man. Just be a fucking quiet tiger, OK?'

GREG FULLER: I'd spent the remainder of the morning in the car park. Sonia possessed the sensitive touch of a rivet gun and her massage had left me more tense rather than less. My stress only subsided when I watched Norman shove handfuls of sage and onion up half a dozen chickens' arses. I began to see things in perspective. It was just a bunch of ads. Universe of Sofas could wait until the evening. I mentally replayed the messages I'd left Carrie and thought that, however sincere I'd felt, she'd hear only the voice of a mercenary bastard. I wasn't going to compound my lousy image by begging for help again.

CARRIE FULLER: My cab arrived at our house and I asked the driver to wait. I sprinted (at six months pregnant? Think rapid waddle) up the steps and headed for the study. It took me a minute or two to find the Galaxy of Suites ads – they were in the middle drawer, not the bottom one as Greg had said they'd be. I ran back to the cab. 'Hounslow, please,' I said to the driver.

GREG FULLER: After lunch I went back into the studio. I stood next to Yasmin and asked her how it had been going.

'We've set a new world record apparently. Thirty-eight takes for Joe to catch the little ball.'

After her badly concealed nervousness earlier in the week, she was now assuming the cynicism of the shoot-weary vet. She was a quick learner; I imagined she'd go far if she chose to. I noticed that Toddy, who was normally never more than five paces from Kevin, was nowhere to be seen. I asked Yasmin where she was.

'Oh, that was awful. Kevin banned her from the set. She'd left her mobile on and it rang during a take.'

'That's not very Toddy.' I was genuinely incredulous.

'I know. She's normally so professional.'

I amended my appraisal – cynicism tinged with irony: she'd definitely go far.

I thought about finding Toddy to see if she was bearing up – but only for a split second; I must have been over her. Instead I settled back to enjoy the action. It was Joe's and Rebecca's finale from the Bull/Shirer script – the one that ended thus:

Jane laughs at her date's mischievous sense of humour.

JANE: That's amazing, Doug. Excuse me while I powder my nose, and then you can tell me more about your fascinating work.

It had made me wince when I wrote it. To watch it being played out in front of a full crew was truly humiliating. Rebecca was having problems with her character's motivation (and who could blame her?). After a few limp attempts she pulled up.

'I'm sorry, everyone,' she said. 'It's this line.'

That would be my department, I thought, and I hid my face in my hands. So did Joe, but in his case it was histrionic exasperation rather than painful embarrassment.

'It's the "powder my nose" bit,' Rebecca went on, ignoring Joe's audible groan. 'Who says that apart from my mum?'

Kevin, clearly ready to stand as president, secretary and treasurer of the Rebecca Richards fan club, did a very un-French thing and agreed with her. 'That poxy line has been bothering me as well, babe. Let's get the writer to sort it.'

Seeing Kevin and Rebecca cosying up was too much for Joe and he snapped, 'Fuck the rewrites, guys. There's nothing wrong with the line. Face it, Rebecca, every time you screw up you blame the writers.'

I think he was siding with me but, since I wasn't siding with me on this particular bit of wordsmithing, it did nothing to boost my self-esteem.

'That's not fair, Joe,' said Rebecca. Not much of a riposte, but true.

'Not fair? You're so goddamn wooden they yell out "Timber!" when you walk onto a set. . . .' He paused for a laugh, which wasn't forthcoming, and it gave Kevin a chance to step in.

'Joe, mate,' he said, 'I think you should cool it and leave the directing to me.'

'Directing? That's another worry,' said Joe. 'Did I tell you I had a call from John McTiernan? He's got some mind-blowing ideas for *BM II*. Anyway, let's get on with this fucking scene, that's if Rebecca is up to it. No wonder they're burying her in a six-car pile-up next season.'

That was news to everyone, and it obviously wasn't the way Rebecca and her publicists had planned to announce her departure from one of TV's hottest shows. She ran from the studio as fast as her fuck-me pumps would allow. Director, cast and crew glared at Joe as he flashed an if-you-can't-stand-the-heat smirk. Even his manager, his PA and the usually simpering Greta Bastendorff looked disappointed.

My track record in averting walkouts had been 100 per cent to date, so I decided to follow her and coax her back.

CARRIE FULLER: My taxi driver was of the talkative variety. In the time it took to get to Hounslow he treated me to an opinion on asylum-seekers and foreign footballers (too many), bus and taxi lanes (too few), corporate fat cats (too fat by far) and hanging (too good for 'em). I nodded along politely but my brain tuned out. But he got my interest when he said, 'You seen Rebecca Richards in the paper today?'

'No, I didn't,' I replied.

'She should make her mind up what she wants to be. One minute she's laying a left on a defenceless customs woman, and the next she's acting like Mother bloody Teresa. What's she after – a Lonsdale Belt or the Nobel Peace Prize?'

He'd lost me and I said, 'I'm not with you.'

'Take a look for yourself,' he replied, feeding a copy of the *Daily Mirror* through the gap in the partition. I found the Rebecca story. At first I was drawn to the shot of her cuddling a sickly teenager. 'I see what you mean,' I said.

Then I saw it at the bottom of the page. It was only small but there was no misreading Greg's expression. It was the gaze he'd fixed me with the first time we'd met – the one that drilled straight through my eyes, melted its way through my heart and settled between my legs. The difference this time was that he'd dispensed with eye-to-eye contact and had gone straight for Rebecca's breasts. In that instant I knew the truth.

The taxi driver said, 'I can forgive her though. I mean, I wouldn't say no.'

'You're not the only one,' said Unborn.

VERONICA D: I came back from a restroom break. No Rebecca. 'Where's my world famous hairdo?' I asked Yasmin.

'God, it was awful,' she said. 'Joe destroyed her and she ran off. Greg's gone after her.'

'I'd better find her,' I said.

'Leave it to Greg,' Kevin said. 'He's good at this shit.'

'I'll give him fifteen minutes. I'm gonna call Freddie and tell her to get her ass out of that hotel and take some interest in what's left of her client's career.'

TODDY GLUCK: I was in the reception area feeling so, *so* alone. Nobody had ever spoken to me that way. All over a silly little mobile – such an overreaction. How dare he ban me from the set? Who was going to produce the ad now? It could produce itself for all I cared. What hurt far more than Kevin's unprofessionalism was

Greg's indifference. If our relationship had meant anything at all, then surely he would have been straight out to comfort me.

You can imagine my devastation when Rebecca appeared in floods of tears (such a prima) and seconds later Greg popped up and put his arm around her. He was totally oblivious to me sitting only feet away.

GREG FULLER: 'I'm so sorry we had to see that, Rebecca,' I said. 'It was vile and Joe only demeaned himself, not you.' She didn't say anything but just cried. I looked up and saw the paparazzi through the glass doors leading to the street. They could sense a wobbly celebrity lip like sharks scent blood, and they were aiming their lenses at her within seconds.

'Perhaps we should go to your dressing room,' I suggested.

TODDY GLUCK: I watched Greg lead her away and I fell apart.

But I'm strong and within minutes I'd pulled myself together. Now I was simply angry. I was fixing my mascara when Carrie turned up. The security men wouldn't let her in. Why would they? She was frumpy and pregnant – hardly like a film person.

Then it hit me. I'd just found out what a callous, shallow bastard Greg was – it was about time she did too. I got up and went to the door. I put on my best smile, opened the door and said, 'Carrie, what a wonderful surprise.'

CARRIE FULLER: The picture was acid-etched on my mind. I knew that if we ever managed to save our marriage (in between forging a lasting peace in the Middle East and other impossible ambitions), the image wouldn't go away. It would resurface every time he told me he had to go to a 'boring work dinner', one that he 'couldn't possibly get out of'.

Security wouldn't let me in and I was relieved – it gave me an excuse to turn around and go home. Greg didn't deserve my help and I didn't deserve a public humiliation. But the door opened and

Toddy Gluck appeared wearing Ralph Lauren and a collagen-enhanced smile.

'You look absolutely stunning,' she trilled. 'No one would believe you were about to have a baby.'

Maybe it was the Cameron Diaz effect of the mud bath, or perhaps Toddy was every bit as insincere as I'd always assumed her to be.

'What brings you to Hounslow?' she said as she led me in.

'I've got some work Greg needs from home.'

'He'll be thrilled that you're here. He's in a meeting. Just down there.' She pointed along a corridor. 'Turn left at the end and it's the last door. Go on in and see him.'

'It's OK,' I said, 'I'll wait till he's finished.'

'Don't be silly. It's not important, and you know how deathly meetings are.' She gave me a gentle shove towards the corridor.

Moments later I was standing outside a door marked with a star above a strip of card printed with *her* name. I can't go in there, I thought. Picture it: hotshot creative director, impossibly desirable star *that he is almost certainly screwing*, plus other unspecified film types discussing crucial creative issues in star's dressing room; hotshot creative director's swollen-ankled wife-cum-messenger standing in doorway with a tatty brown envelope. Bye-bye, self-esteem.

Toddy must have sensed my discomfort because she appeared at my shoulder like a designer ghost and knocked on the door.

No reply.

'I'll wait till he's finished,' I said again.

'Don't be silly,' she said, pushing the door open.

TODDY GLUCK: I couldn't believe it. I'd thought he'd just be comforting her, dabbing her eyes or whatever. I only wanted to embarrass him. I wasn't prepared for what I saw and it felt like a knife piercing my heart.

CARRIE FULLER: Greg had his back to me and his trousers around his ankles. Rebecca was on her knees in her fetish dress, her face buried between his legs. Maybe Toddy had greater powers of empathy than I'd credited her with, because she slumped to the floor in a faint. The sound broke Greg's concentration and he looked round. His face drained of its flush and his mouth gulped guppy-style for air or words or both. Rebecca, though, maintained her focus like a pro and her head kept up its rhythmic bobbing. I turned and fled. I crashed through a fire door and found myself in a car park.

What stopped me from going into premature labour there and then will be the subject of medical debate for years to come.

twenty-one:

cream horn, bill clinton, meat cleaver

NORMAN THE COOK: Rebecca came out to the truck but she didn't say anything. She helped herself to a coffee and a cake. Then she sat herself down at a table and started to read a bunch of papers she'd brought with her. You never see stars on their own. For them, alone means having an agent, a lawyer, a masseur and probably the masseur's lawyer for company.

'Look at the state of her makeup,' said Wendy. 'Something's up with her, Norm. I'll bet Joe Shirer has been giving her grief. Shall I have a word?'

'No, leave her be,' I said. I know when a bird needs to be alone with her thoughts and a cream horn.

Ten minutes later a woman appeared – a pretty thing in her late thirties with a bun in the oven. She clocked Rebecca and froze. There was something mad-eyed about her. Hey up, I thought, a bunny-boiler – either she's after an autograph or she wants to take Rebecca home and bury her under the floorboards. There was no way of telling so I reached for my cleaver – better safe than landed in another Lennon assassination-type balls-up.

CARRIE FULLER: I couldn't understand what I was seeing: same dress, same legendary hairdo, but she was stuffing her mouth with a cream bun rather than Greg's genitals. Either what I'd witnessed in the dressing room was a deranged hallucination, or this was. I felt a wave of dizziness wash over me. I was going to keel over like Toddy. Rebecca Richards was at my side in a flash and I collapsed onto her. I heard her shout, 'Norman, water. Quick!'

GREG FULLER: What can I say? Guilty as charged. I'm a cunt, your honour.

The events as they happened.

I took Rebecca to her dressing room, where I sat her down and fed her tissues. She was racked with sobs and I figured it must be more than Joe's cheap shots – to say she'd had a duff week was an understatement. At that stage I felt sorry for her. I wasn't thinking lustful thoughts. Honestly I wasn't.

I knelt down and put my hands on her shoulders. I may have said, 'There, there,' or, 'Go on, have a good cry,' or something equally platitudinous. Whatever, it had an effect, because she slumped onto me and sobbed into my shoulder.

I have to confess that as her tits were pressing into me the thought did cross my mind.

Eventually the sobs turned into sniffs and she said, 'You've been really kind. Thank you.'

Her hair was collapsing and her makeup had turned into a Jackson Pollock, but she still looked beautiful. That apart, there is nothing else I can say in mitigation, m'lud.

I leaned into her and she pushed me away so hard that I fell backwards onto my arse.

'What the hell are you doing?' she snapped.

I thought that was obvious. I was attempting to kiss her.

'Jesus,' she continued, 'I can't believe you tried to do that.'

Neither can I, I thought, as I watched her leave the room.

YASMIN FISH: We were waiting for Greg to reappear with Rebecca.

'This is boring, innit?' said Sonia.

'Why don't you go and chat up Kevin?' I suggested. 'You seemed to be getting on OK with him earlier.'

'No, he might be a good career move, but it'd be like blowing ET. I reckon I'll give Greg a test drive. Where is he?'

'He went after Rebecca.'

'I'll see if I can help him. I'll show him my sensitive side and give her a cuddle. We'll look like latex lesbo twins. If that doesn't give him a hard-on he must be dead.'

As she walked off in her rubber dress, I thought she made Bridget Farmer look like a nun.

GREG FULLER: I was still on the floor when I saw Rebecca return out of the corner of my eye – well, it was her dressing room, and if anyone should have left, it should have been me.

But when I looked up I saw Sonia.

'You OK?' she asked.

'Fine,' I said, 'just a trip.'

She helped me to my feet and I sat down in the chair – I wasn't ready to face the world.

'Where's Rebecca?' she asked.

'I've no idea.'

Sonia scanned the room. 'Funny this, innit?'

'How do you mean?' I asked.

'Being here in her dressing room, me being her double.'

She reached for a hanger draped with the dress that Rebecca had worn to work and held it against herself. 'Do you think I look like her?'

'If you didn't you wouldn't have the job,' I said.

She sashayed around the room, modelling the dress. 'So if we were doing it would you be thinking of me or her?'

I didn't answer. At that moment I was only 80 per cent certain she was coming on to me. Seconds later that rose to 100 per cent. She put down the dress and planted herself on my lap. 'I can't,' I said.

'Course you can, Malcolm,' she replied before kissing me.

My token resistance ended when she dropped to her knees and unzipped me. It wasn't quite in the Toddy league, but it was far better than her Indian head massage.

CARRIE FULLER: Rebecca Richards walked me to a table and sat me down. When the guy in the catering truck brought me a cup of water she told him to get a doctor.

'Please don't,' I said. 'I'm fine, honestly. Just let me sit for a minute.'

I watched the cook walk back to his truck and I wondered why he was carrying a meat cleaver – emergency caesarean section? Then Rebecca asked me, 'When's your baby due?'

'Not for another three . . .' I stopped and thought, why am I having this conversation? Wasn't there something a touch more pressing to discuss?

'I just saw you in your dressing room,' I said.

'I was in there ten or fifteen minutes ago.'

'No, two or three minutes ago. You were on your knees giving my husband a blowjob.'

'Excuse me?'

I was angry now. 'You can stop acting. We're not in front of a camera. I *saw* you. You were in that dress, on your fucking knees, giving my . . .'

I couldn't finish and I started to cry. The cook was watching from his truck. He picked up his cleaver but Rebecca raised her hand to him. Then she said, 'Look, I've no idea who your husband is, but I was *not* giving him a blowjob.'

As denials went it qualified as brazen. Maybe I was going mad. Norman's hand twitching over his cleaver suggested I wasn't the only one who thought so.

'But the dress, the hair,' I said. 'It was you.'

'It could have been my body double.'

'Your . . .'

'I have a double. She was hired when I had the allergy.'

'But she looked exactly like you.'

'She's my double. She's supposed to. Did you see her face?'

Now that I thought about it, I hadn't – it had been hidden somewhere it had no business being hidden.

'No, I didn't.'

'There you go,' said Rebecca Richards. 'If you'd seen her face you'd have known. She's only got my figure and hair.'

'But . . .'

'I promise you it wasn't me.'

'This is too weird. . . . You must think I'm mad. . . . I am so sorry. . . . Accusing you like that.'

'I don't think you're mad at all. I think you're a woman who's being cheated on. Believe me, I know what that's like.'

Then Rebecca Richards, reputedly one of Hollywood's flakier, more self-absorbed and, by recent accounts, violent actresses, put her arms around me and I sank into her embrace.

GREG FULLER: I could claim that, being oral, it didn't count (the Bill Clinton defence, which I'm surprised he didn't try to write into the constitution – the Sixty-ninth Amendment). I could, but I won't.

CARRIE FULLER: She gave me a tissue and, as I dried my eyes I said, 'I'm sorry about that.'

'Stop it. If you can't cry now, when can you? Anyway, you're not the only one. I've been at it myself this afternoon, and I think you have far more right to be upset. Look, I've been AWOL for so long they'll be sending out the tracker dogs. I'd better get back. Is there anything I can get you before I go?'

'No, you go. I'll be all right,' I lied.

'OK, I'd better go. I'd sit here for a bit longer, if I were you. I'll make sure Norman looks after you. Hey, do you need transport? I've got a limo hanging around.'

'No thanks,' I said, 'I can take a cab.'

As she stood up, she picked up a sheaf of A4 paper from the table and clutched it to her chest. 'I'll say goodbye then,' she said. 'I hope you're going to be OK.'

I wasn't listening to her, though. I was too busy staring at the title on the top sheet.

GREG FULLER: After Carrie fled I tapped Sonia on the shoulder. She looked up, her mouth still full. 'We've got company,' I said. I pulled out and zipped up. I walked to the door and looked down at Toddy. She stirred. Good, I thought, she isn't dead. Rebecca's hairdresser arrived and not unreasonably asked, 'What the hell's going on?'

'Oh, Toddy's just exhausted,' I replied. 'Would you mind looking after her? There's something I've got to do.'

CARRIE FULLER: 'Where did you get that?' I asked.

'This? Someone left it in the studio. I only picked it up because it's got my name on it.' She held it up and pointed to *Rebecca* on the cover sheet. 'I had some time to kill, so I started to read it. I'd love to know who wrote it.'

'I did,' I said.

'You are kidding,' she squealed. 'You're a writer? This is fucking brilliant – the best thing I've read in ages.'

'I'm not a writer and it's not brilliant. It's rubbish.'

'Who told you that?'

'My husband as it happens.'

'Jesus, who is this guy?'

'The man who wrote the commercial you're appearing in. I'm Carrie Fuller, Greg's wife.'

'How could I have not worked that out?' she said.

Bang on cue Greg appeared at the fire door. He stopped and looked at me. I turned and fled. I heard Rebecca call after me: 'Don't you want your screenplay?' I did want it, but I kept on going.

GREG FULLER: I looked at the two of them together. Coward that I've always been, I wanted to go straight back inside. I didn't, though. I set off after Carrie, but Rebecca strode towards me and grabbed my arm. 'I wouldn't,' she said through gritted teeth. 'She's in the mood to kill you and I'm in the mood to hold you down while she does it.'

Rebecca was still clutching my arm as my wife disappeared from view. I thought then that, in terms of crap happening, the barrel had been scraped spotless.

I was wrong. There was still one big turd lurking at the bottom.

twenty-two:

lesblans, christians, cops

TIM LELYVELDT: In Hollywood, Joe's star was burning white-hot while Rebecca's was being sucked into the black hole that had already claimed Demi, Melanie, Pee-Wee and two sons of Martin Sheen. In career terms I was working for the right guy. In human terms I couldn't have got it more wrong.

Rebecca finally reappeared on the set, and I marvelled again at her resilience. Morton too. 'Jesus, she's armour-fucking-plated,' he gasped. He only swore when he was impressed.

VERONICA D: 'What the hell's been going on?' I asked her.

'Quite a lot. I've fended off a pass, watched a marriage explode and read one of the best scripts ever. Oh, and I managed to fit in a coffee and a cream cake.'

'Tell me, tell me.'

'Later. Just get on with my hair. And call makeup over. My face must look like a train wreck.'

'I gotta tell you I called Freddie.'

'Why the hell did you do that?'

'Whatever she thinks of you, she should be here, not at the hotel lining up fresh clients. You're still paying her, ain't you?'

'Not for much longer. It's time for a fresh start. I'm going to fire her when this job's over.'

TISH WILKIE: Veronica was twiddling with Rebecca's hair and I thought, *at last*. Everyone had been going mad, and finding the right moment to resign had been impossible. I decided to do it before they started shooting. I set off towards her, but when I was twenty feet away one of Jerry Springer's brilliant Final Thoughts literally came flooding back to me. He'd said that if people had 'issues' they had to be 'honest' or they'd never achieve 'closure'.

My letter was *total* lies. My mum was as fit as a fiddle. There was nothing else for it. I'd have to rewrite it. I went to the shops for a new pad.

TIM LELYVELDT: Rebecca did the scene she'd struggled with earlier in two takes. She stormed through the next two set-ups and it looked as if we might actually wrap early. Joe was sinking. He couldn't stomach that she and French were connecting. He might have treated him with disdain all week, but French was *his* director. Joe believed that he'd given him his break on *Body Matter*. The truth was that French was involved with *BM* when Josh Hartnett was slated for the lead – six months before Joe was signed. But never underestimate a star's propensity to demand rewrites to history as if it were just another movie script.

He grabbed me between takes and said, 'Where the fuck is Stryker? I *need* him.'

I'd managed to reach his shrink and persuade him to give up his R&R. He was on his way (along with his wife, four kids and their nanny. That had been the price of sanity: first-class tickets and ten nights at the Dorchester for the Queenan family).

'Don't worry, Joe. I'm sure he'll be here late tonight or early tomorrow,' I said.

He needn't have fretted, though, because an even better saviour was riding into view, this one a card-carrying Christian.

BOB BULL: Roger Knopf, ever punctual, turned up at bang on five.

'This had better not take long,' he told me as I greeted him. 'I've got the weekly sales review at six, and Rhoda and I are hosting our Bible group tonight. I will not be late for that.'

'We'll be in and out in a jiffy,' I said. 'It's just a quick schmooze with the stars – phenomenal talents but fragile egos. They need to feel the love of us senior bods. Joe Shirer is extremely keen to meet you. I think you'll be impressed with him. His commitment is monumental.'

'Let's meet the guy then,' said Roger.

TIM LELYVELDT: I looked at Bull with his boss and said to Morton, 'Looks like you're on. Are you psyched?'

'I guess,' he replied. 'Are you?'

'You're not dragging me into this. I'm just the assistant.'

'Oh, I'll do the talking, but I need some moral support.'

Morton Newman was Hollywood to the core, but some things made even him squeamish.

We went up and introduced ourselves. Morton didn't waste any time in getting to the point.

'Joe is looking forward very much to meeting you, Roger. He has been knocked out by the style of your operation. He is delighted to be endorsing a brand that stands for leading-edge technology as well as a refreshing moral tolerance.'

Knopf looked confused. Moral tolerance? He looked the kind of guy who'd lynch his own son if he turned out to like soft rock. The target was now in sight and Morton picked up momentum. 'The way you guys dealt with the Rebecca revelation was beautiful. It's an attitude that shows the way for other multinationals.'

'Excuse me?' said Knopf, giving us our confirmation that Bull hadn't shared all of the week's events with his CEO.

'The pornographic movie that Rebecca appeared in,' explained Morton. 'Joe was blown away when you guys didn't do the usual corporate knee-jerk and terminate her.'

As the blood drained from Bull's face, Knopf turned to him and said, 'Bob, please tell me what in God's name this man is talking about.'

Morton stood back and warmed his hands on the bonfire he'd lit. I went to inform Joe that the target had been destroyed.

YASMIN FISH: 'They can't do this,' I said to the little spark.

'It stinks, doesn't it?'

'Can't we do something?'

'We could down tools and strike, but I don't think they'd give a toss. It's not like they can use anything that we've shot now, so they'll probably be sending us home early anyway.'

'Well, I'm going to do something,' I said.

I went to find Greg. He was talking to Kevin French and the stupid clients, so I hung around until he was finished. He walked off and I ran behind him.

'This is terrible, Greg. They can't just fire her, can they? How can we finish the ad?'

'We can't finish it without Kevin French either,' he said.

'What do you mean?'

'He's washed his hands of us, Yasmin. I won't be able to talk him out of it this time.'

'What are you going to do?'

'Write a new script tonight and find some poor mug to direct it tomorrow. What else can I do?'

'You could tell Blackstock you're not going to work for them any more – you know, on principle.'

'This is advertising. We don't do those.'

TIM LELYVELDT: Magnanimous in victory. That was Joe. Now that he'd destroyed Rebecca he could act as if he gave a shit and he really laid it on: how unfair it was, how she was strong, she'd bounce back, yadda, yadda, yadda – you don't need me to tell you. We lapped it up as if we were paid to, which, of course, we were.

Kevin burst into the dressing room and launched into Joe before he could say anything.

'Don't insult my fucking intelligence by denying it, Joe, because I know what you've done. These cunts might be climbing your arse like there're condos up there,' he said, gesturing at us, 'but I've had enough. I'm off this job.'

He turned to go and Joe said, 'Leave now and you can forget *BM II*.'

'I hear you, Joe, so why am I still walking?' he said just before he slammed the door.

'Who needs him?' said Danton. 'McTiernan is the Boss.'

Joe was silent. The only call he'd had from John McTiernan had been in his dreams.

Greta had sat quietly on the bed and watched. Joe had worked hard to make sure she hadn't seen the shit he'd pulled but, though she was only seventeen, she was growing up fast.

VERONICA D: Rebecca's dressing room was like a morgue. Despite my 911 to Freddie, the bitch hadn't shown. Tish for once had nothing to say, and packed up Rebecca's things as if they were infected with Ebola. Rebecca was silent – not upset, just silent. There was a knock on the door and I went to answer it: Greta.

'You've got a nerve,' I said to her, but Rebecca was behind me and stopped me going on. The pair of them sat on the sofa and Rebecca put her arm around her. You could push this sainthood thing too far, honey, I was thinking. Just hit the bitch.

'I feel terrible about what's happened,' Greta said.

'Well, don't,' said Rebecca, and I was thinking, yes, do feel terrible, you vicious Lolita. You stole her man and you watched while he destroyed her – if you've got any conscience at all, you should be feeling fucking suicidal. 'This is my fault, Greta,' Rebecca went on. 'Just don't make my mistakes.'

Before she left, Greta came out with what she'd really wanted to talk about. 'Rebecca, you know the rumours about Joe's . . .' She paused to let Rebecca fill in the blank. 'He's sure you started them.'

'Whatever you think of me, I'd never stoop to that.' Greta looked at her for a hint of a lie. 'I swear, Greta.'

'Joe will never believe you, but I think I do.' She stood up to go but there was something else she wanted to say. 'You were still with him when he made *Body Matter*. I've heard gossip. It's probably nothing but . . .'

'You're wondering if Joe did his own stunts?'

Greta nodded.

'I can't lie to you. He didn't.'

Greta may have been elfin sweet, but at that moment she looked ready to murder. Rebecca put her hand on her shoulder and said, 'But please, Greta, don't be too hard on him.'

Now that was a nice touch.

TYRONE EDWARDS: The door is the front line in the Security and Personal Safety Facilitating game. My body's been a coiled spring the whole afternoon. It's been quiet except for a pregnant bird turning up who I thought might not be pregnant – that bump could've been a bomb. Then we get the buzz that Extra-large Tits and Rizlas has got the boot. We're called to the car park to make sure her limo ain't mobbed.

We get there and I'm waiting for her to come out. I'm her personal escort but I ain't excited. I'm a pro and I'm keeping a lid on my emotions. But when she appears I can't stop myself.

'I gotta tell you I seen you at the airport,' I say to her. 'Them bastards was giving you wicked grief. I been through that shit and it ain't cool. I got big respect for the way you dealt with them.'

And then Donkey Dick appears in the door and I panic.

TIM LELYVELDT: Joe insisted on saying goodbye to her. He was hoping she'd lose it and fly at him. Then he could rise above it and he wouldn't even need to say, 'I told you she was fucked up.' It didn't go to plan, though.

TYRONE EDWARDS: She clocks Donkey Dick and then she turns to me. I'm about to run but she takes my hand and says, 'Thank you, that's very sweet. I want you to have something.'

I should get the fuck out of there but I'm thinking, what's she gonna give you, Tyrone, so I stay put. She pulls this big blue sparkler off her finger. She puts it in my hand and it weighs a ton.

'I can't take that,' but I'm thinking, What the fuck you say that for, Tyrone?

'Please, it isn't anything much,' she says. 'Just a stupid present from some schmuck whose name I can't even remember.'

So I close my hand around it and I say, 'Thank you,' but she's in the limo and out of there. It's time for me to scarper, too.

TIM LELYVELDT: That was too much for Joe and he went critical. He recognised the black guy before I did. 'That's the motherfucker that hijacked my limo last night,' he screamed.

TYRONE EDWARDS: I set off like I've got a rocket up my arse. I get to the gates but they're almost closed. I start to climb them but two of Hakkan's boys grab me and pull me down. Ex-pigs. Been giving me the eye all day. Hakkan is staring at me and I know he's thinking, don't do this to me, man, and I'm thinking I didn't do nothing and for once it's the gospel truth. I can hear Donkey Dick shouting, 'I want that mother arrested.'

GREG FULLER: I came outside when I heard Joe having his shitfit. By the time I got there the police were shoving a little black guy into the back of a car. It took me a moment to work out he was the one who'd shunted me at Hyde Park Corner. My first instinct was to tell the police to add leaving the scene of an accident to the charge sheet, but I stopped myself. Like me, the poor sod appeared to have enough on his plate.

VERONICA D: As soon as we'd got Rebecca into her suite, Tish fled. Rebecca slumped onto the sofa and checked her messages.

'You ain't gonna want to hear it,' I said, 'but this shit is gonna fill tomorrow's papers. Like it or not, I think you'd better make up with Freddie. You'll need her help.'

'Problem there,' she said putting the phone down. 'Freddie's on her way to Heathrow. She left a message – her husband's in hospital. Suspected heart attack.'

'My ass. He's an agent too, ain't he? The only problem with his heart will be when the doctors try to find it. I hate to bring up *Titanic* at a time like this, but you know what they say about rats and sinking ships.'

Rebecca ignored me and said, 'What's that?' She pointed at a letter that was sliding under the door. She picked it up and sat down to read it. After a minute she burst out laughing.

'What is it?' I asked.

She couldn't stop laughing, though, and she handed it to me.

Dear ~~Ms Richards~~ Rebecca,

It is so hard to find the right words but I must be totally honest for both our sakes. When I came to work for you I felt that we 'clicked' instantly. As we grew to know each other ~~deeply~~ quite well over the last two and a half weeks, I felt that you weren't only my 'boss' but also my ~~'friend'~~ 'employer'.

However, when I found out about your ~~pornographic sex~~ ~~blue~~ 'adult' film everything changed. This has nothing to do with 'judging' you or anything like that. I completely and totally 1000 per cent respect your choices even if they have involved things that narrow-minded people might call ~~perverted~~ ~~kinky~~ ~~weird~~ unusual.

But knowing that you have 'feelings' towards women of the same sex means that I can no longer work for you. Though I totally have nothing against so-called 'lesbians', knowing that you might be having 'thoughts' would make me worry that you might misunderstand any displays of 'normal' affection from me. The all-important bond of trust between 'assistant' and 'star' would be broken and our relationship would be literally impossible.

I am prepared to carry on working for you until you can find a replacement, though to avoid 'misunderstandings' it might be better if we kept our dealings to phone calls and fax wherever possible.

I hope you are not too upset when you read this.

Yours ~~affectionately sincerely~~ faithfully,

Tish Wilkie

PS – Just a thought. To avoid this situation arising again in the future, perhaps it would be better if your next assistant was a man.

PPS – I'd hate you to think that I'm one of those homophobic people because I am totally not. I have a boxed set of Ellen videos and some of my best friends are literally 'gay'.

'Well, honey, it looks like we're on our own,' I said when I'd finished.

'You're sticking around, Veronica?'

'You might never act again, Becca, but you'll still need someone to fix your hair.'

TISH WILKIE: I *so* wanted to deliver the letter by hand and in person, but I had an appointment and I was late. I was meeting a journalist from the *Daily Mail*. I know what you're thinking: kiss-and-tell – tacky, tacky, tacky. But it was *so* not like that. Definitely, positively not *kiss*-and-tell anyway.

Let me explain. I was, like, 200 per cent comfortable with

Rebecca's 'sexuality'. What she did 'in bed' was literally her choice. As long as she didn't rub it in people's faces (and by 'it' I don't mean 'it'). I was talking to the newspaper for *her* sake. Someone had to put her side of the story. Someone who'd been privy to her most intimate secrets (by 'intimate', of course, I don't mean '*intimate*'). As her *Personal* Assistant of *over* two weeks I felt it was my responsibility to make sure at least one paper didn't write horrid things about her. Since I was literally leaving her in the lurch, it was the absolute least I could do.

The journalist had promised not to write anything sleazy. I had her word on that and I trusted her.

And isn't trust the most important thing of all?

GREG FULLER: I was one of the last people to leave the studio that night, mostly because I had nowhere else to go. As I walked to my taxi, something on the ground caught my eye. I looked down at a scrap of paper resting on a drain grate. It looked familiar and I picked it up. It was half a script for a furniture chain called Galaxy of Suites. The rest of the campaign, I presumed, was drifting gently towards some west London sewage farm.

twenty-three:

straw donkey, suntans, lola's best push-up bra

GREG FULLER: On Friday morning I recalled a comment I'd made to Yasmin the afternoon before – something about having to find a mug to direct the new commercial. I remembered it just before I called action on the first set-up of the day. I was making my directorial debut, shooting a modest (very modest) script that I'd been up slightly more than half the night writing.

The new ad wasn't, as Bob Bull might have had it, an envelope-pusher. It was a workmanlike solution to a particularly sticky problem.

OK, hands up, I admit it was unmitigated bollocks that made my 'powder my nose' effort read like Tom Stoppard.

Joe loved it, though. Well, it featured him at the wheel of an Electric Candy Blue Dodge Viper, and there was no place he'd sooner be. His new co-star, Greta Bastendorff, seemed less enamoured. Perhaps, for jailbait, she had particularly well-honed critical faculties. Alternatively it could have been because she was required to look adoringly at Joe and mouth huskily, 'I feel so safe with you', and I'm not sure that she did any longer.

My client's reaction should have compensated for Greta's misgivings. 'This is state-of-the-art writing, Greg. It's a darn shame we couldn't have got to this sooner instead of wasting dollars on that kinky stuff,' he boomed. This, however, merely confirmed my original opinion of it.

In case you were thinking that Bob Bull had gone all darn American on me, he hadn't. Roger Knopf was there with sleeves rolled up, proving he could get down and dirty in the ad factory. Bob was in attendance but in a menial capacity. And, after the rock 'n' roll excesses of his wardrobe that week, it was comforting to see him in a grey suit again. I suspected that the coffees he fetched for his CEO would be among his final duties at Blackstock. Nothing to gloat over, though – I was certain that when I announced the wrap at the end of the day Fuller Scheidt would be free to tout for a new tyre account.

YASMIN FISH: Everything was different. The extras were gone and the chippies were demolishing the set. The sports car had been parked against a huge plain blue background.

'What's going on?' I asked the little spark.

'Blue screen, love,' he said.

'What's that?'

'They're shooting Joe in the car against the blue screen, and then they magic in a new background in post.'

'What new background?'

'That's the funny bit. They spend fuck knows how much to fly Shirer six thousand miles to Britain, and then they try to make it look like he never left LA. It's going to be the Hollywood Hills.'

'That's mad,' I said.

'No, that's advertising.'

Toddy came up and shoved the new script at me. 'Forty copies, please. One for every crew member.'

As she walked off I read it. One line in I couldn't stop myself saying out loud, 'They can't shoot this. It's rubbish.'

---

fuller scheidt advertising / tv script

CLIENT	BLACKSTOCK TYRES	AC. GROUP HALLEY	
PRODUCT	CORPORATE	**CR TEAM** GREG FULLER	
JOB No.	BS-001		
TITLE	SAFE DRIVING	**PRODUCER** TODDY GLUCK	
LENGTH	30"	**DRAFT No.** 1	

Open on JOE SHIRER at the wheel of a gleaming Dodge Viper. At his side sits GRETA BASTENDORFF. Behind them we see the Hollywood Hills.

    JOE: Shall we hit the road?
  GRETA: Ready when you are, darling.

Joe turns the key and we hear the throaty roar of the Viper's V8 engine. We watch Joe and Greta through the windscreen as he takes the car onto the open road.

    VO: Stars like Joe Shirer and Greta Bastendorff are used
          to protection, twenty-four/seven. But sometimes they
          just want to escape and be footloose and carefree
          like any regular couple.

Joe expertly steers the car through hairpin bends.

    VO: Yet wherever his glamorous life takes him, the
          ultimate in protection is never more than a few feet
          away for Joe Shirer.

On my way to the copier I saw the little spark coiling up cable. He
was singing to himself. He'd been doing that all week. He'd take a
pop song and change the words to fit the mood – 'Living Doll' to
'Rubber Doll', that kind of thing. Now he was singing an old
Motown tune. I only knew it because it was one of my dad's
favourites. He wouldn't have liked the slight change to the title,
though – 'The Tracks of My Tyres'.

GREG FULLER: No longer banned from the set and very much
needed by the greenhorn director, Toddy was in her element. I'd
had to beg her to attend, of course. She wasn't going to let me off
the hook for the body-double incident so easily. But any hurt she
felt over catching me at it would have been counterbalanced by
Schadenfreude towards Carrie – I knew how Toddy's mind worked.
  Talking of doubles, Joe's demand for one of his very own had

been forgotten in the mayhem of the previous day. With a semblance of order now restored, he decided that he couldn't possibly act his way through thirty seconds of TV commercial without the assistance of a thespian twin.

I use the word *twin* in its loosest sense. Joe had reviewed the casting tapes at some length, and had rejected the models that actually looked like him – 'too skinny'. Let me state for the record that Joe had an excellent body – not muscle-bound, but sufficiently sculpted to be an adornment at any Beverly Hills pool party. He was a credit to his personal trainers. As far as he was concerned, though, they'd clearly stopped short of the ideal, and he'd gone for a guy who looked as if he possessed the bodies of both Sly and Arnie, which had somehow been welded together and then fed some steroids for good measure.

'Fuck, it's like looking in the mirror,' Joe gasped, as he scanned the wall of muscle upon muscle of his double. No one contradicted him – they were either catatonic with disbelief, or, like me, several miles past caring. I had no idea how the frame-filling shots of the double would cut together with those of the considerably leaner real thing, but, as I said, I didn't give a shit.

Compared to the four that had preceded it, it was an uneventful day. This was due in no small part to Toddy. It may have been a rotten script, but it still needed producing. She sank to the occasion and produced the hell out of it. Downtime entertainment was provided by the papers. All of them ran the story of Rebecca's dismissal. The *Mirror* beefed up their piece with exclusive and heavily censored stills from *Titanic*. I wondered how they'd acquired those. My favourite coverage, though, was in the *Mail*. They'd managed to sign up the only player with any real insight, who told it like it undoubtedly was beneath the sober headline, 'MY HELL AT THE HEART OF HOLLYWOOD'S SECRET LESBIAN PORN CONSPIRACY'.

Only a couple of things happened to disturb a bog-standard day of filmmaking. The first was when Lola the bounty hunter returned from the Spanish badlands.

NANCY STARK: When my flight touched down at Gatwick my whole body ached. Not from the aeroplane. I was flying business class and, since I'd only ever been on charters before, I was in heaven. No, I hurt thanks to Diego, the barman with the forearms. I'd often used the expression, shagged bandy, but I'd never known what it meant until then.

I got onto the Gatwick Express with my bags and headed back into London. It was time for Stage Two of Operation Three-piece Suite. I flipped open my phone and sent a text.

P+S. LANDED. ETA RENDEZVU 13.00 HRS. DONT B L8. N

Then I opened the *Mirror* and settled back to enjoy the pictures of Rebecca Richards getting it in more ways than even Dieter, Dirk and Diego could have dreamt up.

GREG FULLER: She arrived sporting a rich tan for only three days in the sun. She was also alone. We were in the middle of a set-up, but I called a ten-minute break and ran over to her.

'Lola, please tell me you're not empty-handed.'

'No, I brought you these,' she said. She reached into a carrier and pulled out a bottle of Spanish brandy and a small straw donkey. 'I thought the donkey would look sweet on the shelf next to all your awards.'

'Quit being cute. Where the fuck are they?'

'Paul and Shaun? They bumped into some producer they know on the way in and stopped for a chat.'

I hopped around on the spot for a couple of minutes until Piss and Shit appeared wearing holiday T-shirts, thirty-six-inch sombreros and deeper tans than even Lola had managed. I should have been overjoyed to see them, but actually I just wanted to push them to the ground and kick them about a bit.

'How much?' I said to Lola as they walked towards us.

'The full whack, I'm afraid – fifty per cent.'

'Bastards. No wonder they look so fucking smug,' I said.

Piss was carrying a black zip-up portfolio.

'Is that all their luggage from Spain?' I asked.

'No, they left the rest outside. That's their campaign. And however crap it is you'd better love it. It's your only hope.'

I greeted them and spun them a line about the whole thing being a huge mix-up. They had the good grace not to ask, 'And which bit of "You're fired" did we misunderstand?'

Then we went to the production office and it was down to business. Piss, always the front man, unzipped the folio and made the presentation. I didn't know how they'd managed to squeeze in a fishing trip because they'd done a heap of work. There were layouts for press ads, TV storyboards, radio scripts, in-store posters and what we know in the trade as shelf-wobblers (please, don't ask me to explain). They'd written jingles, put prices in eye-catching starbursts and come up with a snappy slogan – 'Sofa ahead of the rest'.

'Look,' squeaked Lola, 'there's a lovely model on that chesterfield.'

Yes, they even had the regulation blonde.

It was the crassest advertising I'd seen since, well, since I'd last read my new Blackstock script.

'Fantastic, guys, top quality as usual,' I said. 'Do you think you can have it licked into shape by Monday?'

'No problem,' Piss assured me. 'We'll head for the office now and work on it through the weekend.'

The small production office we were in was windowless and the air-conditioning was on the blink. It was stiflingly hot. As they packed up and prepared to leave, I looked at Shit. He was perspiring. He'd always been a naturally sweaty git so this wasn't particularly interesting in itself. But I couldn't help noticing the rivulets that were running down his neck, leaving orange stains on his white Marbella T-shirt.

Stop it, Greg, I told myself. You've got your campaign now – don't even go there.

NANCY STARK: I didn't once say that Paul and Shaun were definitely in Spain, did I? I said that I *thought* they were there and it was true, I did. When Olly del Monte e-mailed the tip to me I passed it on to Greg and, as far as I was concerned, at that point that's where they were.

Then on the Tuesday morning Paul called me. He and Shaun had been away for a long weekend hill-walking in Derbyshire. Most of Greg's creative teams spent their weekends in bed, on drugs or, more likely, both. Paul and Shaun walked up hills. I told you they didn't fit in. Paul had just got home and had listened to the messages I'd left him. I told him that Greg wanted them back and was prepared to prove it to the tune of a twenty-five per cent pay hike. Paul mumbled, 'Dunno, Nancy. I'll have to talk to Shaun,' but I could tell he was chuffed and they'd come back. I was about to pick up the phone and put Greg out of his misery when he called me. Before I could say a word he was telling me that Max was on his case – the only way I could shut him up was to tell him that I was already on my way to Spain. He told me to get off my arse and catch a plane before Max did an office walkabout and caught me at my desk.

OK, you're the boss, I thought, I will.

I called Paul and asked him how he would like it if I could turn a twenty-five per cent pay rise into fifty. When he'd picked himself up off the floor I gave him his orders.

'Lie low until Friday. Don't answer the phone. Don't even come out of your front doors to collect the milk. Just sit tight and write the biggest, juiciest Universe of Sofas campaign ever. Oh, and don't try to call me – I'll be getting a bit of sun.'

All right, so I was dishonest but who lost out? Greg got his campaign, Paul and Shaun got an obscene pay rise and I got a bit of a holiday – which I deserved because I worked so bloody hard *and* covered Greg's arse *and* told God knows how many lies for him. Why am I defending myself? This isn't a court of law.

Anyway, you can't knock a scam when it works so brilliantly, can you? I can hear the judge now: 'You are a cheeky monkey, Nancy Stark. I especially enjoyed the little touch of buying the souvenir T-shirts and novelty sombreros for the lads to wear at the meeting. You nearly blew it with the fake tan, though – you should have remembered what a sweaty so and so your accomplice was. Now run along and don't do it again.'

GREG FULLER: Piss and Shit left and I said to Lola, 'Aren't you going back to the office with them?'

'I'm knackered,' she said. 'This business travel shags you out, doesn't it? I'll never have a go at you and your imaginary jet lag again. I thought I'd hang out here for a bit and then go home. Anyway, bring me up to date.'

'Well, yesterday Rebecca –'

'Not with the shoot. I've got the papers for that. I want to know if you've sorted things out with Carrie.'

'Not exactly,' I said.

CARRIE FULLER: I was determined not to answer the phone on Friday. Greg left three pleading messages. He was very sorry, of course, and he said we had to talk. As far as I was concerned, though, any dialogue would take place through lawyers. I didn't want to speak to anyone. Unborn sensed my mood and refrained from giving me the benefit of his wisdom.

Nancy called after lunch. Her message went, 'Carrie, it's me. Greg told me what happened. Don't worry, I'm not going to make excuses for him. He's a stupid bastard and he doesn't deserve you. If you want me as a witness at the divorce/helper at the castration I'll be more than happy. I'm not joking for once. Anyway, if you need anything, call me. Any time. I'm thinking about you – bye.'

Ten minutes later the phone rang again. The machine cut in with Greg's taped voice: 'We're not here. You know what to do', followed by the tone. Then this: 'Hi, I don't know if you're in, Carrie, but, if you are, pick up ... OK, you're either out or you don't want to talk. I'll try you la –' I grabbed the receiver.

'Hi, don't hang up. How on earth did you get my number?'

'I'm a Hollywood star. I get whatever I want. Actually it was easy. I've still got my call sheet from the shoot. Your number's on it.'

'What can I do for you, Rebecca?'

'I was wondering what I could do for you.'

'Aren't you going back to the States now?'

'You heard, then.'

'I could hardly miss it – breakfast TV, every paper, even Radio Four. Was that really your PA in the *Mail*?'

'I haven't dared read that one yet.'

'You must be going through hell.'

'I've been dreading this ever since I made that film but, now it's happened, it's more a relief than anything. Anyway, my situation is nothing compared to yours. What you saw yesterday was hateful. How are you coping?'

We talked for nearly an hour about the bastard.

'He is more of a shit than I ever thought possible,' I summed up, 'and I've only seen the tip of the bloody iceberg.'

'Don't talk to me about icebergs.'

'Sorry, the thingy film, I was forgetting.'

'Let's change the subject. *Your* film.'

'Oh, that. I should have grabbed it off you yesterday.'

'I'm glad you didn't. Kevin French came to my hotel for dinner last night. I hope you don't mind but I showed it to him.'

'God, I'm so embarrassed.'

'Don't be. He loves it.'

'You're joking.'

'Look, he may be a Brit but he's Hollywood now, so it's imposs-ible to know whether he's genuine or full of crap. But I'll tell you verbatim what he told me: "Rebecca, I've *got* to shoot this fucking script."'

'You're joking,' I repeated limply.

'Don't let it go to your head. It's not all good news. He hates the title. He also said the third act is "a cow's arse".'

'I told you, it's rubbish,' I said.

'Carrie, there's no rubbish in what you've written. I may be Hollywood as well, but I'm not bullshitting you. This will sound really lame – I mean, it's what every pushy actress says to anyone with a part to cast – but Rebecca Edwards is so *me*. She even has my name, for God's sake. This is fate.'

Not fate, I thought, just coincidence.

Then she went off the line and I could hear muffled talking. She came back and said, 'I'm sorry, Carrie, got to go. You won't believe this but the police want to talk to me. I'll call you later. And remember, don't let the bastard get to you. You're bigger and more talented than he'll ever be.'

As I put the phone down, Unborn must have sensed my spirits lift and he muttered, 'Starfucker.'

DETECTIVE SERGEANT COLIN PARKIN, HOUNSLOW POLICE STATION:
'This interview is being recorded at two-thirty pm on Friday the twenty-fourth of May. I am questioning Tyrone Edwards of fourteen B Bunny Wailer House, the Bob Marley Estate, New Cross. Mr Edwards has waived his right to legal representation. Also present is Detective Constable Lisa Henneberry. . . . Tyrone, you're in a bit of a fix, aren't you?'

'I've explained a million times. Straight up, I ain't done nothing.'

'Of course you haven't. Let's just go through your statement again and see if we can iron out the wrinkles. You claim that on Wednesday night you and your girlfriend, Yvonne Garfield, were going about your business when you saw Joe Shirer and his party having some bother with a group of local youths.'

'That's right.'

'Next, after first making sure that your girlfriend was at a safe distance, you intervened and saved Mr Shirer from receiving a "proper kicking".'

'I got no argument with that.'

'After which you offered to drive Mr Shirer to the Chinese Elvis restaurant. However, you were delayed when the limousine became inadvertently stuck between width restriction posts.'

'Them limos is wider than they look, man.'

'So there's absolutely nothing in Mr Shirer's claim that you deliberately jammed his car in the gap and held him hostage while you waited for your accomplices to arrive.'

'How could I hold him hostage, man? It was just me and Yvonne and she wouldn't hurt a fly. Shirer had *six* guys with him.'

'All of whom were frightened and disoriented after becoming hopelessly lost in an unfamiliar part of London.'

'A bloody scary part as well, sir. There's more crack on that estate than on a builder's arse.'

'Lyrically put, Henneberry. Let's move on to the more serious matter: this ... I am now showing Mr Edwards a ring – a large single sapphire in a platinum setting.'

'I told you, she gave it to me.'

'Of course she did. This famous actress who didn't know you from a black Adam "*just gave*" you a bloody huge and extremely sparkly sapphire in a shiny platinum setting which happens to be worth ... what's the report say, Henneberry?'

'Rare Kashmir sapphire, three point four-one carats, platinum ...'

'Cut to the bottom line, please.'

'Value for insurance purposes, ninety-eight and a bit grand, sir.'

'*Ninety-eight grand*, Tyrone ... The clattering sound that's audible on the tape is Mr Edwards falling backwards off his chair. This was not, I repeat, *was not* caused by either DC Henneberry or myself laying so much as a finger on him. I will now halt the interview while Mr Edwards sorts himself out.'

GREG FULLER: The day's other highlight was the visit of Max with Mario Tigana, the superbly turned out, urbane, charismatic Italian CEO of Gruppo Tigana. Actually, he was short, inarticulate and, for an Italian, surprisingly scruffy, but he was the man who was about to dump serious wads into Max's and my bank accounts. The visit had been planned for weeks. When Max had first suggested it I'd thought it an excellent schmooze – impress suitor with exclusive peek at sexy London creative director hard at work supervising Hollywood director as latter shoots ultra-creative script with top international stars.

DETECTIVE SERGEANT COLIN PARKIN: 'I am resuming the interview with Tyrone Edwards. . . . Now, you still claim she gave you the ring?'

'Would I make something like that up, man?'

'Of course not. Happens all the time. Did Henneberry show you her diamond necklace with matching earrings? Landed on her doormat in a Jiffy Bag a couple of days ago. They were from Harrison Ford.'

'She just gave it to me, honest to fucking God.'

'For the record, Mr Edwards is now crossing himself repeatedly.'

'Anyway, I told you, me and Big Ti . . . me and Rebecca do know each other. Kind of. We met at the airport.'

'Ah, yes, you were on your way back from your little holiday in Jamaica. I'd love to have a root through your cases to see what charming examples of the local handicrafts you brought back, but I suppose it's a bit late for that now.'

'We're not getting anything here, Sarge. Can't we just give him a slap?'

'Patience, patience, we'll wear the bastard down yet.'

'She gave me the fucking ring, I swear. Ask her yourself.'

'Oh, don't worry, Tyrone. One of our finest is paying her a visit as we speak. Lucky bloody copper he is – he gets Rebecca Richards and I get a squirt like you.'

GREG FULLER: I'd never have said yes to Tigana's visit if I'd known the shoot would turn out so pear-shaped that the pears were close to suing for defamation.

Max knew the worst, but he felt it was too late to cancel. He didn't know how cheesy the new script was, but I wasn't too bothered about that. Mario's standards couldn't be that high, I thought – have you ever seen Italian TV advertising? Besides, he spoke piss-poor English and he'd be lucky to understand a word of what was going on.

When they arrived I pulled Max aside and told him that our Universe of Sofas prayers had been answered.

'You'd better not be bullshitting me, Greg.'

'I promise you, Paul and Shaun are back at the ranch working on it. I've seen the campaign. It's an absolute belter.'

'Big prices?'

'Fucking monolithic.'

'Starbursts?'

'Can't move for them.'

'Blonde?'

'There's one parked on every sofa.'

'Maybe this week won't be such a fiasco after all,' he sighed.

I sat Max and Mario at ringside in a couple of canvas chairs and got back to work. Ever the optimist, I was hoping that the fact I was a copywriter who could also direct (after a fashion) would take away any of Mario's disappointment that the shoot didn't quite live up to its star billing.

I should really have learned enough by then to have knocked the optimism on the head.

TYRONE EDWARDS: The pig stops the interview and leaves me sweating. I hate police stations. Most people hate hospitals but with me it's the nick. I know I ain't done nothing wrong, but I'm thinking this must be God paying me back for all the times I did and didn't get done. Then the DS comes back and says, 'Heaven is smiling on you today, Tyrone. Apparently Mr Shirer has had a rethink and no longer wishes to press charges. Probably thinks the image of him cowering in a car isn't very Clint Eastwood.'

'Yeah, but you're still gonna have me for the ring,' I say. 'I swear she gave it to me.'

'Hard to credit it, but she swears she did too.'

'You're kidding, man.'

'I wish I were, believe me I do. But you can stop wasting our precious time and the taxpayers' money and go home.'

I walk out into the sunshine and he shouts out after me, 'Aren't you forgetting something?' I turn round and he holds out the ring. 'Yours, I believe.'

I grab it and run down the street before he can think of something else to bang me up for. I stop and look at it. Ninety-eight grand of fuck-off sparkler and I'm punching the air.

Then I think, fuck, Yvonne. How am I gonna explain this one? First thing she'll say is it's nicked and she'll kill me. But when I tell her it's from Extra-large Tits and Rizlas she'll double kill me.

GREG FULLER: Joe and Greta were settling themselves in the Viper. I was about to turn over on them when I heard a commotion behind me. It had a distinctly Latin flavour. I turned round and saw Mario gesticulating wildly to his translator. Max came over and I asked him what was happening.

'He's only just twigged that there's no Rebecca Richards.'

'But we can give him Greta Bastendorff.'

'He twigged when he saw her. He asked who's that whatever the Italian is for stick insect.'

Mario was performing the universally understood fruit-weighing gesture. I also caught the word '*melones*'.

'Oh Christ,' I said to Max as the truth dawned, 'he's a bloody tit man.'

'Big time.'

Lola had been outside getting a coffee, but her antennae must have sensed the brewing rumble. She reappeared in the studio and appraised the situation. Then she moved in on Mario.

As she walked past me she muttered, 'I don't know why the hell

I'm doing this. You don't deserve anyone's help right now.'

I didn't know why she was doing it either, but I hoped she had a plan.

NANCY STARK: Apart from *lasagne, ciao* and Paolo Maldini, I didn't speak a word of Italian, but after three nights with Dieter, Dirk and Diego, I was fluent in the international language of love. I also had a full tank of pheromones, my best push-up bra and a nicely tanned cleavage.

Mario Tigana was going to be easy, and I moved in for the kill. As I flirted with the dumpy Italian letch I was thinking that Greg owed me a very fat bonus when his deal went through.

GREG FULLER: We finished the ad ahead of time and I called a wrap for the final time that week. Another commercial shot and ready for the editor.

Over.

Done.

Finito.

A very boring and blissfully uneventful day.

Oh, I almost forgot. The wrap party.

twenty-four:

cake, canapés, cocktail gherkins

NORMAN THE COOK: Live and let live, that's my motto. I like pretty much everyone and, apart from Chinese metabolic bollocks merchants, there's only one sort that really gets on my tits.

Producers.

You know their trouble? They always know best. Only they don't, do they? If they did they'd never have lumbered us with *Absolute Beginners*, *Rancid Aluminium* or *Captain Corelli's* twatting *Mandolin*.

I only have to deal with Chinese metabolic bollocks merchants once in a blue moon, but producers are in my face on a daily basis. I have to keep it zipped, though – they're the bastards that decide whether the job goes to yours truly or some other mug in a three-ton truck with a serving hatch. Toddy Gluck was the worst of the breed. The crew had been griping about her since day one. Beyond watching her poke at my salad selection, I hadn't had much to do with her, though.

That changed on the Friday morning when she marched up to my truck and demanded a cake.

'Tea and stickies are at four as per usual, darling, but I'll let you have a custard Danish now if you don't let on,' I told her.

'No, a proper cake for the wrap party.'

'I wouldn't have thought there's much cause for a knees-up after a week like this one.'

'Well, it's not every day that you shoot an ad with Joe Shirer and Greta Bastendorff, is it?'

'And it's not every day you lose both your director and your first-choice leading lady either,' I said. 'But what do I know? I just sling the sausages.'

'Precisely, and I am the producer. I want a cake.'

As you can imagine, I was getting a tiny bit narked at this point, but I kept my cool. 'It is a bit short notice, but I can probably get a couple of fruit slabs in,' I said.

'Fruit slabs? Hardly A-list. This *is* Joe Shirer we're talking about. I was thinking more along the lines of a light Victoria sponge – big enough for forty.'

'By the end of play? You're having a laugh.'

'You know, that's the trouble with the British worker,' she said. 'Plumbers, mechanics, film crew, you're all the same. You stroke your chins and mumble that it can't be done. Well, it can. You've got to be proactive, show a bit of initiative. Now, can you do me a cake or can't you?'

'Blimey, you'll be wanting it iced next,' I said.

'Of course.'

'I was joking, darling.'

'I wasn't. A fondant Joe would be perfect. Him and Greta would be even better. Why don't you show me some designs at lunchtime? And keep it tasteful – no building-site humour.'

Then she was off to harass some other poor sod.

'What the hell's she got shoved up her arse?' said Wendy as we watched her walk away.

'I don't know, but if she wants a cake, we'll give her a fucking cake. We got any self-raising in?'

GREG FULLER: From the moment Toddy had the idea of a party, she was a woman possessed. That was her true vocation – party planner. I said as much to the first and I heard him mutter, 'I wish she'd piss off and be a party planner then.'

I pulled her aside and said, 'It's hardly been a week of cinematic triumph to rank with *Gladiator*. Can't you keep this low-key?'

'What's the point of having a party if it's low-key? Besides, it's not just for Joe and Greta. Your senior client is here, as well as Max and Mario Tigana. Anyway, just because you want to slink away and pretend this week never happened, doesn't mean that the rest of us do.'

I shut up after that and let her get on with ordering champagne, canapés and hand-cooked crisps. Or rather get on with ordering others to do the ordering.

NORMAN THE COOK: Yasmin tipped up not long after the cake incident. 'Toddy wants to know if you can do three hundred assorted canapés.'

'She's sending you to do her dirty work now, is she? You can tell the stuck-up cow that if she wants canapés she can go to the sodding Marks and Sparks on the high street. She's not getting another sausage fucking roll out of me.'

'With pleasure,' she said. 'Do you want me to include the fucking?'

NANCY STARK: Super Mario and his interpreter stuck to me like glue that afternoon. The translator was obviously used to business situations rather than pulling girls – after he'd got hold of his boss's pick-up lines they sounded like items on an agenda. If Super Mario had ever managed to get me into bed (never in a million years, I swear), he'd probably have brought him along – 'Signor Tigana wishes to know if you are sufficiently lubricated to attempt full-scale penetration?'

By the time Greg yelled, 'It's a wrap,' I reckoned I was owed at least ten per cent of his seven mill. It was party time then, and I was relieved. Not because I was dying to rave – I thought it might be a chance to lose Super Mario in the crowd.

BOB BULL: Morton Newman and I had formed quite a team over the week, and he latched onto me as soon as the celebration was under way.

'We finally made it, Bobby,' he said, chinking his plastic cup against mine.

'I always knew we would, Morty. My faith never wavered.'

'The new script is sensational.'

'Phenomenal, isn't it?' I agreed. 'You know, working with ad agencies is like pulling teeth, but we got them there in the end. Mark my words, the little envelope-pusher we shot today will write a new chapter in the history of automotive advertising.'

'It's a benchmark movie, Bobby, for sure. Hey, you seemed a little quiet today. Everything cool between you and Roger?'

'Absolutely. Roger is very much a big picture chap. I'm indispensable to him when it comes down to brass tacks at the brand/ consumer interface. I just took a step back today, let the man feel like he's in charge,' I explained.

'Smart move, Bobby. You're clearly at home in the corporate shark tank. Blackstock is lucky to have you.'

'Good of you to say so. I'm ready for pastures new though. I'm a great believer in shipping out when I'm on the upward curve.'

'I hear you,' said Mort. 'You and I should stay in touch. You'd love LA. A left-brain guy like you would fit right in.'

'You think so?'

'No question. If you like I'll talk to some people, see if I can kick open some doors.'

As we went to congratulate our star on his stunning performance,

I thought about what Morton had said. I felt that I'd achieved all I could in the tyre and related products arena, and I was ready to make a clean breast. Morton had given me some gourmet food for thought, career strategy-wise. I pictured the Family Bull on Malibu Beach – the sprogs with their surfboards and Jane in a bright red costume. If she'd still have me, that is. I'd done some serious soul-searching over the last twenty-four hours and I'd made a big decision, wedded bliss-wise.

TIM LELYVELDT: Joe acted blasé, but he was glad they were throwing the party. It wouldn't have been the same if Rebecca had been there and he'd had to share the glory. Greta may have performed with him that day, but he was in the driving seat in their relationship just as he was on the set – it was Joe's party.

   As soon as the first cork popped the two Blackstock guys homed in on Joe and the adoration began. I heard Knopf admire his 'manly, clean-living image' at least twice, and Bull kept pace with him on the bullshit count.

GREG FULLER: I must confess to joining the moth-like throng around Joe and Greta. Who doesn't like flirting with celebrity? Joe indulged us with some Jack Nicholson anecdotes. However famous you are, there's always someone starrier whose home number in your Rolodex provides cachet. I wonder who adds kudos to Nicholson's life? Who is the ultimate starfuck? I suppose that is the exclusive property of the Pope. His Holiness may no longer be A-list, but he remains the one true player, being on backslapping terms with God.

TIM LELYVELDT: Joe was wearying of the Blackstock and agency people. He wanted to widen the circle of worship. His chance came when the cake was wheeled in.

NORMAN THE COOK: Toddy scurried out to have one last gander at her cake. Even though I say so myself, I'd done a bang-up job – four twelve-inch sponges stuck side by side and covered in icing. Cake decorating is a bit Jane Asher for me, but I'd managed to do her fondant Joe and Greta.

'Not bad,' she said. I think she was well pissed off that she couldn't find fault. 'Although Joe's nose is –'

'It's fine,' I said. I admit, it was on the Jimmy Durante side, but it balanced Greta's baps, which I'd made a couple of sizes bigger than they were in reality.

'OK,' she said. 'Shall we take it in?'

'Yeah, but I've had an idea, darling.'

'Oh.' She looked shocked.

'Well, I thought I'd be proactive, show some initiative. I thought we could stick a tablecloth on it and make it more of a surprise. The crowd will go wild when you whip it off.'

'Fantastic idea,' she said.

I covered the cake, and as she wheeled it off on the trolley, Wendy whispered, 'You can't do it, Norm.'

'Just watch me,' I replied.

YASMIN FISH: Toddy wheeled the cake in like she'd baked it herself. Norman was behind her with a big grin on his face. What are you up to, I thought. When she reached Joe she called for silence and the little spark shouted out, 'Speech, speech!'

Greg moved forward – he was either trying to save her embarrassment or he thought he should make the speech since he was director for the day. Before he got a chance to butt in, though, she'd launched into it.

'OK, OK, if I must. I'm not very good at this so I'll make it short. I believe I can speak for everyone in saying that this has been a very challenging week.'

'I dunno,' whispered the little spark, 'I think it's been pretty bloody entertaining.'

'Events have unfolded in ways that none of us could have foreseen. But Joe has never let his total professionalism slip. Today, aided by Greta, he showed inspirational courage in seeing the job through. Joe Shirer and Greta Bastendorff, you are true stars and we would like to present you with this . . .'

She pulled the cloth off the cake with a flourish.

'. . . Where the fuck did that come from?'

NORMAN THE COOK: If you want someone to produce an egg out of your earhole, I'm your man. OK, I'm no Paul Daniels, but slipping the banana under the tablecloth when it went over the cake was a piece of piss. The hard part was arranging it so one end was stuck nicely into fondant Joe's groin. When I was setting it up in the afternoon I was going to have fondant Greta going down on it, but Wendy wouldn't let me.

GREG FULLER: Toddy froze in horror over the cake, her mouth hanging open. It was an image which, combined with the banana, brought back memories that I didn't want to relive at that particular moment. I scanned the crowd, most of whom were cheering ecstatically. I looked at Roger Knopf and knew then we'd be lucky to get our commercial to its first edit without being fired. I saw Max, who had his hand clasped over his eyes. Beside him was Mario Tigana, who seemed not to have noticed the banana – he was too busy marvelling at Greta's icing *melones*. Then I looked at Joe.

TIM LELYVELDT: Would he do the right thing? It was a close call. The crew's clapping pushed him to the verge of a *Letterman*-esque walk-out but when Greta started to giggle he reconsidered. He forced a smile and joined the applause. Well done, Joe, I thought, maybe you've learned something this week.

NORMAN THE COOK: Toddy pulled herself together and stormed up to me. Come on then, I thought, come and have a go if you think you're hard enough.

'I will personally make sure that you never, *ever* work on a job of mine again.'

Which suited me down to the ground.

GREG FULLER: As Joe cut the cake, Max joined me. 'I've just had a bizarre conversation with Bob Bull,' he said. 'He told me we could do what we like with the videotape because he's decided to come clean and tell his wife about – how did he put it? – "The completely innocent thing with the business studies student in the thong." Have you the foggiest what he's talking about?'

I shook my head.

'Well, he's been putting away the bubbly. Maybe he's delusional.'

From across the studio Bob shot me a poisonous glance as he drained his plastic cup. I'd wanted to escape for a while. Now my departure was imperative.

NANCY STARK: I'd lost Super Mario at the cake. He was so busy bagsying a slice with Greta's boob on it that he didn't notice me slip away. I went to find Greg.

'I'm going now, sweet pea,' he said.

'But where?'

'I have to try and talk to Carrie.'

'Only six months too late,' I said. 'Good luck, though.'

He kissed me on the cheek and said, 'Thanks for everything this week.'

'Oh, it was a pleasure – mostly. Aren't you going to say goodbye to the big knobs?' I asked, nodding towards the clients who were still grovelling round Joe and Greta.

'No, fuck 'em.'

It was good that he was leaving, but it was also a shame because he missed the best bit.

YASMIN FISH: After Norman's banana stunt, Joe became the centre of attention. All of a sudden he was the greatest because he could take a joke. I'd seen enough of what he was like that week, though. He was spoilt, selfish, and spiteful. The others were either too stupid to notice or they just didn't care. Whatever, it made me sick.

Starfuckers.

The little spark came up to me and asked, 'What's your next job then?'

'Homebase probably.'

'Who's directing?'

'Not ads,' I explained. 'The store in Streatham.'

NANCY STARK: Joe was holding court and it was like one of those *An Audience With . . .* TV shows. You know, a plant in the celeb audience asks a question, the celeb on stage answers like he never guessed anyone would come out with that one, celeb audience laughs like it's the best ad lib they've ever heard. The chat didn't take long to turn to the only thing anyone was interested in: *Body Matter.* Was there going to be a sequel?, someone asked.

TIM LELYVELDT: 'We're close to a go on the script and Kev is ninety-nine per cent committed to directing,' said Joe. Would that be the same script you've thrown out for rewrites and the same Kev that walked out on you last night?, I wondered.

Then someone asked about the stunts. Please don't go there, Joe, I thought. Crews turn up to work in jackets and T-shirts emblazoned with the movies they've helped make – they wear them like war vets wear their medals. Over the week I'd spotted all the recent Bonds, a couple of *Gladiators* and at least one *Private Ryan*, all stunt-heavy pictures. They were an experienced bunch and I had good reason to want Joe to stay off the subject.

At first he played it modest, keeping away from specifics. But, with such an adoring audience, his confidence soon rose and he mutated into Pepsi Max Dude.

That's when the gopher who'd been fetching his mineral water all week asked, 'Joe, why don't you do one now?'

He laughed and said, 'Show me a three-hundred-foot tower and a chopper and I'll show you a stunt.'

YASMIN FISH: I'd had enough of listening to him lie through his arse. When he tried to laugh it off I said, 'What about one of the others? I loved the one where you jumped off the bridge and landed in the moving car. *Absolutely brilliant.*'

'Hey, we've even got the motor,' said the little spark without realising he was helping me out. 'Same one too. You drove a Viper in *Body Matter*, didn't you, Joe?'

'Yeah, but –'

'Oh, go on, please . . . *pleeeease*,' I begged like I used to when I was six.

'Love to, guys, but I couldn't. You'll have to go rent the DVD,' he said and my heart sank.

TIM LELYVELDT: He'd have been home free if it hadn't been for Greta: 'You know, I'd love to see you in action. I so missed out not being with you when you were shooting *BM*.' She was innocence personified, but at that moment I was convinced it was an act.

The crew started to chant, 'Joe, Joe, Joe,' and it was another Hollywood moment – two in one week.

'No, I couldn't,' Joe protested, but the chants grew louder and he was weakening, starting to fall for his own hype.

'*Pleeeeease*,' pleaded the gopher.

'C'mon, Joe, do it for me,' begged Greta.

'Joe, Joe, Joe, Joe,' cheered the crew.

'OK,' he said, 'but no retakes if I screw it up.'

Joe Shirer, physical coward, a man who couldn't tie his shoelaces without risking a vertigo attack, was about to do a moderately-to-severely-dangerous stunt. I don't believe in anything that remotely resembles God, but I was praying for a miracle.

The crew worked faster than they'd done all week, and it didn't take long to set up. In the middle of the studio they built a rig –

a bridge that the Viper would coast beneath. It was maybe fifteen feet high, half the height his double had jumped from in *BM*. The carpenters constructed a shallow ramp to roll the car down. In the movie it had hit thirty, but here it would be lucky to touch five.

Maybe, just maybe he'll get through this, I thought.

When they were ready Joe stood at the foot of the rig and briefed the guys like he'd spent his career as a stunt wrangler. 'Have the engine running but make sure she's in neutral. I'll slam it into gear when my ass hits the seat and take it to the other side of the studio. And don't let the car go before my signal. This is all about mental prepping and I've got to be ready up there.'

He started to climb but stopped at two feet up. I told you, vertigo tying his shoes.

YASMIN FISH: 'He's gonna bottle it,' said the little spark.

'I hope so,' I muttered.

But he didn't, and after a few seconds he started climbing again. He reached the top and slowly worked his way to the middle of the bridge. When looked down he was white – no LA tan any more. I thought he was going to be sick, which might actually have made a better ending.

TIM LELYVELDT: He hung there for maybe a minute, though it seemed longer. I could tell how dry-mouthed he was because his 'OK, roll it' wasn't much more than a rasp. One of the guys on the ramp said, 'Was that a go?'

'Yes, *go* for fuck's sake,' shouted another and they gave the car a shove. I turned away. I couldn't watch.

YASMIN FISH: Most people were watching the car but I was watching him. His eyes rolled towards the back of his head and by the time it was underneath him he'd fainted. He dropped like a sack of spuds – my mum and dad are greengrocers so I know about sacks of spuds. He landed in the car and his head disappeared below the door. His body must have knocked it into gear because it shot off like a rocket towards the big studio door.

NORMAN THE COOK: They say your life flashes before you at times like that, but what I saw was a re-run of the Spurs v. Man C cup final replay of eighty-one. It was like a dream. One minute, I'm standing in the truck doing a stint with the Mr Muscle. The next, Ricky Villa is off like a dago ferret through the City defence.

I don't remember what happened after the studio door splintered. I obviously jumped clear because, when I came to my senses, I was flat on my arse on the tarmac and there was a car in my truck. Everyone piled out after it and Toddy Gluck screamed, 'My God, there's blood everywhere!' Silly cow – a case of ketchup had gone for a Burton. Heinz as well. I should have known better than to buy the premium stuff for a bloody commercial.

I picked myself up and walked over to my poor old truck. The car had hit it slap bang where I'd been standing. That's when it struck me how lucky I'd been. Wendy too – she'd gone to the bog, saved by a bladder that shrinks to the size of a pea after a sip of champagne. The Blackstock idiot staggered over and looked at the wreckage in a daze. Pissed as a fart.

'American car, American tyres, mate,' I told him. 'Now if that motor had been fitted with British Dunlops it might have been a different story.'

'Joe Shirer was in that car,' he sobbed.

'Well, why the fuck didn't someone say? We'd better get the poor sod out.'

TIM LELYVELDT: It took the firefighters an hour to lift the debris off his body. The fridge was the toughest. It had jammed itself in the cockpit across his legs. When they finally lifted it clear, Joe was covered in a paste of bolognese, sour cream and chives, ratatouille and mashed potato. I could also make out grated cheese, olives and canned peach slices.

NANCY STARK: I stood at the back of the crowd while the firemen cut Joe free. I couldn't see much but it didn't look good. I felt a tap on my shoulder and looked round. A lost-looking bloke was behind me with his wife, four kids and what looked like a Filipino nanny. 'Excuse me,' he said in a soft American accent, 'I'm looking for Joe Shirer. I'm Stryker Queenan, his analyst.'

'He's over there,' I told him, 'but I think he'll need more than a session on the couch.'

TIM LELYVELDT: Joe screamed when they lifted him onto a stretcher. Both his legs were severely broken. The paramedics needed to put temporary splints on them but, with the coating of food on his body, they couldn't see what they were doing.

'We're going to have to cut him out of these jeans,' one of them said.

Joe lifted his oxygen mask and gasped, 'Please don't.'

They'd cost over $400, but it wasn't the jeans he was worried about.

YASMIN FISH: No one said a word when they got his trousers off. Except for Norman. Not very loud, but I heard because he was next to me. 'Fuck me sideways,' he said, 'I've seen bigger cocktail gherkins.'

TISH WILKIE: I was running late and had to eat breakfast on the go again. I dashed into the kitchen to grab a high-fibre cereal bar, a Chunky Kit-Kat and a family-size bag of cheese and onion. Mum and Dad were watching GMTV on the portable and I *so* couldn't believe who was on the famous pinky-red sofa: Joe Shirer! He hadn't worked in two years and now he'd bravely come back to Britain to promote his incredible new charity. I *had* to watch. He looked different – wiser and more vulnerable. His crutches were beside him, a heart-rending reminder of how close the world came to tragically losing one of its greatest young stars.

'I said it then and I'll say it now,' Dad muttered. 'That car was a death trap. If they'd listened to me he might not –'

'Shush, Dad, I'm watching,' I said. 'He's literally a saint. He's raised an absolute ton for stuntmen's widows.'

'Is that what Stunt Aid does?' said my mum. 'I thought it had something to do with thingy enlargement.'

'No, that was just the *Sun* being nasty,' I explained. God, parents – so, like, *duh*.

They shut up and I managed to listen to Joe. 'The last two years have been amazing,' he said bravely. 'I've grown as a person and now I've got Hollywood in perspective. I'm totally focused on getting to work again, but I know that fame is meaningless unless you use it to make a real difference as a human being.'

'He seems like a lovely young man,' said Mum.

'He's a fool. He'd have two good legs if he'd listened to me,' said Dad.

'Have you seen the time, Tish?' said Mum.

'God, I'm supposed to be there in half an hour. The ribbon-cutting is at ten and Vanessa will kill me if I'm late.'

I grabbed my pile of lists and flew out of the house. Being Personal Assistant to Britain's most in-demand (heterosexual) supermarket-opening person was non-stop. Literally.

TIM LELYVELDT: A gopher walked Joe back to the hospitality room where Morton and I were waiting for him.

'You were stupendous out there, Joe – a very moving interview,' Mort said as he slapped him on the back.

Joe ignored him and snarled, 'I look like George fucking Hamilton in this makeup. Why didn't you fly my own girl over?'

'I don't see how we could have justified it, Joe,' Morton said. 'The Shirer Foundation is covering the costs of the trip.'

'What's the point of a charitable foundation if I can't load the payroll with my own people?'

'We've got to get out of here, guys,' I interrupted. 'We're due at Great Ormond Street in less than an hour.'

'I'm too stressed to look at a bunch of dying fucking kids. Phone and tell them I'm ill – migraine, stomach, whatever.'

Joe *was* stressed. When we'd arrived at the TV studio, Morton and I hadn't been quick enough to hide the newspapers in the hospitality room. Before he went on, Joe had seen the pictures of

Tom Cruise. Joe hated him as it was. Seeing long-lens shots of him strolling on a Caribbean beach with Greta Bastendorff on his arm must have stung like hell.

YASMIN FISH: I was starving and I went to get a Big Mac. I walked out of Homebase and past the Universe of Sofas next door. Some film trucks were parked out front. One of them had Check the Plate painted on its side. I walked across the car park and looked through the hatch.

'Hi, Norman,' I shouted.

He looked round and said, 'Do I know you, darling?'

'French Films. Blackstock Tyres. Two years ago.'

'Blimey, you're . . . you're . . .'

'Yasmin, the runner.'

'Yasmin, that's right. Bloody hell, you've grown up.'

'I'm nearly twenty now. Anyway, what are you doing here?'

'They're shooting an ad in the store. A load of old pony with titsy blondes on sofas.'

'Hey, doesn't the agency that made the tyre ad do them?'

'No, this is some other bunch of wankers. It all went pear-shaped for that lot. They lost Universe of Sofas at pretty much the same time as Blackstock fired them.' He looked at the badge on my uniform. 'Trainee Manager – very bleeding posh. So you got out of films then?'

'You said it yourself, Norman. Too many wankers. I do miss the buzz sometimes, but at least now I can get through the day without some stuck-up cow shouting at me about mineral water.'

'That Toddy Gluck, eh? I heard she's gone on to bigger and better things.'

'I know. I saw *Hello!* "London society's top party planner shows us round her stunning Belgravia home and tells us about the special man in her life, her conversion to Buddhism and her hopes for world peace." I nearly threw up.'

'You're right, Yasmin, you're well shot of it.'

'I haven't lost touch completely though,' I said. 'I've been invited to the premiere of *Who'd Have Believed?* tonight.'

'That Rebecca Richards, eh?' he sighed.

'Didn't you just know she'd bounce back?'

'No offence, darling, but with the way she's stacked, bouncing was just about her only option.'

CARRIE FULLER: I got back to the Mondrian and looked in the bathroom mirror. I couldn't believe my hair. The people at Miramax would think I was Ivana Trump rather than a middle-aged British mum desperately trying to be taken seriously as a screenwriter. I had thirty minutes before I had to leave for my meeting. They wanted to discuss the rewrites on my second screenplay. I'd tried my hand at comedy, and had written one that was only faintly autobiographical – its working title was *Starfuckers*. I knew that if it ever got made, this would change, and I was resigned to it. I promised myself that I wouldn't be upset, as I had been when Kevin French had insisted that *Rebecca Edwards* became *Who'd Have Believed?*

Before I changed, I picked up the phone and checked my messages. There were two.

'Carrie, I can't believe I'm here and you're in LA. Tonight. Big red carpet. Charles and Camilla. Odeon Leicester Square. The UK premiere of your first film. And you're missing it. I've been doing wall-to-wall interviews. All they want to talk about is the usual hairdo/love life/blah, blah, blah, but I've been getting in a few plugs for the writer. Hope Veronica didn't get carried away – she tends to go a bit Ivana with her more *mature* clients. Love you. Call me.'

VERONICA D: After Carrie had gone I swept up the hair from my bathroom floor. Then I made a coffee, sat on my bed and emptied the garbage sack of clothes that Rebecca had given me before she'd left for London. She would clear out her closets once a year and let her friends pick over her trash like fashion vultures. It wasn't charity in any regular sense – you could open a store on Rodeo Drive with what a movie star like Rebecca wears once and throws away. The first thing that caught my eye was a gorgeous denim jacket – Dior, all rhinestones and embroidery. I'd wanted it from the moment I'd seen Beyoncé Knowles wear it to the Sky Bar. I didn't even know Rebecca had it. I put it on and stood in front of the mirror. 'Veronica Dingolldongersonn, you are to *die* for,' I said out loud. Then I saw something sticking out of the breast pocket. A little card, the kind that comes with a bouquet. I pulled it out and read it.

Rebecca – I owe you. The flowers are just a deposit – Erika

There must have been hundreds of Erikas in LA and I truly had no idea which one owed Rebecca. It couldn't possibly be the Erika that wrote for the *Enquirer*, the one that had got the original exclusive on the Shirer schlong.

Couldn't *possibly* be her.

CARRIE FULLER: The second message was also from London.

'Hi, only me. Just calling to wish you luck with Miramax. Miss you. Kids do too. Ryan is pissed off because he was substituted in his match yesterday. Blames me for telling him to track back. I have no idea what track back means but I heard Alan Hansen say it on the telly. Hope cut her leg in the playground. Don't worry – it looks worse than it is and I took her to the hospital for a tetanus. Call me when you can. I love you. So does Axel. He's now going to sing "The Wheels on the Bus" down the phone. I've listened to it fifty sodding times today so I think you should have to put up with it once ... go on, Ax ... go on ...'

I listened to the Toddler Formerly Known as Unborn sing to

me. Apart from one mighty belch when he'd been four months old, he'd never sounded a bit like Ben Kingsley in *Sexy Beast*.

GREG FULLER: Axel made it to the end of the verse and I stuck him in front of Cartoon Network. Experience had taught me that *Scooby Doo* would keep him quiet for up to twenty minutes and give me the chance to work.

Not for Fuller Scheidt though. The agency still existed but I'd discovered the hard way that even having your name over the door doesn't make you indispensable. Carrie and I had rescued our marriage but my other one to Max didn't survive. We might have been able to cope with the loss of Blackstock and Universe of Sofas but, when our Italian suitor walked off with his loot, divorce was inevitable. It wasn't amicable. Max treated me far more vindictively than Carrie ever did.

But before you write him off as utterly heartless, he did let me keep one of the Jags, the one that lost its bumper on Hyde Park Corner. The last time I saw the guy that hit me, he was generously agreeing to help the police with their enquiries. I occasionally wondered what had happened to him.

TYRONE EDWARDS: I'm lying on the beach at Ochy and I'm thinking it's the first time I've been to JA without it being a business trip, if you know what I mean. Yvonne is by my side and everything is sweet. I know what you're thinking, man. You're saying, c'mon, Tyrone, what bird ain't gonna be sweet when you sell your hundred grand sparkler, set her up in her own nail-sculpting empire, and buy her all the clothes and presents and holidays in the sun she wants?

But it ain't like that, I swear. Me and Yvonne have a love that's for real. We is the Puffy and Naomi of New Cross, man.

'Hey, babe, whack some of that oil on my back,' I say, and I feel her loving hands go to work. 'Mmm ... That's gooood ...

Ow, what the fuck are you doing? You wanna break my spine?'

'You ain't changed a bit, Tyrone Edwards,' she says. 'Don't think I don't see you staring at the tits on that cheap white slut.'

'I can't help it, Yvonne. We is on a beach. Everywhere I look there's tits.'

She don't say nothing. She just whacks me on the back of my head. OK, maybe we is more like the Ike and Tina of New Cross. And, yeah, Yvonne is Ike.

GREG FULLER: After Max dumped me I went out of fashion faster than puffball skirts. Agencies wouldn't touch me with a shitty stick. It was a double stroke of luck that Carrie was not only prepared to keep me but was also in a position to. Two-hour features pay even better than thirty-second TV ads.

After a couple of years in the wilderness I was in the process of reconstructing. I'd set up Fuller Creative Consultants. Strictly that should have been Consultant – there was only me. I had an office on Greek Street but, with Carrie being away so much, I did a lot of work from home. Lola ran things when I wasn't there, though for reasons that need no explanation she now insisted I called her Nancy.

In between looking after Axel, I'd spent the day of Carrie's premiere on a new business drive. This consisted of calling old clients and pretending that their voices were the most pleasing sound on earth. I sat at my desk for twenty minutes of schmoozing before *Scooby*-fatigue set in. I flicked through the Rolodex and it fell open at B: Barclays Bank, Bird's Eye, Blackstock – Bob Bull's direct line. He was no longer there, of course. After Knopf fired him, he went to LA. He was probably still out there chasing the ultimate starfuck.

I didn't have time to dwell on him, though. The sitter arrived. It was two o'clock and time for my appointment with my counsellor. With his help, Carrie's goodwill, Nancy's constant vigilance and supreme self-restraint on my part, I'd managed to keep my dick in my pants for two years, three weeks, six days and fourteen hours.

THE REVEREND ROBERT G BULL, SENIOR VICE PRESIDENT OF MARKETING, PROMOTION AND PRAYER, EVERLASTING LOVE TV, BAKERSFIELD, CALIFORNIA: It was time to take a break from organising the two-year marketing plan of the West Coast's fastest-growing evangelical cable station and have a well-earned sandwich at my desk. First, though, I got down on my knees and spent a moment with the Lord.

'Heavenly Father, I thank you for the opportunity to perform your good works on Earth for as long as you see fit. I also thank you for the twenty-three per cent year-on-year subscription base growth enjoyed by Everlasting Love TV over the last fiscal, which has allowed us to thrash our rivals at JC-♥s-U-TV.

'I pray for the soul of Roger Knopf, towards whom I bear no resentment for our mutual and amicable decision to part company as part of a carefully considered corporate restructure.

'I pray for Greg Fuller. May your phenomenally ineffable goodness flow like sweet honey into his heart and teach him the error of his sinful ways.

'I pray for the soul of Jane, now known as Fletcher, the name of her new husband, although being omniscient, oh Lord, you will, of course, already know this. I give thanks for the fact that she took me to the cleaners, alimony-wise, and so made me see the falseness of material things.

'And I pray for the soul of Morton Newman, for whom I feel only love even though he never came through with the promised job in entertainment and/or related fields.

'Finally I give thanks for the delicious and wholesome sandwich that I am about to enjoy – Amen.'

Chinwag with the Almighty over, I took a sip of Diet Coke and reflected that He did indeed work in mysterious ways. Had He not sent Morton to tempt me like the serpent tempted Eve, I would never have ended up in a lonely room at the Snoozrite Motel with only a bottle of whisky and a cancelled credit card for company. It was there that I tuned in to Everlasting Love TV and experienced the miracle of rebirth.

You really should get to know Him – a phenomenal guy, literally phenomenal.

e

Matt Beaumont

e is a tapestry of insincerity, backstabbing and bare-faced bitchiness – just everyday office politics.

Meet:

- a CEO with an MBA from the Joseph Stalin School of Management
- a director who is a genius, if only in his own head
- creatives with remarkable brains, if only in their trousers
- a copywriter with the two things no adwoman should ever show – underarm hair and a conscience
- secretaries who drip honey and spit cyanide
- the sad git in accounts

Consisting entirely of e-mails, *e* spends a week in the company of Miller Shanks, an advertising agency embarked upon the quest to land Coca-Cola – the account they would sell their collective grandmothers in a car boot sale to acquire. This is one pitch that nobody will ever forget . . .

'Depicts the Machiavellian scheming and summary sackings of the ad world in withering detail and with no shortage of dead-eye wit'
The Times

'Groundbreaking . . . an internet-enabled *Clarissa* for the 21st century'
Evening Standard

ISBN 0 00 710068 X

For further adventures in adland,
competitions and extra information, go to:
www.millershanks.com

The e before Christmas

Matt Beaumont

'I want a party that our staff will talk about for years to come.'

These are the prophetic words that begin the quest for the perfect office bash. The e before Christmas follows a twisted trail that leads in the only direction Miller Shanks advertising seems capable of heading – downhill. The familiar cast of liars, skivers and shagaholics plays out the fiasco with predictable flair. Cameo performances are given by Vinnie Jones, Jarvis Cocker and a militant lesbian Barbie doll.

'Tis the season to be merry, but peace and goodwill have no business at Miller Shanks. Or as resident deviant Vince Douglas would write (if only he could), 'May all your Christmases be shite.'

Acclaim for Matt Beaumont:

'Lively, viciously funny and about as switched on as a novel can be.'   *Mirror*

' A genuinely enjoyable page-turner.'   *The Times*

'Hilarious.'   *Cosmpolitan*

ISBN 0 00 711487 7